# I Kissed a Dog

Carol Van Atta

Enjoy,
Carol Van Atta

Werewolves of the West
Book One

Copyright © 2012 Carol Van Atta. All rights reserved.

Names, characters, and incidents depicted in this book are products of the author's imagination or are used fictitiously. Any resemblance to actual events, locales, organizations, or persons, living or dead, is entirely coincidental and beyond the intent of the author or the publisher.

No part of this publication may be reproduced, stored in a retrieval system, or transmitted, in any form or by any means, electronic, mechanical, photocopying, recording, or otherwise, without the written prior permission of the author.

I Kissed a Dog / Carol Van Atta
First Edition Paperback: October 2012
ISBN 13: 978-1-936185-72-6
ISBN 10: 1-936185-72-5

Editor: Mary Belk
Interior Design: Roger Hunt
Cover Design: Ann Falcone

Readers may contact the author at:
www.werewolvesofthewest.com

Published by Charles River Press, LLC
www.CharlesRiverPress.com

Dedication

I dedicate this book to you, Jordyn and Jade, for putting up with all my whims and wackiness when I'm writing, and the rest of the time too. You are the best kids a mom could have. And to my mom, who instilled the love of reading in my life at a young age. Reading is better than TV, hands down. And lastly, and most importantly, to my Awesome God who gave me any talents I might have. Without You, I would be lost.

Acknowledgments

There are so many people to thank, individuals who helped make *I Kissed a Dog* come to life. If you played a role in this book's publishing process please know I appreciate all your help. It must be said: without seeing Tessa Dawn's book ad on Facebook, I might not have discovered my wonderful publisher, Charles River Press/Cambridge Press US. Her book promotion prompted me to buy her book, which led me to Charles River Press and the purchase of more books, where, ultimately, I realized I'd found a great place for my own series, if they'd have me. Thankfully, Jon Womack, a talented author in his own right, gave the green light for the book you're reading. Thank you to the Dogman! To Mary Belk, editor extraordinaire, thank you for continually reminding me that more isn't always better; you made the clean up process fun. Packaging a book is always important. Having a cover I love, but more importantly one that grabs you, the reader, enough to peek inside is a gift. This gift was made possible by my talented and creative cover designer Anne Falcone. Roger Hunt, your skills made the pages inside the cover reader-ready, thank you. Lastly, I want to mention those early readers who encouraged me to keep writing and gave invaluable feedback along the way: Jade (my daughter), Sean (who is always scaring me), Mariah,

Michael, Becky, and my mom, and to author of the *Blood Curse Series*, Tessa Dawn, for her kindness and input with post writing tips and suggestions for marketing and more. A book is without a doubt a team effort, and I needed all of you!

One

June 12, 2011 – The Oregon Coast

The lion paced to the left, top lip curled back, revealing his pointed teeth; he snarled at me for good measure.

Wary, I watched as his tail whipped from side to side, and he shifted into a crouching position, his eyes never once straying from mine. He was perched above me on the rocky ledge where he spent hours lounging in the sun.

Planting my fists on my hips, I stood taller, squaring my shoulders, and glared up at Butch, a regal three-year-old lion I'd known since I first started working for Luke Snider at the Plum Beach Wildlife Park, over two years ago. Never had I experienced the wrath of this particular animal, and I wasn't enjoying being on the receiving end of the young cat's fury.

Fred, one of the park's volunteers, had gotten the absurd notion that lions were just bigger versions of their housecat cousins, and based on the faulty information, decided to enter the cage for a feel of their fur.

The two females were eating and ignored the intruder. Butch, always curious and fiercely territorial, wasn't quite as welcoming. He'd cornered Fred and was preparing to paw at him when I'd noticed his dilemma. Counting on my positive relationship with Butch, I'd helped Fred escape and was turning to leave.

Butch had other ideas and decided to get frisky with me. Something I hadn't anticipated.

Now I was stuck and angry. How dare Butch treat me like a prospective snack?

I could hear Luke, off to my right, warning me to exit the cage — now, but I refused to surrender to my growling challenger. This was one battle I didn't intend to lose.

It appeared Butch felt the same.

My pride alone wasn't holding me back; I wasn't one hundred percent convinced I could escape unharmed and wasn't ready to risk it.

To make matters worse, I'd become the animal park's featured entertainment.

A considerable, mid-afternoon crowd swarmed the lions' enclosure eager for some action. As if the town's recent murders weren't enough. Granted, most of the park's patrons were tourists with their cell phones raised in hopes of capturing footage worth posting online later.

If I had any say, it wouldn't be me dangling from the jaws of my former feline friend. Some vacation memory that would be for the kids watching.

Butch roared, sending a wave of nerve-induced nausea crashing through my midsection. His hindquarters quivered in preparation for the sure-to-come pounce. If I was going to divert a catastrophe, and my funeral, I had to act now.

Backing away, I used my coma-acquired communication skills, and sent what I hoped was a soothing mantra into the lion's mind: *You're okay. It's me, Chloe. Calm down. Relax. I have treats for you. Relax. Good boy. That's it. Relax.*

Butch cocked his head, responding to my calming thoughts. He looked, for a brief moment, more like a dog with a mane than a menacing lion. I sensed him relaxing, his rage receding, but before I could release the lung-tormenting breath I'd been holding, a child screamed loud enough to crack glass, inspiring several more children to add their piercing shrieks to his, creating a chaotic chorus.

The lion, startled by the commotion, roared a final warning and sprang, arcing toward me; front paws, lined with stabbing claws, extended my direction.

To avoid direct impact, I dove to the ground, bundling myself into a ball, making sure to cover any vital organs and the soft flesh of my neck.

With my head tucked to my knees, I shielded the back of my head with my arms, and waited.

And waited …

Instead of the lion's victorious roar and sounds of my tearing flesh, loud applause and cheers erupted around me. Encouraged, I raised my head, peering out from the mass of unruly curls that had escaped their ponytail.

Cameras flashed while camcorders and cell phones filmed the extraordinary ending to a daring rescue, performed by the most delectable specimen of manhood I'd ever had the pleasure of ogling. Appalled by my sinful assessment, I was quick to blame it on shock; after all, I'd almost died — again.

Almost dying was becoming a bad habit. A habit I needed to break before my luck ran out.

Turning my attention back to my savior, I watched my boss

shake his hand. I had no idea how he'd stopped the lion, now pacing in an isolation cage attached to the enclosure. A line of well-wishers had accumulated and were waiting to congratulate him. It was then I realized I'd somehow been removed from the cage, without my permission or knowledge, and people, now surrounded me.

My co-worker, Rhonda, leaned in close. "Just had to find a way to get the hot guy's attention, didn't you?" Her sneer drew my attention to her makeup-caked face.

Rhonda was my high school nemesis reincarnated. I refused to give her the satisfaction of seeing me squirm. Like my former rival, her bark tended to be much worse than her bite. As long as she was center stage, she was content. Right now, I was the center of attention, guaranteeing her displeasure.

Ignoring her question, I accepted a water bottle and several concerned pats on the back before circling around behind the lions' enclosure where I could gather my wits. I was more shaken than I cared to admit. At last alone, my scattered thoughts narrowed to Senior Prom 2004, another prime example of how my coma-acquired-ability caused a major commotion while leading to an overwhelming sense of discomfort.

Darlene Davenport, the school's self-proclaimed fashion authority, who could've been Rhonda's twin sister, had manipulated our vice principal into letting her bring Queenie, a miniature poodle, to the prom, by insisting the ball-of-fluff was a necessary accessory for her already-garish fuchsia gown.

Peeking from a sequined handbag, the dog looked cute enough — so cute that my normal fear of dogs was absent for the evening, causing me to forget about Darlene's ongoing desire to dethrone me from my ever-tentative popular-girl status.

Like her successor, Darlene Davenport was no fan of mine.

In fact, she was one of three girls who made it their priority to gossip and grumble about me anytime anyone would listen, which was too often for my liking.

Bob, my stepdad, a police officer, the always-conservative and overprotective parent, banned any article of clothing that might accentuate my figure. Form-fitting or low-cut were not in my clothing vocabulary, or closet, leaving me little to wear that was teenage-girl approved.

Sure, my clothes were cute, practical, and probably cost more than the fashionista's, Darlene's. However, Darlene and her few followers made their disapproval known in a number of creative ways that I'd prefer to forget.

Still admired in spite of my conservative attire and their unrestrained bad mouthing, I was up for the coveted title of prom queen. My chief competitor was, of course, none other than Ms. Diva Davenport.

Hoping to tame my hair, I met up with Darlene primping in front of a mirror. Her precious baby, Queenie, succumbed to my mental probing with ease. Queenie's doggy thoughts revealed that Darlene and her gal pals had bribed one of the stage hands into hanging a bucket of Queenie's poo poo over a letter X, chalked on the exact spot where the elected queen would make her royal appearance. The whole scene was reminiscent of a 1970's horror movie that left the prom queen in a telekinetic frenzy.

And if that wasn't enough to churn my stomach, Queenie's vision featured me bowing to receive the crown, followed by the bucket tipping. The squishy brown downpour made me gag.

Should by chance Darlene win, the bucket would remain upright and unused.

I Kissed a Dog

How convenient.

Let's just say that when all was said and done, I won the crown and Darlene was covered in her beloved pooch's poop.

"How did you know?" she'd screeched through the stinking mess.

Making sure to smile and pat Queenie's head, I replied cheerfully, "Your dog told me." After all, Queenie had saved the queen.

The Monday following prom, Darlene told anyone who would listen that I was a mind-reading witch and explained how her parents were suing me for the irreparable damage to her dress. In the end, she succeeded in making herself look crazier; and I became, much to her chagrin, even more popular.

Rhonda experienced the exact problem as Darlene. The more she tried to destroy my reputation and make my life miserable, the less people liked her. After two years, she still couldn't figure out why everyone favored me.

I remembered the gorgeous stranger who Rhonda favored, and who'd saved me. I felt sorry for him. Given the chance, Rhonda would pursue him like he was the last man alive.

Damn! With all the craziness, I'd failed to thank him for his lion taming heroics. I assumed Luke would know how to reach him. The least he deserved was a kind word.

With the shock subsiding, it occurred to me it was my day off. I should have stayed home. At least I'd have been safer there. With me, absolute safety was never an option.

"Ms. Carpenter, can I get a word with you?" an unfamiliar voice called from behind.

Waving him off, I exited through the side gate. Monday would be here soon enough. I trusted it would be better than today.

Two

Monday, June 13, 2011 – The Oregon Coast

When my dog, Buddy Boy, communicated with me for the first time, following what I now refer to as "the incident," AKA coma catastrophe, I decided a smaller community was the best place for someone with my disability, or talent, to put down roots following high school and a few unsuccessful years of city living.

What I think about my special ability changes day to day, all depending on what type of trouble I end up in because of it. So far, it's been a pretty good summer, but it's only the second week in June. A lot can happen before September. I've found that out over the years.

Luke Snider loves my talent. I've saved him tons of money since I started working for him. At first, like everyone else I've told — Mom, Bob, Melanie, and Jordon — he doubted my ability. After I diagnosed his male tiger with depression and provided the solution, he was real appreciative. He knows the entire story. The other employees understand that I have a unique connection with the animals, but they give me a pretty wide berth.

I Kissed a Dog

The animals have shown me how they (humans) gossip — about me.

It's something I've come to expect and accept. True, my ability isn't quite as threatening as mind reading. Yet imagine if a friend (or enemy) was complaining about you, your dog overheard, and could show you the unpleasant scene's images and audio. *Pretty* uncomfortable.

Yesterday had been beyond uncomfortable, but gossiping coworkers were always preferable to a near mauling. The naughty lion would be getting a serious scolding today, and I could count on Rhonda to spend more time complaining about me than working. I'd choose confronting a lion over dealing with her any day.

Cracking the window, the fresh ocean air poured in, refreshing me. I found myself replaying that fateful spring day when my life came to a screeching stop and made a U-turn toward a traumatic death. The unforeseen events from 2002 were etched in my memory:

Free from our final class, I glanced at my BFF, Melanie, and I decided a little girl-time on my fifteenth birthday might be fun. "Hey, want to walk home with me?"

"I would, but my mom wants me to help her at the grocery store. When's your party?" Melanie said the party word loud enough to turn a few heads as we made our way into the crowded hallway.

Great, now I'd have to deflect the interest directed my way. "Uh, I'm not sure. I'll let everyone know." I made sure to say everyone in a way that demonstrated my inclusive nature, all while knowing there wouldn't be any big birthday bash.

An event involving boys would never gain Bob's approval. My mom would find the idea uncomfortable, her tag word for anything she wanted to avoid, which was pretty much everything.

"Call me later," Melanie commanded, before digging into her locker.

I knew if I didn't, she would. Melanie wasn't just persistent about parties.

Leaving her to sort through the mess in her locker, I hurried outside, eager to embrace the sunny spring afternoon. Celebrating my birthday by taking the longer route home, through a small, wooded area, seemed like a safe way to rebel against my stepdad while enjoying the scenery.

Taking the long way wasn't my parents' idea of safe or responsible behavior. Bob was near neurotic about my walking alone. He'd seen too many crime scene photos. My mom went along with him to avoid creating any waves. She was vigorous when it came to maintaining an environment void of any unnecessary discomfort.

I refused to let their paranoia infect me. It was like a plague to be avoided at all costs. Doing something they wouldn't approve of was how I inoculated myself from their fears. I didn't push the limit too far, just enough to maintain my independence.

Flinging their warnings aside, I marched through the school's manicured lawn toward the tree line where the brush parted and a trail waited.

I turned onto the narrow path. I could hear a baseball game starting back at the ball field and school buses chugging away to nearby neighborhoods — safe sounds. Basking in the moment, I took several graceful spins and celebrated my few minutes away from prying eyes.

The afternoon sunlight filtered through the trees' canopy, giving the path an other worldly appearance. Birds chirped and the *wind rustled the leaves. Talk about a fairytale scene. At the trail's end, the foliage parted, revealing a suburban Troutdale neighborhood, and a huge growling dog.*

I wasn't familiar with the breed, but recognized, at first glance, its eyes were full of suspicion, and its lips were curled back and trembling, revealing two gleaming canines.

A five-foot fence, just to the left, would have to serve as my escape.

I lunged toward it.

Snarling, the dog charged forward, planning to intercept me.

I scrambled over the railing, thankful for my long legs and above average height. My gratitude was cut short when, to my displeasure, I landed with a painful thud on concrete. My head spun as I tried to right myself. Instead of standing, I collapsed —this time plummeting into the icy depths of a stranger's uncovered swimming pool.

My head thudded against the wall.

Little pins of light blinked behind my eyelids, giving way to murky darkness.

Several disjointed thoughts managed to linger in the moment before blackness swallowed me whole. Happy Birthday, Chloe. Today you die. Cause of death: Attacked by a dog; drowned in a pool. Not so cool.

I'd always heard that near-death experiences were strange. People have no idea just how strange. Being in a coma for seven months can also be considered more than extraordinary.

Lucky me, I experienced both.

To everyone's surprise, I woke up with total recollection of the events leading to my coma.

After all the ooing and ah-h-hing over my miraculous recovery subsided; my parents relented and told me the whole story. I learned from Bob I'd been under water for about fifteen minutes; they'd restarted my heart three times. I should have been brain dead, if not dead-dead. They were advised several times to pull life support, even referring to me as a vegetable. In other words, I was a goner. But here I am breathing, talking, and doing all the stuff *alive* people do.

When I finally left the hospital, after suffering through every test imaginable, I was at last able to accept and celebrate I was alive. I recall having difficulty believing that there were no lingering side effects. I'd read Pet Cemetery like five times, and dead things never came back to life right.

Despite my worries, I couldn't wait to see what the future had in store for me. As long as it didn't include more danger — or dogs — I'd be just fine.

It was after I saw my very own, man's-best-friend, Buddy Boy, I grasped the entire truth — things would never be *fine* again.

Danger and dogs have continued to haunt and harass me since that historic day, and considering my commute to work takes over an hour on Highway101, I have tons of time to reminisce and often end up revisiting my perilous past.

Once at work, the impressions from the animals are my main concern, making it difficult to sort through my own thoughts. When people question why I don't move closer to the wildlife park, I'm able to tell the truth — the long drive relaxes me; it helps me process my past and plan for my future.

Glancing in the rearview mirror, I smoothed a stray ringlet behind my ear. I wished the early nineties spiral perms would come back in style. My long curls were the source of many compliments, mostly from women with super-straight hair.

It's funny how women, me included, are never satisfied with their looks. My eyes, emerald green, are my best asset, although a few men might tell you otherwise. Not that they've seen more than me in a swimsuit sunning myself. Lean and lithe, but with a fanny I consider too rounded, I move with grace. However, I'm clumsy. That's right; a graceful woman prone to accidents, yet another "gift" I unwrapped following my coma.

The cell phone's buzz tugged me away from my self-appraisal. "I'm on my way, Luke," I confirmed, trying not to sound snippy. He made it a habit to check in at least once during my drive to Plum Beach.

"Of course you are. When is my Dr. Doolittle ever late? By the way, you took off yesterday before I could check on you; did you get my messages last night?"

"Yes, I'm fine, and you're right about one thing: I'm never late," I replied dutifully. It was a childish game we played; making small talk when a ton of sexual heat sizzled between us.

As one of the last known virgins over twenty, I still notice that my employer is an attractive man. Who wouldn't? Six feet tall, sun-streaked hair, and sea-blue eyes make him the all-American dream boy. Mom is always quick to remind me, during our Sunday evening phone calls, how attractive and established Mr. Snider is. She also points out the fact that he is single.

"Not true, Chloe, you were not only late, but also missed work with that flu bug."

"Six months ago, for two days. Everyone else milked you

for a week of sick time," I reminded him. Ensuring he appreciated my integrity, I rubbed in my superior work habits every available opportunity.

"See you." He hung up, ending our everyday debate.

I was relieved. He'd avoided quizzing me about my latest incident in The Lion's Den. I doubted anyone else would be as considerate.

Outside the passenger window, the Pacific Ocean glimmered in the Monday morning sunlight. The water shimmered inviting me into blue depths for a swim. I was a certified sun-lover. Weather like today reminded me of new beginnings. Maybe this would be the day someone or something would bring a little spark of excitement to light up my life. A girl could wish, right? Dealing with angry lions wasn't the type of excitement I was seeking.

The siren and flashing lights behind me were the first indication that this might be *the day*.

As always, I'd left home in plenty of time to account for any unexpected issues. Waiting for the patrolman, his paunch leading the way, to reach my window wasn't the spark I'd been hoping for.

"Good morning, Miss. I'm Officer Tate. Do you realize you have a broken left tail light and you were going seven miles over the posted speed limit?"

I decided to keep it simple and avoid any sarcasm.

"I didn't realize …"

Woof! Woof! A dog barked from the cruiser, sounding fierce. My guts clenched in response. Dogs always had that annoying affect on me.

"Pipe down, Barney!" Officer Tate hollered back.

Woof!

The dog didn't seem to be minding his manners. I decided to see what had Barney all riled up.

Relaxing my mind, I listened. The process worked better if I could look into an animal's eyes, but I could still glean enough from the barks to get a picture. My brain did its special thing and the images started flowing. Barney was in pain. A tumor, the size of a small apple was growing near his testicles. Ouch!

"Sir, did you know your dog is sick?" I decided to be direct. He could contact Luke if he needed confirmation.

"Excuse me? What are you talking about?" He took a step back, looking like he'd seen a ghost, or worse.

"I don't have time to explain; I'm going to be late to my job at the Plum Beach Wildlife Park. I work there diagnosing animal problems." I hoped I sounded half-believable. I wasn't sure how else to describe what I did without going into a drawn out explanation about my special skills. It was doubtful he'd believe me. If our roles were switched, I wouldn't.

"Your dog has a definite tone to his bark," I improvised. "That tone makes me think he might have some sort of a tumor, near his groin."

"I'm familiar with the park, and Luke Snider. I'll make sure to check it out. Heard you all had a problem yesterday, something about the lions?"

"Problem solved," I said, refusing to elaborate. "Thanks for getting Barney looked at. He'll appreciate it." I hoped my free diagnosis would earn me the honor of keeping my perfect driving record intact.

"You go on now. Take care of that taillight and slow down.

There are too many campers and trailers out here. And watch out for frisky lions." He winked.

"Thanks!" I called, my voice syrupy with false cheer. "You have a good Monday."

Eager to forget my brush with the law, I switched on the radio, tuning in the local station. I was just in time for the news.

"At last night's press conference, Police Chief, Robert Daily, admitted for the first time, a connection between the two male victims. Both men were found in their respective homes, stabbed."

Groaning, I changed stations. I needed cheerful not dreadful.

"Plum Beach may have its very first serial killer. Police aren't confirming —"

So much for my sunny morning disposition — getting pulled over, even though the results were positive, and now murder and mayhem so close to home, gave me warning willies. I should have known after yesterday that my good streak wouldn't last.

It never did.

Three

When I pulled into my self-proclaimed parking spot, my outlook had improved dramatically. I was looking forward to my schedule.

On Mondays I spent time with the park's Capybaras, the world's largest rodents. The new capy babies squealed in delight anytime I approached. I know for certain their cries equal delight, because I can see what they're thinking. My smiling face to them is all about food and a good behind-the-ear-scratching-session. Not to mention, the jumbo-sized rodents wouldn't try to maul me like Butch.

I grabbed my bag from the backseat and stretched, taking a moment to soak in some morning rays.

"You're looking pretty pleased with yourself," Rhonda scoffed with a sneer, her backside glued to the hood of her older model Jetta. She sucked down smoke as if tar and nicotine were the elixir for eternal life.

Geeze I'd expected her to pick up where she'd left off, but not before I left the parking lot. If I wasn't careful, she'd deflate my good mood like a pin popping a balloon.

"I thought *you* were going to quit?" I snapped. According to Hank the Chimpanzee, Rhonda was enemy numero uno. He'd get no argument from me on that revelation.

She'd planted herself in front of Hank's enclosure and proceeded to have a nice, long chat with herself — about little ole me. Hank, with the promise of a ripe banana, had shown me the one-sided conversation in its entirety. In addition to her raging jealousy, Rhonda pretty much thinks I'm a crazy bitch with the ability to manipulate Luke into obeying my every whim. Don't I wish! Luke obeying me would be damn convenient.

"Any theories on who's killing those guys?" Rhonda flicked her cigarette away. "I knew them both."

So much for not brooding over the stabbings; Rhonda wouldn't be the only one analyzing the unsolved crimes today.

To my relief, our conversation was cut short by the purring engine of a vintage Corvette. The Wildlife Park wouldn't open for an hour. This gleaming red car didn't belong to any local resident. I would have remembered that muscular arm resting in the open window...

"Wow! That's what I call a *real* man." Rhonda stared, her gaze hungry.

"Good morning, ladies." A deep voice drew my attention away from the pristine paint job.

After a quick glance at our visitor, and a near heart attack, I bolted toward the entrance, hating myself for my ridiculous reaction.

Rhonda offered her eager assistance.

There was no denying he was the same smoldering, hot hero who just yesterday saved my butt from a good lion chewing. I'd seen plenty of good looking men, even dated a few, but for some reason, the stranger in the parking lot had rendered me speechless, and feeling stupid.

As a rule, I'm quick with my words and have no trouble socializing with the male species. Not that I've found one worthy of my undivided time and attention, but I enjoyed flirting.

What I'd just seen of our guest made my stomach twist and my heart race. I could feel the heat rising up my neck. At least my toffee-colored skin would camouflage the evidence of my blush.

Talk about a schoolgirl reaction.

The newcomer had to be at least six five, with piercing brown eyes and strong arched eyebrows. Those chiseled cheekbones made the bottom frame for those eyes.

Glancing back, I caught another peek at my lion-rescuer. He was also blessed with long, tousled, blue-black waves that spilled over his broad shoulders, as untamed as the lion. I forced my eyes away from the broad shoulders that tapered into a narrow waist and rock hard butt and hurried through the familiar park entrance, abandoning my need to thank him.

"Here's my favorite girl." Luke unlocked the gate, holding it open in his normal, gentlemanly fashion. I stumbled in, almost meeting the pavement with my face.

Used to my clumsiness, Luke scooped me up at the last moment. "Chloe, Chloe." He shook his head, reminding me how much I depended on him.

Knowing he wouldn't expect a thank you, I demanded, "Who's the big dude with the rock star hair?" I needed to know. How could I focus with Mr. Muscle around? The more nervous I was, the more dangerously clumsy I became. "Why is he here today?"

"Big dude with the hair, that would be me," a smug masculine voice replied from behind.

If I had been a flower, I'd have wilted on the spot.

Somehow, I managed to locate my composure and put on my biggest, brightest, and fakest smile — courtesy of my mother's handy, hide your emotions "training."

"And who might *you* be?" I demanded, raising my gaze to meet his. I tried to keep my focus on his mouth so his eyes wouldn't distract me. I failed.

"I'm Dr. Zane Marshall, the new vet." He held my gaze. His eyes, flicked with gold, were almost as dark as his hair. He raised an eyebrow.

"Isn't this great!" Rhonda squealed, oblivious to my discomfort. "Our very own hero."

I spun to face my boss who had a sheepish grin on his All-American face.

"When were you going to tell me I was getting a new partner?" I blurted.

"Hold on, Chloe; no one knew. Dr. Marshall gave me his answer an hour ago. It's about time we have a full-time vet.

You can diagnose the animals' problems, but then we have to call in people to fix those problems. Our system worked fine during the winter, but summer's too busy. Besides, he did you quite the favor yesterday."

Luke was right on both accounts. Zane had done me a huge favor — keeping me alive. There were very few wildlife vets that worked on call anymore. It was expensive to get one here right away. We'd been using a retired wildlife veterinarian who'd been mauled to death by his own cougar.

Luke turned his attention back to the new vet. "Now that we've figured out why Dr. Marshall ..."

"Mr. Snider, I prefer Zane."

"I'll make you a deal, call me Luke and I'll call you Zane," Luke suggested, sounding pleased with his newest employee.

"Call me confused," I huffed. "I've got a busy day. The Capys need my attention."

"Hold on. *Today*, you can show Mr. ... Zane around and get him acquainted with our park procedures." I could tell by Luke's crossed arms and narrowed eyes that this was an order not a suggestion.

With a loud sigh, I communicated my disapproval and marched off to my storage cubby. I could hear other employees arriving, followed by more introductions.

Why did this Zane have to be drop dead gorgeous wearing Levis that hugged his muscular legs? I'm a leg girl. Powerful legs and a tight bum were a major turn on. His presence gave me heartburn. It looked like I'd have to invest in some strong antacids.

As a rule, I don't worry much about my appearance during work hours, but today was different. Dr. Zane Marshall had changed all that when he roared into Plum Beach in his spiffy sports car. My always-trustworthy instincts screamed warnings, while my body shouted something downright pornographic.

This newfound physical attraction was just plain inconvenient. Staying distant and professional was going to be a top priority. Especially since the other time I'd experienced a reaction even close to this was with Jordon, and that hadn't ended well for either of us. I still had some serious emotional ghosts, as Melanie called them, haunting my heart.

"Hey, I didn't mean to be so gruff." Luke caught up as I tried to slink from the women's restroom, where I'd applied lipstick, for the first time I could remember. I moved on to the coffee maker.

He was pretty much in tune to my routine. Organize cubby. Visit the restroom. Drink too much coffee. Then work. Always in that order.

Predictability was one theme I appreciated about my job. The information the animals broadcasted had the potential to interrupt my calm façade, but otherwise, work was my safe place. Now, without warning, a new man had upset the one place where routines kept me grounded and semi-sane. Sure, on my extended commute I'd wished for something exciting to happen, but Zane wasn't what I had in mind, and work wasn't the place.

"I'm sorry," Luke pressed, eager to restore peace.

"You didn't even tell me you'd interviewed someone," I accused. Luke had always been upfront with me. I guess I felt slighted, although I knew that was silly. Consulting with me wasn't in his job description. But, still —

"I'm not sure what it is about our new employee that has you so rattled. I figured you'd like the help. This guy is good. You should see his references."

"I'm not worried about his references or his skill level. I'm worried about his cocky, know-it-all attitude," I huffed.

How else could I explain what I was feeling?

I Kissed a Dog

Gee, Luke, the guy is the hottest thing I've seen, ever. He makes me uncomfortable. Yep, that word — uncomfortable — still harassed me like an un-exorcised demon. And I owe him my life, that's always a plus in any relationship.

"Everyone else seems to like him." Luke filled another cup with steaming coffee. He had the nerve to sound offended.

His unexpected defense of Zane infuriated me more.

"Good for them! I don't." I knew I was acting like a spoiled brat, but I didn't care.

Grabbing my mug, I marched away, not bothering to clean up the brown liquid I sloshed onto the floor. I could imagine what Luke was thinking. He was aware I was prone to an occasional emotional tirade, but my rant today far exceeded anything he'd witnessed. He'd have something more to say later, once he figured out how to approach me.

I could count on it.

Careful to calm myself before entering the central courtyard, I tried breathing through my nose then out my mouth, while counting from one to ten. Most of the time, the method worked. Realizing ten wouldn't be enough, I continued to twenty, which proved to be the magic number, allowing me to walk, not stalk, to my usual bench.

The concrete slab featured a name plaque engraved with one of the wildlife park's founding families. I avoided sitting on the engraved wording. Not only did it offend my behind, but it also felt kind of sacrilegious.

From my perch, I sipped my coffee, wishing for more sugar, and listened to the awakening animals. Chirps, growls, and a few roars chorused, signaling the start of a new day at Plum Beach Wildlife Park.

For a blessed moment, I forgot my new partner.

My bliss flipped to frustration as Dr. Zane Marshal strode into the courtyard surrounded by several admiring female workers, including Rhonda, and a small troop of men eager to prove their worthiness to this god of men. Ridiculous! It was like high school all over again.

Attempting to ignore the commotion, I willed myself to listen to the animals, hoping to catch a clear impression. In most cases, I had to be focused on one specific creature, yet the canine patrol dog had confirmed I was getting better at communicating from afar.

Shutting my eyes, I forced all nagging thoughts away and listened.

She's one beautiful bitch.

What —? My eyes flew open in time to see one of the park's free-wandering goat's lips part, ready to nibble.

I lifted the goat's head and gazed into her eyes.

I'm so hungry. I'm so hungry. Just a little bite ... The goat's mind reflected her desire to chew on my clothing, just as I'd expected. Goats weren't the most intelligent beasts on the block.

I scanned the area. The one animal looking my way was a beastly but very human veterinarian.

I couldn't read humans, no matter how hard I tried. After discovering my post-coma ability, I'd expended a ton of energy attempting to reach my own species. It just didn't work. So, what or *who* had formulated such a crude thought?

For the first time, which added to the mystery, there weren't any pictures accompanying the words. In general, animals didn't use words in the traditional sense. Their thinking revolved around their senses, and what they both saw and heard, sort of like a video preview. With this latest development, I'd entered uncharted territory.

Today, I'd heard, without a doubt, the *worded* thought of an animal. My gift was expanding, transforming again. The capricious ability seemed to evolve without notice. An animal using the "B" word was beyond baffling. It was bizarre.

"Sorry to interrupt your coffee break, but I thought we should get moving. We've got a lot of ground to cover." Zane's commanding tone implied that he was used to getting what he wanted.

I gasped, almost spilling my coffee.

Towering over me, it was evident he'd left his newfound followers to their own work.

How such a large man could approach with such stealth was unnerving. He'd advanced without my knowledge — something that never happened. Having a cop for a parent had taught me to be ultra-vigilant. Bottom line: I should have heard him.

"Excuse me, but I'm not on a break, as you so quickly assumed. My shift," I glanced meaningfully at my watch, "doesn't start for ten more minutes." I swallowed my uneasiness with a long drink.

"Fine, I'll join you." Without waiting for an invitation, he took a seat on the bench. Stretching his legs, he rotated his shoulders. I was overwhelmed by a masculine, musky fragrance. Shampoo? Whatever it was smelled way too good. I inched away, hoping to put a safer distance between us.

What's with her? Do I stink?

"What?" I stammered. This couldn't be happening. Of all people, why him?

Seeming to realize that I'd infiltrated his thoughts, he grimaced.

Just Great! Considering we'd be working together, good ole Luke had explained my talent to our newest employee. But why Zane would assume that my animal-reading-ability extended to him, a human being, was beyond me.

I leaned closer, this time forgetting to hide my intentions.

Attempting to slide into his mind, I was met with a brick wall — a very vivid image of a brick barrier blocked my probing, making it impossible to sense anything.

I was shut out, on purpose, it seemed.

No animal had ever stopped my snooping. They seemed eager to comply. Apparently, humans were different.

Between my latest encounter with death, my ever-expanding talents, the murders, and Zane's sudden appearance, I felt my stress level rising. I had to make a decision: Stuff my feelings until later, when I could sort through them alone, or go bonkers and lose my job.

The example my parents' had set once again guided my decision. For now, I'd ignore the strange incidents and pretend my world was standing right side up.

Gulping down the last of my coffee, I handed Zane a park map. "Let's go."

Forcing myself to treat Zane as I would any new employee, I babbled on about the various animals, citing their unique traits, histories, and dispositions. Zane took careful notes and remained silent other than a number of questions about the black bears. I was grateful that he hadn't attempted to bring up our earlier mind reading encounter or yesterday's lion taming/Chloe shaming incident.

The few times I tried to tune in to his thoughts left me disappointed. The brick wall remained strong, shielding his mind. The good news — he didn't seem aware of my failed intrusions, at least he didn't acknowledge them. Maybe the barrier he'd managed to erect was permanent, although I wasn't sure how that would work. It wasn't like I'd found a how-to-manual for my condition.

"What's going up over there?" Zane stopped to watch several men working on a new exhibit building.

"Come on. I'll show you." I hurried ahead eager to see the latest developments.

Luke's dream to add a mini-aquarium was becoming a reality. I was amazed by the progress.

"Hey, Chloe!" Joel, one of the younger workers, turned to wave from his rooftop perch, bumping several nearby metal poles in the process.

One of the huge rods was catapulted my direction.

With no time to move away, I dropped to my knees, covering my head with my arms. I felt a gust of air.

I froze, waiting for impact. Nothing hit me but relief and curiosity.

I opened one eye than the other.

What I saw made no sense. Zane was lowering several poles to the ground without any effort.

"Man! How'd you do that?" The worker stared at the rods, awed.

"You should worry less about me, kid, and more about keeping this work site safe. You could have killed her." Zane glanced back, his concern obvious, causing my heart to do an unfamiliar flip flop.

Severe shock, again … that would explain my increased heart

rate. Of course, I was in shock. What else could it be? The guy had saved my life twice in less than twenty-four hours.

Before I could even begin finding my feet, Zane was lifting me up, holding my elbow to keep me steady. My legs wobbled, but with his help, I remained standing.

Several workers offered apologies.

Joel rushed to my side. "Chloe, I'm so sorry. I messed up. Can you forgive me?"

I nodded and turned toward Zane, more interested in his heroic actions. "How did you get to me in time?" I asked, lowering my voice.

I tried to gauge the distance he must have traveled to reach me. Last I remembered he'd been several long paces away, and I was convinced the steel beams weighed far more than any one man could lift. He'd laid them down like putting pencils on a desk.

This latest occurrence reminded me of yesterday's rapid rescue effort, and it made no sense. Men just didn't move that fast, nor could they subdue lions with their bare hands. The whole incident seemed to have a surreal quality to it. And to think I'd wished for excitement.

"Well?" I pressed, waiting for his explanation.

"I've been known to respond with adrenaline a time or two." He shrugged. "No big deal."

"No big deal. You're kidding, right? You saved my life, not once, but twice." The idea that I was indebted to this massive man didn't sit well in my gut. "Thank you," I stammered.

Seeming to read my mind, he shrugged. "I'd have done it for anyone. In spite of what you might think about me, I'm a pretty helpful guy." He released my arm.

"You can help me anytime," I said, making sure I sounded serious; because I was.

"You can count on it." Looking uncomfortable, he turned to gather my scattered papers.

"Do you want to continue the tour?" I asked, hoping we could move on. I didn't want to dwell on my latest dance with death.

"If you're able, I'm willing." He smiled, a broad smile that reached his eyes, softening his features.

"Thanks to you, I'm able." I accepted my paperwork and moved to the next exhibit, trying to ignore the warmth spreading through me like liquid heat. His smile had the same effect on me as the sun had earlier.

Sun lover equals Zane lover? No way! Not a chance. I shoved the ridiculous idea away.

We'd reached the wolves, one of my favorite exhibits in spite of my aversion to dogs. A male and three females lived in the wilderness-inspired enclosure.

Unlike many zoos, the park's animals had large areas to explore, making their confined existence more bearable. At this point, all the animals had been born in captivity, and I'd never heard any complain about their surroundings.

For the most part, the wolves watched from a distance. They stuck together and avoided human contact, forming their own little pack. Feeding time was the one exception.

Zane fixed his gaze on the big male and made a funny growling noise deep in his throat. Much to my surprise the grey wolf trotted toward us.

"Magnificent creature," Zane acknowledged. He squatted and faced the wolf through the gaps in the fencing.

After a few minutes of silent staring, the wolf retreated.

Randall, I spoke the wolf's name in my mind. *What did the man say?*

All I could decipher was a picture of an enormous black wolf and the word, *brother.* Another actual word? My ability was morphing from the caterpillar phase into a fully developed butterfly, and I had no clue how or why it was happening, or when it would stop.

"You're not the only one with a special animal connection," Zane boasted.

"I've never claimed to be the one and only!" I shot back, feeling defensive.

Regardless of his rescue efforts, he still annoyed me on several levels. Later, I'd give Luke my ultimatum: Zane or me. As for the wolf's strange mental impression, I'd explore that later as well, right along with my growing list of crazy and impossible things to consider.

"You are high-spirited, aren't you?" he teased.

"What did you expect, another pining woman?" Why did I feel the need to be so mean? He'd saved my life — two times. It wasn't his fault more of my coma-acquired-gift was being unwrapped without my permission.

"Chloe, I've managed to offend you. I'm sorry. I'd hoped for a compatible partnership with a coworker. I'm guessing that's not in the stars." He sounded disappointed.

Before I could process his apology, he reached for my hand. "Hello, my name is Zane Marshall. Can we start over?"

The moment our hands touched an electrical current, coursed through my veins like an illicit drug. I quivered as I stumbled backward, almost falling. The strained look on his face was evidence enough that he, too, had felt the intoxicating sensation.

As much as I hated to admit it, there was something both alluring and odd about Zane Marshall. And I was desperate to know more.

Zane tensed. Our *moment* ended as Rhonda, a cat in heat, sashayed toward us,

"How's it going? Enjoying your tour?"

"Very much so." His eyes traveled down my frame, lingering on my breasts then legs. My face burned in what was surely a very brazen blush. I doubted my darker coloring could hide my heated reaction this time around. I didn't care.

It gave me an odd sense of power to see him focused on me with the curvy, platinum-blonde batting her lashes. When Rhonda found a man she wanted, she made no effort to hide her intentions. Zane was the latest man on her hit list of hunks.

"What are you doing for lunch?" Her question was for Zane alone. She made that clear by sliding closer to him while ignoring my presence. I should have been happy to see him vanish for awhile, but instead, an unexpected stab of jealousy pierced between my ribs.

The next words tumbled out of my mouth shocking us all. "Zane's having lunch with me. We've still got some animals to visit anyway." I waited for his sure-to-follow rejection. Why would he want to have lunch with a sourpuss like me when Rhonda would stroke his ego and a whole lot more if he desired.

"That's right, I'm sorry, but Chloe and I have more work to complete before we can head out. If you'd like to join us, it'll be awhile." His attempt at diplomacy was lost on Rhonda.

Her face scrunched into a mask of fury.

I knew right then that our treaty of common dislike had just expanded to hatred on her part. I'd have to watch my back more than ever.

"I'll take a rain check." She softened her features before turning to smile at Zane, and then strode away, making sure to sway her ample hips.

"Wow — is she always like that?" Zane grimaced.

"Do I have to answer?" I tried to conceal the excitement I felt knowing that this Hercules of a Man preferred me over a sure roll in the sack. This latest development added to my growing belief that there was more to Dr. Marshall than I'd originally thought.

"So, you're treating me to lunch?" His face lit up with a boyish grin that just about won me over on the spot.

"Co-workers go Dutch. That's the rule around here," I joked.

"Fair enough. I saw a little seafood place down the road."

"Which one?" This was the Oregon Coast. Seafood was the main staple. Where was this guy from anyway — Mars? I'd once read a book about men being from Mars.

He seemed to catch my attempt at humor slash sarcasm. "All right now, play nice. I'm the outsider. You pick."

Twenty minutes later, we were seated across from each other at the Plum Beach Fish and Steak House. I eyed the menu, trying to keep from gawking at Zane, who looked larger than life in the small booth. Every female in the place was stealing glances our way. Zane seemed oblivious to the attention, another plus for my new partner.

An afternoon newsbreak filled the flat screens mounted on various walls throughout the restaurant. Several patrons called for the staff to turn up the volume.

Police Chief, Robert Daily, dabbing his face with a handkerchief, waited behind the podium, prepared to make an official statement. He shuffled through a pile of papers. Another man, wearing a tasteful business suit that boasted a major designer's label, waited nearby. He gripped his own stack of papers.

I didn't recognize him. Of the two men, he appeared the calmest.

"Friends," Chief Daily began. "It is times like these, when drawing closer as a community is more important than ever. As you are aware, two of our town's young men were needlessly murdered."

The word *needlessly* struck me as the wrong word to use when describing a murder victim; however, Police Chief Daily wasn't the type of person that garnered respect. Today was no exception. He'd always seemed out of his league making public announcements. If the situation weren't so dire, I might feel sorry for him.

"We are working overtime to solve these cases and bring justice for these crimes and peace back to Plum Beach. I understand your concerns about the tourist season, and realize that many of your livelihoods are being affected by these events. …"

"Why can't you catch this creep?" Someone yelled from the crowd of onlookers surrounding the podium.

"We heard there was another killing!" a woman shouted.

"Hold on, folks, please, let me finish," his voice trembled.

I looked at Zane to see if he was watching the news like everyone else. Sensing my scrutiny, he turned away from the screen. "Did you know either of these men?" His eyes mirrored the concern in his voice.

Thankfully, I could answer no. We turned back to the

report in time to see the well-dressed man replace the chief at the podium.

"My name is Agent Green. I'm from the Portland FBI Field Office. I will be working with your local police department to bring a rapid resolution to these events. To answer your question about an additional murder; you are correct."

People gasped, both on and off the screens. Hushed conversations broke out around the restaurant. I held my breath waiting for the details, hoping that once again I'd be a stranger to the victim.

I should have known my luck would run out.

"Our latest victim has been identified by family members as Seth Johnson, a local fisherman who worked part time for Tim's Tackle and Treasures. If you are a single man, between the ages of eighteen and thirty, we advise you to remain vigilant."

A throng of reporters pushed forward as the officers turned to leave. The local anchorman returned, providing a press conference summary.

"I knew Seth Johnson," I said, surprised by the hitch in my throat. "It wasn't like we were close or anything, but he helped me pick out fishing gear for my stepdad when he visited last summer. Seth was just a kid. He couldn't be, *have been*, more than eighteen or nineteen."

"I'm sorry. Do you want to leave?" He asked with genuine concern.

"I don't think so. My stomach's still growling and there's nothing not eating will fix." I hoped I didn't sound callous, but by the twinkle in his eyes, I knew he agreed.

Avoiding any further discussion about the murders, we instead discussed park procedures between huge bites of grilled salmon and steak, cleaning our plates like two people ravished by an inhuman hunger. I almost choked, considering just how much I'd like to be ravished by the man inclined over his plate.

Seeming to read my thoughts, he glanced up, running his tongue over his upper lip. I couldn't help imagining what his tongue would feel like gliding down me.

I scolded myself. Thoughts like those belonged to a sex-starved woman, not a twenty-four-year-old-virgin. I had every intention of keeping my purity intact until my wedding night, but for the first time, ever, I wondered if I'd make it.

Zane, if he uncovered my internal battle, was certain to rise to the challenge of deflowering me. Keeping a safe distance had become more important.

Being raised a good Baptist girl made an impact on my beliefs. My religious upbringing was like a safety net keeping me from losing control and following after what my mother referred to as desires of the flesh. I'd never understood the whole temptation principle, until this moment. I wished now that I'd paid closer attention in church.

"Delicious!" He reached for his water.

"Amen to that!" I agreed, sounding far more spiritual than I felt.

Zane gave me a lopsided grin. I couldn't blame him. Typically, I didn't shout amen after a meal — although my steak had been flame-broiled to perfection.

"Can I tell you a secret?" His eyes twinkled with mischief.

I leaned forward, eager to learn what type of secret a man like Zane might reveal.

"I love a woman who's not afraid to eat when she's hungry."

Not sure whether to feel insulted or pleased, I decided on pleased. I'd always hated phony women who refused to eat in front of men. "Thanks, I think. I enjoy food."

"That's just one of many things we have in common."

"I'm sorry. Did I miss something?" Now I was baffled. I barely knew Zane Marshall. Although, I was beginning to hope that would change despite my internal warning system flashing red.

"We both care about animals. We've determined we enjoy food, *and* we like each other." His expression dared me to say otherwise.

"I think you're overestimating our very short acquaintance. To be honest, earlier, I was leaning toward the not-liking-you side. Your car caught my attention, though. Oh, and the fact you kept me from getting mauled and crushed helped."

"See! We both like my car!" He laughed loud enough that a few heads turned our direction. He lowered his voice, "I do like you, Chloe. I have what you might call a sixth sense about people. You're a good woman, but you don't believe it."

Stunned by his assessment, and how close our faces were, I pulled back. No one had ever called me a good woman, and he was right, believing it wasn't easy for me. My former teenage confidence had diminished after my dramatic breakup with Jordon, amongst other things better forgotten.

Not comfortable with the emotions he'd triggered, and intending to keep my commitment by paying my own tab, I reached for my purse.

"I don't believe in going Dutch." He pulled a shiny gold card from his wallet.

"Oh, I see." My protective defenses slammed into place.

"Women aren't capable of paying their own way. You think I'm some damsel in distress looking for a big strong man to save me."

My comment drew the ire of two older women seated at the table next to us. They looked appalled by my outburst.

I had no reference point for Zane. A man who looked like a movie star, but was also insightful, humorous, and seemed to care, was beyond comprehension.

Too good to be true was exactly that: too good to be true.

I'd been hurt by a so-called perfect man once before. It wouldn't happen again.

"How was your lunch?" A pretty waitress accepted his card. Like every woman who came within ten feet of Zane, she made no attempt to hide her approval.

Crossing my arms, I waited, wishing I'd driven. Oh, no; I just had to ride in the Corvette.

When the waitress returned, she scribbled what I imagined was her phone number, before handing over the receipt. Zane gave her a blinding smile.

What a dog! I thought. *Typical male.*

Luke was going to have to choose between his newest employee and me after all. Plum Beach Wildlife Park wasn't big enough for both of us. I hoped my seniority and Luke's long-term crush would give me the edge I needed.

We'd know soon enough.

Four

Managing to remain silent on our drive back to the park was more difficult than I'd expected. Zane, on the other hand, seemed unaffected by my simmering rage. His slight grin signaled he was enjoying life — including no significant worries about my unpredictable emotions. He tried once to apologize. I didn't give him a chance.

Pressed against the passenger door, I pictured myself with steam shooting out my ears and a torrent of unladylike words pouring from my mouth. Instead, I kept my mouth clamped shut and plotted what I'd say to Luke when I issued my ultimatum.

Zane broke the silence, his smile vanishing. "Not good."

Startled, I peered out the window. There were three police cruisers and one unmarked car by the wildlife park's front entrance. People milled around, some looking dazed.

Zane parked and we waited by his car.

"Not good at all," I agreed, wondering if one of our predators had somehow gotten loose and attacked a visitor. A vision of a vicious Butch the Lion crossed my mind.

I Kissed a Dog

Spotting Zane's car, Luke broke away from the group and jogged over. "Chloe, I don't know how to tell you this." He kept his head down, unable to make eye contact.

"What?" Panic's cold hand squeezed my windpipe. I gasped, but couldn't catch my breath.

The last thing I saw before succumbing to darkness was Zane's face leaning over me.

"She's coming around," a relieved voice announced.

My first thought was one of absolute embarrassment. I'd swooned in front of half the town, a ton of tourists, law enforcement officials, and worst of all — Zane — had once again caught me in his arms. That thought gave me a twinge of unwanted pleasure.

"What happened?" I remembered why I'd had a panic attack in the first place. Luke had been sharing bad news. When no one answered, I pushed myself into a sitting position. "Please, I'm fine."

Glancing around the room, I realized I was in Luke's office on his leather couch. Zane, Luke, and Officer Tate from this morning, were looking down at me.

Luke pulled up a chair and took my hand.

This was getting weirder by the minute. Why couldn't they just get it over with? I'd already determined there'd been another murder — a person I knew on a personal level.

"Will ..." Luke looked at Officer Tate.

"Miss, I'm sorry to meet you again under these circumstances, but Will Mills was found stabbed in his bed, about sixty minutes ago."

"How? Who found him?" Confusion wrapped around me

like a thick fog. Fearing I might faint again, I squeezed Luke's hand.

Not Will. It couldn't be true. I'd dated him a few times. Nothing serious, but he was a good friend. We worked together. I liked him.

"When he didn't show up for work, and I couldn't reach him, I called his brother." Luke shook his head, but didn't relax his grip on my hand.

"He never misses work," I said absently.

"That's what concerned me," Luke agreed.

I knew this was difficult for Luke too. He made a point of being concerned about all his employees. As much as we all bickered, we were one big family. Will had been the one that kept us laughing.

"I know you're all grieving and in shock," Officer Tate said, lowering his voice. "But, Ms. Carpenter, your boss shared a little more about your special ability. By the way, you were right about Barney."

I nodded, anticipating his next words. Using my talent for police business wasn't something I'd ever wanted, or considered. I'd refused my stepdad's requests for help on cases several times.

"We'd like you to come to Will's house, hoping you might spend some time with his dog and …"

I groaned. Not a dog! Why couldn't it be a parrot, maybe a goldfish?

"Are you o —?"

"Go on," I sighed. Of course I'd have to chat with a dog. Danger and dogs, the two things that I'd sworn off that just kept coming back to torment me.

"He had a dog and cat. Can you communicate with both?"

I Kissed a Dog

"Yes. Can we get this over with? I'm pretty overwhelmed right now." That was an understatement.

"I'll go with you," Zane offered, extending his hand.

Stunned by his suggestion, I wasn't sure how to respond. Last I checked I was furious with him. And now I'd have to delay my heart-to-heart with Luke. Today wasn't the day for employee quarrels. Under the circumstances, I realized how petty I'd behaved at the restaurant. A man had wanted to pay for my lunch. Like that was a crime.

Aware three men were waiting for my answer, I snapped at Zane, "If you insist."

Ignoring his hand I stood, my legs trembling. I couldn't handle a repeat of our earlier electric encounter. Touching was off limits when it came to Zane Marshall, no matter how tempted I was to test whatever it was I felt between us.

I hated to admit, despite the craziness unfolding around us, I was undeniably curious about Zane's motives for wanting to accompany me and was shocked by what he said next.

"I thought I might offer to care for Will's pets, if the family doesn't want them." He shrugged. "I've got a thing for animals."

Every time I was ready to write Zane off, he said or did something chivalrous. Maybe I'd find a daisy on the way back so I could play the old "he loves me; he loves me not" game with the words changed to: "I love him; I love him not."

Much to my relief, I rode in the squad car's front seat with Officer Tate. Zane looked cramped in the back. I was beginning to understand he would look confined just about anywhere. He was an imposing man. *I love him not;* I reminded myself for the umpteenth time since we'd left work.

We pulled into Will's gravel driveway about thirty minutes

later. I could see his treasured quads parked off to the side of the garage. He'd been a great driver, somewhat of a daredevil, but good enough to convince me into taking a long thrill ride on the dunes last summer. It was almost impossible for me to accept that he was dead — killed — and would never ride again.

The police team swarming over his property like flies on a corpse were what convinced me.

"This way," Officer Tate directed.

Several colleagues acknowledged him but gave me cautious looks. I wondered if they knew the reason for my presence. If so, they weren't sold on my special skills. I recognized the FBI agent from the news. He glanced our way without any official acknowledgment.

My arm hairs stood at full attention when his eyes met mine. He gave me what my mom referred to as the major heebie jeebies. I decided right then I didn't like or trust Agent Green. Zane wasn't the only one with good instincts.

"You ready?" Before I realized what he was doing, Zane rested his hand on my arm. The electricity remained, but this time it felt less intense, yet no less pleasurable. His touch provided a calm and confident feeling I was grateful for.

You are a good woman echoed through my tumultuous thoughts. As much as I'd like to believe otherwise, Zane was the reassuring presence I was desperate for right now.

Remembering why I was here, I nodded at Officer Tate. "Take me to talk with the animals." I hoped I sounded halfway pleasant — anything to slice through the gloom that hung over the crime scene. My earlier morning cheer had been replaced by a grim sense of duty.

Exiting Will's house, a woman approached. "You must be

Chloe Carpenter. I'm Detective Davis. You are?" She looked at Zane with open approval.

"Dr. Marshall. I'm the new wildlife vet down at the park." He extended his hand.

She disregarded it and jotted something in her flip pad; the evidence of her approval gone like it'd never existed, replaced with suspicion. "I may want to talk with you later, Dr. Marshall."

I attempted to swallow my surprise. So, not all women were automatically under his spell. Even more unexpected, though, was my intense desire to protect him from her probing eyes. As if aware of my intentions, she gave a curt nod and strode away.

Inside the house, everything appeared undisturbed. A man was dusting for prints and other law enforcement personnel were removing plastic bags of evidence.

I couldn't begin to imagine how I'd feel right now had we been lovers. Once again, my commitment to maintaining my virginity had saved me from additional heartache.

"Here's Junior. The cat took off." Another officer led a young pit bull into the room.

I confirmed the puppy's leash was secure. I'd never forgotten or forgiven the pit bull that had escaped with my favorite shoe.

"Hey, little guy." I had to admit he was adorable. His stubbed-tail wiggled and he yipped, excited by the attention. "You sure are cute." He squirmed and pranced around us more like a pony than a pit. I realized I'd have to hold him and get him settled down if I was going to retrieve any information other than: *Pet me! Pet me! I like you! Pet me!*

After some reassuring whispers and gentle strokes, Junior calmed; his round puppy-eyes melting into mine. For a brief scary second, I couldn't see or hear anything. Then the memories roared into my mind like a tornado. *Woman. Sex. She smelled like a dog.* The pictures were beyond my wildest and most horrifying nightmares.

A redheaded woman was clinging to Will like a rider on a bucking bronco, her head thrown back in ecstasy. Following their vigorous coupling, everything blurred. She changed into something I couldn't explain. Either that or she'd let a wolf the size of a grizzly into the bedroom.

All I knew for certain was that Will hadn't been stabbed.

He'd been ripped to shreds.

"Oh. My. God." I couldn't begin to barricade the pain exploding from my mouth in waves of wailing.

Zane lifted me to my feet, pulling me against his hard chest, cradling me. He let me sob; winding his fingers through my curls, while I released every painful memory I'd unwittingly clung to until now. Feeling safe in his arms, I dared to wonder what might happen next.

How would I explain what the dog had so vividly communicated? Who would believe me?

☙

The rest of the day passed in a blur.

The park stayed open. With the tourist season in jeopardy, it would have been unwise for Luke to shut down. Business soared. People were fascinated by death and destruction. And our little serial killer, who I now believed was female, was attracting plenty of attention.

With hesitation, I'd revealed every detail of my grisly vision with Detective Davis and Agent Green. Both, to my amazement, appeared to believe me, at least they hadn't locked me in a rubber room. Agent Green had demanded additional details about the woman, for some reason hung up on the color and style of her hair.

Zane had listened to my summary with his jaw twitching and fists clenched. He seemed to be experiencing an internal battle, remaining sullen.

As I'd expected, there were a number of key elements being kept from the media. Agent Green did go on record with the information about a woman being involved in the slayings. All other details had been kept confidential.

Luke found me alone by my cubby. I stared at the wall unsure what to do next, dreading my evening commute back to Florence.

Luke patted my shoulder. "You okay?"

Tempted to snap at him for his ridiculous question, I bit my lip instead, deciding he didn't have a clue what else to say. Conversations were always strained following a death. Not just any death, but the brutal killing of a mutual friend.

"I'm okay," I lied, relieved that what felt like the longest day of my life was over.

"It'll be different around here." He leaned against his desk, watching me clean out my cubby. "Do you want to grab a drink?"

I paused. We'd never had a drink together. I wasn't sure if I wanted to spend my personal time with Luke. I understood his reasoning. With Will dead, and our unacknowledged attraction, it made sense. Still, my internal alarm system was chiming away. Warning that in my current condition I might turn to Luke for comfort. I'd regret that big time.

No. I wanted to go home — alone — and cry.

"Thanks for the offer, but not tonight." I could tell he was disappointed.

"Well, all right. If you need tomorrow off, I understand," he offered sounding drained.

"I'll be here." Staying home stewing about what I'd witnessed wasn't an option. "You take care."

When I reached my car, I was shocked to see Zane's Corvette next to mine. He stood by the rear bumper, staring into the distance. "Good, you're here."

"And?" I tried to hide my excitement, and frustration. How could one man conjure such opposing feelings? I'd just rejected a man I'd known and liked for years, but was giddy over an almost stranger.

"I just figured you could use a friend." He shrugged. "We could go Dutch on drinks." His dark eyes bore into mine, sending chills down my spine.

Ignoring the fact that moments ago I'd told Luke no, I decided to throw caution to the wind. "Sure. Where?"

"You live in Florence, right?"

"I do, but you haven't told me where you're staying." I still knew nothing of substance about Zane Marshall.

Well, that wasn't one-hundred-percent true. I knew he liked me and considered me a good woman. I knew he had the power to enrage or encourage me. Most important, I knew there was a connection between us unlike anything I'd ever experienced. I just didn't know where he lived.

"I'm not sure about a permanent location. For now, I rented a place a few miles out of town. I'll find a good deal on a house soon."

Satisfied with his answer, I decided to choose a spot where

I Kissed a Dog

I felt comfortable and was close to home, ensuring I could take my own car. "If you don't mind following me up to Florence and backtracking after, we could go to Joni's Bar and Grill. They have good specials."

An hour later, we were once again seated across from each other in a corner booth. This time, the lights were dim and tendrils of smoke curled upward from the crowded tables. The smell of liquor and boisterous laughter filled the rustic bar giving it a certain appeal.

"Is this becoming a habit?" Zane grinned from behind his menu.

"No!" It's just been a strange day."

Because the truth was, no matter how strange a day, or how much I resisted Zane, spending time with him was enjoyable, and watching the women watch him added an interesting twist, one I hadn't experienced on this level before. Not that the guys I'd dated before were bad looking, they just couldn't compare to Zane. I wasn't sure any man could, and I knew it wasn't just his good looks I appreciated.

"Strange yes, but I've never enjoyed the company so much."

A perky waitress, I didn't recognize, saved me from responding. As expected, she almost drooled at the sight of Zane, who ordered without hesitation, "I'll take the largest steak on the menu, very rare, and whatever beer you have on tap."

"Chef Salad," I piped up, realizing she was still staring at my companion, ignoring my presence. Was I invisible? Considering the number of men who dared sneak a look my direction, I guessed not.

"You sure have your share of admirers," Zane noted with a hint of annoyance.

"Nothing compared to you. I thought our waitress might

slobber or hang her tongue out. I bet she's still panting." I watched as she moved to another table, reluctant to turn away.

"Are you jealous?" He asked; his lopsided grin back on display, dimples and all.

Was I? I hadn't been jealous for a long time.

"Well hello, Zane," a sultry female voice interrupted our banter. "How unexpected to find you *here*." Her eyes traveled over the room with obvious distaste.

"Jazmine," he growled, not pleased by her intrusion.

"Mind if I join you?" Without hesitating, she glided into the booth beside him, resting a hand on his bicep. Her bright crimson nails shimmered; her malice-filled eyes, dark like Zane's, gleamed at me.

"Can I get you anything?" The perky waitress returned, looking as aggravated by the new woman's presence as I was.

"I'll be just a moment." A curt wave dismissed the girl. Ms. Perky marched off. I sympathized with the waitress' wounded pride.

Jazmine was as stunning as she was ice-cold. I didn't need to see the tags to know she was a Designer Fashion Week regular. Her sheen black hair was cut in a neat geometrical bob that framed her face, drawing attention to her sculpted cheekbones and heart-shaped lips. Her makeup was applied with such obvious expertise that I thought of a model I'd seen on the cover of *Vogue*.

That model had looked genuinely happy, this woman oozed of cruel intent.

"You've been avoiding my calls." Jazmine sulked, caressing Zane's arm with her graceful fingers. He shook her off.

You'll be my mate. Tradition requires it. Her eyes flashed with a myriad of emotions.

My jaw dropped, turning my gaping mouth into a capital O. The woman's bizarre thought had permeated my mind. Realizing how I must look, I shut my mouth and reached for a slice of bread.

"I told you I'm busy with business. We'll talk at the scheduled time. And be aware; your behavior is not earning you any points," Zane snapped.

"Oh, now I have to earn points." She tsked. "I'd hate for you to lose ..."

"Enough!" he growled.

With one final, scathing glance my direction, she rose fluidly and vanished out the door

Following her exit, the noise returned to the room.

It was then I recognized that following her arrival, everything had somehow revolved around her. She reminded me of a predator stalking its prey. All the other "animals", had remained silent, hoping to avoid the hunter's detection.

I hadn't succeeded in avoiding anything.

She was well-aware of my existence, and she already abhorred me. In one meeting I'd become the mysterious woman's enemy. Between her and Rhonda, I was pretty unpopular.

"Don't mind Jazmine." Zane guzzled his beer.

Stunned by his casual comment, I leaned forward, ready to battle. "You're kidding, right?" I didn't wait for an answer. "Some crazy woman, with eyes like a rabid dog, comes in, and from what I could tell, pretty much threatens you. Oh, and I guess you didn't notice the way she looked at me."

"Your dinners." The waitress slid our heaping platters in front of us and hurried away. Smart woman!

Zane grabbed his knife and fork and sliced into a steak big enough to feed four. He tore off a huge chunk of bloody beef and swallowed it whole.

I struggled not to gag. Sure, I liked red meat, but not when it was still mooing.

"I'll deal with Jazmine. She's just a business partner. She likes me; I don't like her. End of story." He tore off another piece, blood trickling from the corner of his mouth. Realizing I was watching him with disgust, he grabbed a napkin and wiped his chin.

"What type of business?" I couldn't begin to eat until Zane finished. At least he had one glaringly imperfect trait, he ate like a savage. He must have been on better behavior during lunch.

Leaning back for a minute, he considered his words. "We both do work for a chain of casino resorts in Washington and Nevada. We've had some issues with one of our Washington locations."

"Which one?" I half remembered reading something about a Washington Indian tribe hoping to develop casino sites off their reservation. I also recalled there'd been an alleged murder associated with the request.

"Wild Winds."

"Wasn't there a murder up there last year?" Of course I'd remembered. My memory was impeccable.

"Will anything I say convince you I'm just a regular guy with a normal, sometimes dysfunctional life?"

"It's the dysfunctional part that concerns me." I tried not to smile. Zane had devoured his steak and seemed eager to put an end to my questioning. Maybe I could let go of my suspicious nature for the rest of the evening. After all, I'd have day after day at work to scrutinize him.

"And you're not at all dysfunctional?" He cocked his head, reminding me of the cute Pit-bull puppy I'd interviewed earlier.

"Fine! You win!" I stabbed at my salad, no longer able to ignore the painful grumbles. "If I had a middle name, it would be dysfunctional."

Several drinks later, we were chatting away like old friends, Jazmine and his gruesome eating habits forgotten.

For the first time since I could remember, I shared the entire coma *incident* story. Zane was an adept listener, nodding at the right times and commenting when appropriate. For the most part, he let me talk. I'd forgotten how good it felt to open up with no agenda. Talking about my gift was a huge relief.

"You're a pretty darn good listener, Zane Marshall." I could tell the glasses of wine had done their magic, lubricating my libido. As a very sporadic drinker, it didn't take much.

"Why thank you, lovely lady. By the way, your skin tone is fabulous. May I ask your background?"

Usually people ho-hummed around, afraid to ask questions about my ethnicity. I'd always wondered what the big deal was. My caramel coloring was courtesy of my Caucasian mother and my real dad's half African half Native American heritage. Bob, my illustrious stepfather, was as white as white can be.

"I'm a smorgasbord." I giggled, realizing my mistake too late.

"Um, I love a good smorgasbord," he all but groaned, his eyes growing smoky. *I want her.*

I felt a jolt of primal hunger so intense I was afraid I might climb across the table and into his lap. Astonished that those three simple words had managed to escape from behind his mental barrier, I tried to listen for more. The wall had returned, but his eyes smoldered with anticipation.

All I had to do was reach for him.

My breathing grew ragged as he watched my internal struggle.

"I need to get home," I managed to stutter. "Work," I apologized, as if he didn't know my schedule. Defying my still-pounding heart was as impossible as ignoring a stampede of wild horses. I wondered if he could sense my desire and uncertainty.

"As you wish," he said, his voice husky.

I jumped up before I could change my mind. "I need to use the ladies room."

Touching up my makeup, I tried to find my usual composure. It wasn't easy. Closing my eyes, I breathed in through my nose, starting my proverbial counting routine.

As soon as my mind relaxed, a flood of words rushed in.

He's in there. I saw Jazmine leave. She looked pretty pissed.

What's new? She's a bitch.

Laughter.

Let's deliver our message to Zane and have a little fun with his female.

She's human.

Your point?

How many were there? I wasn't sure, but at least three men were waiting outside the bar, and their intentions for us were far from honorable.

Zane was finishing his beer when I rejoined him. He sensed my mood change.

I Kissed a Dog

"What happened?" He slammed his glass down. "Did she come back?"

"No, but someone wants to hurt you. There's a group of men outside waiting for us. Don't ask me how I know, because until today, I could only read animals, but somehow I can now hear specific people. They mentioned Jazmine."

"Great. I didn't want to drag you into my personal problems."

"I take it this is part of the dysfunctional stuff," I snapped, feeling let down.. Though a part of me wanted to believe he was protecting me.

"You stay in here. I'll handle this."

"Oh no! You're not leaving me behind. What if something happens to you?" Just then it occurred to me that there were people trained to deal with stalking psychopaths. "Why don't we call the police?"

"Not a good idea." Zane was on his feet. His features had morphed from relaxed to intense. He reminded me of a vicious dog. "Is there any way you can sense where they're positioned?" He sniffed the air.

"I'm not sure. I can try." I closed my eyes and attempted to erase the terrifying images I'd already conjured in my mind. The voices returned. I could visualize the men. There were three — one by the Corvette; two in the woods behind the restaurant, around thirty feet from our vehicles. They were contemplating entering the bar.

"They're tired of waiting," I warned. "Three males, all near our cars. Two out of sight, hiding in the brush."

"Them coming in here is not an option." He swung around giving the room a once over. "Too many people."

"Zane, some of these locals are pretty tough. Why not get some help?" I couldn't fathom why he was so hung up on doing this alone.

Before I could comment further, he stalked from the bar, ignoring my calls for him to wait.

Men! I decided to do the one thing I could — eavesdrop.

Seeing the check had been paid, I grabbed my purse and hurried to the entrance. There were benches hugging the lobby walls and the area was deserted. Away from the crowded bar, I could pay better attention to what was happening outside.

Who sent you? Zane demanded.

Don't play coy, Marshall. The Indians are on to you. They don't like our kind.

Your kind is the problem! Zane growled, sounding more feral than human.

That's right. I forgot; you're one of those high and mighty purebreds. In their eyes we're all the same.

The talking stopped and fighting started.

In my vision, I heard a series of vicious dog-like snarls and an ear-shattering roar, followed by what sounded like bones snapping.

Too afraid to do nothing, I charged for the door, forgetting my aversion to dogs and danger.

The ferocious snarls and a few whimpers were coming from the wooded area off to the bar's right side.

I dodged between vehicles, searching for what I knew were four men in a barbaric death match.

An overpowering need to protect Zane increased with every step.

My lone weapon, from Bob, of course, was a never-before-used canister of mace. Until this moment, I'd never had reason to wield it. With my hands shaking, I held it in front of me like a too-heavy sword. I slunk into the woods, ready to fire into an attacker's eyes given the chance.

What I saw in a small clearing rocked my understanding of reality as I'd known it.

Two men lay twisted and bloody on the ground.

Intestines spilled from one man's torn abdomen, darkening the ground with a foul, clumpy fluid. A third struggled to his feet, aiming a gun at what appeared to be a humungous black bear standing at least seven feet tall on two hind legs.

It was not a bear.

The creature looked like a wolf hybrid from some horror movie with topnotch special effects. Its muzzle, longer than an average wolf's, rippled, and its lips curled back, revealing long spiked fangs, still covered with its victim's juices. Blood poured from a jagged gash on its massive shoulder.

I didn't see Zane anywhere.

The strange man and monster circled each other like two wrestlers in a ring.

The man was built like Zane, with cropped yellow hair. He carried himself with confidence even while facing the lethal beast. It was easy to see without the gushing wound, the wolf-thing would have already disarmed and destroyed its human adversary, regardless of the man's courageous demeanor.

"Back down! I don't want to do this!" the man yelled, shaking the pistol.

The wolf-creature appeared to drop lower in what I

assumed was a posture of belated surrender. The man seemed to agree with my assessment and lowered his weapon. A relieved sigh escaped through my clenched teeth.

Any relief was short-lived.

The wolf, moving swifter than anything I'd ever seen, ripped into his final opponent's throat, tearing the flesh open.

Shrieking, the blond man crumpled to the ground, his blood staining the grass.

His head tumbled from his slumped shoulders, rolling to rest just an inch from my toes.

My own screams sliced through the darkness, silencing the remaining night sounds. I knew the music in the bar was too loud. No one could hear me. Unless maybe an exiting or entering customer happened upon me, I was alone with the murderous wolf creature.

What could a mere man do to help anyway? He'd end up slaughtered like the others.

The beast at last dropped to all fours, giving it a more wolf-like appearance. Its glowing eyes stared with longing in my direction. Was it going to eat me? Kill me?

Instead, a mournful howl erupted from its cavernous mouth before it lunged into the deeper foliage.

Later, back home, I sat slumped in my favorite *L-Z-Boy* recliner, feet up. Every few minutes I'd shake all over. And in a few short hours, I'd become a shell of my normal cheery self.

Disgusted for not calling the police sooner, I reached for the phone then pulled back.

What would I say? How could I explain the evening's events? I had the FBI agent's card, but couldn't bring myself to look for it.

For some ridiculous reason, I still felt protective of Zane. I had no idea where he'd disappeared to or if he'd somehow managed to survive the unearthly encounter. What if I inadvertently implicated him?

All I knew for certain: the universe was home to things far more foreign than my unusual ability to communicate with animals.

Right now was one time I wished I had closer friendships. I could call Luke, but then I'd have to explain my time with Zane. I hadn't spoken with Melanie since her divorce last month. With her personal beliefs and paranormal stories gaining popularity, she'd at least hear me out. My parents were not an option.

Unable to sleep and not sure what else to do, I flipped open my laptop and logged online.

Wolfman, I typed and watched the links pop up. It was then I realized the one word I'd been searching for: *Werewolf.*

That had to be it! I'd seen a real, honest to God, werewolf.

Just reading the word prompted an avalanche of memories from my day — hearing what must have been Zane's "beautiful bitch" comment; the park's wolf, Randall, and his vision of a huge black wolf that he'd referred to as *brother*; Zane's odd interaction with the very same wolf; Zane's superhuman speed and strength; Jazmine's reference to her future *mate*; the three men's comments about me being a human; the vision of the monster in Will's bedroom; the brutal murders. It all made sense now, sort of. Zane, my potential dream man, was a werewolf. He'd beheaded someone with his own teeth. He was a vicious killer and the full moon stories had nothing to do with his ability to change. He'd shifted at will.

There was more. I remembered the three would-be

assailants referring to Zane as a purebred. What did that make them?

They weren't human.

I'd tried earlier today, with no success, to read my very human coworkers. No wonder I'd heard the thugs! They were part animal! What did that make Jazmine? — One scary bitch.

Horror and anger collided as I remembered the hatred in Jazmine's eyes, sending my body into a series of spasms. My teeth chattered as the tears flowed again. I thought I'd released every fear and tear back at Will's. Apparently not. I made no effort to hold back now.

What I'd endured in less than twenty four hours was enough to make the toughest diehard crazy with fright. Without my special ability, I'd have continued my life unaware of the supernatural world around me. I felt better knowing. Knowing meant I could prepare and take precautions to protect myself and the people I cared about.

Still too wired to sleep after the tears subsided, and desperate to know more, my fingers flew across the keyboard as I conducted my first ever research project on werewolves.

Of course I'd fall for a dog, a damn dog. Talk about irony. Someone out there had a sick sense of humor. I hadn't bargained for this when I'd said my half-hearted prayer for excitement yesterday morning.

Bob had always warned us to be careful what we wished for, another life lesson I'd ignored.

As expected, the Internet was filled with abundant folklore in relation to werewolves, or lycanthropes, as they were referred to in Greek. Some were said to have mystical powers, including superb senses and strength. But the stories, overall, featured dramatic differences, making it difficult to determine the facts, if any, that were relevant to all so-called werewolves.

I wondered if one of Zane's powers was his ability to break a woman's heart in forty-eight hours or less. It would seem if my heart was any indication, he was heartbreak material.

Looking back, his protective nature was without a doubt lupine. My old mutt, Buddy Boy, would have fought off Butch the lion to save me, given the chance. Zane had been protective from the start. That thought gave me some comfort. He hadn't been running around rescuing anyone else.

Sometime before dawn on Tuesday, with my thoughts becoming even more incoherent, I closed my computer.

That was the last I remembered of my longest Monday ever.

◉

The ringing phone jarred me awake.

I tore myself from the chair where I'd fallen asleep. My wall clock read 9:11 AM. I was over an hour late for work.

"Luke, I don't know what happened!" I half screeched, not yet awake.

"I told you to take the day off. Zane's here. He can handle things. Stay home. It's an order."

"No way! Let me hop in the shower, and I'll be there." I hung up before he could protest further.

This I had to see.

Mr. Werewolf had made it to work after a long night of pillaging and killing. We had a number of things to discuss. First item on my to-discuss-list was his identity — the real one.

After showering in record time, I paid careful attention to applying my makeup just so, enhancing my features. I made up my eyes like I'd seen in a copy of *Vogue*, giving them a cat-like appearance. I intended to use every possible angle, including my womanly wiles, to persuade Zane into spilling the gory details of his existence.

Any lustful feelings I might have entertained had been severed, right along with the blond stranger's head.

Following an uneventful commute, I pulled into my usual space, noting the parking lot was already filling up. A steady stream of people flowed through the front entrance. The theory that our summer business faced extinction was proven wrong by the diverse crowd willing to brave the thick morning fog.

Rushing through the gate, I hurried to complete my normal routine. I'd have to forfeit my usual coffee-on-the-bench time — one of the major reasons I was never late. Starting work on the run held no appeal for me.

The moment I spotted Zane talking with Rhonda and Luke, I regretted coming in. My earlier bravado was replaced by a sense of revulsion at the sight of our veterinarian/werewolf. By wearing the extra makeup and sequined jeans I now felt cheap and overdone rather than cute and confident. Who was I kidding? I was way out of my league. Women like Jazmine belonged with wolfy-men like Zane. He'd see right through my little ruse.

Determining I had just minutes, even seconds, before Zane and the others noticed my arrival; I decided to see if Zane's mental block was operational. Maybe he allowed himself a reprieve from the mental warfare without me around.

I concentrated, pushing away any distracting sounds. It took a second and I was in.

I've got to talk with Chloe. She saw me. What am I going to do? Jazmine will find a way to implicate her, especially if I keep avoiding the mating ceremony. How could something so simple turn into such a mess? The meeting is next week. That's all the time I have…

"Chloe! I didn't know you were here." Another employee, John Mitchell, greeted me, looking puzzled by my strange behavior. I was half-hiding behind the wallaby enclosure staring at Zane.

"I figured you'd taken the day off." He followed the direction of my gaze.

"I should have. It's so strange without Will." I hoped John would take that as a cue to move on and mind his own business.

"He was a good guy. Sorry, gotta run! Time to display the babies." He zigzagged his way through the visitors toward the nursery.

As a longtime employee, John had one of the cushiest jobs in the park. His biggest stressor was ensuring that everyone had a chance to pet the fuzzy critters. I avoided the nursery. Baby animals didn't have much to say other than feed me; pet me.

Zane on the other hand had quite a bit to say in the short time I'd managed to infiltrate his thoughts. Making sense of his disjointed thinking was a whole different matter.

"I thought I told you to stay home!" Luke, being the first to notice my arrival, scolded. "You're so damn stubborn, Chloe."

"Since when is that a problem?" My eyes darted to the spot

Zane had been standing. Both he and Rhonda were gone. "Where did my illustrious partner go?"

Luke peered at his always-present clipboard. "Where he's supposed to be, the exam room. Please don't tell me you're still worked up about him," he paused, looking guilty. "I'm sorry I yelled at you. With Will and all —"

"No." I stopped him. "You're right. I was being childish. There's a serial killer roaming our streets. My issues with Zane are nothing I can't deal with. Don't apologize." I hoped I sounded more sincere than I felt. My problems with Zane were far from over. Oh no, we were just beginning to scratch the surface.

"Good. He'll be glad you're here. One of the zebras was limping."

"I'm on it, and, please, stop worrying about me. Okay?' I felt bad for Luke. He was a great boss and a good guy. Sometimes I took his kindness for granted.

"You look fantastic. What's with the makeup?" He gave me a knowing look, tinged with a hint of jealous speculation.

"Can't a girl play with her cosmetics now and then?" I tried to joke off his not-so-subtle insinuation.

"Luke! I'm out of ones!" Christy, our gift shop cashier, hollered from inside, waving. A half-circle of restless customers surrounded her counter.

Relieved by the distraction, I swallowed my rising worries, and headed to the exam room.

Five

"Calm down, Missy." Zane hovered over the female Zebra. His current caring demeanor belied his feral nature as a werewolf.

Standing just inside the door, I could sense Missy's terror. She saw Zane as a hunter not a healer. I wondered if he was even a real veterinarian.

"Are you planning to help or just watch me struggle?' Zane asked, eyebrows raised.

"Oh, I don't know. She thinks you're going to eat her for breakfast."

"You think you're so cute, don't you? Do you have any idea what you've got us into?" He moved away from the squirming filly to face me.

"Me?" How in the world could he blame me for his brutal rampage? And why did I still find him so darn delectable? My so-called disgust had vanished, replaced by an unacceptable craving to feel his mouth on mine. I forced myself to think of the bloody men in the field. That did the trick. My loathing returned.

"Yes! You! When I said 'stay in the bar,' did that not mean *stay in the bar*?" He stepped closer, glaring down at me, his eyes wild with fury and something I couldn't discern.

Backing up, I found myself pressed against the wall. Icy fear froze my mouth, keeping me from spouting off.

"What have you done to me, Chloe Carpenter?" Taking another step, he reduced the distance between us. I could smell his musky cologne and feel his body heat.

"You're scaring me," I peeped.

"It's about time something scared you."

Without warning, he reached around the back of my head with one vast hand, drawing my mouth to his.

His lips pressed against mine; I melted — my knees all rubbery. Sensing my dilemma, his other hand slid around my waist pulling me closer.

To my dismay, he was hard — everywhere.

A little moan escaped from the back of my throat as I parted my lips, allowing him to explore my mouth. Sighing with pleasure, my hands moved of their own accord, finding their way around his neck and into the thickness of his dark waves. His hair was as I'd imagined, soft yet dense.

A delicious wildness hummed between us, I was reeling from its intensity.

Missy's distinct braying-bark tore through my mind, reminding me I was locking lips with a vicious, inhuman beast, all while the zebra looked on, fearing not only for her own safety, but also, from the images she was firing my way, for mine.

"The zebra needs you," I whispered.

"From what I can tell, *you* need me more." Zane smirked.

"O-o-o-o-o … you." The words wouldn't form.

So much for self-control.

Deciding to hammer my raging hormones into submission, I approached Missy with caution. I could see the pain and terror in her eyes. Apprehensive, she snorted as Zane moved closer.

"You're scaring her. How can you be a vet when the animals see you as a predator?"

"I'm great with lions, tigers, and bears, oh my."

For a moment I just stared — a werewolf joking about the *Wizard of Oz*. Could things get any stranger?

I should have known better than even to think the question.

"How about you being *Little Red Riding Hood* and I'll be the big bad wolf," he roared with laughter, sending Missy into a braying fit.

"Is everything all right?" Luke pushed through the swinging doors. Worry etched across his face.

"Our new vet seems to have an obsession with fairytales." I stopped to glare in his direction. "And a desire to torment me and our poor zebra."

"Zane, I have to tell you, I heard you laughing like …"

"A maniac," I finished, pleased to have Luke on my side at last.

"I was going to say, like he was having a good time. It was Missy's discomfort I was worried about, not yours, Chloe." Luke looked between us.

Ignoring Luke's mutiny, I faced the zebra. She'd waited long enough for our diagnosis.

I rested one hand on her side and stroked her neck with the other, making sure to gain direct eye contact. The graphic images she released were disgusting, fitting with the horror-movie-theme from my previous day.

A well-muscled man, hidden inside a hooded sweatshirt, tore across the zebra's meadow, remaining crouched, low to the ground as he ran. It was nighttime, and I could feel the horror as the human-beast ambushed Missy, slamming her to the ground.

The zebra screamed. Snarling, the *thing* sank his teeth into Missy's leg, sucking and pulling blood from the thrashing zebra.

Forcing myself to stay with the scene, I felt a stream of fiery bile flood my mouth as the man-beast raised his head, blood covering his face. He howled a deep guttural cry that caused me to fall back from the zebra, almost collapsing.

Zane did his normal hero-rescue-thing and captured me in his arms, keeping me from hitting the floor.

"We have to stop meeting like this," he whispered for my ears alone.

"Not a problem," I stammered, wishing for more oomph behind my words.

"What was it?" Luke helped Zane get me to a stool. "What did you see?"

"Water?" I croaked, still dangerously close to losing my breakfast.

Zane vanished and returned with a fresh water bottle. I let the water soothe my throat.

"Let me check something." I forced myself to stand and examine Missy's right rear leg. Sure enough, I located a large bruised patch that resembled a human hickey. I motioned the men over.

"I've never seen anything like this," Luke said.

I have. Zane thought, glancing at me. *I'll explain later.*

"Okay …" I forgot to mind message.

I Kissed a Dog

"Okay, what?" Luke looked doubly confused.

"Okay, here's the deal." I determined right then I couldn't tell my boss everything I'd seen. He wouldn't understand. Shoot! I didn't understand. I did understand one thing though: Zane didn't want me sharing all the gruesome details with Luke.

"All I know for certain is some animal attacked Missy." I paused, choosing my next words with care. "It was gnawing and sucking on her leg. She was so frightened I couldn't get a clear picture. We should treat her for possible infection and pain." I nodded at Zane who was already moving toward the large, glass, medicine cabinet.

"Maybe it's time I hire more than a sit-down security person," Luke pondered. "With our animals at risk … well, it seems prudent."

We'd hired Henry, a retired San Francisco beat cop, to spend the nights in the front ticket booth. The booth was a small room with a cot that opened into a single bed. A TV and DVD player were added bonuses. Henry could access the gift shop area, restrooms, coffeemakers, and all the essentials, through a side entrance into the main building.

There were also a number of video cameras placed strategically throughout the park, but not enough to film everything at once.

If Henry suspected a major disturbance, he'd contact local police. Other than a few high school kids looking for trouble, nothing major had ever occurred, until now.

"What are you thinking, a nighttime patrol?" I tried to hide my alarm. With what I now knew about werewolves and their blood-drinking counterparts, the idea of some poor, underpaid soul traipsing around after dark didn't sit well with me.

Add an estranged serial killer to the mix, and you had a big fat recipe for disaster.

"I'm not so sure about that," Zane mirrored my apprehension. "With our local serial killer and all — "

"I'm open to suggestions." Luke shrugged. "We've got to do something. I'll try to move a camera closer to the zebras, but what if other animals are being attacked?"

"If you don't have anything major for us, Zane and I can interview the animals," I suggested. Who better to talk with than the actual witnesses?

Pleased with my idea, Luke returned to his normal duties.

"Well?" I turned to Zane who was giving poor Missy a shot of antibiotic mixed with a pain medication.

"Working here," he grunted.

"Meet me on the bench when you finish," I commanded, before stomping away, maddened by his nonchalant attitude.

At last, I was sipping a sugar-filled cup of coffee. I almost never took my fifteen minute breaks, but today was an exception. Between Zane's conflicting attitudes and the zebra's nightmarish experience, my Tuesday was becoming as bizarre as my Monday; and it wasn't even noon yet.

To make matters worse, Rhonda sauntered over. "I suppose you've heard." She tilted her head and puckered her silicon-stuffed lips, feigning sadness. I could tell she was itching to spill the latest gossip or something worse.

"What now?" Fear clutched my heart like a vice as I envisioned another victim torn to shreds.

"You don't have to bite my head off," she snapped. "Some woman called for Zane. She said she was his fiancée. He doesn't seem like the marrying type. I'd gotten the feeling he was interested in me."

"You're telling me this *because?*" I tried to hide my annoyance. Jazmine, of course, came to mind. She'd referred to Zane as her potential mate. I guessed that would suffice as fiancée in the werewolf world.

"Well, you're with him a lot at work. I wondered if he'd mentioned me or this future wife."

"Ladies." Zane strode up, his Levis embracing every masculine bulge.

I couldn't tear my eyes from the area just below his belt. I suspected Rhonda was leering too — as if that made it any less unacceptable. By the glint in his eyes, it was easy to see just how aware he was of our staring.

"Zane," Rhonda purred. "When's the wedding?"

I froze — my gawking indiscretion all but forgotten. Did this woman have no tact? I wondered how Zane would explain Jazmine.

"Where'd you hear that nonsense?" He asked with obvious irritation.

"Your lady friend called. She happened to mention you were her husband-to-be. For us single girls, it's a major disappointment."

"Don't include me in your disappointed group of single girls," I quipped..

Zane shot me an "if looks could kill" look. *Love you, too, Babe.*

Eck! This mind-messaging was becoming as cumbersome as text-messaging. Why couldn't we just talk like two normal adults? *Because we're not normal adults*, I chided myself. One werewolf plus one animal-reading-freak equaled a major mismatch.

"Chloe, we'd better get to work." He raised his wrist, revealing a watch. "As for future wives, Rhonda; I promise nothing is signed in blood."

Clasping her hands, Rhonda giggled, unable to hide her pleasure. With a near-perfect runway pivot she spun toward the courtyard, making her exit dramatic as usual.

She, of course, hadn't picked up on the ominous way he'd said *blood*.

"I think we need to have our own talk prior to any animal conversations," Zane said minus any hidden innuendos I could identify.

"Where to?" The stone bench didn't seem private enough. Too many tourists.

"The wolves. Where else?"

"Where else," I agreed.

⁂

Zane led the way around the wolf exhibit to a concealed bench at the enclosure's far end. He motioned for me to sit.

"I'd hate to have you fainting again," he teased.

"I'm not a child," I muttered. I was starting to feel like the damsel-in-distress I'd worked so hard not to become.

"Oh, I'm well aware of your womanhood." He slid close enough that our thighs brushed. The electrical current tingled down my right leg.

"And, I've had to catch you more times in two days than I've caught any woman in my lifetime." He grinned. I noticed for the first time just how pointy his incisors were, not full-fledged fangs, but sharp nevertheless.

I tried without success to ignore his closeness. "You wanted to talk, and I'm all ears. By the way, you're over-using our little mind telepathy thing."

"I find it very convenient and stimulating." He sounded like he meant it.

In truth, there was a part of me that found our private communications stimulating as well. Not that I'd let Zane know. That would give him more unwanted power over me.

"Since you've seen more than any human should, I'll give you a rundown of what's going on. First, you should know, if you haven't already figured it out, you're in grave danger."

"You think?"

Danger pretty much oozed from Zane. Every moment in his presence was dangerous for me. Except I couldn't quite accept this gorgeous, very human-looking man, was the same monstrous killing machine I'd seen in the clearing.

"For once, can you just listen without getting all defensive?"

I nodded. If I wanted to learn about werewolves and the impact they'd have on my life, I'd have to surrender my sarcasm.

He continued. "As you've discovered, I'm not human. I'm a werewolf. I can change at will, anytime, anywhere, and I'm lethal in my changed forms. I protect what is mine with my life, and I destroy anyone or anything that challenges my pack's safety."

"*Your pack?*" I wondered if he'd protect me with his life. So far, he'd proven to be my personal rescuer, a great listener; he'd even called me a good woman. Every time I tried to remain focused on his evilness, I was bombarded by his goodness.

"Werewolves are divided into packs, some larger than others. I'm the Pacific Pack's Chief Enforcer. I'm second in command to our pack alpha, Logan Sanders, who is running one of our casinos in Vegas. Our pack is the largest on the West Coast. We live along the coast range, in Oregon and Washington, with a small contingent in California and Nevada.

Jazmine, who you were unlucky enough to meet, was selected to be my mate when I was just a pup. She, too, is a purebred. I despise her. There was a time, when we were younger, that I was drawn to her, but that all changed when I saw the *real* Jazmine, who is none too charming."

My curiosity got the better of me and I cut in, "She still wants to be your mate, doesn't she?" I couldn't deny that the idea of Jazmine cuddled up to Zane infuriated me.

"Not for the normal sentimental reasons. For her it's all about power. Mated to me she'd have substantial … privileges."

I decided to wait before asking more about the so-called mating privileges. I didn't want to appear eager to become a werewolf's mate.

Still experiencing some major anxiety about last night, I fired off a series of other must-know questions. "Who were those men that assaulted you? Why did they look so human? What about the Zebra's attacker?"

"Whoa, slow down, I promise I'll explain everything," he reassured.

I wished there was a way to speed up our conversation. There was a way. "Since you seem to like the convenience of our mental chit chat, what if you just *thought* everything you wanted to say. That way, I'll see the images." This seemed like the perfect communication solution under the circumstances.

"Maybe I'd prefer to talk, you know, like two normal people." He shrugged.

"Face it; we're not your average Joe and Jane."

"Take my hand." He reached over, his unique musky scent filling my senses.

"Is this necessary?" Holding hands seemed way too intimate. After our recent kissing session, my potential reaction to his touch worried me, making it difficult to discount my feelings for him.

Ignoring my question, he grinned what seemed a very wolfy grin. In fact, I could see the wolf in all his expressions. Instead of repelling me, I was even more curious.

"Okay." I allowed his massive hand to cover my much smaller one.

His heat penetrated through my fingers, warming areas of my body never touched by a man. I gulped, unable to look away from his gaze. The golden flecks in his eyes expanded, his wildness captivating me.

The images he transferred into my mind were crystal clear, squelching any sensuous feelings, and instead overwhelming my senses with the sights, smells, and sounds of a large gathering.

Men, women, and children mingled; eating, drinking, and dancing to the folksy songs of several musicians. Flowing skirts, cowboy hats, and denim coveralls were the fashion trend. A scene from the late 1800's or early 1900's had unfolded before me.

Following polite applause, the families seated themselves on long benches and wooden stools. A powerful looking man, with dark hair like Zane's, moved with surprising stealth to the front and faced the crowd.

"Friends and family, I'm proud, as your leader, to reestablish our peace treaty with the local Indian tribes. Earlier today, we signed this document." He held up a tanned parchment. "This agreement is based on our ability, as the purebred pack, to maintain control of the mutants, who have of late become very bothersome to our copper-skinned friends.

Ladies and children, if you'd be so kind to let the men move to the meeting room."

The women clustered together, talking in hushed tones as the men followed their leader through a side door. One lone boy, who resembled the pack's leader, stood off to the side. His gaze followed the trail of departing men.

"Go on, boy. Your father agreed." A gorgeous woman, with two smaller children clinging to her skirt, prodded the older boy forward. After a brief hesitation, he dashed through the entrance to join the men in the other room.

"Who is the boy?" I asked; certain he was a relation of Zane's.

"My father. The leader, of course, was my granddad. This event marked our renewed partnership with the Native American population. An agreement that's stayed intact until now."

"What do you mean, *until now?*"

"Keep watching." He squeezed my hand.

Following their meeting, the men exited the building, trudging in a triangular formation into the darkness. They hiked deep into the forest, stopping outside a grassy clearing occupied by a half-circle of misshapen lean-to's that faced several glowing bonfires.

Around the fires, figures crouched, feasting on dead carcasses — some animals — others human. Their hands and faces were splattered with gore.

Sensing the purebred pack, their lips receded. A series of snarls erupted from the camp.

I Kissed a Dog

Zane's pack shifted with unparalleled speed. A visual vibration surrounded them as bones broke, split, and refitted together; faces stretched, forming the elongated muzzles I recognized from last night. The pack's height increased, giving them the appearance of towering, fur-covered giants. Fangs glistened in the moonlight.

The nighttime peace was shattered by roars, snarls, and vicious growls as the two sides launched into battle, their bodies forming a sea of fur and flesh.

From the start, the purebreds maintained a considerable advantage.

Able to change without a full moon, they dominated the mutants, pressing their advantage. Flesh tearing and blood spraying, Zane's pack moved through the camp like conquering barbarians. The most attractive females, a group of ancient males, and the children, were spared.

"They became our slaves. Some of our males chose their women as mates. It was a bad idea. We should have complied with the Indians and destroyed them all. Then, maybe, we wouldn't be in the situation we're in now," Zane added, his expression grim.

"What situation?" I found myself hanging on Zane's explanations.

"When you leave enemies amongst you, in time, they find a way to rebel. In the late sixties, we agreed to let the mutants move on. The ones remaining in the wild, so to speak, had been staying away from humans, trying to blend into society like the rest of us.

With the Indians' approval, we decided to allow them limited freedom. Our pack chose the strongest males to enforce the long-established law — no feeding off humans or human-owned livestock. Unlike us, mutants have greater difficulty ignoring the bloodlust, particularly during a full moon."

"So these mutants became mutants in the first place because you guys snacked on them? You haven't explained how they came into existence other than saying they were 'bitten.'" I struggled to keep everything straight.

"Let's just say our ancient ancestors discovered that by biting humans they could convert them into wolf-like creatures — to do their dirty work. They hoped these mixed-breeds would serve as additional warriors and slaves.

Instead of building a loyal army, they ended up creating an enemy. For centuries, we've paid for our relatives' mistakes." He looked down, as if to gather his thoughts.

"In recent years, we've been able to keep things under control. Now we've come to believe that some of our own are partnering with the mutants to stir up trouble with the Indians, hoping to take a bite of our financial success while destroying our overall credibility."

"Where does Ms. Jazmine fit into all this?" My brain was reaching its capacity, but I couldn't rest without knowing about my arch rival.

"Like I mentioned last night, she works for our casinos. I serve on the Board of Directors, an honor she's always wanted. Our parents presented us as future mates before the combined Native American Werewolf Council when we were about seven or eight. Regardless of my aversion to her, tradition requires that unless another true partner is revealed, we must mate, or, as you humans say, marry."

"Oh." I couldn't think of anything else to say. Marrying without love sounded like the worst possible fate.

"She showed up here, because when I turn twenty-eight

next month, we're supposed to present ourselves before the council elders as mates. Believe me; I'm trying everything to get out of this archaic agreement. If I can prove she's up to something that endangers the pack's well-being, in any way, I'm free from her — forever." He sighed. "That's the proven way, unless my true, fated mate appears, although that's not likely. Most of our kind never locates their actual mates."

His last words provided an unexpected solution along with a flood of nervous jitters. I could be the woman to save him from Jazmine.

Ridiculous! I couldn't marry, mate, or whatever it entailed with Zane. He was a werewolf. With my assorted background I was all for interracial relationships. Interspecies? — The jury was still out on that possibility.

I forced my thoughts back to the Jazmine issue.

"What do you think she's doing to threaten the pack?" I asked, hoping for an answer I could understand. Helping Zane expose her plan seemed like a pretty noble cause. Anything to keep Ms. Jazmine far-far away from Plum Beach — and me — was well worth my time.

"I'm not sure. She's always been manipulative. What are you thinking?" Zane drew me closer, my hand still in his.

"That I don't like her, and I still don't know why those men showed up at the bar." He'd failed to explain *that* little, very important piece of the puzzle. "And what about the bodies?" I was shocked the story hadn't been splashed across the front page of today's paper.

"Good eye for details, Princess. Those dead dogs were here to deliver a little warning." He grimaced. "The mutants aren't the only ones scheming and positioning for power and money. I've been assigned to investigate the suspicious murders in Plum Beach, but Logan also believes that several Indian elders may be double-crossing the pack. Jazmine fits into all this somehow. The news is out now that I'm sniffing around.

Since I've eliminated the messengers, things will heat up that much faster. As for the remains, I have a friend who handles clean up."

"Well, I think you've got pretty good instincts for a werewolf," I said, hoping I sounded confident. I was pretty spooked about everything, and the idea of more danger didn't help.

I'd already decided I didn't want to know anything else about his little clean up committee. What I did want to learn more about was Jazmine. I knew for certain that she was somehow up to her fangs in whatever was happening.

To conclude our discussion, Randall, the wolf, howled an eerie wail that sent chills winding down my spine, reminding me — Jazmine was a werewolf to be reckoned with — a werewolf I'd do just about anything, including howling at the moon, to keep away from Zane.

Six

Following the heart-to-heart about Zane's background, I hated to admit I was coming to respect this strange wolf/man. Sure he was prideful, pushy, and pretty much a male chauvinist, but he cared about his pack and their ability to live in harmony with humans. That commitment earned high marks in my book of *what to look for in a "good" man—er—werewolf.*

We spent the workday's remaining hours interviewing the park's diverse animal residents. None had seen the vicious intruder, though most had heard the zebra's screams and the merciless sounds of her attacker.

The animals shared a mutual feeling of panic. The predators alone felt semi-secure. I didn't blame them. From what I'd seen, the creature, which I now assumed was a mutant, had no qualms about his supremacy.

"Chloe, you're thinking so hard that your brain might crack," Zane teased.

"What are you trying to say, big guy? That my mind is fragile?" Feeling playful, I elbowed him below the ribs. I was enjoying his attention and glad for a reprieve from all the scary stuff.

The day had flown by, and I'd discovered, in spite of everything, just how much I liked his company. Having him around was enjoyable in the midst of all the madness.

"I'd never say fragile, quite the opposite. You're very intelligent," he said.

"Thank you."

"And sexy." He grinned, his eyes shifting again from brown to golden. A little growl rumbled deep in his throat.

He moved closer, until he was standing just a few inches away. I could feel his body heat and smell his enticing spicy scent.

Uncomfortable with his piercing gaze and proximity, I blurted out the one question I'd failed to ask earlier. "Are there other supernatural creatures?"

Looking surprised by my mood-deflating query, he roared with laughter, startling the nearby tigers who roared back. "If I didn't know better, Ms. Carpenter, I'd think you were a complete innocent."

"Excuse me? What's wrong with being innocent?"

"Well, by the way you respond to me at times, you seem almost a prude, but the way you kissed …"

"Wait a minute, buddy, you kissed me!" How dare he? He was the one with all the untamed sexual energy.

"Yes, I kissed you. And you, Princess, kissed me back with a high level of expertise, I might add."

Expertise? I couldn't imagine appearing to be an expert in

the kissing department. I'd never kissed a man, not even Jordon, the way I'd kissed Zane in the exam room. Did he think I was some Rhonda-type hussy?

"So, you think I'm a whore?" I protested, my fists now grinding into my hips.

"Whoa ... slow down. Where in the world did you —?"

"The park will be closing in thirty minutes. Please move toward the exits, and if you'd like to visit our gift shop please do so at this time," Luke's voice announced via our park-wide intercom system.

"Good! This day's done," I quipped, turning to flee.

Grabbing my arm, Zane spun me around and pulled me with an unexpected urgency to his chest. "You never allowed me to answer your last question," he whispered, his lips warm against my ear. "I don't think you're a whore, not even close. I find you beautiful, smart, sexy, and a little too headstrong, but that I can live with. And, yes, there are other supernatural beings."

Shocked by his answer, I lifted my chin, meeting his gaze.

His eyes shimmered gold.

Figuring the color change had to do with amorous emotions I tried to pull away, afraid of succumbing to certain seduction. Intent on my surrender, his head dipped down and his lips crushed against mine, leaving me breathless as I melted against him, my tongue finding a perfect rhythm with his.

Forgetting we were in a public place, I ran my hands down his muscular arms, causing him to growl, a low feral vibration that sent shivers of pleasure everywhere at once. His skillful hands caressed my back, sliding lower.

"E-hem!" A phony throat-clearing cough interrupted his roaming hands.

Jumping back, I was more than a little miffed to see Rhonda and a fuming Jazmine standing nearby. If Rhonda knew she was playing sidekick to a werewolf in heat, she'd run the other way.

Zane took the interruption in stride, appearing unruffled, yet allowing the disapproval of his future mate to slither through his words. "Jazmine, how not-so-nice to see you again. Didn't I make it clear enough last night that I would find you at the appointed time?"

"You should know by now that I'm not so good about following rules." Her eyes narrowed, glowing red rather than amber. Maybe red was for pissed off. I hoped I'd be alive to ask later.

If Rhonda's expression of hatred was any indication, I was in trouble. It was painfully clear these two women ought not to be hanging out together, with their sole focus being my demise.

Remembering my ability to listen to werewolves, I honed in on Jazmine's thoughts. *So this is the little bitch keeping my mate from me. How will he feel when she's a mutant and he's required to kill her? Or, I could do the killing myself.*

Without pause, I flashed the thought to Zane, who heard me loud and clear. His lip curled in response. The look he shot Jazmine would have been enough to send me scurrying for safety. Her expression changed from smug defiance to fear, but was replaced by her usual haughtiness a blink later.

"I guess I'll have to find a way to teach an old dog some of my best new tricks," she purred, eyes gleaming at Zane. "Come on, Rhonda."

Like the follower she was, Rhonda stomped off behind Jazmine, not quite able to keep up with her lupine counterpart.

"That's it," Zane said, his expression thoughtful. "You're staying with me."

"Crazy werewolf say what?" I mimicked my cousin's favorite teen idol.

No way. Danger or not, I was not going straight to the dragon's (or dog's) lair where I'd be devoured.

"You're not safe at home. Jazmine is wicked and conniving, and you heard as well as I did that she wants you dead or mutanized. By the way, great idea mind-messaging me." He pointed at his head.

"Mutanized," I forced a laugh. "Is that a real word or did you just make it up?" I, too, was thankful we could use mental communication. The ability might prove lifesaving, considering our combined list of increasing enemies.

"It's not a word, but rather a state of being; a being that I'll do everything in my power to keep you from becoming." He looked so fierce and very determined. I couldn't stop the pleasure I felt knowing his desire to keep me safe.

"What will people think?" I sputtered out of the blue, more worried about my reputation than staying alive.

"What would they think if you were killed and I had the power to protect you? In fact, maybe we should get out of town for a few days. Ever been to Vegas?" He pulled a cell phone from his back pocket before I could respond.

"Whoa, werewolf. Slow down a minute. Vegas? First it was

your house, now Nevada?" This was getting ridiculous. I couldn't go to Las Vegas.

"Logan, it's me. Things are getting more complicated in Plum Beach; can I bring a friend who needs some serious guarding?" He paused listening. "Call Mack. We'll need him pronto." Zane stopped to listen. "See you soon."

"Did you just make arrangements for both of us? Because, I sure don't remember agreeing to *your* vacation plans." My previous irritation with Zane had returned.

"Chloe, can you be reasonable? Remember when I told you there were more supernatural creatures than just werewolves? There's a whole lot more. Right now, I'm not sure who's slashing your local men to shreds, and I'm not even a hundred percent convinced a mutant gave your zebra that nasty hickey. I do know Jazmine, though. Trust me. I want you alive. I promise to keep my hands off you, if that's what it takes." His expression left no room for argument.

Jazmine's intentions were obvious. I knew he was right. I had plenty of vacation time saved up. Luke would accept my request, especially after Will's murder. I suspected Zane would come up with some viable explanation for himself.

"Fine, I'll go; but you keep your hands *and* your paws off me." I crossed my arms attempting to look firmer than I felt.

"Paws too, wolf's honor."

"Five minutes until closing. Please exit the park," Luke announced for the final time.

"Who will watch the animals?" I'd almost forgotten with both of us gone the park's animals would be without proper care. Not that we didn't have other animal specialists, but no one like me.

Zane nodded. "I've already taken care of that. Mack and his son, Michael ..."

"*Mack* and *Michael*?" I interrupted.

"They like M-names, what can I say? Anyway, Mack is a healer and Mike is another pack enforcer. They can keep an eye on things while we're away."

As we rushed past the exhibits, to the main office, I informed all the animals I could about our travel plans. They weren't thrilled by my pending departure, but they'd survive — I hoped. If Mack and his son were anything like Zane, I knew they'd be well-protected.

"You two have been busy. Did you take a lunch?" Luke was hunched over his desk, doing his one-finger computer work.

I could hear subdued conversations as the other employees performed their closing duties. Closing time was traditionally filled with an overabundance of laughter.

Will's murder had changed all that.

Zane glanced my way. *Go on. Ask him.*

I raised my eyebrows, hoping he'd take the lead instead.

"You're right about no lunch. We were too busy to eat, but we still didn't learn as much as we'd hoped to.

A good portion of the animals overheard the zebra attack, but none saw the perpetrator. I've got a good friend, another vet, who'll be in town for a few days. He's got a ton of prior investigative experience. I was hoping he and his son could help out while I'm gone," Zane suggested..

"Gone?" Luke stopped typing and looked up. I could tell he was more than a little curious. "You just got here."

"You do remember me mentioning my prior commitments

to the casino board. There's an emergency I have to address. I'll be gone a few days, a week at the most."

"Well, we've got Chloe and that friend of yours. We should be fine." Luke glanced back at his notebook.

"Uh, Luke," I squirmed. Asking for time off wasn't easy for me under the circumstances. I was sure Luke would see through our little charade.

"What Ms. Never-Miss-Work is trying to say — I convinced her to take some much overdue time off. She's too embarrassed to admit the murders have her shook up. Blame me. I told her to follow up on your offer for rest." Zane shrugged his left shoulder, feigning a guilty expression.

"I can't believe you were able to convince her. I've been trying for the last year. If your friends are as good as you say, we should be fine. I give you my boss' blessing, Chloe. Go. Rest. Take a break." He waved us off. "Get out of here. You're stalling."

I couldn't leave without more assurance. "Are you …"

"He's sure. Get going. I'll walk you out." Zane pressed his palm against the small of my back, guiding me to the door.

"Oh, Zane, I met your fiancé today. She's a real pretty gal." Luke flashed Zane the I-approve-of-your-woman smile.

Curious how Zane would pull this one off, I faced the men. Maybe werewolves were also good actors. They seemed skilled at everything else.

"She's adorable. Although my feet are getting colder the closer the day gets."

"Don't let her get away." Luke's eyes darted my direction then away.

"Thanks for the advice. I'll be in touch." Zane followed me out the door.

Stepping into the parking lot, I breathed in the salty air. I felt free. I was off work. A gorgeous man slash wolf was my personal bodyguard, and we were headed to Las Vegas.

"Do I sense excitement?" Zane leaned back and sniffed, his nose twitching.

"Is it that obvious? I guess I don't, as they say, get out much."

"That, my Princess, is about to change."

Before I could respond, Rhonda's Jetta screeched out from behind the park's company van, swerving toward us. Grabbing me up, Zane leaped over her car faster than an action hero jumping from one rooftop to another.

The wheels skidded as she spun around and raced past. I could see Jazmine in the passenger seat, her vicious laughter pouring from an open window.

Gasping, I clung to my savior. Without his werewolf reflexes, I'd be a bloody pancake on the pavement.

Not even forty-eight hours since my Monday morning commute, and my request for excitement had already been fulfilled in ways I couldn't have predicted.

Although horrified, I'd already determined Zane's arms provided the most excitement and protection any woman could hope to find.

༄

Zane paced somewhere not far behind me as I gathered the few belongings I needed for our trip. I had one sequined cocktail dress, a couple of cute skirts, and several sheer matching blouses that I hoped would be dressy enough for the infamous and always glitzy Sin City.

Dressing up was something way out of the ordinary and even further out of my comfort zone. I was a jeans and t-shirt kind of gal.

A few days ago, I couldn't have begun to foresee my current reality. For one, taking a vacation from work was mind boggling in itself. Add traveling to another state with a man who wasn't a man added to my new dreamlike existence.

Without the foot tapping coming from the far corner of my bedroom, where Zane now loomed, I might have been tempted to pinch myself.

"If you forget something, we'll pick it up when we get there." He sounded impatient, and worried.

"Can I grab my toiletries?" I didn't have a ton of money to be splurging on new makeup.

"Can you do everything in five minutes or less?" he demanded.

"Can you stop rushing me? I'm almost finished." His brusque manner made me more anxious than I already was. I scurried to the bathroom and tossed the essentials into a smaller bag.

"What about my car? What if someone sees it and wonders why I'm not in it or why I don't answer the door?" I didn't want to raise any suspicions. "Luke might figure out we're together. That would be … uncomfortable."

"Do you think he'll come by?" Zane asked. "He likes you a lot."

"I doubt it. Maybe I'm just being paranoid. He'll think I went to visit my folks. My mom's been known to whisk me away for a weekend." I ignored his comment about Luke's feelings. I had no intention of exploring *that* situation tonight.

"How would you feel about the two M's staying here and keeping an eye on your place?" Zane suggested, changing the subject.

Having two werewolves as house sitters seemed a little bizarre, but they'd be closer to the animal park this way and more able to protect my property from any intruders.

"Sure," I agreed, adding, "I think I'll call Luke, let him know I'm with my parents. That'll take care of the car being here with me gone." I hated the idea of lying to Luke, but had convinced myself I'd hurt him more by revealing the truth.

"Call him from my place." Zane lifted my heavy, old-fashioned suitcase like it weighed next to nothing.

After a quick once-over, I realized there was nothing else for me to do. I'd already preset two timers on my table lamps, and now that Zane's friends were staying, I felt more confident leaving my personal sanctuary.

Forty minutes later, we pulled up in front of a small, run-down four-plex. The place looked deserted, creepy. Regardless, I was relieved to escape the confining Corvette. I'd never seen Zane so withdrawn. He hadn't appreciated my attempts at scanning his thoughts either, and my enjoyment over his protectiveness had vanished, to be replaced by the nagging thought I'd become his biggest burden.

I decided to stay quiet and out of his way. Considering the limited space in his apartment, it wouldn't be easy. Vegas sounded better by the moment.

"You can take the bedroom. I'll stay out here and keep watch." He placed my luggage by the front door. Grateful I'd worn sweats, I could go to bed without disturbing anything.

"I appreciate you doing all this, but I can handle things. I could go to my parents," I said, hating how feeble I sounded.

"We've already been through our options. The last thing you want is your parents in a standoff with mutant werewolves. Believe me, the bad guys will find a way to locate everyone who's important to you."

A fist of terror punched into my gut. "What do you mean? Should I warn my family? Friends?" I thought of Melanie.

"If they don't register your scent or find you there, they'll move on. I don't think anyone wants this exploding in the media. Staying undetected is still a top priority for everyone involved. The consequences for revealing our existence to humans are … unpleasant."

I decided not to ask for the extended version. After all, the sole consequence I was aware of didn't leave room for any others. I'd defeated death more than once and had no intention of trying again. Still, there was one person I figured we could reach out to for added assurance.

"My stepdad's a cop. Maybe we could trust him …"

"With what? The fact you're running from a supernatural serial killer, a vengeful woman werewolf, and her mutant warriors, with your new werewolf companion?"

I hated to admit he was right. Bob was way too practical even to consider something as farfetched as ghosts and goblins, let alone monster-sized wolves howling at the moon. For my family, ignorance wasn't bliss, but it was the safer choice.

"You never told me what other supernatural creatures exist." I glanced at the window certain there were ferocious fiends hovering just beyond the glass.

I couldn't seem to escape the vivid memory of Missy the Zebra's ruthless assailant, blood drenching his face.

Seeing my discomfort, Zane closed the mismatched curtains. Considering his status in the pack, I was baffled by his sparse living arrangements. His car screamed of wealth, power, and prestige. These tiny quarters told a far different story.

Keeping a low profile was the explanation that made sense. I realized again how little I knew about my current companion. I wasn't even sure what to refer to him as — coworker, life-saver, friend, boyfriend, veterinarian, werewolf buddy, future lover …

"*Now* you want a bedtime story about things that go bump in the night?" The corner of his mouth twitched like he was fighting the urge to smile. "Can I tuck you in too?" A full grin followed.

Thankful for another reprieve from thinking about what Zane meant to me, and relieved to see him back to his normal flirty self, I sunk into the worn sofa. "That depends on how good the stories are."

Rather than responding with his usual sarcastic-laced enthusiasm, his smile vanished. He froze, listening.

Following his example, I turned my attention to anyone in the vicinity. After a few seconds, I was rewarded with several non-threatening images.

He's not expecting us.

I hope he doesn't mind we're early. Zane isn't one for surprises.

"I think your friends are here," I whispered.

"They're not trying to hide their presence, that's for sure." A loud crash confirmed Zane's observation.

"Ouch!" Several curses followed.

Almost faster than my mind could register his movements, Zane opened the door and vanished. Laughter and friendly greetings broke the silence. I questioned how Mack and

Michael had managed to arrive so fast. It didn't take a rocket scientist to conclude that traditional travel methods weren't a feasible option.

"I hate teleporting," a smooth masculine voice answered my unspoken questions.

The explanation wasn't what I'd expected.

"It was your idea," either Mack or Mike chided the other.

"Nothing changes. Always bickering," Zane chuckled. "You picked a great time to show up."

"Ah, that's right. You're protecting the *human* woman …"

"I can hear you," I called through the door, not wanting to listen while pretending I wasn't. The way they said *human* was borderline insulting.

"She can hear in more ways than one," Zane agreed, affirming my unique talents.

"I'm Mack," a monstrous and very attractive man, with shoulder-length, blonde hair, announced. He filled the doorframe.

No wonder they called him Mack. He was built like a Mack Truck. Too bad the werewolves couldn't form a professional football team.

Sensing my appraisal, Mack flashed a wide grin my direction.

"And I'm Michael. The. Younger. One," he boasted, dodging his father's grasp. The two looked more like brothers than father and son.

Zane shook his head, looking from one man to the other. "Need I say more?"

"Did someone say *teleporting*?" I pressed, ignoring Zane.

Mack glanced at Michael, who looked at Zane. *How much does she know?* Mack speculated without speaking.

"A lot," I replied. "We were just starting our discussion on the wide range of existing supernatural creatures."

Mack and Michael grinned, looking even more alike.

Zane glanced my way. "She's a pushy one."

I couldn't let that comment go. "Hey! Who's pushy?"

The two M's sniggered. Zane scowled.

"I like a woman who knows what she wants," said Mack with approval.

Zane tilted his head, tightening his lips into a hard line.

"Come on, man. We're just playing. I forgot how fast you jump from fun and games to teasing and tormenting," Mack scolded.

I determined right then that Mack would be an ally. By the way Zane glared his direction, I assumed he knew too.

Sensing a standoff, Michael joined in, "You want me to tell about the others?"

"Thank you. That's what I wanted all along. Zane keeps topic hopping," I teased, hoping to deflate the tension. It worked. In unison, the two older men inhaled and relaxed.

"If Zane doesn't mind," Mack said, head inclined, acknowledging his lesser status in the pack.

"Michael, feel free. Just don't scare her," Zane warned, refusing to meet my gaze.

"It's not his fault if I'm scared. He's not responsible for my reactions." I tried to keep my voice steady. Zane's overbearing manner was getting on my nerves.

"Michael's storytelling skills are renowned," said Zane.

"He's trying to say I exaggerate," Michael agreed sheepishly. "Anyway, first, let me ask *you* something." He glanced at Zane for what I guessed was approval. Zane nodded. "What do *you* think exists?"

Surprised by the question, I thought back to several scary movies I'd seen, without my parents' permission of course. "Vampires, witches, goblins ... "

"You're doing great," Michael grinned. "Go on."

"Since there are werewolves and mutants, I'm guessing there might be other creatures, oh, what are they called?" I tried to remember the creatures that I'd read about in my study of Indian legends. "Shapeshifters!" I yelled out as if we were playing monster charades.

"Real," Zane confirmed, at last relaxing.

"What about angels and demons?" I wondered, hoping my biblical training wasn't based on myth.

"The Bible is real. Remember, there are a number of additional books the Bible either references or alludes to, like the *Book of Jasher* and the *Book of Enoch*. If uncovered by humans, these ancient texts would expose the supernatural communities. In fact, the Bible talks about fallen angels, or sons of God and human woman creating a new race of giants. Many of us are offspring of those ancient races."

Still confused, I felt more relieved knowing the Bible was true. There just happened to be additional information that was dispersed on a need-to-know basis.

"You doing okay?" Zane asked, looking apprehensive.

"Of course," I fibbed, unwilling to halt the discussion because of Zane's over protectiveness and my increasing squirminess. "Tell me about vampires," I insisted.

"Let's stick with vampire basics." Michael glanced at Zane, who again nodded.

I was starting to see just how serious the werewolf hierarchy thing was. Zane held a powerful position in his pack. I assumed that Logan alone outranked him. Though, according to family history, Zane should be the alpha male. His grandfather, then his father had held those positions. Why not Zane? I understood those questions would have to wait until we were alone.

Noticing my companions' stares, I agreed. "I'm ready for vampire 101." All three werewolves chuckled. I wished my own species found me so amusing.

"The first vampires resulted from fallen angels copulating with human women. As I mentioned, they were just one of the many offspring from these illicit unions, often referred to as the Nephilim. For whatever reason, this finicky family line had no desire for traditional food sources. They craved blood. Human blood. This desire made them pretty unpopular with the others …"

"Short version," Mack interrupted.

"I'm just trying to give a little background. Anyway, these blood drinkers formed their own clan and became nomads traveling from place to place in order to avoid detection. They hunted solely at night and stayed hidden during daylight hours. This pattern caused them to become what legends often refer to as children of the night.

Like most creatures, though, there are exceptions to the rule. Some vampires can survive during the day. They have to wear sunglasses to cover their light-sensitive eyes, but nowadays, they blend in. Sure, they're paler than the normal person, but they are beautiful to look at."

"Do they still drink human blood?" I was fascinated.

"There are different populations of vampires. Some have found a way to exist on animal blood. Others feed off criminals. And, yes, there are still vampires that thrive on seducing humans. A few have specialized powers like flying, mindreading, mind control, even the ability to teleport from one place to another."

"Is that how you got here so fast?" I asked, reminded of their unconventional travel method.

Michael's eyes darted to Mack, who turned to Zane.

"Well?" I looked toward Zane since he seemed to be my sole hope of an honest answer to this particular question.

"A vampire friend teleported them here. We work closely with some of the vampires," Zane admitted with reluctance.

"The vegetarians and the ones who feed off the bad guys," Michael explained, as if my knowing that little tidbit would make their partnership more tolerable.

Curious to know more than he was revealing, I pushed through Michael's ineffective mental barrier. He was recalling the memory of teleporting. An attractive twenty-something man, with black sunglasses, rested his hands on Michael and his father. In a blink, they vanished. The next picture revealed the three of them standing by Zane's mailbox.

"There was a vampire *here*?" The idea repulsed me. Vegetarian or not, the image of a bloodsucker was just too much. Maybe a vampire had attacked Missy. "The zebra's blood …"

"No," Zane said. "Like werewolves and well-behaved mutants, human-owned animals are off limits for vampires to hunt"

"I thought you said there were exceptions to the rules. Maybe a rogue vampire?" I wasn't convinced.

"We're done with this discussion. You're going to have to trust me, Chloe. I will protect you. You know more than any human should. This knowledge puts you in greater danger."

"You can't make up your mind, can you?" I snapped; regretting my disrespectful tone in front of his guests.

"I think it's best you get some sleep," he said, his irritation obvious. "I'll wake you in time for our flight."

Wishing I could teleport far away from the scrutinizing gazes of three werewolves, one in particular, I struggled up from the sunken couch and rammed my little toe against the coffee table's protruding leg. Refusing to acknowledge the biting pain, I hobbled to the bedroom door, where I tripped over a tear in the worn carpet and found myself sailing across the room. I collided with the bed, face first.

My clumsiness was becoming quite the nuisance. Humiliated more than hurt, I dragged myself onto the bed. Zane's musky scent enveloping me.

"Are you all right?"

I didn't need to look to know Zane was hovering above me. I heard the door click shut.

"I'm sorry. I didn't mean to challenge your pack authority. I …"

"Chloe, you're not a werewolf. I'm not your leader. I appreciate the sentiment, but both Mack and Michael realize you're human. Humans aren't even supposed to know we exist, let alone understand our code of behavior." He lowered himself to sit beside me.

"You deserve to know the rest. The supernatural population is diverse; our history is extensive, and far more complex than I could begin to explain right now. Just know there is an unnoticed world right in the midst of yours. Other than angels and demons, werewolves, mutants, and vampires are the largest sub-groups, though there are many others. We go to great lengths to remain anonymous, but as you know, scores of stories and myths about our kind exist. Though many are false, due to our meddling, some contain bits of truth.

There are indeed humans who do know about us. Some are more sensitive to the supernatural. Others hunt us.

Most of us try to live amongst your kind in peace, even protecting your race. But, like humans, we have our own bad guys. Covering their tracks in order to maintain our anonymity while making sure justice is served are top priorities."

"Really?" I rolled over and sat up, feeling vulnerable lying down with him so near. "I feel inadequate, lost even. This is all so overwhelming. I keep forgetting it isn't a dream." A fresh wave of uncertainty threatened to drag me under.

"You're not inadequate. It's not a dream. I'm real. And you're very, very real." He cupped my face.

The kiss was different from the others. He handled me like a fragile treasure, pressing kisses across my cheeks, eyelids, and forehead. I clung to him like a life preserver, afraid if I let go I'd drown.

All I wanted was him.

Sensing my need, he found my mouth and pulled me onto his lap. The electrical current of insatiable desire, raging like a wildfire between us, exceeded any pleasure I'd ever experienced. I wondered if a vampire's need for blood surpassed my need for this half-man half wolf. Somehow I doubted it.

I loosened the leather cord that bound his hair, releasing an avalanche of raven waves. I wound my fingers through the dark mane. His hands mimicked mine, clutching and pulling my curls as our kiss deepened.

A little moan escaped my lips, surprising me. I'd never felt so out of control.

Forgetting my virginal vow, I let my hands trail down, reveling in the sensation of his muscular arms under my fingertips. His skin was fiery hot and smooth. The musky, earthy scent that was all Zane wrapped around me.

"Are you sure, Princess?" He whispered; his golden eyes focused on my face.

Unable to tear myself from his gaze, I responded by scooting off his lap and stretching out beside him. Faster than lightning, he positioned himself just above me, his hair spilling around my face. When he lowered his mouth to my neck, I arched, winding my arms around him, pulling him closer.

"Zane! We've got company!" Mack bellowed from the front room.

Zane, on his feet in an instant, commanded: "Into the closet! Go! Now!"

I was frozen on the bed, unable to obey. My body felt like melting butter, ready for loving not running.

Then the funny rippling thing was happening all around him. Terrified to see him again in his wolf form, I sprang toward the closet.

Crouched below several long-sleeved shirts and jackets, I reached with shaking hands for the doorknob, but hesitated. Zane had morphed into a humongous, sable, wolf–like creature. His thick fur spiked outward, making him appear even more formidable. A menacing growl rippled through him, a chilling challenge to anyone *or* anything foolish enough to mess with him.

For a time-stopping moment, he was motionless like a statue. His ears twitched, followed by another deep rumble. Slamming through the bedroom door, he shattered it into pieces.

Seven

I heard the roars and snarls and flashed into Zane's mind. No brick wall in sight.

Trying to make sense of the morphing images was difficult, and I struggled through a minute of dizziness before honing in on the repulsive scene. Zane was flanked by a smaller russet wolf and a large grey beast. With their lips curled back, the three looked beyond intimidating.

"I knew what you were the first time we met." A woman stepped into the werewolves' path.

I couldn't fathom why any sane human would face off with the feral purebreds.

For a split second, the scene vanished as a crimson haze shaded my eyes, and then everything morphed. I was no longer watching the action as an observer.

I. Was. There.

I could see through Zane's eyes as if they were my own.

Curious, I shifted my vision and glanced down to confirm I was once again viewing my own reality — inside the closet. Then, with what felt like a mental flip of a switch, I was back inside Zane's viewpoint — amazing.

Watching the woman approach through Zane's eyes was beyond peculiar. Everything remained tinted beneath a reddish film. I could still identify natural colors, but his vision was altered while he was in wolf form.

My ability had evolved from hearing and seeing Zane's thoughts. I was now able to hitch a ride through his senses — all of them. His fury slithered through me like a spiraling serpent.

Before I could further explore our advanced connection, the woman took another *very* foolish step forward.

Recognition dawned; it was Detective Davis from Will's house. The woman who'd scrutinized Zane. As before, an overpowering need to protect him rose up inside me.

"I'm alone. Feel free to change back so we can chat," she suggested casually, unafraid of the ferocious wolves, who even on all fours reached her chest.

Don't do it, Zane. Something's wrong. I forced my warning into Zane's mind.

No kidding. Can you sense anyone else?

My initial reaction was no, but I concentrated harder. There was something about this woman that just wasn't right. She didn't seem human, yet she wasn't an animal.

I probed her mind. She stiffened, her eyes darting around the yard. I couldn't see or hear her thoughts; but was assaulted by her emotions — the primary an overwhelming sense of confidence. There was just a hint of well-warranted fear. Everything else seemed hazy and like jumbled puzzle inside her mind. I pulled out, troubled by what I'd felt.

Not human, but something else. I silenced my mind and listened, knowing I might be searching for another creature like her.

I Kissed a Dog

Sure enough, similar to last night at the bar, I located the energy of several unidentified beings. They waited in the shadows by an old pole barn. I could sense their tension and eagerness to join the group.

There are more of whatever she is. They're hiding by the barn. What are they?

I don't have a clue. This is something new.

"Are you trying to figure me out, wolf?" she asked, keeping her gaze fixed on Zane. "Because you won't."

Another threatening rumble was his response.

Unable to control my increasing anxiety, I slipped from the closet.

What did his neighbors think about these strange happenings? I'd remember to ask Zane more about his living arrangements, later, after this current wave of danger passed … if it passed.

Ahead of me, the front door yawned open, revealing the three wolves facing Detective Davis. I couldn't hear what she was saying, but she was gesturing dramatically. The wolves continued that low throat rumble that I'd come to recognize as a major warning signal. I was surprised the detective wasn't minus her head or at least a limb by now.

Crouching low, I peered out the open door.

"*You*, my dear, should have stayed in the closet," said a pleasant but unfamiliar voice.

Bewildered more than scared, I turned to face the source of the deep British accent, which under normal circumstances, I would have found enticing.

"You're the vampire," I whisper-hissed at the sight of his pallid face so close to mine. His eyes were a shocking blue, like pools of liquid turquoise. I recognized him as the teleporter.

"So glad you noticed." His mouth bowed into a wide grin revealing two gleaming fangs.

"Your teeth are so white." I couldn't help myself. I'd never seen such polished teeth. Maybe vampires had their own special teeth-whitening products.

"You're the first human in five centuries to comment on the whiteness of my teeth. They're more focused on their sharpness," he paused, inhaling. "I must say, Chloe, you smell divine."

Unsure whether to thank him or scream; I decided to acknowledge his fangs with flattery. "Your fangs *are* so sharp, *and* you know my name. Are you friend or foe?" I figured I'd know the answer to the second question soon enough, but his polite demeanor stirred just enough courage for me to ask.

"My name is Alcuin. I was named after the British scholar known as the 'Alcuin of York.' As for your second query, in this case, I am friend; though that could change rather quickly depending on the circumstances."

I exhaled; relieved at least for the moment the vampire was a friend. He remained crouched just behind me, stirring something akin to desire, yet nothing like what I felt with Zane.

"I find you quite desirable as well, Ms. Chloe. Should you tire of the wolf, I'm available," he whispered closer to my neck now.

"All righty, moving on now to the standoff outside," I winced, ashamed of my impure thoughts. "What's happening? Why are they here? And, *what* are they?"

"Direct, aren't you?" Alcuin nodded his approval. "The

woman who calls herself, Detective Davis, is a supernatural-hybrid. I've just recently detected their existence."

"I don't understand." It didn't help that my latest companion didn't seem to know anything more than I did.

"Maybe the faes have decided to get involved, or …"

"As in Faeries?" My brain had reached the shutdown point hours ago. The vampire's attempt to explain what he didn't understand added to my frayed nerves. I knew that Tinker Bell wasn't one of the faeries he was referring to.

"Oh, my. You've assimilated far too much information for one day." Sounding sympathetic, he turned his attention back to the scene outside.

Following his gaze, I spotted four shadowy figures skulking around the pole barn. Somehow I'd miscounted. "Zane! Lookout!" I screamed, realizing too late how ridiculous my warning was. The werewolves would have spotted the intruders long before I did.

Every werewolf and hybrid head swung my way. I could see Detective Davis' eyes glowing blood red. "Uh oh," I fell back.

"It's a good thing I stuck around. Hold on!" My new vampire friend yanked me to his hard chest, squeezing me close. Unlike Zane's extreme warmth, he was icy cold.

Fighting not to vomit, I squeezed my eyelids shut as we spun in what felt like every direction at once. A deafening buzzing, like a million bumble bees gone mad, wrapped around us. Then – nothing.

"Please don't throw up on my shoes," Alcuin pleaded.

Not bothering to see where we'd landed, I bent forward, hands on my knees and retched. Considering the lack of complaints, I assumed I'd missed his treasured shoes.

"I didn't have time to prepare you for your first teleport."

"No kidding," I gagged again.

"Since I can guess your next question will include something about where we are, look around."

With caution, I inched up into a semi-standing position. Because of a low, slanted roof, I was unable to stand.

"We're in a tree house," I concluded, able to see the pole barn in the distance.

"I figured you'd want to remain close to your wolf, and knowing Zane, he'd be none too happy had I taken you elsewhere. You, however, need to gain better control of your emotions should you continue to associate with us."

As usual, my intense emotional responses were not earning me brownie points. Deciding to ignore the angry words threatening to explode at my latest rescuer, I strained my eyes seeking the werewolves.

Sensing my dilemma, Alcuin leaned out the tiny entrance and stared into the distance. "They're gone."

"The strangers?" I hoped.

"They delivered their message." He said minus expression.

"Bring her down!" Zane commanded from the darkness below. "Alcuin! Now!"

"He's so bossy," I apologized, but had to admit I was relieved to hear his voice.

"Don't I know?" the vampire agreed.

"I heard that," Zane grumbled.

"Of course you did," Alcuin said. "May I?" He extended a pale hand.

I stared at it reluctantly, afraid to take hold. "We're not …" My stomach responded with a lurch.

I Kissed a Dog

"No, Doll, we're not teleporting. We're jumping."

Attempting to shield my eyes from the morning brightness, I searched for a clock. I could hear birds singing and dogs barking somewhere in the distance. Awakening to a dog — my Wednesday was off to a great start.

Day three of my new existence had arrived right on schedule. This new version of my life included far more than lions and tigers and bears, oh my, as Zane had so eloquently stated. It included a bunch of supernatural creatures and their hybrid counterparts upsetting any prior predictability I might have enjoyed. Figuring out their vast differences, diverse diets, and uncanny abilities would have to wait.

I was going to Vegas.

"I thought I felt you wake up." Zane strode into the room, oversized coffee mug in hand.

"Gimmie," I begged, forgetting how that one word could be misconstrued by my wannabe-lupine-lover. I couldn't recall a cup of morning java smelling so inviting. Even more inviting was the man sipping it.

Ignoring my plea for caffeine, he maneuvered his muscular frame into the room's one chair. His gaze trained on me. "You met Alcuin?" It was a statement more than a question.

"You already know the answer."

"Indeed; and what did you think?" he probed.

"About what — the mysterious non-human non-animal visitors, or my first experience teleporting? Wait. Maybe you're wondering how I felt about flying through the air when I jumped from the tree house. I did think Alcuin was helpful keeping me on my feet for a rather spectacular landing. What do you think? Do I get a ten?" For a moment, I pictured three werewolf judges holding up score signs displaying the number ten for a cheering audience. That would be one highly-rated reality show.

"I'd say you get a ten in my book for all your moves." He leaned back, looking pleased. I'd passed some sort of test.

"Did I hear a request for coffee?" Michael danced into the room and handed me my own super-sized mug of steaming pleasure, before adding, "There's bagels and OJ in the kitchen."

Peering at Zane over my cup, I realized for the umpteenth time I was far more interested in the steaming pleasure he could provide.

"Oh, I called Luke for you."

My steamy thoughts collided with my pride; I snapped, "I said that *I* would call. Wasn't that a little strange, your calling for me like a parent calling the teacher?"

"It made perfect sense. I called to explain that Mack and Michael would be over to the park by 9:30 and that I'd heard you mention a little vacation with your mom. I thought I did you a favor."

Michael hurried from the room, eager to get away from our latest disagreement. He turned to shut the door before realizing the door no longer existed. I noticed then that someone had taken time to clean up the mangled pieces of wood from last night's door-busting heroics.

I grudgingly accepted my overreaction, forcing myself to apologize, "I'm sorry; you did do me a big favor. I'm beyond overwhelmed. Even your vampire friend recommended that I get my erratic emotions reigned in."

As always, my emotions were causing discomfort, not just

for my new friends, but for me. I wanted off the rollercoaster of extremes once and for all. But considering my present predicament, I was certain that counting to ten, or even one hundred, wouldn't do the trick. Maybe a few days in Vegas would.

"Your emotions make you unique. Maybe I'm biased, but I don't know many humans who could handle what you have in such a short time. You're too hard on yourself," Zane said.

"There you go again, surprising me," I said keeping it light, when in truth, Zane's words did far more than surprise me. They reassured me that being me was okay; something no one had bothered to tell me growing up.

"Chloe, Princess, you've just discovered monsters are real, yet you're more concerned about what we think about you. Don't you find that a little odd?" His eyes locked with mine.

Deciding to ignore his last question, I changed the subject. "I'm shocked your neighbors didn't call in the reserves last night. We were pretty loud out there."

"Don't think I don't know what you're doing, but I'll bite. Just remember, I have a long memory and I'm keeping tabs of the questions *you* ignore.

I rented the entire property until I could find a nicer home. No neighbors are the best neighbors for a werewolf. Don't tell me you thought I'd choose this primo piece of real-estate as my home sweet home." He raised a brow.

Catching what must have been a tell-tale look, he added, "You *believed* this was my permanent bachelor's cave?"

"Perhaps for a minute, but considering your position in the pack, I assumed it must be a cover or something." I finished my coffee with a final slurp.

"Maybe another cup?" He stretched as he stood.

"Sorry to interrupt." Mack poked his head through the door-less frame. "But you two have a plane to catch, and I have an animal park to protect."

Glad for the reminder and eager for some distance from Zane, I scooted off the bed and padded to my suitcase. "Do I have time to shower?" I hoped so after my late night jog from the tree house.

"Knowing Mack, he's got us ahead of schedule. Right?" Zane asked.

"As long as you're at the airport in an hour," Mack assured.

I stopped, wary. The only major airport that I could think of was Portland International, a good five-plus-hours away. We wouldn't make it driving. That could mean one thing ... my poor stomach.

Alcuin strode through the front door, his sunglasses in place — presenting a very clear confirmation to my travel worries. "It's quite an exquisite morning," he said, sounding more like an old school gentleman than a blood sucking fiend.

Seeing my tortured expression, he stepped back. "You're turning green. I didn't realize I'd had such a profound effect on you, Doll."

"Enough with the doll business, vamp. I'm warning you ..."

Zane growled through clenched teeth. "Be a good dog and fetch me some breakfast. I don't feel like hunting right now." Alcuin crossed his arms. Modeling defiance at its best.

My worry-induced nausea was replaced by awe. Did the vampire have a death wish?

Three, very angry wolf-men glared his direction. I didn't

blame them. Alcuin had pretty much pushed the other species disrespect thing to an all-time low.

"Fetch it yourself, pale-face!" Mack barked, causing his son to crumple to the floor. Michael gripped his sides and rolled around as if in pain. I was getting ready to offer first aide when I realized he was laughing hysterically, not thrashing in agony.

"I was serious about your calling her doll," Zane choked out between snorts and booming laughter.

Watching the four of them howl at one another was a sight. I didn't think their comments warranted such a display of hysterics.

"Look at her face," Alcuin turned toward me. I closed my mouth, but not before realizing it had been hanging open.

"What's wrong with my face," I grimaced.

"You don't know what to make of us." Alcuin shook his head, his mouth curving into the biggest grin with fangs imaginable.

"All I know is I'm not nervous about my personal sanity. I have four supernatural lunatics that are supposed to be protecting me. Don't mind me if I look alarmed." Feeling a sudden sense of righteous authority, I grabbed my clean clothes and stomped to the bathroom, well aware of the gaping mouths that watched my retreat.

Twenty-two minutes later, I emerged dressed and ready to rejoin the men lounging across the tiny front room. Zane was reviewing the wildlife park's map and filling in father and son about the exhibits. Alcuin sat stone-still on the lumpy sofa.

"Please, join me." Alcuin patted the cushion next to him. "Yes, you, Doll."

"How many times ..."

"I know. I know. I'm not supposed to call her doll because she's your princess," the vampire rumbled at Zane.

"How about you both call me Chloe and then we can stop this nonsense." The endearing pet names had outworn their cuteness. Zane calling me princess in private was one thing, but this whole vampire werewolf competition was disturbing. Fortunately, from what I'd gathered, their friendship ran deeper than I'd first assumed. It had to run pretty darn deep for them to put up with each other.

"Agreed, *Chloe*," Alcuin said with added flourish. "Now, please, come here. I have been warned that if I don't prepare you for future teleporting, I will be visiting a dentist that specializes in fang removal."

"I've heard he does great work," Michael chuckled.

To Alcuin's credit, he didn't respond. He seemed to have greater control of his emotions than the werewolves. No wonder he found me overwhelming.

I hesitated by the couch then sat down, careful not to touch him. The clock was ticking, and I needed to be ready to travel supernatural style — without vomiting.

"I'm guessing, you're our ticket to the airport," I acknowledged grimly.

"You guessed right, do … I mean Chloe."

"Good save," I whispered with a smile. I couldn't help myself. I liked Alcuin. While impressive, he could never measure up to Zane. But I couldn't help admiring his charming wit, not to mention his lack of emotions had a very calming affect on my more unruly ones.

"I don't enjoy it when the wolf gets his fur all up in a bunch," Alcuin hissed, his eyes darting toward the kitchen.

"Heard that," Zane called from the table.

I Kissed a Dog

Alcuin muttered his derisive reply in a foreign language.

It was then I realized we were taking unnecessary travel measures. "Why are we even bothering with an airplane if you can just beam us to Vegas?" I asked.

Alcuin clasped his hands, nodding with visible approval. "I'm glad you noticed. I rather hoped you would; but, with all due respect, you must realize by now that you're a pretty hot commodity. You've got half-breed hybrids or whatever they were, werewolves, and mutants all interested in you. For these reasons, we must give the appearance of normalcy."

"Normalcy? You're kidding me," I scoffed at the idea. I'd never been normal, and considering the direction my life was heading, normalcy was as farfetched as me walking a dog on the moon.

"I guess no one filled you in on last night's little warning," Alciun said, sounding annoyed by my lack of knowledge.

Before I registered his movement, Zane was crouched in front of us. "I'll share the message."

"Alcuin said a warning," I reminded, still not used to Zane's shocking speed.

Ignoring my comment he continued. "We're not sure whose side Detective Davis and her sidekicks are on, but she came out here last night to either arrest me or talk to me. She ended up telling us about the increasing unease in the larger supernatural community over the unsolved Plum Beach murders. The supe community, supe being our abbreviation for supernatural, is very worried the mutilation and murders might draw unwanted attention, leading to more in-depth investigations.

She was put on the case by another multi-species council.

Her job is to ensure the killer is apprehended and stopped. Until last night, she believed I was somehow involved. Someone out there has been pretty persistent about pointing the finger my way."

"How many types of councils are there? Who gave *her* the authority?" I asked. It sounded like the so-called supes had a more puzzling government structure than humans. Packs, werewolf and Native American partnerships, and now these other so-called councils, this was too much. Did they have a president?

"Just like your human government has a lot of checks and balances, we end up with councils trying to oversee everybody else. Each species has its own individual council. Then, of course, werewolves have packs, vampires have …"

"We don't have time for this," Mack said sounding urgent. "You two can talk government on the plane."

Zane stopped to glance at his watch and shot into the bedroom. I could hear him sliding hangers to one side of the closet.

Alcuin, remembering my initial question about teleporting to Vegas, finished his just-be-normal speech: "Trust me, Chloe; it looks good for you to do something human, like riding on a plane for the better part of your trip. It's best that others don't realize how much you're hanging out with the likes of me."

"Fine. Teach me to teleport without hurling."

Eight

Without Zane's untiring confidence, the Vegas airport would have been a nightmare.

He navigated through the throngs of tourists with a level of expertise reserved for those who had a certain familiarity with Sin City. His assurance and striking good looks had women stopping to ogle. One middle-aged brunette stumbled over her carry-on as he strode past.

Zane, on the other hand, made sure to point out the number of men gawking at me. I had to admit, my count of admirers was at least equal to his. He wasn't too pleased.

"Between the two of us, I bet we could convince someone to buy us lunch and cocktails," I joked. I could imagine how someone like Jazmine would use her persuasive talents and exotic appearance to get everything she wanted out of Vegas.

"I don't intend to prostitute either of us for what's already free." He growled, picking up the pace, and making it difficult to match his stride.

"I was just kidding!" I half-shouted. I'd take care never to mention using my looks as the means to an end again.

Even though I felt like a Plain-Jane next to Zane he failed to find a speck of humor in anything related to my appearance. For me, usually a jealous man was a major turnoff. In his case, I found it somehow exhilarating.

Changing tactics, I teased, "Can you slow down? Please? Human girl about to collapse." I hoped to lighten the mood; something I found myself doing often around Zane. Napping on the flight had restored my energy. I wanted to enjoy my time, not spend my first day in Vegas bickering.

"Sorry. I forget how fast I am." He slowed his gait. "You're probably starving. You didn't eat a thing on the plane."

He was right. I hadn't eaten since my morning bagel. Several hours had passed, and I needed nourishment. What I wanted more, though, was to claim our luggage and get to the hotel. "I can wait."

"You sure?" He looked doubtful.

"I want to get out of here." The airport and all the staring people were starting to annoy me. "Geez you'd think these people had never seen an attractive young couple."

"Young couple … is that what we are?" Zane's tension had vanished; a huge grin replaced his frown.

"Well, uh …"

"Just give up, Chloe. You and I both know there's something between us. You can't keep pretending it doesn't exist …"

"Mr. Marshall! I've gathered your luggage!" An odd little man waved and hurried toward us. "Logan sent me with the limo. He figured you might want some help."

"I already like Logan," I said, relieved to be another step closer to peace and quiet — and food.

I Kissed a Dog

"This is Giffin, assistant to Logan Sanders. Where Logan is, you'll find Griffin," Zane admitted. It was clear he was well acquainted with the man.

So she's the one. All this fuss over one little human. She may be pretty, but that's not everything. Her talents must be vital to the pack for Logan to go through all this. Griffin broadcasted his thoughts while towing the bags, not realizing that his mental chit chat was loud enough to be considered obnoxious.

I decided to ignore my negative feelings and see what else he might reveal.

By the time we were seated in the black stretch limo, I was certain there was far more to Zane's initial motives than he'd bothered telling me.

From what I could see in Giffin's head, my werewolf sweetheart had traveled to Plum Beach for more than a murder investigation. I wasn't certain, but it seemed he'd come to locate me. If what I was starting to believe had any truth to it, there was a good chance he was using my abilities for the good of his pack. Our little attraction was just an added bonus for him, unless, of course, that was an act too.

"What do you think?" Zane motioned to the tinted window. "Would you like me to open it so you can see the strip? I know it's not as magnificent during the daylight, but you can still see some of its grandeur."

Ignoring my suspicions, I forced myself to act normal. I leaned closer to the window.

Taking my interest as a yes, Zane insisted Griffin lower not only the side window, but also open the oversized sunroof. Warm air poured in along with the scent of spicy food, desert flora, exhaust, and something unidentifiable that I assumed was unique to Vegas.

Huge hotels, casinos, even the original Statue of Liberty's giant replica lined the street. Las Vegas Boulevard and familiar resort names like *Treasure Island, The Mirage, and Hotel Excalibur* (my personal favorite) reminded me that I wasn't in Oregon any more.

Storing my latest impressions of Zane away for later, I soaked in the wonders of Nevada's very own "City that Never Sleeps." From what I'd read, New York had nothing on Vegas in terms of nightlife.

The men had enough common sense to know I was enthralled by my surroundings, and left me alone until we pulled into a long drive lined with palm trees.

Fountains and tropical flowers were placed strategically between the palms with life-like animal statues scattered throughout. It was as if the animals from the wildlife park had been released to stand guard along the winding hotel entryway.

As we inched closer to the building, I positioned myself to do something I'd always dreamed about. Before either man could protest, I climbed on the center table and pulled myself up through the sunroof until everything above my waist was outside the limo.

I tilted my head back to look at the massive structure. It was a jungle-themed palace. Vines were suspended from the windows and sculpted replicas of monkeys and exotic birds either dangled or perched on the vines.

"It's incredible," I gasped, wishing I could pretend to be

I Kissed a Dog

Jane and climb a vine to Tarzan's room, knowing darn well my Tarzan's name started with a Z.

"I'm glad you approve." Zane slid his arm around my waist as he joined me. "Welcome to the Jungle Jamboree Family Resort," he announced. "A place where kids play while parents gamble."

I laughed. "That's some tagline."

"You think the board will like it?"

"It's catchy."

Griffin cleared his throat. "Can I get you two to exit the limo? There are cars waiting," he said, sounding perturbed by our childish antics. His earlier eagerness to assist had been replaced with a condescending manner that I found offensive in light of my excitement.

"Come on!" Zane pulled me back into the limo. "Wait till you see our room."

"*Our* room?" Zane's room-comment erased my desire to chastise Griffin.

Rather than respond, Zane exploded through the limo door the minute it opened. He rushed to my side and helped me out. "Welcome to paradise, Princess."

"I'll send up your luggage," Griffin said, sounding suddenly formal.

As thrilled as I was about our unfamiliar surroundings, I couldn't let Zane off the hook. "You said something about 'our room.' Would you care to elaborate?"

"I'm your bodyguard; therefore, I stay close to you."

"But ..."

"Chloe, please, remember why we're here. The suite has a huge bedroom and a smaller one. Does that make things easier for you to deal with?" He said, cutting me off.

Unable to find any reasonable argument, I nodded. "That'll work. I guess." I wasn't going to admit I was more afraid of spending the night behind closed doors with him than being attacked by deranged mutants.

A stocky porter approached. "Mr. Marshall, so glad to see you. Mr. Sanders is ready to receive you in his office." He cocked his head, studying me. "The lady's presence is requested as well." He backed up with a little bow than hurried the other direction.

I made a half-hearted attempt to infiltrate his thoughts, but was met with a strong barrier, signaling that he, too, was of the supernatural persuasion. I couldn't help but wonder if the hotel even bothered hiring humans.

Zane took my hand as we approached the glass elevator centrally positioned in the enormous oval-shaped lobby.

Before I could formulate a question about the hotel's shady hiring requirements, I was again awed by my surroundings. Covered in jungle foliage and vines, the elevator was a sight to behold. Two monkey replicas were suspended from two of the larger vines. I craned my neck to look up.

Not a fan of heights, I wasn't happy to see how high the elevator could travel. There were other elevators off to the side of the lobby, but this amazing creation was designed to rise straight up through the grand hotel's center. The upper floors formed a circle of doors with attached hanging bridges crisscrossing the center space at each level, one main bridge connecting to the elevator on every floor.

I'd never seen such a bizarre layout. The architect must have been on some major, mind-altering chemicals to come up with such extravagance.

"Is it safe?" I questioned, unable to tear my eyes away.

I Kissed a Dog

"I promise; the bridges are well crafted. They're supposed to give guests a *Swiss Family Robinson* feel," he explained. "Would I take you on something that wasn't safe?"

"You make it sound like you're taking me on a ride at an amusement part."

Zane laughed his eyes full of mischief. "You're scared of some fancy construction, but you're okay with supernaturals."

I stepped through the yawning glass door, feigning bravado that I didn't feel. "Fine, big boy, let's ride." Not entering the elevator was no longer an option.

Zane had a curious way of provoking me, making me see everything as a challenge. I pondered his comment. Why was I so reasonable when it came to vampires and werewolves, yet everyday things continued to unravel me? I wasn't sure I wanted the answer. Maybe I was just happy to meet others who were stranger than me.

Once across the *Swiss Family Robinson* bridge, on our floor, I realized that I preferred teleporting over the elevator ride. My stomach felt queasy. I was worried I might do one of my fainting numbers. Zane read the signs and curled a protective arm around my waist, drawing me closer, and supporting my weight.

As usual, his touch released a collection of butterflies in my midsection and sent a wave of desire crashing over me. I was thankful to be stopping somewhere other than our private suite. Alone with Zane, right now, could prove disastrous.

My attraction for him was far from diminishing. It was as if someone was playing a cruel cosmic joke on me, making my lifeless libido go haywire around Zane.

All tempting thoughts were silenced when we entered the alpha wolf's massive suite turned office.

My initial response to Logan Sanders was embarrassment.

I noticed right away, that just like his counterparts, the alpha werewolf was gorgeous and powerful. He, too, wore his hair long and pulled back. But unlike Zane, his hair was a chocolate brown, and streaked with gold. My embarrassment was caused by what he was thinking about me. His thoughts revealed a semi-accurate assessment of my current emotional state.

Another human with no steel. Such a weak creature. Upset by a simple elevator.

"I am not weak!" I protested. I didn't bother arguing about the elevator.

Logan grinned, appreciative. "Good, I can see you weren't exaggerating her abilities." His eyes traveled over me, causing a jolt of apprehension to replace my embarrassment.

Zane noticed too. His smile dissolved into a scowl.

"Since when do I embellish?" Zane scowled; unwilling to forgive his leader's visual indulgence.

Unmoved by our reactions, Logan slid into a leather chair, positioned like a throne behind his expansive, marble-topped desk. "Sit." He motioned toward two equally plush chairs.

Delighted to obey and put an end to my lingering dizziness, and Logan's roaming eyes, I chose the chair nearest the floor-to-ceiling window. Prepared for a dull briefing about pack business, I could look outside if things got too boring.

"I can see she is everything we hoped." Logan sounded pleased.

Zane shifted in his seat. "She's much more."

I couldn't help wondering what Zane's words implied. I hoped they confirmed he was falling for me as hard as I was for him.

Logan looked lost. His puzzled expression, reminded me there was more going on than I was privy to. Just like Griffin, Logan had alluded to my special skills.

Something was wrong. I could feel it. I wouldn't like whatever was waiting to be revealed.

"She's been briefed?" Logan questioned Zane, who responded with uncomfortable silence, which only prompted another question. "What have you shared with Ms. Carpenter?"

Zane gave me a solemn look before launching into a sporadic update. "She knows our history. As you know, she's been stalked by Jazmine, who has mutants at her disposal, eager to do her bidding if the mating ceremony is delayed. She has come face to face with Jazmine on two occasions already; neither were positive encounters."

"I'd say," I muttered.

"Using her ability, Chloe recognized that a woman werewolf is the killer, however, it wasn't Jazmine. I still suspect she's involved somehow …"

Tired of hearing my life explained at a rate too slow for my taste, I jumped in. "I've learned to teleport; I had the honor of meeting Mack and his son, Michael; and I ran into my first vampire, Alcuin." I figured that about summed things up.

"Your world has changed quite a bit in the past few days," Logan said, his expression revealing his interest and what looked like a hint of compassion. "But what do you think of your involvement in our search?"

"Logan, can we talk — alone?" Zane asked, avoiding my gaze.

The pack leader appeared unfazed, as if anticipating Zane's

request. His answer was to send me to my room. "Chloe, your room is four doors down." He handed me a cardkey. "Zane will make sure you get in."

Not willing to be shut out without an explanation, I stood my ground. "If you're planning on discussing me, I'd like to stay. Make sure you're getting things right."

Logan's eyes narrowed. "Zane …"

Taking my elbow, Zane guided me toward the door. "This is personal pack business. I'll explain. Later." His tone gave no room for argument.

Oh, I'd let him go to his little "business" meeting, but I intended to get all the details when he returned.

When he leaned down to kiss me, I presented my cheek.

He didn't press the issue.

I waited as he strode down the hall. He glanced back before disappearing into the pack leader's office. Seeing the alarm written across his rugged features was unexpected and downright unnerving.

I didn't know if he was scared for me or himself — or both of us.

⊚

After seeing Zane's tortured expression, I waited just inside our suite, hoping to eavesdrop on his and Logan's now private debriefing. I honed in on Zane first. The brick wall was up in full force, his mind off limits. Logan's thoughts were barricaded too. The werewolf leadership-duo wanted to keep their conversation private.

Something was troubling Zane, which in turn, worried me. He was keeping secrets.

I Kissed a Dog

From what I could tell, the pack wanted to use my ability. I knew they were anxious about the mutants plotting with the Indian elders, but I wasn't sure how I could help with the situation.

What I didn't like (maybe even hated) was the lying.

Zane had come to Plum Beach for more than the murder investigation. He'd known about me before arriving. That fact was obvious now. Why would he keep the knowledge hidden?

I had to make a choice. I could embrace the feeling of impatience threatening to overtake me, while plotting our inevitable showdown, or, I could explore the suite and take my mind off all the craziness.

I decided on the latter and moved from the entryway into the main living area.

Like Logan's office, the oval-shaped room featured a floor-to-ceiling window that provided a postcard view of the Vegas skyline. I determined we were at least twenty floors up, although I wasn't certain. I'd kept my eyes squeezed shut on the elevator.

The spacious room, in harmony with the hotel's theme, had décor that reflected a jungle scene. The lavish furniture was leopard and zebra printed. A faux-fur rug covered a good portion of the shiny marble flooring. Exotic plants and artwork, worth more than my annual salary, added yet another eye-pleasing element.

I marveled at the creativity, vision, and unbridled imagination that had influenced the hotel's designer. He or she was unbelievably talented. I still dreamed of finding my own niche, a platform to use my abilities in such a distinguished way.

Adjacent to the main suite, I discovered the hallway leading to the master bedroom. Finding my future noble cause was discarded at the sight of the room's richness.

My suitcase and carry-on had been placed just inside the door. The area reminded me of a unique blending of African Safari and South American jungle. It was easy to see how the design work and decorative features would delight both children and adults, and I had no problem imagining myself remaining in the tropical fantasy world indefinitely.

The king-sized bed, featuring richly patterned red and cocoa fabrics shaped into a stunning crown bed canopy was pure temptation. Just looking at it convinced me I was tired and needed rest before Zane returned.

Slipping off my shoes, I crawled up the looming structure and sank into its softness. I'd relax for a few minutes before freshening up.

I was too aggravated to sleep; so I'd thought.

"Princess." Hearing Zane's voice startled me awake.

"What are you doing?" I asked, for a brief moment unsure of my whereabouts.

Vegas, the big comfy bed — how could I forget such memorable surroundings?

"Hoping to wake you gently." His finger trailed down my cheek, igniting a welcome blaze along the way.

Pushing myself up and away from him, I went for the juggler. "You knew all about me and my animal mindreading abilities before we met, right?" I didn't know why I even bothered asking. I already knew the answer, but I wanted to hear it from him.

"I did," he said, meeting my gaze.

I narrowed my eyes. His candid response was not what I'd expected. Not that I thought he'd outright lie, but I'd anticipated some long drawn-out explanation.

"Why? I told you my entire life story. You acted so interested in it, *in me*." I realized as I said the words that I sounded as wounded as I felt.

"Princess ..."

"I'm not your princess." How dare he continue to treat this situation like no big deal? Fuming, I vaulted from the bed to pace by the window, no longer able to make eye contact.

Betrayal was something I'd grown used to in my brief experiences with the opposite sex, Jordon in particular. Why I'd expected Zane to be any different was beyond me. It appeared werewolves were true dogs at heart. Bow-wow.

"You're making more out of this than you need to." His gruffness was evidence of his rising defensiveness.

"I am? Just tell me, was *everything* you said a lie?" I faced the window keeping my back to him. I could feel his eyes boring into me from behind, daring me to face him. I knew better than to look into those dark eyes streaked with sunshine.

"In spite of what you believe, everything I said was true. I merely failed to mention *all* my reasons for coming to Plum Beach."

"How comforting. When were you planning to share this with me? From what I heard in Logan's office, he seemed to think you'd already filled me in." Part of me wanted to bolt from the room, but I needed to know the real reason he'd wanted to locate me.

"I'm sharing it now. I should have told you from the start. That was my intention. However, if you remember, you weren't real thrilled about my arrival. I was trying to gain your trust, get to know you."

I refused to admit what he said made sense. I had been pretty difficult in the beginning. Still, that didn't give him a reason to lie. Did it?

"Logan had heard from another purebred living in Plum Beach …"

"What purebred in Plum Beach?" I wondered how many of my co-workers and acquaintances were of the supernatural affiliation. Maybe it was better if I didn't know.

"If you'd let me finish."

"Go on." I forced myself to focus, pushing away my desire to pummel him with questions (or my fists) if he didn't fess up fast.

"One of the park's delivery drivers is part of our pack. He's more of a loner and not involved in the casino or resort business. He mentioned a woman that could communicate with animals. I, of course, thought he was full of it. Logan, on the other hand, believed you might be able to help us by listening in on some of the board members' dogs."

"You wanted me to spy on someone's pets?" I couldn't believe what I was hearing. Maybe he was joking. His serious expression led me to believe otherwise.

He continued without a hint of humor. "We wanted you to spy on the owners through their pets. We were hoping to bring you to an upcoming board meeting.

I Kissed a Dog

There are several members that bring their dogs everywhere, even to our meetings. Logan figured we'd just say you were our new secretary. He fired the last one. The board is already used to her taking notes and typing up minutes."

Their plan sounded feasible enough, and he was right, had he blurted this all out at our first meeting I would have run the other direction thinking he was a lunatic. No questions asked.

"I don't know, Zane. You had plenty of opportunities to tell me. I'm not sure how I feel right now." Wasn't that the truth? I had no idea what to feel about anything, in particular, my werewolf companion. "I need some time."

I felt him move to stand behind me. Ignoring his distinctive scent was difficult with him so close.

"I'm safe in the hotel?" I didn't wait for him to answer. "I'm going downstairs to the bar for a drink. Alone."

"I don't think ..."

"Either I have some much-needed time alone to think, or I call my stepdad and tell him I'm being held hostage by some maniac that thinks he's a wolfman." The idea sounded plausible considering my current dilemma.

"Have it your way," Zane agreed, his reluctance marked by his softening tone. "Will you look at me, please?"

I turned and looked up, into his eyes, not sure what to expect.

I was shocked to see his eyes were tinged a subtle red hue. Not crimson like Jazmine's, thank goodness, but it was obvious that he was pretty unhappy with me too. Knowing what I did about Zane's protective nature, I could deduce how anxious the idea of my little excursion downstairs — alone — made him feel.

Pushing my concerns about his feelings aside, I marched to my suitcase and tossed it on the bed. I planned to dress up and make the most of my evening out. Maybe I'd try my luck at the slot machines.

One thing I knew for certain — I was going to do whatever it took to vanquish Zane Marshall from my mind, if only for a few hours.

"Woman preparing to dress. Would you mind showing yourself out? I'm sure there's some secret camera or something you can use to follow my every move," I quipped, hating to admit I'd feel safer knowing he was still keeping tabs on me from a distance.

"We have plenty of security here. Most are purebreds. Should anyone give you trouble, they'll take care of it. I'm going out myself. I have a few old friends to visit."

"Have a nice evening." I was surprised by how clipped my words came out. I sounded like a jealous girlfriend.

"Enjoy yourself and try not to trip over anything," he said, making a swift exit from my room.

Clenching my fists, I struggled to remain silent. A door clicked shut somewhere in the suite, closing off any opportunity to voice my disapproval.

The idea of his visiting *old friends* stirred my guts into a frenzy of nerves. I could imagine what type of friends he was referring to — probably some exotic dancer, or sexy cocktail waitress. Why did it matter?

He wasn't my man, nor would he be — ever.

I didn't date liars with hidden motives. I didn't date werewolves that maimed and killed their enemies. In fact, last time I checked — I didn't date.

The past few days had been beyond bewildering, but that

I Kissed a Dog

was all behind me now. Zane was a temporary bodyguard — nothing more. In a few weeks, he'd be mated to a psycho she-wolf, just his type, and I'd be back at work enjoying my predictable life hanging out with regular old animals.

Maybe I'd take Luke up on his offer for an evening out. I'd been waiting for something or someone exciting, when that person had been right in front of me all along. In this case, my mother really did know best. Luke was just the caliber of man I needed.

If only I could believe that.

Following a quick shower, I applied my cosmetics with great care, jelled my hair into loose curls, and wiggled into every woman's must-have nightwear staple — a clingy, glittery, little-black-dress. My shapely legs were on full display.

Slipping on a pair of three-inch, black sling-back sandals, I stood in front of the full-length mirror. Pleased with my reflection, I decided to explore the hotel, grab dinner, and head to the bar featuring live entertainment. It was still afternoon, but I knew that here in Vegas my attire was appropriate no matter what the hour.

I wished for an escort, an arm to link mine through. Too bad I wasn't on Zane's arm. Eck! Why did my thoughts always return to him?

Committing to have fun (without my wolfy counterpart) I straightened my shoulders and strutted into the living area, making sure to practice the runway technique of crossing one foot in front of the other to create a seductive sway.

Not expecting to see Zane sprawled shirtless on the zebra-printed couch, I nearly tripped over the furry throw rug at the sight of his tanned and toned abdomen. His broad chest and shoulders didn't make staying upright any easier.

"Didn't I warn you about tripping?" He raised an eyebrow, his eyes now golden.

Not sure how to respond, I kept staring.

His loose hair framed his face like a mane. The crooked grin made him look sexier, if that were possible.

From the hungry look in his eyes, it was clear that my little black number had garnered his full attention. At least I wasn't the only one overcome by our chemistry.

I understood that if I didn't leave in the next minute, more than his shirt would be missing, and my dress would be a glittery heap on the floor.

"You have fun," I said, pasting on a bright smile.

Rather than bother with words, he growled. His mental message almost changed my mind. *You're all the fun I need, Chloe. When will you figure it out? I. Want. You.*

With energy I didn't recognize as my own, I commanded my legs to move, and managed to walk myself to the door and stumble out. When I heard Zane's pained but feral roar, I knew I'd made a huge mistake.

If only I could put my pride to rest and return to his arms.

Nine

The applause was already deafening, but I joined the enthusiastic crowd, my claps lost in the mix. I even added my trademark piercing whistle to the avalanche of noise.

Following a few stray hoots and hollers, the band resumed their set of popular cover songs. The music brought back memories, most of them positive for a change. A majority of the diverse crowd had been lured onto the dance floor by the familiar songs. I was an exception, lounging in a shadowy corner booth, my feet keeping time to the beat.

"Can I get you another?" the flashy server asked through ruby lips.

"Why not?' I couldn't remember ever drinking this much. Men had been buying me drinks all evening, and I'd won a whopping three-hundred dollars playing the slot machines.

"You got it, sweetie. This one's from tall, dark, and handsome at the end of the long bar." She sauntered away.

A pang of hope made it impossible not to investigate my latest suitor. Maybe Zane had come to claim me. A girl could hope. Because I'd figured out that no matter how much liquor I consumed, I couldn't get his image out of my mind.

He'd been right about one thing. Anytime I seemed the least bit uncomfortable with an admirer, a security werewolf, in human-form, of course, rushed to my side, removing the *cause* of my discomfort with discretion. How convenient. I would have welcomed their protective services in high school.

Before I was able to check out my latest cocktail-contributor, he glided into my booth, making himself comfortable at my side rather than taking the traditional place across the table.

"Thanks for the drink," I said, awed by his alluring presence and striking appearance.

His hair was darker than Zane's. It was hard to describe the style, but there was something surreal about him that caused me to envision castles and armored warriors wielding gleaming swords.

His eyes were hypnotic, mesmerizing — a dazzling shade of icy blue, framed with thick, inky lashes; they drew me in, soothing me, and complimenting the alcohol's effects.

"You are very welcome. May I ask your name?" He leaned closer, his mouth brushing my throat.

His intimate actions and dramatic demeanor reminded me of someone whose identity remained just out of reach, hidden behind a haze of booze inspired bliss.

"I'm Chloe Carpenter," I whispered, allowing my eyes to travel over his lean form. His skin appeared almost translucent in the club's special lighting. He was breathtaking, different from Zane, more elegant, more refined.

An unfamiliar predatory urge to sink my teeth into him should have warned me away. Instead, I examined his attire, which served to intensify his appeal. He was exceedingly masculine in a black leather coat, matching pants, and deep burgundy shirt. An ancient-looking insignia hung from a chain around his neck. Both of his ears were pierced. Like Zane, danger clung to him tighter than his leather pants, which appeared to be poured on, accentuating his manliness.

The waitress delivered our drinks, giving me a sly look before slipping into the crowd. For some unfathomable reason, my werewolf guards had yet to interfere. I was grateful for their current lack of attention. This was one suitor I wanted by my side.

"Chloe, what a lovely name for a very delectable woman," his voice caressed my mind, pulling me into a trancelike state.

He was irresistible.

Even so, I understood on some level that something was wrong.

This was no ordinary man. Everything about him screamed supernatural. I was blinded by the booze and his special, mind-swaying talent. I felt powerless to fight. I wasn't sure I wanted to.

"My name is Valamir." Taking my hand he kissed it, his eyes locked on my mine as he looked up through dark lashes. I melted, wanting nothing more than his mouth on mine.

Suddenly unsure of myself, I reached for my cocktail and drank it in two long gulps. Valamir seemed amused by my actions. "I think you may want to slow down," he chuckled.

Slowing down my drinking, not a problem. What I wanted to taste was this man with the foreign name.

Discerning my desire, he pushed me deeper into the booth. Dropping his head, he kissed me, savoring my mouth like an exquisite dessert. Forgetting where we were, I slid my hands under his jacket, digging into his hard back with my nails. Unlike Zane, who was hot like fire, Valamir's touch was wintry, yet at the same time scorching.

"You are luscious, Chloe. You are mine." He gazed at me with hooded eyes, before his mouth claimed me in a most unexpected way.

Sharp pain followed by blissful warmth, tortured, and teased my neck. I pressed closer, purposefully rubbing my breasts against his chest. Compelling and erotic images flooded my mind as he continued to suckle my neck.

Groaning, he released his mouth; his tongue lapped my tender skin.

Something — an inner knowing — told me that stopping had not been easy for him.

Any pain I thought I'd felt subsided beneath the soft stroke of his tongue. When his mouth returned to mine, I tasted something coppery like pennies with a dash of fine wine.

It was in that moment when I realized who Valamir reminded me of — Alciun — a vampire.

"Enough …!" a familiar voice roared, pulling me away from Valamir.

"No!" I protested, flailing my arms against the man who dared interrupt the most sensuous experience of my life. "Valamir!" I cried, returning to my senses just enough to see Zane snarling at the vampire, whose lips were now curled back revealing his own fangs. He crouched, arms extended, ready to strike Zane, who'd pushed me behind him.

Zane started to vibrate. The atmosphere around him shimmered.

I Kissed a Dog

Responding to the escalating crisis, a group of security guards surrounded our table like a wall, blocking us from the curious crowd.

"Both of you! Stop!" Logan stepped into the circle, grabbing Zane. "Control yourself, friend. This is not the place."

"You!" Logan turned to the vampire. "Leave this place. Now!" His eyes glowed crimson.

"I will return for you, Chloe," Valamir promised, before dissolving into a cascade of silver stardust. No one else in our little group appeared surprised by his vanishing act.

I half heard Logan instruct Zane to get me upstairs. Zane was disagreeing about something I didn't understand. Their voices sounded like they were coming from underwater.

"She's mine! The mark, it's been revealed," Zane argued.

I was baffled as to why these men continued to refer to me as their possession. The whole "she's mine" thing was annoying. Last time I checked, I wasn't a belonging.

Logan sounded equally agitated. "How can that be?"

"I don't know, but it's there. Do you want to see?"

"I believe you. Find a way to make her understand," Logan commanded.

"There's one thing I can think of to keep her safe," Zane replied with certainty.

Logan nodded. "You have my blessing."

In an alcohol-induced haze, I let Zane support me against his side. He led me from the hotel into the breezy Vegas night. He motioned for a nearby taxi.

Careful not to jostle me, he lifted me into the cab, joining me in the backseat.

"Charity Chapel," he instructed.

136

"How nice," I slurred, "we're going to church." I was surprised that werewolves attended church, especially in Vegas. Since Monday, my life had been full of unexpected surprises.

Feeling seasick, I leaned my head against Zane and watched the blinking lights speed by. "Where are the lights going?" I heard myself ask in a faraway voice, certain we were now riding in a boat.

"Goodness, Chloe; I can't leave you for a minute," he grumbled. "We're the ones moving, not the lights."

That made sense, sort of.

Uncertain how long we'd traveled, I found myself struggling to see through a misty veil that cloaked my vision. No longer moving, I was standing at the front of what appeared to be a chapel. Zane gripped my hand. A moment later we were facing an elaborate altar overflowing with floral arrangements. The room smelled sickly sweet like stale perfume which made the inside of my nose tickle.

I suspected now that I'd passed out and was dreaming.

"Is this an evangelical church?" I asked, trying not to sneeze. The Baptist church back home was nothing like this colorful place.

A man, I assumed was the pastor, approached and stood in front of us on a little platform. I couldn't quite hear what he was saying — something about in sickness and health and for better or worse.

"I do," Zane said.

Next, the man asked me a question and Zane nudged me. "Say *I do*, Princess."

"I do, Princess," I repeated, too disorientated to question his strange demand.

I Kissed a Dog

The pastor-man's mouth continued to move in a rapid blur; I still had no idea what he was saying. I didn't care. Another wave of nausea threatened to drown me. Zane held firm. At last, the man stopped talking and smiled.

Zane bent down and kissed me tenderly on the lips.

"My head," I moaned, not used to the pounding of drums between my ears. "O-h-h-h … I hurt."

I forced one eyelid up. The brightness spilling through the windows was more than I could tolerate. I pulled the blankets over my head.

Where was I? The hospital seemed likely considering how ill I felt.

"Good morning, Mrs. Marshall," Zane whispered in my ear. "You celebrated a little too hard last night," he chuckled.

"What are you talking about?" I gasped, very aware of his warm skin against mine.

"How soon you forget something as important as our wedding."

Fighting the throbbing pain, I opened my eyes to see if what I suspected was true. "You're naked!" I screeched.

So was I.

"You're my wife. Of course, I'm naked. Our honeymoon night was fantastic." He moved to kiss my cheek. "Don't worry; we'll have an extended honeymoon soon, maybe a trip to Europe."

Throwing off the covers, I dashed for the bathroom. This was impossible! There was no way in hell that I would have married a werewolf. I had to get a grip and think.

What happened last night?

I'd put on my little black dress after an argument with Zane and had gone to one of the hotel's in-house clubs for some live music.

Drinks. Lots and lots of drinks. Men had kept buying them for me, and I'd kept drinking.

Valamir — the vampire — he'd dazzled my mind with some form of vamp magic and kissed me. After that, everything got fuzzy.

My reflection caught my attention, reminding me of my horrible predicament. Dear Lord. The mirror revealed an exhausted-looking woman with dark half-moons under both eyes. I shook my head. The reflection shook hers. No doubt about it — I was the bedraggled woman in the mirror.

One thing was clear; I didn't look anything like a blissful newlywed.

I was miserable inside and out. Besides the blistering headache, my stomach was churning, and I felt all wobbly. Even worse, if what Zane said was true, I was no longer a virgin, *and* I didn't even remember my wedding night.

"Babe, come on. Let's talk. Don't get all shy now," Zane called. "I had the maid come and change the bedding. Please, I promise; it was incredible."

Inhaling, and then blowing air out my nose like a raging bull, I slid into the hotel-provided bathrobe and cinched the waist with its tie. Flinging open the door so hard it battered the wall, I stormed into the room, ignoring the drumbeat in my head.

In the short time that I'd been secluded in the bathroom, the bed had been remade and Zane was lounging across it with his arms behind his head. His long hair spilled over his shoulders. He'd put on a pair of athletic shorts. They didn't begin to hide his muscular form. My breath caught in my throat. Had I made love with this man and forgotten?

I got it now that drinking, for me, was no longer an option, at least not in public, and not without a very sober chaperone.

"How could you? *Why* would you?" I pleaded, letting my revulsion rise to the surface.

"That's two questions, Princess." He smirked, still looking delicious.

"I'm going to sit down," I announced, afraid I would vomit should I continue standing. He patted the bed, imploring me with his eyes.

I ignored the gesture and chose a chair by the window. "Why would you take advantage of me? Why?" I tried to keep the tears behind my eyes where they belonged. It didn't work. I could feel the liquid trails winding down my cheeks, increasing my humiliation.

"Babe, please, don't cry. I thought you wanted this. You agreed to the marriage. You were so happy last night."

"I was so drunk," I sobbed, no longer able to control my emotions.

"You'd had a few too many, but I had no idea you wouldn't remember. I would never …"

"Yes, you would have! You know my religious upbringing. Thanks to you, I can't even get an annulment and feel right about it. Couldn't you wait until I was sober before we, we did *that*." I cried harder, choking down sobs. I couldn't remember anything about what was supposed to be the most memorable night in a woman's life. I deserved to cry.

Did he even consider how his actions might be regarded as rape?

He moved with stealth, like always, and was kneeling beside me before I could begin to protest. Wrapping his arms around me, he held me while I wept. "Hey, hey, I promise; it'll be all right. I'll make it okay."

The realization that I was clinging to the cause of my anguish, startled me into action. Pushing him away, I leapt to my feet; I pummeled his bare chest with my fists.

"You can't make it okay. Don't you understand? I will never experience that experience again. Ever. You stole something precious from me, married or not," I cried.

"I'm sorry, Chloe. So sorry." From the depth of pain evident in his eyes, I almost believed him. Sadly, his regret couldn't repair my grief or return my virginity.

Yet, on some level, I felt just a smidgen of relief. His emotional responses and my woman's intuition assured me that he'd, without doubt, believed me to be a willing participant last night, and I knew enough about Zane to know he wasn't the type to resort to rape. Still, I felt violated, and he would have to pay somehow, someway, for his indiscretion.

He'd soon discover that being married to me wasn't going to be a walk in the park.

I'd make sure of that.

◎

Several aspirin, washed down with a secret hangover remedy, courtesy of Logan Sanders' younger sister, Misty, had me feeling almost normal.

Now it was time to get tough and keep the crying to a minimum. I was married to a werewolf, after all. I'd resolved earlier to make the best of my dismal situation, while ensuring that Zane forever regretted his selfish decision to coerce me into this perverted version of Holy Matrimony.

Despite my fury over Zane's lack of discretion, helping the pack wasn't negotiable. If I wanted freedom from a vicious killer and the mutant hybrids, my participation was critical.

After a lengthy and much-needed discussion with Logan and several high-ranking pack members, I'd committed to using my talents not only to help find Plum Beach's allusive serial killer, but also to snoop around at their upcoming board meeting. I hated to think what scary secrets the participants' pets would divulge.

Even our well-laid plans did little to quell my fear.

One unpleasant question nipped at the edge of my thoughts — how would Jazmine respond to the impromptu wedding? My new status as Zane's wife wouldn't help matters. She was already hell-bent on destroying me and taking Zane as her mate.

Much to my relief, I didn't have to stew alone. Misty had agreed to keep me company for the remainder of the afternoon and answer some of my questions while the men further plotted their strategies. I hoped our girl-time bonding-session would provide an opportunity for me to learn more about the whole werewolf mating phenomenon.

I still wasn't sure if our recent marriage equaled a formal mating ceremony, or if something additional was required. From what I'd gathered during our group discussion, Jazmine could no longer claim Zane as her mate, as I was now his one and only ... whatever that meant. My questions would have to wait, though. Hunger pangs had driven any lingering nausea away, making the search for food my number one priority.

The official lunch hour had long passed, but once again, the time didn't matter. It was Las Vegas. Days merged with nights and vice versa. And from what I could tell by the other hotel patron's rumpled attire and drooping eyes, I wasn't the only one none too thrilled with my previous night's conduct. For most of them, their nighttime indiscretions had been dragged into today, right along with their over-worn clothing.

I'd at least made the effort to clean up in an attempt to hide my recklessness.

"People don't sleep much around here," I acknowledged to myself, not sure yet how I felt about Misty. At least she understood my initial distress over the sudden change in my marital status. She'd stood up to Logan and Zane, voicing her sympathy for my predicament.

"Sleep is overrated," she said. "Casino owners count on guests that gamble until they drop. Tired gamblers make desperate decisions that tend to increase our profits."

"Can we eat here?" Longing for food, I stared through one of the hotel restaurants' open doors. An overflowing buffet table was calling my name. The inviting aromas were enough to drive me forward without her approval.

"You sure your stomach is ready for all that?" Misty studied me. "You were still pretty pasty an hour ago."

Appreciating her concern, I gave her my most sincere smile. "I promise if I get sick, which is happening a lot lately, I'll take the blame." I understood on some level that Misty was for the moment in charge of my wellbeing. Zane wouldn't take kindly to my being returned worse off than I'd been before leaving. If anything, since last night, his protectiveness had increased.

"You're catching on quick." She gave me a grateful look. "I'll grab a table."

After filling my plate to capacity, I joined my first ever female werewolf acquaintance, who I hoped in the future I could refer to as a friend. She seemed nice enough.

We ate for a few minutes in comfortable silence, both of us lost in our thoughts. She was the one to speak first. "How much did Zane tell you about the mating process?'

"Not much." Wasn't that the truth? Yesterday I was single. Today I was married to a werewolf and trying to accept that I'd had sex with said werewolf without my knowledge. I'd apparently given permission and enjoyed the monumental event.

During the morning meeting, I'd caught a vivid flash from Zane's memory that showed me kissing him with great enthusiasm on the bed. I could understand how he would have considered me a willing wife.

"Chloe ..." Misty called me back to the present.

"Sorry, please, go on."

"Male werewolves know when they've found their true mate. Normally, a female werewolf," She explained. "I've seen just one human werewolf mating ... it didn't end well."

"Why?" I was almost too scared to ask.

"She died in childbirth. Her body wasn't equipped to handle the pregnancy. Some say it was because she'd never received the mark."

"The mark?"

"Didn't you wonder how Zane knew you were his mate? Why he rushed you off to get married?" Misty asked her voice softer.

I doubted she'd accept my true thoughts on the matter, but I shared them anyway. "I assumed he was being selfish and controlling."

"You don't remember what happened before your nuptials, do you?"

I closed my eyes and inhaled. "I've never been so intoxicated in my life. I don't remember much." That fact troubled me.

Something significant had happened before my interlude with Zane. I vaguely remembered a vampire at my table. Just thinking about him caused my heart rate to quicken. I'd kissed him. *That* I was sure of. I'd enjoyed it too.

"Let me fill you in then. You were wrapped up in the arms of a master vampire. Thankfully, he didn't get a taste of your blood."

A sense of foreboding slithered through me in response to her last words. I'd know if a vampire had pierced my flesh. Wouldn't I?

"Are you okay?" Misty leaned forward, pushing her empty plate away.

"I feel like there's a memory missing. Like it's been erased." I shivered in spite of the warmth.

She nodded. "Master vampires have the power to dazzle your mind. They confuse your thoughts, drug you in a sense. No wonder you were so sick. Drunk *and* dazzled — definitely not a good combination."

Rather than reply, I considered my life four short days ago.

I Kissed a Dog

I could never have predicted on Monday that by Thursday I'd be in Las Vegas, married to a werewolf, following a make-out session with an ancient vampire, who may or may not have tasted my blood. I also realized that most of my rage toward Zane had vanished to be replaced instead by a mind-dulling numbness.

For the first time, my ability to communicate with animals seemed less important in the big scheme of things, but I knew otherwise. It was *that* so-called talent that had landed me in my existing predicament. Had I been a normal woman, none of this would have happened.

"Earth to Chloe …"

"Sorry. Again." I forced myself to refocus. "Tell me how Zane knew I was the one." *This* I had to know. We had experienced an abnormal attraction starting from the moment we'd met. I could attest to that.

"On his ankle, a symbol appeared. This symbol shows up within seventy-two hours of meeting a mate. By claiming you and marrying you in the traditional way, he has given you his name, and his protection."

I leaned down and twisted my legs, looking for any anomaly. Nothing. There were no symbols on either of my ankles. "What about me? Shouldn't I have a mark or something?"

"It's different for females. Men don't have a choice. You do. Should you determine in your heart that you want to be mated to Zane, and proclaim your love for him, you'll receive the mark."

I could tell she was leaving out something important. "And if I fail to reciprocate?"

"Zane will be alone for the remainder of his life.

Werewolves can only have one mate. And once they're marked, they are, as you humans say, 'off the market'."

This still didn't explain Jazmine and Zane's previous commitment though. "How then could Zane and Jazmine have been promised to each other as mates? He doesn't even like her." I remembered Zane's explanation, but I was curious to see if Misty confirmed it.

"Should a male and female be pledged as mates, a ceremony can still take place. They forfeit the opportunity of finding their true, fated mates. This is how alliances are formed. Alliances often without love.

Parents may choose this path for their children in order to strengthen their pack. Finding your destined mate isn't always easy. Some never do," Misty sighed. "Had Zane already been mated to Jazmine, he wouldn't have recognized you as his real mate."

"Do you have a mate, Misty?"

Her expression revealed the answer before her words. "The one I wanted found his true mate. They're very happy." She looked down, cheeks blazing.

"I'm so sorry. Here I am with a mate that I'm not sure I want, and you desire someone you can't have." I shook my head amazed by the irony.

Misty was a beautiful young woman, close to my age. She wore her fiery hair in a textured shag that framed her waiflike features. Her skin was creamy, free of any blemishes. Like me, she had emerald eyes. She was petite, with narrow hips and small breasts. I always felt too shapely around pixies like Misty. Any man would be thrilled to have a woman (werewolf) like her.

I Kissed a Dog

"Goodness! I didn't mean to get all mushy about my ..." She looked up, embarrassed.

"Forget it," I countered. "I'm the master of mushy. Ask Zane."

"Speaking of Zane," she paused, her tentative expression revealing the uncertainty she felt broaching the subject. "He loves you ..."

I started to interrupt but thought better of it when I noticed the gleam in Misty's eyes. She was determined to have her say.

"He was never really interested in Jazmine. Numerous females have tried to seduce Zane. Many have been disappointed. Any female I know would be honored to have Zane Marshall for a mate or husband."

"Those females are the same species. I'm human. This match just isn't right." I struggled to remember the reasons why a relationship with Zane wasn't acceptable. The biggest barrier I could come up with was his bull-headedness, which if I were honest with myself, rivaled my own. Admitting how much we were alike wasn't easy.

"You love him. I can see it in the way you look at him when you think no one is watching. Passion sizzles between you two like bacon in a frying pan."

The bacon comparison was too much. I couldn't stop the laughter. It intruded into our serious discussion, causing Misty to double over; her own melodic giggles sending me into a renewed frenzy. Several customers shot annoyed glances our way as we continued to escalate, releasing any previous tension that might have lingered between us.

Choking back tears, I somehow sputtered, "Bacon? I can't believe you described our attraction as sizzling bacon."

"So maybe it was a bit melodramatic," she said, still fighting for control.

Much to the pleasure of the nearby tables, a stern-faced waiter chose that moment to deliver our check. Grabbing my arm, Misty led me to the cashier and signed her name on the bill. "Being the owner's sister has certain benefits."

"Free food is always a perk," I agreed, pleased to have met Misty. Laughter in the midst of my present situation was good medicine.

"Would you like to walk around the grounds outside? It's like exploring a jungle without the danger," she offered. "I promise that my brother and your mat … husband will be wrapped up in their plotting session for hours."

Knowing she was probably right and eager to have some danger-free fun, I found myself agreeing.

It was apparent that Misty had been right in her description of the resort's grounds. They were amazing, especially the sound effects. An authentic roar caused me to grab Misty's arm. Instead of laughing at my reaction, she tensed, raising a finger to her lips.

In the same fluid manner that I'd seen Zane move, she lowered herself into a defensive crouch. Like Zane, her eyes changed to scarlet as she surveyed our surroundings.

Remembering my own talent, I probed the area with my mind, seeking anything out of the ordinary. It didn't take long to locate another nonhuman presence.

She smells so good. I want to taste her flesh, her blood. But, no-o-o-o-o, Jazmine needs the little bitch intact. Maybe one bite?

Hoping that Zane would hear me at this distance, I blasted the thought to him. Logan had suggested that as mates our telepathic communication abilities might increase.

"Get behind me!" Misty hissed.

The familiar vibration hummed through the air, preceding an explosion of clothes from her tiny frame. For a brief second I saw her nakedness; then she was on all fours covered in luscious grey and silver fur. Though not as big as the male wolves, she was still magnificent.

A snarl tore from her throat as our enemy stalked from the brush. So much for no danger in the make-believe jungle.

"Just give the human to me and I'll let you live," the hulk-of-a-man growled. "You hardly know her. She's just a pitiful little girl." Flashing a knife, he grinned menacingly, taunting us.

Seeing the crazed look on his face had the opposite effect on me than it should have. Instead of scaring me, he'd managed to piss me off.

I stepped forward. "I'm not some little girl, you stupid freak." To demonstrate just how furious his threats had made me, I targeted his mind with a barrage of humiliating thoughts aimed to castrate his masculinity.

Startled by my mental ambush, he grabbed his head and shook it crazily, attempting to disengage from the scorching visions.

The blade clattered on the paved pathway near his feet. I pressed harder, tightening my focus and shooting daggers of disgust in deeper. It was obvious by his tormented expression the daggers were hitting their intended targets. *Bull's-eye!*

Seeing her opportunity, Misty sprang at the man. Her front paws plowed into his chest, knocking him backward. Arms flailed as he struggled to keep his balance. A second later, his throat was a bloody gash. I turned away as she finished the job. Zane's arms were around me in the same instant.

"I'm sorry I didn't get here sooner. Although it looks like you two make a pretty good team," he said; his voice a mixture of worry and pride.

"I thought you might need this." Logan handed over a hotel robe to his sister. She covered herself, after a brief glance at her tattered clothes.

"Thank you, Misty," I whispered; fear had caught up with me and was squeezing the air from my lungs.

I was uncertain how we'd managed to defeat the huge man without any help from our male protectors. His massive bulk had been beyond threatening. The idea of meeting him in mutant form under a full moon sent shivers scurrying down my spine.

"You saved my life." My respect for my lupine friend had increased ten-fold in the last ten minutes.

"No. Thank *you*," she said grinning, brushing off my compliments. "Without your very effective mind games, we would've been doomed."

Trying to ignore the splashes of crimson on her face, I turned back to Zane, accepting his offer of support. His arm around me was the one thing holding me together.

All I wanted now was to go home. The intrigue of Vegas had died right along with my mutant attacker.

Ten

Our return trip to Oregon was uneventful. I was able to unwind on the plane and enjoy the superb service.

Our current attendant was an energetic young man. Despite his enthusiasm, I was more pleased with the empty First Class section; giving us some much-needed privacy. Zane seemed relieved that no one was kicking at the back of his seat.

"Where do we go from here?" I asked, curious how we would present ourselves at work. I'd decided to stay focused on facts and push my erratic feelings aside.

Back at the hotel, Zane had insisted we make every effort to demonstrate our commitment to each other by being candid about our elopement. I still wasn't convinced that everyone in Plum Beach needed to know about our marital status.

Wife. Mate. Neither title suited me. I doubted that I'd ever accept either label with good grace.

Zane gave me a pointed look. "I thought we already went through this. We couldn't ignore the whole love-at-first-sight-thing, and we followed through on those loving feelings. It happens all the time."

"Except there's a slight problem — everyone knows my practical personality. They know I'm not a person prone to impulsive decisions." At least I hadn't been impulsive prior to meeting my alleged mate.

Instead of answering, he let his gaze wander over my face and down my neck, leaving a trail of scorching desire in its wake. I trembled, imagining what our first night together must have been like. I could only imagine the pleasure he'd inflicted on my body.

Just contemplating our wedding night provoked a renewed storm of anger, slamming the door on any amorous feelings.

"You love the fact that I'm putty in your presence. It's the power over me that excites you," I taunted.

His lustful expression evaporated into a mask of consternation. If I wasn't aware of his misshapen motives, I might have believed my words had wounded him. More likely, they'd stung his pride.

He shook his head and looked away.

I didn't understand why, but I felt an overwhelming need to apologize. My emotions were more uncontrollable around Zane than they'd ever been. Taking Alcuin's prior advice to chill out wasn't possible, not now, maybe never.

Hoping I sounded more contrite than I felt, I forced an apology, "I'm sorry. I just can't get over missing such an intimate experience."

I knew I didn't need to explain to which experience I was referring. He had what I assumed were very fresh and detailed memories of our post-wedding intimacy.

Zane straightened and faced me. "I can't erase my mistake. You must realize, had I known the extent of your inebriation, I would never have made love to you. Maybe someday you'll give me another opportunity, but from this point forward, I'll wait for you." He closed his eyes and leaned back.

His words left me speechless. I couldn't deny the sincerity behind them. When he spoke with such tender frankness, I found myself questioning how I would survive without his tantalizing glances and heart-stopping kisses.

But this was what *I* wanted, right? To be left alone. And he was leaving me alone, allowing me to choose the time and place for any future encounters, and according to Misty, he was utterly, without any recourse, bonded to me.

Without my surrender, he was destined to remain alone — untouched, unloved.

Maybe it served him right.

I knew better. He couldn't stop the mating mark from appearing any more than he could help what he'd been born to become. All I had to do was accept his love and protection, and we could have many more nights together that I would remember.

What was holding me back from what seemed inevitable?

I doubted any so-called *normal* man could handle my post-coma talents with Zane's grace and admiration. My former relationship had been proof enough that my animal reading gift caused major relationship discomfort.

I'd discovered Jordon's infidelity one evening while feeding his cat like a good girlfriend. He was away on a business trip … the infamous meet-the-other-woman-trip.

When we ended our relationship, a week later, in a storm of harsh words and accusations, Jordon made sure to let me know I was a psychotic weirdo, as well as boring because I refused to sleep with him. He was, after all, a man with needs.

When he kicked his helpless cat for tattling, I kicked him in the shin — hard.

Jordon hopping around on his uninjured leg screaming obscenities was my last memory of him.

And I'd thought he was my Knight in Shining Armor? Talk about a major misjudgment of character.

I spent the remainder of the flight plagued by one question. What would be so horrible about a man like Zane loving and protecting me?

Considering my unpleasant history with the *human* male, it was difficult to establish what exactly was keeping me from embracing the werewolf resting beside me.

Two hours later, we waited vigilantly with our fellow passengers at the luggage carrousel. Suitcase after suitcase rolled by, the majority of them black. Zane spotted his bags first and separated them from the sea of similar baggage. I followed suit, recognizing my old beat-up case and travel bag. Prepared to snatch mine from the circling belt, I was startled when a pale hand beat me to them.

Alcuin! I never thought I'd be so pleased to see a vampire.

"I thought you two might want to avoid six hours in a rental car," Alcuin said, setting my bags on the floor.

Zane relaxed, smiling his approval.

His response caused my heart to do little somersaults. I hated to admit how much I disliked seeing him unhappy. I was spending so much time worried about him exerting his power over me that I'd failed to acknowledge the extent of my influence over him.

"You're such a mind reader," Zane joked, still grinning at his friend.

Alcuin stopped.

Standing stiffly; he looked over the rims of his dark sunglasses and focused his piercing gaze on my neck. Self-consciously, I started to reach up, and just as quickly dropped my hand, fighting not to fidget under his sudden scrutiny.

Ignoring my discomfort, he walked a slow circle around me, sniffing like a dog. "Something is different about you," he stated without emotion.

"I'm mated to Zane now," I said trying to sound pleasant; certain he had used his supernatural senses to detect a lingering trace of Valamir.

I glanced at Zane who appeared puzzled by his friend's actions.

"We're married, and I'm marked. That's what you're feeling," Zane clarified, allowing his amber eyes to rake over me, sending the usual trails of heat down my spine.

Feigning indifference, I shrugged, turning my attention to my purse that I pretended to search. It was hard not to feel ruffled with the two of them intently staring.

"Where are we going when we get back in town?" I decided to change the subject while applying the lip gloss I'd managed to retrieve. We hadn't talked about our future plans other than publicly announcing our marriage.

At last, after another endless moment of examination, Alcuin turned away. "She has a good question."

I allowed relief to wash over me as we returned to a more normal line of conversation. I couldn't help feeling as if I'd escaped the lion's den without a scratch — this time, anyway.

Miraculously, Zane took the bait too. "We need to go to Chloe's place first. We'll figure out the next step from there."

Finding a secluded spot away from the airport crowds, we team-teleported back to my beach house in Florence. It appeared I'd conquered all disagreeable reactions to my latest mode of traveling. On the down side, I hated to admit that I was getting quite comfortable going wherever I wanted with the blink of an eye. This was no *I Dream of Genie*, though. All the blinking was courtesy of my new fanged friend.

Glancing again at Alcuin, I concluded that in addition to my newfound acceptance of teleportation, I had indeed misplaced some essential memories back in Vegas.

Although different in appearance, Alcuin reminded me of the regal vampire — Valamir. I could still recall his haunting face. My neck tingled just thinking about our short time together in the bar. I wished I could confide in Alcuin, but I didn't dare. Not now. I had no idea how he would respond, and I wanted, at all cost, to avoid the negative impact that discussing the ancient vampire would have on Zane.

Seeing Zane's bulky form in my living room yanked me back to the moment.

To begin with, Luke would be shocked to see us strolling into work hand in hand. Just imagining the expression on his face when he heard the "good news" was enough to send me to bed for a month. Yet as anxious as I was about my boss' reaction to my shotgun wedding, I was more concerned about Jazmine and the mutants. Considering how they'd tracked me all the way to Sin City, preparing to combat future attacks on the home front seemed prudent.

"Your bags are on your bed," Zane said from behind.

Just the silky sound of his voice was like liquid honey to my ears, calming my jumbled thoughts. I wished he'd forget his vow and take me in his arms. Somehow, though, I understood as difficult as it was for him to resist, he meant business this time. I'd have to make the first move.

"Thanks," I half-whispered, looking for Alcuin. "Where'd our transporter disappear to?" I was beginning to understand that vampires were prone to popping in and out at will. They didn't seem too inclined to explain their whereabouts, and I wasn't sure if knowing was such a good idea.

"Even though he can survive the daylight, he prefers the dark. I suspect he's taking a vampire rest." Zane shrugged.

I almost asked what a vampire rest entailed, but decided against it. We had more important things to deal with.

The blinking light on my archaic answering machine caught my attention. Curious, I darted around Zane's bulky mass and hit the button.

"You have three new messages…"

"Hi, Chloe. It's me, Luke. I know you're out of town, but I wanted you to know it's been real quiet since you left. No new murders. So far, no new leads either. At least, we've had some peace.

Zane's friends have done a great job. They installed new security cameras, and, the even better news — they've agreed to stay on as additional security until we get a handle on our animal attacker. Well, I miss you."

Before I could ponder his words, the second message was retrieved. "You little whore. So you can talk to animals. How quaint. Have they told you how you're going to die like a slaughtered cow? You should ask around, clues can be found in the oddest places."

Hitting the pause button, I faced Zane, surprised by my detached observation. "That voice ... it's familiar, but I can't place it. It sounded like he was trying to disguise himself."

"Another reason why we'll be staying at my place until this is resolved. The M's can remain here." Seeing my narrowed eyes he added, "My promise of chastity extends to my bedroom. Besides, living together makes more sense in light of our recent matrimony. We are man and wife."

More like wolf and woman, I almost said, but stopped myself. He was trying to be kind and protective.

The final message belonged to my always-anxious mother. "Honey, it's me. Where are you? Are you in some kind of trouble? Two men stopped by yesterday asking for you. I told them you didn't live here. They were very nice-looking, but a little on the grouchy side. Do you owe money? If you do, please don't be afraid to ask for help. Your father and I understand how hard these economic times are. Your machine's cutting me off ..."

I sighed, dreading the next conversation with my parents. I wondered if they'd called work looking for me. If so, they'd blown my cover with Luke to smithereens. Why I still cared was a mystery. He'd know my marital status within the hour, if he didn't already.

"I told you that not telling your folks was best," Zane said carefully, watching for my reaction to the latest message.

Instead of snapping back at his I-told-you-so comment, I lifted the phone.

Before it was halfway to my ear, Zane took it from me. "Not now, Chloe. You can call them later. Let's get your stuff and get out of here. We need to connect with Mack and Michael, not to mention, our boss."

I had to agree. Home no longer felt safe. I wondered what returning to work would feel like.

I'd know soon enough.

Eleven

It was Friday, and everyone would be back from lunch by now, eager to collect their paychecks.

This knowledge did little to calm my nerves.

In a few minutes, the entire Plum Beach Wildlife Park's staff would be privy to my new relationship. Rhonda's reaction was the one worth watching. Her jealousy was bound to be entertaining, at least until she rejoined forces with Jazmine. I wondered how their blossoming friendship was progressing.

"You okay?" Zane asked, squeezing my hand tighter.

Regardless of my conflicting feelings about my new husband, I felt more secure with my hand tucked in his. "Fine. Just stay close." My confident words did little to belie the undercurrent of fear lurking just below my upbeat surface.

"I'll be right here, Princess."

Our unique connection made it easy for me to sense the humming vibration surrounding him like a supernatural shield. I knew that he'd change to his werewolf form if it ensured my safety. Granted, I didn't anticipate any physical threat from our coworkers. A few shocked faces — absolutely, I was prepared for that.

"Hey, you two lovebirds!" Mack called from the park's main entrance booth. "We've rented The Crab Cove for your reception tonight. Though no one knows what we're celebrating, Logan sent some extra funding to make it happen."

"Gee, I can't wait," I murmured before flashing the big blonde wolf my famous phony smile.

"He's following orders," Zane reminded, releasing my hand to slip his arm around my waist.

I tried, without a smidgen of success, to ignore the tummy-flops his latest affections produced. No matter how hard I tried, I couldn't deny that I was besotted with him. Staying angry required too much energy. Besides, we had to convince an entire town that we were madly in love.

Mack continued, "Here's the scoop. Everyone has been told that there's a big announcement planned for this afternoon. The staff thinks we're celebrating the new aquarium's opening …"

"Won't they be surprised?" I interrupted.

Overlooking my sarcasm, he glanced at Zane, who just shook his head.

"Can I please finish up here before that next carload of customers needs my attention?" Mack pressed.

"Sorry." I could hear several car doors slamming and kids laughing.

"Luke has no clue what's going on. I'm afraid he might think the party is for him. He mentioned that most of the staff forgot his birthday last month."

"This is going to break his heart in so many ways." I almost turned to leave, but the group of boisterous kids had reached the gate and they were wiggling around behind us.

Accepting our fate, I pushed through the turnstile and waited for Zane. He whispered something to Mack and was by my side before I could blink. I doubted I'd ever get used to his super-speed and agility.

"Dad, did you see that guy? He moved faster than the speed of light." The young boy sounded impressed.

"I told you he's been reading too many comics," a woman scolded.

That's my guy, a comic book superhero. I sent the thought silently, hoping to surprise him.

I'm glad you think I'm the hero not the villain. Zane squeezed me closer. *You also called me — your guy.*

"Today, you're in the hero category."

He guided me to the central courtyard. "I'm trying to be your hero every day."

Remaining silent was the best response to his latest insinuation. Violence and lust rested just beneath the surface of his cooling smile. When he was on edge like this, I could feel the magnetic pull of his power, wrapping its otherworldly tentacles around me, drawing me in.

If I had my way, I'd forget this whole new-couple-introduction-crap and wrap my legs around him and forget everything scary that went bump in the night. Wait. He was one of those things bumping around in the night.

"Well, I'll be damned!" Rhonda's shrill voice just about bowled me over, reminding me that my leg-wrapping fantasy wasn't about to become reality anytime soon.

Luke hurried from the gift shop. "Rhonda! There are customers …" His words faded as his eyes met mine. He glanced from me to Zane and back.

I knew the exact moment that Luke Snider, my favorite

boss and longtime crush, put everything together. Zane tensed, ready for battle. Rhonda continued to mutter obscenities despite Luke's warning about the customers, and the other employees were mysteriously drawn to the courtyard like flies to a spider's web. Talk about uncomfortable.

Michael chose that moment to bounce (I have no other way to describe his energetic way of walking) into the middle of the increasing crowd. "Congratulations, you two! You had us all fooled pretty good."

"I'll say," Luke agreed, looking madder than I'd ever seen him.

"I can explain," I started, before Zane interrupted.

He faced Luke and Rhonda; I assumed because they were the two making such a ruckus. "Thank you, Michael. Yes, Chloe and I are married."

Gasps and a few giggles rippled through the group of park employees, and I couldn't help noticing that a number of customers had stopped to watch the unfolding drama. They were getting their money's worth.

"We were just as surprised as you are about the intensity of our feelings. I didn't expect to fall in love when I took this job, but what can I say?" He gazed down at me.

I determined right then that Zane truly loved me, or he was destined for an Oscar nomination.

Michael again did the unexpected and started clapping. The courtyard erupted in applause and more than a few whistles, turning the tense atmosphere into a celebration as people moved forward to offer their congratulations. The two who didn't look pleased were Luke and Rhonda.

Luke stalked away and Rhonda flipped open her cell phone. I hated to imagine who she was calling.

I hadn't realized how many people could cram into The Crab Cove. Every chair was occupied and people leaned against the walls. The dance floor was gaining popularity as our guests enjoyed the free-flowing champagne. Wildlife Park employees helped fill the room, minus Luke and Rhonda. I was disappointed in Luke. I'd expected him to be more mature about the whole marriage thing. Obviously, I'd underestimated the extent of his feelings for me, *and* his level of maturity.

Zane, on the other hand, had support from his werewolf (and vampire) family. Logan, Misty, Mack, Michael, and Alcuin stood out from the crowd no matter how hard they tried to blend in and mingle. All gorgeous and mysterious, they drew curious glances from the local guests. The bolder ones couldn't keep their eyes off my new friends. I couldn't blame them for staring. I understood their fascination.

Initially, I'd been surprised by Logan and Misty's presence, but that was before I realized they'd teleported. Thankfully, no one had enough insight to question their sudden arrival.

I hadn't notified my family yet. The timing wasn't right, and I didn't have a clue how to tell my parents. Waiting until after the danger passed seemed logical. My mom would be devastated, probably scarred for life.

She'd been waiting for me to get married since birth it seemed. Married without a big formal wedding would be considered high treason in her eyes. Bob, on the other hand, would be frustrated that he hadn't had an opportunity to run a thorough background check on Zane.

I Kissed a Dog

I dreaded their first meeting. It had the potential to be one of those family fiascos perfect for Hollywood movies. Maybe we could do a reality show on the aftermath, or better yet, a reality program starring supernatural characters. Considering the supes had their own government, maybe they had their own cable channel floating around out there somewhere in TV land. I'd remember to ask Zane later. I still knew very little about the world he came from.

Distracting me with her too-flowery perfume, Misty materialized at my side. She gave me an extended once over. "Girl, you look stunning," she sighed, admiring my new dress, yet another wedding gift from her brother. Apparently pack leaders took their responsibilities pretty seriously. From our evening attire to the food, Logan's taste was impeccable.

Our wedding cake towered on a nearby table waiting to be cut and devoured. Zane informed me that Logan had paid the bill for the whole affair. I wondered if this was the alpha wolf's way of paying in advance for my animal eavesdropping services.

"E-hem!" Misty cleared her throat, a reminder she'd been complimenting my dress.

"Oh! Sorry. Lovely, isn't it?" Sexy and sleek, my post-wedding gown shimmered. I knew it hugged me in all the right places. Zane, along with every other man in the vicinity, couldn't keep his eyes off me.

Even more unsettling than the hungry male stares were the longing gazes from the women when they thought I wasn't looking. The green-eyed monster was trolling tonight in all his covetous glory. Again, I couldn't blame the ladies. Zane was downright delicious. Who wouldn't be jealous of my catch — and dress?

"You actually look like a blushing bride," Misty continued. "I suppose you've noticed everyone here is eyeballing you and Zane."

Of course, Misty, with her keen werewolf senses, would have picked up on all the heated glances and accompanying emotions. A low growl rumbled in her throat. She gave me a little nudge.

Oops. I just couldn't stay focused on what she was saying. "Sorry, I'm spacing out. Too much stimulus for one day. *And I'm not some giddy, blushing bride,*" I snipped without meaning to. "I'm just so hot; you'd think they'd turned up the heat."

A trickle of sweat was winding down my cheek. Ug! Not the face I wanted captured in our first family photos. Considering the event photographer, another paid-for-product, courtesy of Logan Sanders, was erecting his equipment by the cake table, my distress wasn't exaggerated.

According to Zane's last update, we had a few minutes to spare before the official cake-cutting ceremony — giving me just enough time to sneak a breath of cool ocean air.

"I'm sorry. I'm going to step outside." I hoped Misty wouldn't ask to join me. I was overheating, and starting to feel claustrophobic. Too many people stuffed in one place made my skin crawl. I'd never been one for big crowds.

"Go on. You're forgiven." Misty grinned before dancing off.

At least someone was having fun.

The familiar scents of salt water, rotting sea kelp, and what

I've come to refer to as "beach air" were what I noticed when I stepped out of the crowded Crab Cove. The deck was deserted, and I took that as a sign I'd picked the right time to escape my well-meaning, but increasingly annoying reception guests.

Leaning against the deck's wooden rail, I gazed into the line of trees and foliage that separated the restaurant from the beach and pounding surf.

The moon was bright, and I spotted one of several paths that wound through the brush leading to the soft sand beyond. The temptation to slip off my jeweled-stilettos and make a dash for the beach almost proved too enticing resist. It felt as if someone had beguiled my senses and was beckoning me to leave my party and dance to the more natural night melodies.

An involuntary shudder swept through me as the moisture-tinged breeze rustled the trees. The compelling need to leave the lighted patio's protection was growing stronger the longer I remained.

A movement on the nearest path seized my attention. I strained to see who or what was standing just beyond the light, obscured in the shadows.

"Hello … is anyone there?" I heard myself ask.

A man stepped forward, his skin illuminant in the moonlight. "I can come no closer, Chloe. This place has been warded by magic to keep uninvited guests away. You, however, could invite me to cross the ward."

Wards? Magic? Why was I even surprised? I'd learned more about the unseen world that existed around me this past week than a heroine in a paranormal novel.

"Please, I must speak with you. I have information that will help you," the stranger said, his voice sending shivers down my spine. My neck tingled in anticipation. I wanted the man in the moonlight to put his mouth on my throat, although I couldn't fathom why.

"Yes, Chloe, you remember. That moment in Las Vegas was but a taste of the pleasure I can give you."

My heart raced faster in response. I opened my mouth to do as he asked.

"Hurry! Someone is coming!" he commanded, fiercer this time.

Suddenly uncertain, I froze. My indecision was just long enough to allow another figure to burst through the trees and onto the moonlit lawn.

Stooped and reeking of fresh blood, the newcomer released a ferocious growl and lunged toward Valamir. Valamir! — My warrior vampire from the Vegas nightclub. How could I have mistaken the seducing creature for anyone else?

The snarling, slobbering mutant-monster was horrifying. about as far from appealing as you could get. Saliva and blood dripped from his jagged fangs. Who had he been eating?

Furious, the thing snapped at the air just in front of Valamir, who with his lightening speed countered each attempt. The mutant, enraged by his adversary's offensive prowess, roared and dove for the vampire. Instead of sinking his massive claws into his prey, the mutant found himself hugging a swirling cloud of glittery silver.

I didn't bother turning when the double doors behind me burst open. I was too mystified by Valamir's hasty vanishing act. Apparently, the mutant wolf was too. He swung his massive head both directions seeking his missing prey. One second Valamir had been in the clearing, wanting me; now he'd disappeared leaving me with an unexplainable unexpected sense of emptiness.

Why did I feel empty? How could he make me forget Zane for even a second? I wasn't in love with the vampire; nor was I a fickle woman.

"What the hell?" Zane shouted before catapulting over the railing. He landed with an ominous thud in front of the mutant.

"Get in the bar!" Zane roared at me. Then, so fast that I barely registered the movement, he pulled out a gleaming blade concealed beneath his pant leg.

He plunged the blade into the mutant's neck. Dark crimson spewed from the fatal wound, darkening Zane's white dress shirt.

In a flash of shimmering light, Alcuin appeared next to the fallen creature. He gripped its arm and they both vanished in a cascade of silver sparkles that reminded me not only of the fake fairy dust I used to keep in a little bottle as a child, but also of Valamir's departure a few moments earlier. One thing was obvious; both vamps shared the same traveling techniques and special effects.

The whole incident had happened so fast a camera probably would have missed it. My feet were frozen. I couldn't move and certainly not have run inside.

"What's going on out here?" several voices chorused, as more footsteps rushed onto the deck.

"Animal attack," Zane pronounced. "A large cougar was stalking Chloe. I got here before it pounced."

"Thank God you're all right; someone inside mentioned spotting a big cat recently." Misty patted my shoulder. I couldn't tell if she was buying Zane's story or helping him make it more believable. I assumed the later.

"Should we hunt it?" someone asked. "We could get our guns."

"There's no need. I got it good with my hunting knife. I keep it with me at all times. I've learned the hard way that nature doesn't always behave the way we expect." Zane brushed off his jacket and stalked up the steps at the patio's far end, the crimson stain on his shirt the preternatural struggle's last remaining evidence.

"Are you okay, Princess?" *I thought I told you to get inside.*

Choosing to ignore his second comment, I nodded, still not sure what to say. For some irrational reason, I'd already decided to keep my Valamir-sighting to myself. The thought of enduring the barrage of questions Zane and his pack were bound to ask seemed too overwhelming. Besides, Valamir was trying to help me. Maybe he knew something about the murders. I also knew if Zane found out about Valamir's presence he'd get all over-protective and forbid me to talk with the vampire. Overprotection was really going to be a challenge. Very nice when I was agreeable but hell when I wasn't.

Zane looked down at his dress shirt. "Let me change. The cake is waiting."

I just nodded, still unable to make my mouth form words.

Our guests appeared unruffled and were already returning to the party. Free drinks had that effect. People would forget the excitement if it meant an opportunity to consume unlimited quantities of alcohol on somebody else's dime. And unlike me, they hadn't witnessed the brutal fight between a mutant and vampire. I doubted even free booze would not have done the job had they caught a peek of the otherworldly spectacle.

Now the last remaining evidence of the violence was the blood soaking Zane's shirt. In a few minutes that would be gone too, and for most people the incident would be forgotten.

Not for me.

"Misty …" Zane nodded in my direction.

"I got her." Misty shook her head at his retreating form. "Come on, blushing bride; let's get you ready for your cake-cutting photo-op."

I allowed her to lead me inside and through the tangle of dancing, drinking bodies. Even in my current zombie-like state I knew that it was important for me to learn about the so-called magic and wards that Valamir had mentioned. But asking one of my werewolf companions was out of the question.

Maybe it was time I trusted Alciun with my secret.

Waking up in Zane's bed didn't seem as strange as I'd expected. I'd already spent one memorable night in his lackluster apartment, but not as his new bride.

That first night we'd had some pretty intense kissing action before our supernatural encounter with Detective Davis and her hybrid flunkies. This time, as promised, he'd kept his hands to himself leaving me huddled on the bed's right side (far right, I might add) fighting for my share of the blankets. Summer on the Oregon Coast was unpredictable, making it top priority that I figure out some way to stay warm during the long nighttime hours. I wanted to curl up in his arms. However, we hadn't stopped long enough for me to come to terms with the fact I was married to a werewolf. It all happened so fast. I needed to catch my breath and think.

At last night's reception, we'd managed to complete the cake cutting ceremony with no additional drama.. Our intoxicated guests hadn't seemed at all bothered by our early departure. After all, we were newlyweds, supposedly madly in love.

If they knew how I'd spent my second night as a new bride debating whether or not to kill my husband — or seduce him — they might have questioned our rush to escape the festivities.

In reality, it was jealously not love that drove us out the doors before midnight.

Zane had grown impatient with all the male attention I was receiving. It seemed the longer the liquor flowed, the bolder the men became. Zane had no sense of humor when it came to me being ogled by other males. I guessed it was a wolf thing, because I'd never known a man to be so territorial. On some level, his possessive behavior scared me, yet at the same time made me feel valued, even cherished. As long as he didn't start lifting his leg to mark his territory, we'd manage.

His actions would always illicit conflicting emotions, but boredom wasn't something I'd ever have to worry about.

"Coffee?" he called from the kitchenette.

I was surprised to hear him already banging around in his kitchen. It was 8:00 AM on Saturday. We were off work for the weekend, and, as far as I knew, we had no major plans until Monday's board meeting.

Thankful to be wearing sweats in the morning chill, I padded as noiselessly into the kitchen as I could. I wanted to see him at work doing something other than beating up bad guys or bad dogs.

"Trying to sneak up on me, weren't you?" He leaned against the kitchen's sole counter, arms crossed.

"Supersonic hearing, how could I forget? Just curious what you're doing in here."

His lip twitched in a way that I was beginning to recognize as Zane's method of "smile control." Looking overly happy wasn't in his nature.

"You *were* sneaking, hoping to catch me doing something domestic," he teased.

"No comment? Since when is Princess Chloe so quiet? I was expecting a sarcastic comeback." He turned to stir something on the two-burner stove.

A whiff of sure-to-be tasty spices sent my stomach into a fit of growls and gurgles.

"My mate is hungry. I hope you like biscuits and gravy made from scratch."

I nodded.

His cooking expertise was a very pleasant and unexpected surprise. If the women at last night's party had known about this particular trait, they'd probably have plotted something unthinkable, and very illegal, to get me out of the picture for good. A gorgeous, masculine man who cooks; that was a lethal combination any woman would appreciate and admire.

"I admit; I'm impressed."

Zane grinned. His pleasure at my words was undeniable, causing me to draw in a quick breath. Goodness! A simple smile and I was left breathless. I needed to find a way to control my betraying emotions. I'd committed to making this marriage miserable for him, not a relationship full of compliments and early morning cheer.

Sensitive to my underlying feelings, he refrained from making any additional remarks. Opening the oven, he pulled out a tray of biscuits. "I hope you're hungry."

"We are!" Mack called from outside, his booming voice penetrating through the closed door. "Open up or I'll huff and I'll puff and I'll blow …"

"Yeah, yeah. This big bad wolf is not in the mood for visitors. I'm a married man now. So take your hungry pup and go someplace where you two can super-size your meals," Zane called out the open window.

Under normal circumstances I would have been annoyed by the intrusion, but having the father son duo in for breakfast would help relieve the tension and temptation that lingered in the kitchen.

"You might as well let them in. We don't want two hungry wolves patrolling the park today," I said.

"You heard the lady, breakfast is served." Several plates clanked together, as Zane reached for more dishes. I was surprised by how quickly he'd agreed. Maybe he was as uncertain about how to deal with me as I was him.

"Thanks, Chloe. We owe you," Michael laughed as I swung the door open.

"We thought you might want an update," Michael added.

For the first ten minutes, nobody spoke. We all shoveled Zane's biscuits and gravy into our mouths like we'd never seen food before. I'd never tasted such a scrumptious breakfast. Not even my step dad's homemade waffles could compare.

Long before the men finished with their third helpings, I'd

pushed my plate away and was rubbing my swollen stomach. I was certain someone might mistake me for a woman in her second trimester of pregnancy. Despite my fullness, my taste buds were still screaming for more food while my insides protested.

Being around wolves wasn't good for the waistline. I'd have to watch what I ate if I wanted to keep my figure. I assumed that werewolves burned huge quantities of calories during the shifting process. Presumably, running around in wolf form also burned a fair share. If I could be so lucky.

What was I thinking? I'd never consider becoming a werewolf. And taking into consideration my human status, if bitten, I'd turn into a freakish mutant. I'd have to find another, more acceptable way to burn off my extra caloric intake. Maybe Zane had a gym membership. We could work out together.

Abruptly, Zane made a satisfied groaning sound. He tipped his chair back and wiped his mouth with another napkin. He and Mack had accumulated quite a pile of napkins between their two plates. At least Michael seemed to have more refined table manners.

"Good stuff," Mack confirmed. "Where did you learn to cook like that?"

"Who cares?" Michael interrupted. "As long as we get to reap the rewards."

"Both my mother and my father were good cooks. So was my sister."

"Well, good for all of you," Mack managed to say before taking another huge bite.

A few minutes later, the men joined me in rubbing their stomachs and looking stuffed at last. Though I doubted they minded the "ready to burst" feeling as much as I did.

Mack, now settled with his feet up, explained that Officer Tate had visited the park on two occasions, and that Agent Green had stopped in once. They'd also received a late night visit from Detective Davis and her mystical minions. They all had been seeking more answers and were eager to know when Zane and I would return.

Both Michael and Mack sensed that Officer Tate and Detective Davis had no qualms with Zane or me. But the shifty FBI agent seemed suspicious of us both — in particular — me.

Why would anyone think that I had a part in the murders? Sure, I'd known two of the victims, and I'd dated Will, but it was a small town where everyone knew everyone. Paths were bound to cross often.

Will hadn't exactly been a prude either. Last summer he'd spent some very intimate one-on-one time with Rhonda following our short-lived relationship, if you could even call it a relationship. She'd made certain that the entire park staff knew the details of their escapades.

Why didn't Agent Green take a long look her way?

Rhonda had been furious when Will had decided to cut her off. And far more important than Rhonda's unlikely involvement was the fact that any halfway intelligent person would know I didn't have the physical strength, let alone a motive, to carry out such heinous crimes.

Just like the crime dramas my step dad was addicted to —

something just didn't add up. But unlike the TV shows, figuring out who-done-it wouldn't be neatly gift-wrapped with a bow and delivered in sixty minutes or less.

"Why me?" I looked up at Zane as he took a seat next to me on his lumpy sofa.

His eyes drifted to my clenched hands. "Who knows? This whole thing reeks of the supernatural. Based on the info you pulled from Will's pit bull, it's probable that a mutant is the cause of the actual killing, and a rogue werewolf, a female, is somehow involved. Why they'd even suspect a human is beyond me."

"Zane, have you forgotten, not everyone knows about the supernatural world? A few days ago, I would have thought you were all insane for even mentioning werewolves and vampires. Why would Agent Green, a plain old human being, think that anything other than a human or wild animal was the culprit?

They probably don't believe the puppy told me anything. Or, worse, they think I'm lying to protect the killer. Possibly one of us." The more I thought about the out-of-town FBI agent, the more unsettled I felt. He gave me the creeps times ten.

"What about the park animals?" Zane turned to Michael, since he'd been the one watching over them while his father was manning the front booth and handling other security issues.

"They seemed calm for the most part. A little nervous at nightfall, but, overall, everything was normal."

Michael's update added to my theory that we'd been implicated. "No wonder they're suspicious of us. We leave town and everything stops. No new murders; no animal attacks; nothing." Why did it still feel like I was missing an important piece, something obvious?

"I still think Jazmine is involved. How, I can't put it together, but I will." Zane's eyes narrowed.

"Down big guy," Mack soothed. "We know how you feel about Jazmine, but really, why would she waste her time on something like this. Small town murders aren't her specialty. She's all about making money and gaining power."

I wanted to remind Mack that killing for a killer was a sure path to power.

I listened while the men hashed out their theories and talked about the upcoming board meeting.

Logan was getting ready to present his ideas about expanding their hotels in the Pacific Northwest off the reservations, focusing less on gambling and more on family activities.

I couldn't help remembering the very public murder associated with a similar request in the past. Everything was somehow connected, figuring out how was proving far more difficult than anyone had expected.

Twelve

Taking a tour of the recent murder scenes was not my idea of a relaxing Saturday afternoon, especially after last night's stress-inducing wedding reception. I agreed with Zane's plan to launch our own investigation because I wasn't going to relax until we solved these murders and I cleared my name of wrong doing and my head of everything but Zane.

Could he be God's will for my life?

I don't understand why I can communicate with animals, but I have accepted that gift. Was Zane another puzzling gift? My stomach's insistent growls overrode my questions, for now, anyway. After recovering from our homemade Breakfast of Champions, and seeing the two M's off to work, we decided to snoop, or, in Zane's case, sniff around the crime scenes, starting with the oldest first.

I discovered Zane, being a purebred werewolf, had two options for shifting shapes. He could manifest into the wolfy, humanoid form I'd seen that first night behind the bar. In that formable shape, he appeared more closely related to the mutants. But, unlike his malformed counterparts, he could function on all fours too, making him a versatile killing machine.

Today, he'd morphed into an enormous, black wolf with bright amber eyes that mirrored intelligence not typical for any animal. His intimidating size made him significantly larger than any wolf I'd seen, giving me pause when he first emerged from the brush.

Before his change, he'd made sure to explain that his sense of smell was sharper when he was in his most natural form. Also, should anyone stumble upon us, he'd pass as an ordinary wolf.

"You think you are an *ordinary* wolf?" I laughed.

After watching me watch him, he padded over to my side, inclining his massive head. *Yes, you can pet me.*

That was the encouragement I needed. Dropping to my knees, I buried my face into the thick, mane-like fur around his neck. He pressed himself against me, allowing me to explore his supple coat. I ran my hands down his back and hugged him closer. He made as a happy growl. Being with him in his wolf form put me at ease. There was gentleness under the wildness. Gentleness I'd detected in his human form, but was too afraid of being vulnerable to acknowledge.

Despite my fear of emotional exposure, I allowed myself the luxury of praising his magnificence. "*You* are incredible," I cooed, scratching behind his ears.

He nudged me playfully with his muzzle. Losing my balance, I toppled over. "Hey! We've got work to do."

Scrambling to my feet I brushed a few stray leaves off my backside, noticing the way his eyes traveled over me. Even in wolf form he was still a flirt. I was relieved to see his new hands-off-policy didn't stop his appreciative glances.

I was enjoying being checked out by an animal. Something I'd never admit.

Okay, Miss Bossy, he teased silently. *What do you know about our first victim?*

Prior to our excursion, I'd spent a good hour on the Internet searching for any information. Victim number one — Jordon Smart — had been a part time dad; he'd just turned twenty-nine. As a special education aide, he'd worked in the fifth-grade classroom at the local grade school. Nothing about him appeared out of the ordinary, at first glance.

I had developed a whole new regard for first impressions. Just because Mr. Smart *appeared* normal, didn't mean he had been. I wasn't even sure how to define normal anymore.

His son, a sixth grader, had alternated between both parents' homes. Mom also worked in the education field, at the nearby administrative building.

The boy had discovered the grisly remains of his father. So traumatized, he was now residing in one of Portland's psychiatric facilities for youth. According to news' sources, he hadn't said a word since the gruesome discovery. Getting him to speak was my personal project. Only Zane didn't know it yet. I wasn't sure why I felt compelled to help the kid, but I did. I'd figure out how later.

After explaining what I'd discovered, we hiked through the overgrown grass and circled around the ranch style home. Nothing seemed out of place. The yellow tape was long gone and everything appeared peaceful.

Zane raised his muzzle. He closed his eyes, sniffing, before lowering his snout to the ground. Alert, he slunk toward the back door.

By the way, Princess, I have a few extra abilities I haven't told you about. Instead of elaborating, the doorknob turned as if gripped by an invisible hand. A click followed and it cracked open.

When were you planning to tell me what else you can do, Wolfman? Awed and angry, I fired the thought into his mind, recalling why he aggravated me — too many secrets.

He lifted his front paw and cocked his enormous head. *Each shape I take includes a few extra perks. That little trick makes up for the lack of hands.* He wiggled his paw.

Seeing his display of such human antics dissolved my anger. *How could an animal be so damn charming!*

Too late, I realized I'd sent my thought right into his furry head, officially making Zane the first wolf I'd seen grin. His tail wagged enthusiastically.

A crash from inside warned us that we weren't alone and whatever was inside probably wasn't friendly.

Zane's fur stood on end and his gums receded, revealing a set of fangs any vampire would envy. He crouched, ready to spring.

Immobilized, I waited and forced my mind to tune into the intruder. What I latched on to was unlike any animal mind I'd ever explored. It wasn't like any supe mind either, at least not the supernaturals I'd met.

A swirling red and black mass of repugnant and jumbled thoughts poured into my mind. I pushed harder, urging myself to delve deeper. My efforts were rewarded by visions of blood stained walls, disemboweled men, and the redheaded woman screeching orders at men in medical scrubs.

An inhuman wail severed me from the images. Before I could reattach, a cloaked shape burst from the house.

I Kissed a Dog

Zane lunged. His teeth latched onto its robe, tearing a piece from its shriveled body. Bald and wrinkled, the thing looked like an elderly baby. It keened again and vanished.

"What the hell!" I stared at Zane. A long shred of material dangled from his mouth.

Possibly something from the Fae world. Another mutant life form ...

I interrupted, "In other words, you don't know."

He shook his head. *We still need to go in. There's no one left here that I can sense.*

Unwilling to trust his instincts, I scanned the area for additional energy sources. Zane waited for my assessment. Once satisfied, I snatched the burgundy material from his mouth. It was a rougher fabric than I'd expected, and touching it made me cringe. Disturbing images of the stooped, naked creature would haunt me for a long time.

When I looked up, Zane was already nudging the backdoor open with his nose. Not wanting to be left alone for even a second, I bounded up the stairs.

Just inside, he bristled. I waited behind him, following as he made his way across the kitchen. Glancing over my shoulder, I expected to see the creature reaching for what was left of his tattered robe. All I observed was a semi-sunny sky and grass bending in the breeze. Taking a deep breath through my nose and then exhaling, I continued behind Zane as he padded further into the house.

Accepting we were alone, Zane seemed to relax and darted around the room, his nose to the carpet.

I felt drawn to the master bedroom where the murder had taken place. Not sure what I'd find, I started down the hall trying to imagine what the Smart boy had experienced. He'd most likely entered his home expecting to find his father waiting with dinner on the table, eager to hear about the game.

The newspaper had described Joshua Smart as an outgoing boy who excelled at baseball. According to the press, Jordon Smart had died at approximately 4:30 PM. Joshua's game finished up around 7:30 PM.

Joshua, expecting a warm welcome from his father, had been met with excruciating silence . There would have been a horrific odor. The metallic smell of blood combined with the pungent stench of death — it was no wonder the boy wasn't talking.

My thoughts reverted to the gruesome scene Josh's puppy had imprinted on my mind, and my soul. Queasy, I spun around prepared to escape.

How would I help Joshua Smart if I fled now?

Drawing a ragged breath, I prepared myself to enter the bedroom. Zane brushed against my leg and whimpered. Grateful for his support, even in wolf form, I rested my hand on his thick neck and let him lead the way.

It was evident that a crime scene clean up service had already performed their special brand of magic. The blood and gore had been removed, leaving the former murder scene spotless. An offensive odor remained, though mild, it still triggered my gag reflex.

Zane with his heightened senses prowled through the room.

No matter how long I live, I'll never get used to the smell of death. I flashed to age thirteen. Our cat was locked in the car

I Kissed a Dog

on a hundred-degree day. The car had to be sold. Nothing could rid it of the stench — or memories.

No doubt, Zane agreed. *The cleaning people did well, but that lingering odor ... I'm sorry, maybe this wasn't such a good idea.*

Appreciative of his support, I patted his head. *We're here, so let's look around.*

Zane kept his muzzle glued to the carpet as he rounded the room. When he reached the corner, by the bed's left side, he paused. *Can you take a closer look at this plant?*

The fake tree in the corner was one of several. Mr. Smart must've liked a green touch without watering. They were dust-free and shiny-green courtesy of whatever cleaning products the crew had used.

For one brief terrible moment, before pawing through the branches and leaves, I imagined the tree painted with blood. Blinking away the picture, I sifted through the fake moss.

Anything? Zane questioned.

Not that I can see. What did you smell? I didn't know where else to look.

Something that shouldn't be here, but I don't recognize it.

I stared at the tree wishing it would speak. My eyes glided from top to bottom. Bottom! Ignoring Zane's questioning look, I stood up and tugged the tree from its wicker container, yanking the moss out with it. I peered into the basket.

At first glance; nothing; but with closer examination I spotted a tarnished coin, five times the size of a quarter. It was covered with exotic symbols.

Gleeful, I shouted: "Ah ha!" *Why not use a microphone?* My wolfy husband shook his massive head.

Sorry. I didn't expect to find anything.

I see; you doubted my tracking abilities?

Debating his tracking abilities, where a man had been shredded to pieces, wasn't practical. *Can we clean up and get out of here?*

Zane turned and trotted toward the door leaving me to clean up the mess.

What a dog.

Thirteen

Driving Zane's Corvette gave me a feeling of power. It roared down 101 like a beast on wheels, devouring the road. I could tame this beast without getting my heart broken or my body parts munched on for dinner.

Back in human form, Zane examined the coin on the way to our next stop — Miles McCray's trailer park — Plum Beach murder victim number two's less than pristine property.

Miles, a high school dropout, had been working at the local ARCO station for the past ten years, content to stay close to his parents. One news clip stated his mother still referred to him as her "little champ." Family members observed that Miles was what you might call simple or slow; a man still dependent on his mom. Friends called him an all-around nice guy.

After pouring over a blurry satellite photo, I'd dug up on the Internet, it was clear just how overcrowded the trailer park was. Zane determined with so many trailers jammed into such a crowded space we'd be safer waiting for nightfall before entering Miles' singlewide. He'd also enlisted help from Alcuin, whose vampire talents would provide the edge we needed.

The vampire would manipulate the thoughts of nearby

neighbors, while shielding us from any observant onlookers. Well known for its all-night parties and drug deals, it was doubtful neighbors went to bed before dawn.

Zane thought it was wise for us to drive through and examine the layout prior to our evening excursion.

"Slow down. There! The gravel road." He motioned me right, clenching the coin.

"Thanks," I grumped, still annoyed by his behavior at the Smart's place. He'd somewhat redeemed himself using his little handless trick to clean up the potted tree, but I hadn't completely forgiven his attitude.

"Can we call a truce? It's hard enough visiting murder scenes without us fighting," he suggested, sounding remorseful.

He was right, now wasn't the time to nurse any left over grudges. I nodded and forced a smile. "You're forgiven, for the moment." I realized I didn't so much doubt his skills as I hated not knowing what *extra* talents remained hidden. My tolerance for surprises, and secrets, had reached an all-time low." Spotting the turnoff, I flipped the blinker.

"Pull over!" His eyes narrowed. "There are mutants here. I feel them."

Obeying without question, I parked as close as I could to the entrance without drawing attention.

I sent out my own mental feelers and validated Zane's suspicions. The mutants hadn't bothered shielding their thoughts. They weren't expecting company. Good news for us. Wanting to take advantage of our momentary luck, I probed the creature's minds and prepared to transmit my findings into Zane's. I was stunned to realize my special abilities had expanded again.

This time, I was able to hitch a ride in one of the mutant's minds, similar to what I'd done with Zane during the Detective Davis Fiasco at his place. I could actually feel what the creature felt, see everything he saw, *and* hear what he heard. Talk about a triple threat.

It took me a minute to digest the multitude of unfamiliar sensations bombarding my senses and filter the information in a logical way that Zane could grasp.

I was viewing my surroundings from inside one of three mutants who crouched in the cramped trailer digging through drawers and a large box. I assumed the confined space belonged to murder victim number two: Miles McCray.

The terrible trio's elongated snouts lifted in unison, twitching as they sought any foreign scents. I feared they'd pinpointed us.

Relieved to be wrong, I sighed when they resumed searching.

My newfound ability to listen from inside a mutant wasn't the same as *being* the mutant. I had the capacity to view the entire scene and remain in total control of myself. Influencing the monster's thoughts or actions wasn't possible either. For that I was grateful. Managing that kind of power wasn't something I wanted. Especially since I couldn't begin to grasp what I was doing anymore.

Leaving my analysis for later, I honed in on my environment as experienced through my mutant host.

The largest of the three beasts stood with a guttural grunt. He towered in the cluttered trailer; his pointy ears brushing the ceiling. This massive and cruelly malformed man-wolf filled the limited space.

What should have been hands were a grotesque permutation of paws and claws; just a hint of humanness remained.

The five twisted appendages, featuring an oversized thumb, scarcely mirrored a human hand riddled with arthritis. Filthy, spike-like-nails protruded from the furry tips — nails that would slit a throat like a hot knife slicing butter.

Had we been friends, I would have recommended, without delay, a manicure for all three.

"Stryder, are you certain this is the place?" the creature standing faced the mutant called Stryder, the one whose eyes I was hiding behind.

"That's what she said," Stryder snarled.

I could sense his frustration with the situation and the larger beast. I didn't blame him. The biggest mutant was a menace; more so than his companions. I could feel the difference.

The third added, "We've looked everywhere. Maybe someone got to it first." *You stupid mongrel,* he added telepathically. Like Stryder, his irritation was directed at the mutant looming over them.

It was evident that mutant number two and three did not like number one in charge. Making matters worse for us all, number one stank like rotting fish. Had I been able to manipulate Stryder, he would have recoiled at the stench. It seemed he was immune to the odor.

"Who could have gotten here first? And what about the protective wards?" Stinky Mutant asked.

Wards and spells, there's always a loophole, Stryder thought. *No ward is impenetrable. Someone with stronger magic can break through. As if you'd think of that!* His eyes flashed red, leaving no doubt where his piercing stare and degrading thought was focused — on the revolting swine in charge of their failed search.

I Kissed a Dog

Are you getting all this? I mind-messaged Zane, ensuring he could see the mutants as well as hear them. *There's some serious trouble in paradise.*

It makes no sense. Unless the coin we found is what they're referring to. But what does it have to do with the murders?

"The Mistress will be furious by our lack of success," Stryder growled. *I can't wait till that bitch gets bitten. She's the one who deserves to die.*

With Stryder's last thought, the red-headed woman's picture scrolled through his mind; proving that everything was in some way connected to her.

Maybe she was a real witch not just a bitch. I'd seen stranger this week. Why not add a witch into the mix? If I could find a *Witches and Wards Book for Dummies* I'd be set. In truth, I was lacking, in a major way, the knowledge to fight effectively against my supernatural opponents.

"Do you two have a problem with me?" the massive mutant challenged his subordinates, making me forget my concerns about witches. He glared down at Stryder who glowered back, undaunted.

Faster than I imagined in such a small space, Stryder was up snout to snout with his comrade. "I have a problem with the entire situation. The Mistress is making too many mistakes, and I don't want to suffer the consequences for her inability to clean up *her* messes."

"Questioning our Mistress is not in your best interest," Stinky Mutant (that was my new name for him) cautioned. "I realize this is frustrating, but we must follow orders. We're done here."

"Go!" Zane shouted, dragging my mind back to the car. "We don't want to be sitting here when they come out."

Slamming the car in reverse, I spun around and headed back the way we'd come. I didn't want them to see us drive past the entrance. Zane's Corvette was more than memorable, and Jazmine was well aware of what vehicle he drove, making it all the more probable the mutants knew too.

Taking any unnecessary risks seemed reckless. I'd already resolved Jazmine was in cahoots with the evil redhead, making our situation all the more precarious. We had more enemies than we could handle, and likely others we hadn't met.

Zane grinned, an unexpected gesture under the circumstances. "Good driving, Princess. Ever consider racing?"

"You're kidding, right?" It was just like him to be yelling one second and praising me the next. Besides, escaping mutinous monsters was good motivation for becoming a driving daredevil.

"Seriously, you can drive. I'm impressed." His grin widened. "Maybe you should consider a future with NASCAR."

Ignoring the little twinge of pride his praise ignited was pretty much impossible. Zane didn't make a habit of handing out compliments. I knew if he said my driving was impressive, he meant it.

At last I could thank good old Bob for something — teaching me to drive like a dangerous felon was hot on my tail. His lessons had paid off today.

Today?

Uh oh … Something was very wrong.

Mutants were captive to the full moon. They couldn't shift at will like purebreds — unless something had changed — radically. Without the daylight advantage the playing field would be leveled.

"Did you notice anything different about our mutant friends?" I asked. Afraid to blurt out what I suspected.

I stayed quiet while he mulled over today's events. It didn't take him long.

"This is bad." A scowl replaced his smile. "I have a feeling these coins might shed some light on what's going on. I'm also inclined to believe there's a coin hidden at every murder scene. We just have to locate them before the bad guys, which won't be easy since we can no longer count daylight to our advantage."

"Why the coins, or whatever they are?" I was baffled. The inscriptions on the coin had given me a prickly all-over feeling. And I could tell by the way Zane continued to examine it, he was equally mystified.

Storing my questions, I maneuvered around a deep pothole and continued toward our next stop … murder victim number-three's townhouse.

We'd have to handle this visit delicately. Seth Johnson's parents were apt to be home, and they wouldn't be too keen on letting virtual strangers into their home, especially under the circumstances. I didn't blame them.

Glancing at the dashboard's digital clock, I realized the answer would reveal itself in about fifteen minutes.

Fifteen minutes too soon as far as I was concerned.

"Get the hell off my property!" Mr. Johnson yelled from the front porch. He gripped a hunting rifle in both hands. The muzzle was lowered — for now anyway. His wife huddled behind him. She appeared more worried than hostile.

"We're sick of reporters. Don't you have someone else to harass?" he raged. The rifle vibrated in time to his trembling hands. His frustration laced with anxiety could easily escalate a tense situation into a tragic one if we weren't careful.

I prayed they would hear me out. "Please, I'm so sorry for your loss. Seth was a great guy. He helped my dad pick out some gear last year. We're not reporters," I hurried to get the words out, "but I think we might be able to help. Zane," I nodded his direction, "is a part time private investigator. He believes the police have missed vital information that could help lead to your son's killer."

They spoke in hushed tones. Mr. Johnson gestured and paced, his position not influenced by my plea.

Occupied with their debate, they didn't notice when a golden retriever trotted out of the garage, his tail wagging. He sidled right up to Zane and gazed up at him with a puppy-in-love expression.

I'll pet; you have a little chat with him. Zane sent the mind message and kneeled to face his canine admirer. I was again grateful for our private communication option, something I'd resented a few days ago.

I targeted my energy on Seth's former companion. Making eye contact or maintaining touch was no longer necessary. The range had been expanding all week, right along with the other advances.

Can you show me what happened to your master?

The retriever's markings were exquisite and he appeared to be well cared for. Only one thing detracted from his perfection, a shaved area above his right leg. I could see evidence of fresh stitches. The wound seemed to be healing well.

I Kissed a Dog

I took a breath, preparing myself for the bloody vision he'd undoubtedly reveal. Instead, the dog whimpered, hesitant. Zane whispered something I couldn't understand and rumpled his fur, calming him for me.

Please, we want to catch the people who did this to Seth. You can help us. I made myself pause, careful to remain calm.

The dog's sad eyes found mine, and his mind opened like a book. The visions came on with a vengeance. What I observed sent my stomach reeling.

As with Will, a gorgeous redhead was the gruesome show's star. She approached Seth leisurely licking her pouty lips. He lurched sideways and braced himself against a pool table. They were in an average-sized bedroom turned entertainment room. *A Werewolf in London* played across the big screen, sound blaring.

Where Will had been enthralled by the wicked woman, Seth looked appalled by her overt sexuality. Back pressed against the pool table, he jerked his head sideways and raised both hands to push her way. Ignoring his rejection, she shimmied closer. Before he could protest further, the vibrating thing happened, and she shifted into the frightening werewolf I'd come to abhor.

It was then I noticed the retriever. He sprang from a nearby chair, sinking his fangs into the creature's arm. He stayed latched to the beast for a few short seconds before she disengaged him with a vicious swipe.

He hit the floor with a yelp, but maintained consciousness. His eyes remained half open as the horror escalated. Helpless, he whimpered while his master was brutalized beyond recognition.

I had to give Seth credit. He didn't go down easily. It helped that he hadn't been engaged in the same pre-murder activities that had distracted and debilitated Will.

Grabbing a pool stick, Seth jabbed at her chest. She ripped it from his hands and snapped it in half. The same stick-snapping-routine had been repeated hundreds of times by every big-screen karate-hero to date, reminding me of an action movie rerun.

What followed in the next two minutes wouldn't survive any movie rating system. It would sicken even the most avid blood and gore connoisseur.

Looking for another opening, Seth spun to the side and launched a swift kick at his attacker's midsection. This time he connected before she retaliated.

Bored with the foreplay, she lunged for the jugular.

When Seth's head toppled from his shoulders, landing with an ominous thud, I gagged, but managed to stay attached to the vision.

Mercifully, other, less horrific scenes now played through the dog's mind — police swarming through the house; people crying and consoling one another; a cleanup team scrubbing blood splatters off the big screen; more police searching for clues; Agent Green and Detective Davis walking through the home; reporters crowding the street; a hideous cloaked man …?

Talk about a coincidence. The same wrinkled creature we'd seen back at the Smart's place was creeping unnoticed through Seth Johnson's house. Could things get any stranger?

Good dog. Slow down. Show me this man, I instructed, eager to get a clearer look at the final intruder.

I Kissed a Dog

The rate slowed and I watched in disbelief as the mysterious supe roamed from room to room. He stopped in the master bedroom — a room untouched by the crime. There he entered the attached bathroom and knelt by a wicker laundry basket. Rotating it sideways, he slipped what I guessed was another coin, in between the weaved-slats. It fit snuggly inside its new hiding spot.

Thank you! I patted the dog.

"Kelsey, come here!" Seth's father hollered.

I wondered how long we'd been standing there. When I was listening telepathically, I lost track of time. In most cases, it lasted just a few minutes, but it always seemed longer.

Ignoring the senior Johnson's request, the dog flopped on Zane's shoes, his tail wagging faster than a windshield wiper on high-speed.

"I'll be. If the dog likes them that much, shouldn't we at least see what they want?" Mrs. Johnson chimed in not a moment too soon. "The police haven't helped, and that high and mighty FBI agent is just plain creepy."

Smart lady. She'd used the same word to describe him as I had. I now determined that Agent Green was cruel and calculating. I suspected he'd prove me right.

Zane tapped my arm, his scowl evidence of his annoyance. *Chloe, help me out here. Say something, please.*

"Uh, really Mr. Johnson, Mrs. Johnson, all we want to do is help," I said, hoping I sounded sincere. What I wanted was to get my hands on that blasted coin.

"Edward, what do you think? They seem nice enough."

"Ah, come on in. *Anyone* willing to help us find some damn justice around here is welcome. My son deserved better than what he got," Edward said, lowering the gun.

Relieved, I followed Zane and Kelsey through the door. We sat a respectful distant from each other on the couch, and listened to the Johnsons tell stories about their son. They pointed out memories captured in a jumbo-sized photo album. Kelsey lounged across Zane's lap. I was reluctant to interrupt their story telling, but could barely contain my anxious energy.

Noticing my apprehension, he nudged Kelsey off his lap and stood, feigning a stretch. "I'm sorry to interrupt, but we're on a tight schedule and I'd like to look around. I know it's hard to believe, but sometimes the cops miss things. Plum Beach has never had a major murder investigation, let alone a serial case. Even with a few outside agents, there's a chance we might find something new."

"Now I remember!" Mrs. Johnson replied, her attention fixed on my face. "You're the animal whisperer. I overheard Officer Tate talking about you to that FBI agent. He suggested they contact you to listen to Kelsey, but the agent declined. He wasn't real impressed by the suggestion."

Not sure how to respond, I glanced at Zane.

"I don't think you'd call her an animal whisperer, but Chloe can catch mental impressions or pictures from animals. She's already provided valuable information on this case. Officer Tate is very open to her talent"

Eager to counter their skepticism, I offered, "Your dog tried to save Seth and was hurt, wasn't he?" I reached down to pet the retriever, who'd decided to snuggle up to me. "He showed me what happened."

Mrs. Johnson pressed her hand to her chest. "The news didn't report that! No one but the police knew about Kelsey's injuries." She shot an anxious glance at Kelsey.

I'll stay and entertain them with my animal stories. I messaged Zane the coin's location. *Whatever this creature is, he prefers wicker containers,* I added. Maybe it was a fluke; maybe not.

After Zane's phony search was completed, close to an hour later, we excused ourselves with the promise of keeping them apprised of anything new, if they in turn agreed to keep our impromptu visit to themselves. I made a point to play on our mutual dislike of Agent Green.

It worked.

They shared a laundry list of reasons why the out-of-town agent was incompetent and uncaring. I listened, careful to affirm their observations. Knowing the agent was spreading his suspicions about me to anyone who'd listen; it seemed fair I return the favor.

Another twenty minutes later, and we were back in the car, with Zane behind the wheel, brooding. I had my first opportunity to examine the coins. They hummed in my hands, and were warm, hot even. Adding to the mystery, the engraved symbols didn't make any sense. Hopefully, someone sympathetic to our cause could.

We still had to meet with Alcuin and the M's back at Zane's before returning to the trailer park and checking out Will's place. If the pattern persisted, we'd have two more coins to add to our collection.

Zane broke the silence. "I need to talk with Logan. He needs to know about the mutants. Their ability to shift without a full moon changes everything. Our pack's protection policy is built around a now faulty belief system. Where there's a fault line, you can expect an earthquake. The earthquake is already shaking our foundation."

His words sent a spike of fear through my chest. It was hard for me to remain confident when Zane, a werewolf enforcer, was troubled.

"What about the coins? They represent something important. They have to. Why else would everyone want them? I think someone is trying to tell us something."

"Maybe they're for the police? Serial killers often have their own signatures."

I wasn't sure how to respond. What he said made sense. Why us and not the police or the mutants?

"Promise you won't laugh," I paused.

"Chloe, you're a trooper and you're damn smart. Laughing at you isn't in my best interest. I'm still trying to get on your good side, remember?" He patted my thigh.

Just the casual touch sent a familiar wave of longing crashing over me, while in the same moment providing enough assurance to finish explaining my theory.

"Keep in mind, I'm speculating, but I keep thinking that the coins, if we could figure out what's engraved on them, will provide a road map of some sort. Directions. Clues. I don't know. Maybe I'm just desperate for answers and have seen too many mystery movies."

"You're not the only one feeling desperate. I've got a bad feeling about all this. It's going to get worse …"

"Before it gets better," I finished.

Fourteen

Back at Zane's, we explained our discoveries to Alcuin, Mack, and Michael. The three sat in rapt attention, all uncharacteristically quiet. Alcuin was taking what appeared to be detailed notes.

Seeing a vampire with such a studious demeanor almost undid the tight knots in my stomach. Zane's intense expression kept me from laughing. His brows were so furrowed I could picture them meeting in the middle. An awful thought, because in my book, men with uni-brows were major turnoffs.

In Zane's case, turning off my intense feelings was the most difficult task I faced. Well, maybe not the *most* difficult. I still needed a full-proof plan, if I was going to get my personal meeting with Joshua Smart, in Portland.

For some inexplicable reason, my thoughts were plagued by visions of the Smart boy locked away in a dreary psychiatric facility, far from his home and family. Did his mother even bother to visit? Was his condition improving?

Joshua Smart was a young boy who might very well have

vital information locked away in his troubled mind. Information we desperately needed.

Getting to The City of Roses for a brief visit on my own would be nearly impossible with my protective alpha male watching my every move. Zane would accompany me if I asked. But what I wanted, and probably needed for my own sanity, was twenty-four hours to myself — a full day to process all the craziness that had invaded my life.

I'd plan my clandestine escape for Monday night, after the big meeting with Logan and the legendary Board of Directors. I prayed that I still had enough pull with Luke to enlist him in my plan.

"I believe you're missing an important detail," Alcuin's assertion sliced through my scheming session.

"Go on," Zane grumbled.

Mack and Michael nodded their agreement.

"You are all forgetting something crucial. From what I've gathered after hearing Chloe's description, this woman, the redhead isn't a mutant. She's a purebred.

The normal separation between mutants and werewolves is changing. These killings are evidence of a much wider arrangement that involves not only a group of rebellious werewolves and mutants, but also your Native American brothers, all working together. This female werewolf is a primary player in their game. I also agree that Jazmine is involved." Alcuin glanced at his notes again.

"Who is this redhead?" Mack asked. "I can't think of any female in our pack that fits her description."

I listened as the men went over the details again and again, reexamining all the key players and points, and always ending up with the same conclusion — they were baffled.

The only good news we'd received all day was a phone message from Luke instructing me and Zane to take the next week off from work — his wedding gift to us.

There was one condition: we remain on call in case of an animal emergency that one of the two M's couldn't resolve. I had enough confidence in the father and son duo to trust that my week off wouldn't be interrupted.

I glanced at my husband. His hair was tied back showing off his rugged features.

Sensing my gaze, he lifted his head, giving me an easy smile. My heart did that crazy fluttering thing and I looked away. At least I hadn't blasted my erotic images into his mind. Though his eyes gave away his intentions; they were as heated as my own private thoughts.

Somehow, even in the midst of our developing crisis, he, too, was distracted by my presence. Just the awareness of his heated feelings sent a rush of power through my veins, like a potent narcotic to a diehard junkie, but better, and without all the deplorable side effects, yet no less addictive.

I wasn't sure if it was the situation bringing us closer, but I knew one thing for certain, I wanted a repeat of my wedding night. The night I couldn't remember. I wanted to trade any remaining regrets for romantic bliss. I wanted to experience whatever pleasures he'd given me all over again with my eyes wide open. But with our world raging out of control, finding the right time would prove difficult.

Alcuin rose to his feet. "Since we're all speechless, I suggest we get busy. I'll teleport over to the late Mr. McCray's trailer and search for another antique coin hiding in some wicker contraption. You two," he nodded at Zane before turning his piercing eyes my direction, "will take a look around Will Mills' household. As for the M-mutts …"

"I resent that," Michael snorted. "I'm not a mutt you frozen freak. You're just jealous of my body temperature. And by the way, I have a security shift to pull at the park. Pops can handle anything."

Mack responded to his son's compliment by inflating his already huge chest.

"If I get too cold, I know where to find a warm wolf coat." Alcuin flashed fang and chuckled.

Mack high-fived the vampire, leading Michael to swipe at his dad.

Tired of their banter, I stood and stretched. "How about we finish with our itinerary? I'm exhausted. Stressed. And a whole lot of other things that don't need mentioning in front of you two." I directed my complaints at the youngest werewolf and Alcuin, who raised an eyebrow.

The vampire's ability to distinguish human emotions was disconcerting in view of my never-ceasing hunger for Zane.

To my relief, Alcuin kept his observations to himself and picked up the map. I'd circled the murder sites with my orange highlighter. I kept forgetting to ask the one thing the circles reminded me of. "Someone please explain this whole warding thing to me."

Alcuin raised his head. "Why wards?"

I hated how he answered my question with another one. "The mutants in the trailer mentioned wards and magic."

Zane answered this time. "Some witches, sorcerers, and all

high court fae are able to create wards. The types of wards you're referring to are ones that protect a specific area or person, keeping any unwelcome visitors away. Most wards are breakable, if a more powerful being wants through."

Michael jumped in. "We haven't seen a powerful fae in years. They're watching though. You can count on it."

"Thanks, that helps," I said not satisfied and still wishing I could ask more pointed questions about the wards that had kept Valamir from entering The Crab Cove.

I'd keep those questions to myself for the time being. Mentioning the master vampire would add more chaos to our crisis. I wondered who had set up the wards for our reception. Just the idea that we had a witch — or worse — in our midst was unsettling.

"Where do you want me?" Mack asked. I could tell he was eager to play a more active role in our search.

Reluctant, Zane handed him the coins. "I need you to take these to Rita. Alcuin can teleport you there before he visits Miles' place."

Alcuin just smirked.

"What?" Zane demanded.

"You assume I'm at your beck and call. I'm quite hungry, and I don't play well when I'm hungry." His icy eyes landed on a spot just below my jaw line.

"Oh no, you don't," I snapped, reaching for my neck.

"Don't flatter yourself. I have plenty of willing donors."

Alcuin almost seemed offended, in an "I've been rejected" kind of way. Mr. Calm, Cool, and Collected had displayed emotions. He was upset because I didn't want him to bite me.

"Can't you wait twenty more minutes?" asked Michael.

"I can wait days if it's required, but I don't want to. You hungry hounds should understand. You all eat like …"

"Enough! Please!" I'd reached my boiling over point. "Let the blood-starved vamp go feed, just don't give me any details. Then we can get to work."

Michael clapped, inspired by my retort. "One for the lady." He stopped clapping to make an imaginary check mark in the air.

Alcuin missed out on the younger wolf's theatrics. He'd already disappeared.

I felt relieved when thirty minutes following his vanishing act, Alcuin reappeared with a smug grin. His eyes were brighter and his presence more imposing. I had to admit, for him, blood did the trick.

Zane nodded toward the door and jingled my car keys. I followed, thrilled to leave the once again bickering boys behind.

While Alcuin had been hunting, Zane had explained how civilized vampires like Alcuin could feed from any human, willing or not, without causing permanent damage. Rogue vampires, on the other hand, were far more likely to drain their food sources, causing problems for vampires trying to maintain a semi-normal existence away from the supernatural community's scrutiny, and from humans' superstitious natures.

I wondered if Valamir bled his victims dry.

"You're in deep thought." Zane's voice alerted me to just how far I'd allowed my mind to drift. With so much new information to absorb it was a wonder I could form complete sentences let alone come up with valuable theories and questions.

"There's so much to think about," I said.

I Kissed a Dog

"We're almost there." Zane tensed, preparing once again to face the unknown.

From what I'd gathered, none of my supernatural cohorts were very comfortable with so many unknown players on the game board. Not knowing who or what they were up against had diminished their overconfidence.

Wanting to get this latest search behind us, I was ready to move forward with our investigation of Will's property.

"You haven't asked me the one question I've been expecting," he said. "Aren't you curious about Rita?"

Without his prompting, I might have forgotten about the woman. "I wouldn't mind knowing," I confirmed, refusing to act all excited by this latest tidbit tossed my way like a bone to a hungry dog.

My dog-induced thoughts weren't stopping anytime soon, regardless of my fearful feelings about the four-legged fiends. I hated to admit, I'd taken a real liking to Kelsey — Seth's retriever — the first ever dog that had caught my fancy, except, of course, the werewolf sitting next to me.

I stifled an unexpected giggle.

Zane gave me his lopsided grin. "I'm glad you find this all so amusing."

"I'm sorry," I fibbed. In truth, I was thankful for my imagination. Having an offbeat sense of humor and always creative mind had proven very helpful over the torture-filled years at school, when snooty girls like Darlene Davenport made it their top priority to shred my self-esteem. Right now, my inner-comedian kept me from drowning in despair.

"No reason to apologize. There's more than enough for us to worry about. As for Rita, she's a retired college professor.

Her area of expertise is the study of ancient and lost languages. She's worked with some of the greats in her field. She's also what you might call a packette."

I pulled over and parked across the road from Will's. "*Now* I'm curious. What's a 'packette'?"

"Werewolf supporter, groupie, fan … someone who has discovered our existence and has committed to maintaining complete confidentiality. In turn we provide protection from those unhappy with her knowledge."

"I guess at this point that title would apply to me?" This was good news; the added protection policy.

"You're *my* mate. You are under *my* protection, making *you* far more valuable than any packette."

"Oh," I squeaked.

Afraid to look at him, I did it anyway. His eyes shimmered golden and his mouth formed a firm line. The myriad of emotions churning under his tight expression said more than any words.

As difficult as it was, he remained bound to his self-imposed, no touching without permission rule. The strain this boundary was causing him had become unbearable, evidenced by the twitch in his jaw, his ragged breathing, and the way his body instinctively leaned toward me.

A little moan sounded deep in my throat as I stretched to reach him. His eyes widened for a split second before his hands cupped my face. "You are everything," he whispered. His mouth descended, pressing, at first tentative, than devouring mine.

This kiss was unlike any prior. It was full of promise, protection, and a hint of pain. The pain he'd felt staying away

I Kissed a Dog

from me melted away as I gave myself over to the exquisite things his mouth was doing to mine. Our tongues danced in perfect rhythm, our mouths expressing the feelings I had been fighting. My, oh my — my wolf could kiss.

He stopped mid-kiss and tensed.

I gripped his shoulders. His stillness told me that we weren't alone.

Fifteen

An instant later, I spotted the cloaked man. He hovered near Will's garage.

Keeping my gaze locked on the hunched intruder, I nudged Zane. He shot me a quick glance, confirming he'd already honed in on our target.

"What now?" I whispered. It appeared we were in an old-fashioned stand-off.

Zane answered. "We wait. Let him make the first move."

I sent my telepathy out and captured the creature's thoughts. He, too, was terrified, and not just by our presence.

His mind was filled with splattered images. Mutants, blood, decaying corpses — the same pictures I'd gleaned during our first encounter. This time I saw a vision with no obvious connection to his other thoughts — a sterile medical facility lined with hospital beds. They were occupied. Young men lay in varying positions on the beds that lined both walls in the long, rectangular room. Some patients were asleep; others stared expectantly at a double door.

I know you're in my thoughts. What do you want?

I gasped, stunned. Zane shot me a worried look.

"He's speaking to me telepathically." I raised my finger to my lips. Zane fixed his eyes on the intruder.

I'm trying to find out who you are and why you're here, I offered.

You don't have much time. Check the chimney, he instructed.

What about the wicker? In light of the situation, I realized how silly my question must sound and felt him laugh in my head. A nice laugh … not evil. Not condescending either. He thought my question was funny.

Not everyone has wicker items in their homes. I must go. They're looking for me. Hurry! You are on the right path. I will find you again. Remember, the chimney.

Wait …!

"He's gone."

"And?" Zane pressed.

"We need to hurry. The coin is hidden in the chimney …"

Zane was out the door before I'd finished explaining. Not sure if I should follow, I waited. Someone needed to keep a watch out for the bad guys. I strained to press my powers outward, seeking anything supernatural.

Got it! He cut into my thoughts. *Start the car.*

A few minutes later, we were speeding back home to wait for Alcuin and Mack. I hoped they'd experienced the same success. Having help from our hairless, hunched, but humorous friend, had made our expedition a whole lot easier. I told Zane about the thing's laughter and his desire to help us.

"I don't know what he is, who he works for, and why he's helping us. Not knowing bothers me. But I trust your judgment. You were the one bouncing around in his head." Zane paced to the kitchen and refilled our coffee cups.

We were both growing uneasy. Alcuin should have returned. It was almost eleven. I wasn't too worried about Mack. His assignment had been pretty straightforward. Michael was at work watching over our animal friends.

When my cell rang, I bumped my mug, spilling hot coffee on my leg. "Ouch! Damn that hurts." It appeared my clumsiness had returned with a scorching vengeance.

Zane retrieved a damp dishtowel and was cleaning me up before I could locate the phone hiding in the cluttered bowels of my purse. No longer ringing, the glowing screen displayed a number I knew all too well but hadn't expected to see this late on a Saturday night — Luke's.

Leaning over me, Zane was quick to identify the glowing digits. "This can't be good."

"Should I?" Calling him back was bound to bring bad news.

"I'm not sure you have a choice, if you want the week off. Remember his conditions?" Zane collapsed on the couch next to me. "How's the leg?" He'd removed the towel and was caressing the damp splotch on my jeans.

"Better, thanks to your quick thinking." Times like this made Zane's werewolf super-speed all the more appealing. "I'm going to change first."

I returned to his side feeling fresh and cozy in one of my old jogging suits, I dialed our boss's familiar number and made sure to press the speaker button.

"Hey, what's …?"

Luke didn't wait for me to finish. "I need you guys here right away. Michael spotted someone lurking around the zebras. He took off faster than an Olympic sprinter and hasn't come back. I tried to reach his dad before calling you. No luck."

I Kissed a Dog

Zane was up and had the keys to the Corvette in his hand. "We're on our way."

Back in the car I tried repeatedly to reach Mack. It seemed he and Rita were too involved in their research to respond. Or worse, maybe he was in trouble too. It wouldn't surprise me. No Alcuin and both M's missing, not a good way to end the evening.

"He'll be okay. I'm sure of it. Michael knows when to back off," Zane said as he touched my thigh.

I hoped he was right. From what I'd seen of Michael led me to believe otherwise. He was an energetic and confident young man who could become a wolf at will — a lethal combination.

Even more lethal was the Corvette's increasing speed.

Zane had a serious heavy foot. We were pushing ninety on a treacherous mile of curving freeway. "Honey, please, we can't help anyone if we're trapped under the car. Dead." I braced, prepared for the inevitable accident.

"I can see these roads well, even at night. Remember, I'm not human." He flashed his teeth, but, to my relief, kept his eyes on the dark road. Traffic was pretty much nonexistent, to our benefit.

I forced myself to relax, heeding Zane's "I'm not human" reminder.

The wailing didn't register at first. Then I realized that the shrilling sound was a police siren. Talk about déjà vu. Pulled over twice in one week, both times for speeding — at least I wouldn't be the one worrying about a ticket this time.

Zane pounded his hands against the steering wheel and pulled onto the shoulder. "I should have listened to my wife," he groaned.

I liked the way he said wife, and was tempted to agree, but decided to keep my mouth shut when I saw the approaching officer in my side mirror. Mr. Creepy FBI agent, from Portland, was walking next to a highway patrolman I didn't recognize.

My body recognized the threat Agent Green presented, and responded by sending a rush of adrenaline and giving me a jolt of energy that coffee shops only wished they could sell in a paper cup.

I inhaled and started my reverse counting routine. I hoped to appear unruffled by their presence.

The unfamiliar officer tapped at the driver's side window. Watching it slide down reminded me of a stage curtain parting to reveal something sinister. A sudden shiver sent goose bumps racing down my arms. These two men gave me the willies.

"Can I help you, officers?" Zane smirked.

I wanted to smack him and tell him to put the testosterone on hold.

"I don't know, Dr. Marshall. *Can you?*" Agent Green sneered, his own testosterone making an ill-timed appearance.

Now there were two manly-men ready to defend their masculinity. I'd watch for an opening to diffuse the situation. I hoped it would come sooner rather than too late.

"I don't mean to be rude, but we had an emergency call from the wildlife park. One of our animals is in danger," Zane explained, sounding more official and less smug.

Agent Green leaned down and peered into the car. He noticed me and smiled. "Ms. Carpenter, how nice to see you again. Any additional *animal visions* to report?" His mocking tone was far from admiring.

A stab of humiliation sliced through me. This was the same man who'd claimed to believe me following my puppy interrogation at Will's.

I struggled to keep my cool. Forget testosterone, hormones could be blamed for the sour words threatening to spew from my mouth. Sensing my dilemma, Zane dropped a bomb.

"You may want to make a note, Agent Green. This lovely lady is no longer a Carpenter." Zane paused for effect. "She's a Marshall."

Outside the car, both men did a double take. I couldn't help myself. I had to smile.

"That's interesting." The agent took Zane's advice and jotted something in his little black flipbook. "I need to ask both of you to keep us informed of your whereabouts.

"With your animal-inspired story being so farfetched, *Mrs. Marshall*, we may need to ask you some additional questions. I'm sure you understand that with an ongoing murder investigation we need everyone to remain available."

I felt Zane tense beside me. He was starting to vibrate. Not a good sign. Fur, claws, and fangs would put an additional damper on our already deteriorating conversation. It was time for my diffusing thing.

"No problem officers. I'd be happy to talk with you again. We need to help Luke down at the park. Are you going to give us a ticket?" I tried to sound sweet and unconcerned about his veiled threat.

Agent Green spoke again. I wondered if the other guy could talk. "You know something … I'm feeling generous tonight. I do like animals, especially the zebras and the wolves. You two go ahead and take care of your business. But, slow down."

"Yeah, slow down," the patrolman added for emphasis, shattering my mute-officer theory.

I nodded vigorously and smiled so big my cheeks hurt. I was mystified by the whole incident, especially the agent's reference to zebras and wolves. What did he know about the wildlife park?

As far as I knew, there'd been no public information about the zebra attack, unless something about tonight had found its way onto Agent Green's personal radar.

Concern for our friends replaced my agonizing over what the agent knew or didn't know. I had to believe that Michael was all right, Alcuin too.

Zane gunned the motor and swung back onto the highway, picking up speed right where he'd left off, taunting the agent to stop us again. Mercifully, their vehicle had vanished over the ridge heading the opposite direction.

Luke, his foot tapping, was waiting for us by the front gate. Noticing headlights in the side mirror, I was relieved to see Mack pull in. Luke's persistent calling had paid off.

"Hey!" I called to Mack. "Glad you made it." He looked worried.

"Thank God you're all here!" Luke exclaimed. "Let's get inside the park." He glanced over his shoulder.

In the courtyard, we formed a small circle. Luke had turned on all the outside lights illuminating the shadowy grounds. On an average night, we kept the lighting low for the animals. Tonight Luke had the place lit up like Times Square on New Year's Eve.

I noticed both Zane and Mack trying to remain discreet while sniffing the air.

Unaware of their unusual antics, Luke rattled on about how he'd tried to follow Michael but couldn't keep up.

"Don't you feel bad, boss. My son can run like the wind." Mack gave Luke a quick pat on the back.

"I'll say," Zane agreed, his nose still twitching. "I doubt many men could keep up with that kid."

Luke explained the events leading up to Michael's mad dash into the darkness.

Michael had been making his rounds when he'd heard unfamiliar growling and scratching. Following the sounds, he'd found himself outside the Zebra's enclosure. He'd radioed Luke for assistance.

Grabbing the shotgun he kept hidden in his office, Luke had hurried out to help him investigate. He was too late. Michael was already pursuing something into heavy foliage behind the park.

"You should have seen him!" Luke boasted. "He hurdled over the electric fence without missing a step. I didn't think jumping like that was possible. "

My eyes darted to Zane, who shrugged.

"Adrenaline can do some pretty funny stuff," Mack offered. "You know the story about the five-foot mother hoisting a car off her child. Things like this are documented. I sure hope adrenaline finds me if I ever need it."

"Luke, why don't you take watch up front? Mack and I will see what we can find out here. Chloe, go with Luke." Zane instructed. *Please, for once do this with debating,* he added for my ears only.

"Can I talk to Missy first?" My question was for Luke who raised an eyebrow at Zane.

Oh my goodness! Did everyone automatically bow to my big bad wolf?

Rather than waiting for his approval, I marched around the enclosure to the far corner where Missy and her mate were huddled. I could hear Luke jogging to catch up. It amazed me how loud a human sounded in comparison to one of the supes, and my athletic boss was no wimp. Stealthy — not so much, evidenced by his labored breathing.

"Since when do you take orders from anyone?" I hissed, aware of a unique opportunity to enlist Luke's help. With all the excitement, I'd almost forgotten my escape plan. Traveling to Portland, Monday evening, remained high on my to-do list.

Looking chagrined, he muttered, "Since *he* became your husband."

Luke made a good point. This was a dangerous situation and my man was all about protecting his prize, Princess Chloe. I hated to admit how much I liked my new royal title and Zane's protective nature. I'd never felt safer or more cherished. Luke was just trying to respect our new relationship.

"I know this was all so sudden …"

"I'll say," he agreed, pausing again to scan the grounds.

I'd grown used to macho supernatural men, who tackled adversity with bold authority. Luke's humanness seemed somewhat inadequate.

Mortified by my degrading thoughts about my own species, I flashed him the biggest grin I could muster under the circumstances. For goodness sake, the man was my former almost-flame. He was a great friend who put up with my glaring deficiencies. He deserved an explanation.

"Luke, I'm so sorry. You know the reason we never dated was because of our work relationship. Sometimes a good friend and excellent working relationship are hard things to give up. Still friends …?"

For the first time since my marriage announcement, the open smile that I'd come to love and expect, spread across his tanned face. "You silly girl, we'll always be friends. And the truth is I like Zane. He's a good guy. A little odd, but he seems to care about you. Congratulations, you deserve to be happy."

Without thinking, I flung my arms around his neck.

"Oh! Sorry! I didn't mean to strangle you," I said backing away, uncomfortable with our physical contact.

He pretended to choke and sputter, "Help! I can't breathe."

I opened my mouth, but the words never came.

An eerie chorus of howls erupted around us, sending the zebras and other nearby animals into a state of frenzied panic.

"Run …" I managed to whisper before the haunting yowls increased in volume, sounding much closer.

I spun back toward the courtyard, not bothering to wait for Luke's response.

When the overhead lights dissolved into darkness, I screamed.

Sixteen

Roars, screeches, and other animal noises filled the darkness. I could hear the chimpanzees protesting in the distance. My heart thudded as I dashed through the familiar landscape. There was scarcely enough moonlight to reveal my course.

"Luke?" I called, slowing my pace. I'd reached the courtyard gift shop and Luke was missing. Realizing I wasn't alone, at the glass door, triggered my inner alarm, awakening a new burst of much-needed adrenaline.

A mutant, its fur a tangled mass of filthy mats, blocked the entrance. Its pitiful condition a glaring contradiction to the other creatures I'd seen. I almost felt sorry for it.

"The little girl who talks to animals," the thing said — its voice a gravelly growl.

I'd never attempted to engage any mutant in conversation, but decided if it might stall my bloody demise it was worth trying.

Where was Zane anyway? And what happened to Luke?

I stood taller, making myself face my gruesome foe. "How

is it you know me and I don't know your name?" My voice sounded much stronger than I'd expected, giving me an air of assurance I didn't feel.

Confused by my calm response, the beast rocked from side to side. It even cocked its massive head like a curious dog. I wondered how much humanness remained beneath its pathetic exterior.

"A *name*. What do you call yourself?" I persisted.

"Don't answer!" a booming voice countered.

In what felt like slow motion, I turned to face my newest adversary. Stryder, the mutant from Miles' trailer park, loomed just behind me.

Talk about surrounded.

"Stryder," I said, hoping to surprise him with an air of familiarity.

It worked.

"How do you know my name, human?" he growled, unable to conceal his stunned expression.

I scanned the mammoth beast, noting his fur was luscious and well-groomed, unlike his counterpart. There was something regal about him. He didn't seem as feral, although I had no doubt he'd kill me with one swipe of his massive claw.

"I've seen more of you than you can imagine," I taunted, remembering the ride I'd hitched in his mind. I realized, too late, how presumptuous I probably sounded.

It also occurred to me Alcuin had been on his way to Miles McCray's trailer in search of a coin. I wanted to ask Stryder if he'd seen anything, but held back. Mentioning the vampire would be like showing my hand during a high stakes poker game — *way* too much information.

Leisurely, Stryder circled me, his snout twitching. He

moved to stand by his subordinate who looked more wretched next to the large more refined mutant.

"Forgive me. I didn't mean to be so rude." I faced the deadly duo.

"I will ask again, human, *how* do you know *my* name?"

Not sure how to answer without giving away the extent of my telepathic gift, I kept it simple. "I overheard you talking at Miles' trailer. I also heard you get angry at your annoying superior."

"What else did you hear?"

"I know about your mistress …"

"You will not speak of her!" Stryder bellowed, lurching forward.

I took a swift step back, keeping my eyes trained on him.

"Chloe! Don't move!" Luke shouted, appearing to my right.

Bad timing. A human male was bound to incite the fury of our furry guests.

Glancing at the mutants, I muttered, "Wouldn't think of moving."

"Don't come near her!" Luke commanded over my shoulder. He slid a protective arm around my waist.

Unbelievably, the mutants stepped back, glancing anxiously around the courtyard. I felt Luke stand taller beside me. Styder stepped to the left. The other creature whimpered. Now he sounded as bad as he looked. Again, I felt a twinge of pity for the forlorn man-beast.

"Keep moving. Away from the door." The one person I'd grown to love and count on demanded. "That's right, Stryder. Your flunkies took off. You and Mr. Tangles are it," Zane added. *Princess, sorry I took so long.*

I thought you'd forgotten me, I scolded mentally.

It was then I understood why the mutants were intimidated. So much for Luke's temporary claim to fame; it had been all about Zane. My boss' shoulders slumped as he realized his mistake.

Chloe, you're unforgettable. Zane maneuvered closer and pulled me to him, disengaging Luke's arm.

To my relief, Alcuin, back at last, joined Mack and Michael who'd emerged from the shadows, forming a tight triangle around our enemies.

Stryder, though outnumbered, maintained his composure. There was something about the mutant that intrigued me. Maybe it was because I knew he was disgruntled with his leadership. And perhaps he could be persuaded to change sides. It happened in the movies and politics all the time.

"You two have a choice to make," Zane said to the captives. "We dispose of you right here right now, or, you accompany us blindfolded, back to my residence, where we have a nice secluded spot for you to think about your next step."

"Go on," Stryder said.

"The way I see it, you have two options. Die for your cause or live for ours."

Stryder looked over our little team, allowing his gaze to rest on each member. It took him a few seconds to ask, "Where's the blindfold?"

With Alcuin's assistance, Zane managed to convince Luke they would handle the intruders. The vampire used some of his nifty mind-magic to make Luke more pliable, ensuring he wouldn't decide to call the police the minute we left him alone. As final insurance, he erased Luke's memories of the wolfy creatures, making certain he remembered them as mischievous men only.

Michael was settled back in his security post when we finally drove off. Alciun had teleported Mack and our two semi-willing prisoners back to home base.

I still had no clue who or what Michael had been pursuing. Now I'd have to wait even longer for his update. At least he was safe at work as if nothing happened.

Alcuin had some explaining to do as well. All I'd been able to garner was that he'd failed to find the coin.

This revelation had surprised us all considering his ability to zap himself from one location to another. His lack of success wasn't something I'd expected. Maybe Stryder and his gang had found it first. At least we had three of the coins in our possession. Thanks to the help from the ugly cloaked man.

So many questions remained unanswered.

Lucky for me, one key question had been answered affirmatively, by Luke.

I'd asked him to accompany me to the bathroom while the others had bound and blindfolded the mutant captives. After a ton of pleading and a few forced tears, I'd convinced him to cover for me Monday night, when I made my escape up north. I didn't have a ton of confidence in our plan, but I couldn't think of anything better.

Once back at Zane's, I escaped into the bedroom, away from the men. There I let my tears flow. Sure, I'd acted all brave when necessary, but now, all I wanted was a hot shower, a warm bed, and at least eight hours of uninterrupted sleep.

Tomorrow was Sunday, the one day my parents had allowed me to sleep in growing up. They pointed to the fact that God commanded a day of rest after six days of hard work. This was one of God's commandments I was more than happy to abide by.

I Kissed a Dog

Thirty minutes later, comfy at last in my pajamas, my teeth brushed, and my hair still damp, I crawled into the bed I would share with Zane until we found a new, more permanent home. We hadn't discussed it, but I didn't see any point in moving until the current mess was resolved.

I was painfully aware of the late hour. Almost three in the morning and the men were out in the pole barn. Doing whatever they did to captured enemies. Exhausted, but too jittery to sleep, I let my mind reach out.

I could sense four of them. Alcuin didn't come up on my radar like the others. I could tell he was there, but no matter how hard I knocked, the door to his mind wouldn't crack. I blamed that little problem on his non-animal status. Undead beings didn't register right, unlike humans, who still remained immune to my talents.

Zane and Mack were closed off, but Stryder was wide open, welcome mat out. I slipped right in and took my place in the front row of his mind. He was tense, refusing to answer Zane's questions. Like so many others, he'd been misled to believe Zane was responsible for the murders, with help from me, of course.

"What about Jazmine?" Zane pressed.

"I told you, I don't know any Jazmine. Man, when will you get it?" Stryder was exhausted, near collapsing. I could feel his twitching muscles and racing heart.

"Why were you at Miles McMcray's trailer? What were you looking for?"

"Just kill me. We're all going to die anyway."

No you're not! None of us will die, dammit! I screeched into Stryder's mind.

"Who said that?" Stryder's eyes darted sideways searching for the source.

"Said what?" Mack asked.

It's me, Chloe, the one who knows your name. Stay with us. Work with us. I know you're not happy with your job.

"Chloe?" Stryder said, his confusion evident.

Zane leapt on the mutant, pinning him to the ground. "What about my mate?" He grasped Stryder's shoulders, shaking him violently.

You stop it right now! I mind-shouted at Zane. He stopped and glanced around, self-conscious.

"Accept my apology. I guess my girl was chatting you up." He pulled Stryder to his feet.

"Isn't she the one who talks to ani … oh, I get it."

They all chuckled. The animal part must have hit home — hard.

"I guess I'm the one acting like a damn rabid animal." Zane sounded repentant. "What was her great idea?"

"She wants us to work together." Stryder shrugged.

"Chloe …!" Zane roared my name loud enough to be heard on the moon.

I yanked the covers over my head and waited.

⟲

Teeth nibbling on my right ear pulled me from the thickness of sleep.

I stayed quiet, keeping my breathing slow and steady. I wanted to keep my now-awake status concealed from Zane so I could enjoy the tempting tortures he'd use to rouse, or, more accurately, *arouse* me.

The room was bright. Even with my eyes closed, I could detect a sunny Sunday morning … or afternoon. I had no idea how long we'd slept.

Following last night's argument about whether or not to form a truce with our mutant prisoners, we'd fallen, mid-sentence, into an all-encompassing and much overdue state of deep sleep. Sex had been the furthest thing from both of our minds, but now, with Zane's tongue winding leisurely down my neck, I felt pretty willing to reestablish our wedding night bliss, the bliss that I'd missed out on the first time around.

Zane nuzzled my neck and nipped at my ear. His hand moved in slow, tantalizing circles over my belly, blazing a trail of heat across my skin. Forgetting my reasons for feigning sleep, I turned on my side, pressing myself against the heat of my husband.

"Ah, Chloe," he murmured, wrapping his arms around me. "I'm sorry about last night."

"No. I should have minded my own business. Dropping into conversations and minds uninvited can be pretty unsettling." I kissed his bare chest, sighing with delight as I ran my tongue down his smooth, warm skin.

We were at last going to consummate our marriage with me fully aware and participating at full capacity. An old love song about afternoon delights drifted through my mind. I moved lower, my tongue winding and flicking along the way.

Before I could straddle the prize, a loud banging shook the front door.

"Dear Lord, now what?" Zane groaned like a man in pain.

More pounding rattled the living room window. I grabbed the alarm clock.

"It's 1:30 PM," I announced, as if that would somehow explain the rude visitors still knocking.

I pushed myself up. "Where's Mack? Michael?" Couldn't they answer the damn door?

Zane was on his feet, "Honey, they don't live here. We needed some alone time."

"Well, it doesn't look like that's going to happen now," I pouted.

"I'll deal with this. You wait here." Zane slid his arm into a sleeve and stalked to the door, pulling the shirt all the way on. "Just a minute!" he barked, with no attempt at civility.

The door swung open with a bang. "What … ?" I heard him stutter.

Grabbing my robe, I dashed to the door. What I witnessed terrified me far more than any blood-thirsty vamp, spell-casting sorcerer, or mad-munching mutant.

My mom and stepdad stood staring up at Zane. Bob reached inside his jacket; where I knew his firearm waited. He scowled, clearly looking for any reason to draw his weapon.

My mom was visibly trembling, holding back a sure stream of tears.

"Why didn't you tell us?" my mom cried. "An elopement … how could you do this to me!"

I glanced at Zane, who gave me a very unhelpful you-get-to-handle-this look.

"Mom, Dad, sometimes things happen fast and you just go with the flow." I knew by my mom's narrowing eyes and Bob's reddening face they weren't buying my simple explanation.

Bob stepped forward. "You've never been a 'go with the flow' kind of gal. Are you in some kind of trouble? We've tried to reach you. After stopping by your house, we tracked down your boss, and he told us you'd gotten married."

"Luke ..." I grumbled to myself. How was I supposed to trust him to help me when he'd blabbed my marital status to my parents?

My mom wiped her eyes with a tissue. "Luke is such a nice man. I always thought ..."

"Mother! Please! I love Zane." Feeling awkward, I looked at Zane. "Mom, Dad — sorry. This is my husband, Zane Marshall. He is a veterinarian. We met at work." I reached for Zane's hand.

My mom was deescalating. I could tell she liked the idea that I'd married a man with a college degree. Her approval would come easier than Bob's. No guy — college educated or not — was good enough for his little girl.

"So, Zane." Bob made his move. "My daughter wasn't worthy of a real family wedding? Why all the rush? Involved in any illegal activity we should know about?"

"Honey, please tell me you're not ..."

I groaned feeling like a teenager caught in the act. "Mom, I'm not pregnant. Dad, I didn't want a big fancy wedding. Mom did."

"That's not ..."

"Yes, it is. You've been talking about *my* big wedding since I was in diapers. Just because *you* never had one." I clapped my hand over my mouth, wishing I could erase those last words.

"Why don't we all calm down, go have a nice lunch, and talk about this. We're sorry about the suddenness, but the romance of Vegas accelerated things. We figured we'd have a big wedding later," Zane explained, an assuring smile pasted on his handsome face.

"I'm sorry, mom. I didn't mean that."

"Yes, you did. I just can't accept this. Something is not right." She crossed her arms, refusing to look at me or Zane.

"What about all the murders, Chloe? I'm not sure it's even safe to live down here anymore." My dad changed tactics. He couldn't handle my mom's messy emotions. It was time for him to retreat to his comfort zone — law enforcement and crime.

"Dad, I know you're already well aware the victims were men. That pretty much rules me out, don't you think?" I couldn't even begin to imagine his response to everything supernatural happening in my life. Seeing him now, like this, gave me another reason to be thankful for Zane's wisdom. At one point, I'd been ready to tell Bob about werewolves.

Ignoring my little appraisal, Bob crossed his arms. "We're leaving. You've upset your mother. When you have time to talk, sensibly, we'll be at our usual hotel for a few days before heading home. And you …" Bob glared up a Zane. "Better take care of my daughter or you'll be answering to the entire Troutdale police force."

Zane tensed, but answered calmly, "Yes, sir. She'll be safe with me. You can count on that."

"That remains to be seen," he added before taking my mom's arm. "Believe me, Mr. Marshall. I will be counting on that. And I *will* be using everything at my disposal to find out who you are."

I didn't like the sound of that. My stepdad was no dummy when it came to technology and he had more than a few favors he could call in. Sending Alcuin to change his perception about this unhappy reunion might be necessary. Messing with his memories wasn't what I wanted, but Bob learning more about Zane was unacceptable. Protecting them from each other was yet another task to add to my lengthy to-do-list, especially with Bob lurking around Plum Beach. I'd try to slip by the hotel later and encourage them to go home; the perfect time for them to meet Alcuin and for him to work his mind magic.

It took three very strong cups of coffee, following their departure, before I felt semi-sane. I hadn't expected my parents to find out about my nuptials from a secondary source, and I kept replaying our horrible conversation over and over in my head. Zane, knowing I needed space, had hurried out to "visit" with our guests. I could no longer refer to them as prisoners. Guests seemed more civil.

How could I have hurt my mom like that? What was wrong with me?

So much for a restful day of exquisite love making with my husband. I stood instead washing the few dishes we'd left in the sink, thinking about tomorrow.

Monday was the big day. We'd teleport to Seattle for the board meeting, and later, I'd try my hand at deceiving Zane. I was already feeling guilty about sneaking off. But now, more than ever, I needed some time away from this supernatural soap opera to think. I'd locate the Smart kid and maybe stop by my parents on the way home. They deserved that much.

"Knock, knock! Anyone home?" Michael called, cheerful as always.

Grateful for the distraction, I hurried to unlock the door. Playing the polite hostess came naturally even when I was wallowing in self pity. I could count on the youngest M to lighten things up. "Coffee?" I was already pouring.

"Sure. You okay?" He pulled out a chair and made himself as comfortable as he could at the tiny table.

"My parents stopped by."

He listened while I poured out my sad story, patting my hand several times.

"How are our mutant friends?" he asked when I was done.

"Zane's out with them now. I think Stryder might prove useful. There's something about him. I don't know why, but I like him."

Michael looked suddenly uncomfortable. "Chloe, I wanted to tell Zane at the same time, but you need to know this. When I vanished at the park, I was chasing something or someone that looked like Agent Green, but not like him. I'm not sure how to explain it, but he was transformed, ready to feast on the zebra again.

It must have been him the first time Missy was attacked. It's too coincidental. But I have no idea what he is or how he figures into all this."

A slow chill spread down my spine. "I guess I'm not surprised. When Mr. FBI pulled us over last night, he mentioned something that seemed strange about the zebras and wolves."

"Did Alcuin talk to you yet?" Michael asked, to my surprise, sounding anxious.

I shook my head.

"He ran into his own trouble out at McCray's trailer park."

"What kind of trouble?" Zane pushed through the front door.

I Kissed a Dog

Michael told Zane the same thing he'd told me about Agent Green and then went on to describe Alcuin's failed attempt to claim the coin. According to Michael, Alcuin had never even made it into the trailer. Another unfamiliar vampire was on the premises and Alcuin had chosen not to engage the outsider.

"That doesn't sound like the Alcuin I know," Zane pondered out loud.

"He didn't say so, but I think he was afraid of the new bloodsucker." Michael looked guilty even suggesting such heresy. "He said that the out-of-town vamp was in the *ultra-ancient* vampire category. Alcuin is old, but not ancient according to vampire history."

For several very obvious reasons, the whole conversation bugged me. I felt as guilty as the young werewolf looked over sharing Alcuin's secret fears. I hadn't told anyone about my most recent vampire rendezvous during the reception, nor had I bothered mentioning the possibility of sharing my blood with that same, ultra-ancient vamp in Vegas. Zane wouldn't be happy to hear any of it.

Now wasn't the time to reveal my Valamir encounters, not with another looming secret so near.

"You okay, Princess?" Zane reached across the table and slid his hand over mine.

Just his touch provoked a myriad of emotions: Love, lust, guilt, fear — a not so nice combination. I'd tell him the truth the minute I returned from my little fact-finding mission. I could blame my behavior on my parents and my desire to make things right with them.

"I'm okay." I heard myself lie. "Mind if I take a nap?" If I stayed with him another second, I was going to blurt out all my secrets, damn the consequences.

He squeezed my hand. "Sleep tight, babe."

"Sleep tight." Michael smiled, weary.

Not tired at all, I tried to read. Something I'd loved doing pre-Zane. Now, with my life as exciting and scary as a bestseller, it was difficult to focus on an author's fictional world.

Tossing the paperback onto the dresser, I paced our small bedroom.

The guys had stepped outside to greet Mack. I assumed Alcuin wouldn't be too far behind. If they stuck to their typical pattern, they'd gather around the table and compare their findings, searching for common themes and suspects.

Zane had mentioned that Rita was working to decode the sigils on the coins. We still needed to find the fourth. Four murders, four coins. Where was my cloaked helper when I needed him?

Chloe, are you there? It's me, Stryder.

What now? Other than Zane, no one had ever sought me out telepathically. How was Stryder able to make the connection with such ease?

I'm here. How did you …

I just focused my thoughts on you and kept repeating my question.

Maybe our unexpected link was the result of my hijacking him at the trailer park. I'd pretty much possessed his mind and all his senses. Yet another reminder that my powers were developing in ways I'd never expected. Making me wish, for the trillionth time, that someone who could explain my gift would appear and offer their wise council.

I decided to use this latest mental enhancement to my benefit. Perhaps I could persuade Styder to join our cause. I'd try keeping the conversation casual for starters, build a rapport.

Wow! This is kind of new for me. Are the guys treating you all right? Focus on his well being, a perfect opening.

As good as can be expected. Better than we'd have treated them, or you.

I didn't have time now to contemplate the implications of *that* statement. I wasn't sure I wanted to.

That's good. I want you to be comfortable. What's your friend's name?

I heard him grumble under his breath. *Tom.*

Tom? Geez, how exotic? Tom the matted mutant.

Like you, we don't choose our names.

I laughed. *I think you've got a sense of humor under all that fur and those sharp teeth.*

Come look at me now. I'm all man.

Oh, boy! I wasn't walking down that conversation path. *Speaking of man, is Tom's hair as tangled as his fur?*

It's in dreadlocks.

That makes sense. I guess.

Not my style, but it suits him. You know, you don't need to waste your time on small talk. I know what you want.

You do? I guessed he did. I wasn't the best at casual chit chat, and now I'd proven counseling wasn't my next best career option.

It doesn't take a PHD to figure out what you're up to. You want to be the welcome committee so I'll join your little team of supernatural misfits.

Misfits! That wasn't very nice. What are you? Wait. I know. You're the misfits' prisoner.

I didn't think he was going to answer, but I refused to apologize for my barb.

You win. I'm more of a misfit than most. I don't follow the rules very well, especially when I don't agree with them. You were also right earlier when you mentioned a crazy woman in charge. None of us lower level scouts have met her. But I can tell you she's a hot redhead, with an appetite for destruction.

You're not kidding about that. I'd seen the kind of destruction she hungered for. It involved severed body parts and lots of blood.

What were you doing in the trailer? I decided to be direct. The worst that could happen — he wouldn't answer.

The same thing you were, looking for some antique coins. Don't bother asking what they're for. I don't know. None of us did. There's not a whole lot of trust on our side of the fence.

What about the ugly man wearing a robe. Did you see him? I needed to find out more about the creature.

I've never seen one, but they're out there. We've been warned by our superiors to stay away from them. You should do the same.

Not sure how to respond to his warning, I plopped on the bed. I'd been pacing like a caged panther for the duration of our conversation. His assumption about the cloaked creature, or as he said, creatures, didn't add up. The one I'd met had been helpful, even timid. I decided to keep that information to myself.

Chloe?

I'm here.

Your friends are on their way for another fun round of questioning.

Play nice, I reminded, before falling back on my pile of pillows, arms stretched over my head.

I always do, he said, his voice like silk and honey.

Men! Mutants. Werewolves. They all had one thing in common. They were big flirts.

Goodbye, Stryder. It was almost as if I was ending a casual phone call.

The good news: I'd accomplished some positive team building. Maybe I'd close my eyes for a few minutes. A quick powernap wouldn't hurt.

After all, tomorrow would be a long, long day.

Seventeen

I felt his presence well before I opened my eyes and saw him silhouetted by the window.

Several perplexing thoughts wound through the sleep-clouded maze in my mind. First: I was alone in the bedroom with a mystery intruder. Second and third: Darkness had replaced daylight, *and* there was no evidence indicating Zane was close enough to rescue me. But in spite of such glaring danger, I wasn't afraid, although I should've been trembling in terror.

My visitor stood unmoving like a statue, hinting at his supernatural status. I didn't know any human that could remain so still for what felt like so long.

Before I could ponder further, the shadow moved closer, so fluidly it was difficult to register until he was standing over the bed, gazing down at me with pale blue eyes.

Rather than speak, he dropped into a crouch, his face now level with mine. I found myself drawn into the pools of blue, lost in their depths. Even Zane's eyes didn't have this effect on me. My little inner voice, the one I tried heed whenever it

I Kissed a Dog

spoke up, told me to look away, but I couldn't tear my eyes from his.

His icy hand brushed my hair away from my neck. He twisted his fingers through my curls and leaned closer. When his lips brushed mine, I sighed. He rose suddenly and pulled me up, clutching me close. I swallowed hard, anticipating his next move.

"You smell so delicious, Chloe. I have been unable to keep you from my thoughts. Never can I recall such an exquisite woman." He leaned in to nuzzle my neck, pulling my hair back and sending jolts of anticipation through every nerve in my body.

When the prick came, my knees buckled. My head swam. I knew on some level he was taking my blood, and not for the first time. I should have been furious, but instead I was enraptured. My body was alive, on fire. An unexpected series of spasms tore through me and I rocked my pelvis against him, riding wave after wave of near excruciating pleasure. My body continued to shudder as he drank what felt like every last drop of my essence.

When I thought I might pass out, he pulled away, but leaned in again to lick my neck. "More," I heard myself beg, still pressing myself against him.

A low chuckle vibrated deep in his chest. "Believe me, I want so much more."

"How long have you been watching me?" I purred, still enthralled by whatever spell he'd cast over me.

"Always, Chloe. You are my destiny. Leave the wolf and come with me. He cannot protect you from the dangers ahead. Neither can he provide you such pleasures." His finger traced my jaw line and trailed down my neck.

Despite his silky caress, my head was clearing. I took a step back, and then another, allowing myself the luxury of visually devouring my vampire suitor.

As in Vegas, he was clad in black. Leather pants, boots, a black T-shirt, a stylish leather jacket, and the same necklace and emblem resting over his chest. His spiky black hair left his angled face in full view.

Seeing my appraisal, his half smile stretched into a full grin. Just the sight of his fangs sent another shiver of excitement down my inner thighs. It took every ounce of self-control I had left, which wasn't much, not to slip back into his arms.

"You want me as much as I do you," he stated with simple sincerity. "Will you join me?"

Fighting that part of me that wanted to do exactly as he requested, I took another careful step away. "I'm mated to Zane now." I didn't say married because I suspected that particular term wouldn't have quite the same impact as its supernatural translation.

"Have you accepted the dog's mark?" His eyes flashed dangerously.

I'd forgotten all about that part of the ritual. I had to officially accept Zane as my mate. I wasn't even sure how to do that. Did I have to lift my leg and mark him as mine?

"I can see you haven't. That is good. You are too wise a woman to do such a despicable thing. You deserve a great deal more than he can give you. I can give you *forever.*"

Forever …? I wasn't even sure I could deal with tomorrow.

I Kissed a Dog

Instead of its desired effect, the forever idea only served to sever any remaining doubt. "I think you better go. The guys will be back soon." I hoped I was right, because the look in his eyes was no longer one of passion. I hated to imagine the pain his fangs could inflict. I had a feeling that pleasure and pain were closely aligned in the mind of a vampire.

Valamir reached inside his coat and pulled out a shiny, round object. "I believe your friend was looking for this?" He extended what had to be the fourth coin.

Hoping I appeared calmer than I felt, I reached out my hand.

Instead of stepping toward me, he flashed. I didn't know what else to call it. One second he was standing a few feet away and the next his face was an inch from mine. He lifted my chin with his finger, his eyes boring into mine. He twirled and twisted the coin between his fingers.

"I am willing to play along for awhile longer. *You* have something I want." He dipped his mouth to mine and kissed me. Without meaning to, I found myself kissing him back. He smelled like leather, spices, and something utterly foreign but absolutely delicious.

I realized in that moment that everything about this vampire was designed to tempt and torture me — his smell, his taste, his kisses, his amazing looks, all of it. He was like a drug. And if I wasn't careful, I'd become hopelessly addicted to him, mated to Zane or not.

He pulled away, leaving my chest heaving. A part of me wanted to tell him off, but the words wouldn't come. He'd literally kissed me quiet. How could I claim to love Zane when I was so easily diverted by the vampire?

"I will have you. You will be mine. To show you how much you already mean to me, here is what you were looking for, I believe." He took my hand in his and pressed the coin in. "Your vampire friend arrived too late. A mutant had already retrieved it. I disposed of the beast and kept your trinket safe."

"Uh, thank you," I whispered. "Do you know what these coins mean? And who the cloaked creatures are?"

"I know many things. Things that I would be willing to reveal should you choose me." He shrugged. "Until then ..." He leaned over and kissed my cheek, then vanished in his trademark glittery swirl.

I collapsed back on the bed. How in the world would I explain this one? For someone who hated secrets, I was sure keeping a list of my own. Visualizing myself telling Zane the truth about *everything* seemed impossible. I could see it now ...

Honey, I was making out with that strange, really ancient vampire, and he gave me the coin because he wants me to leave you and go with him. He rocked my world without even making it to third base.

Like that would go over well. I'd have to leave the coin behind somewhere Zane would find it when I was in Portland. I didn't want to hold up the search because of my own issues. I needed to get out of town now. I needed to think.

There were some major decisions that needed deciding.

Remarkably, I was exhausted, probably due to my impromptu blood donation, expelled sexual energy, and my dazed condition. I slid the coin under the mattress on my side of the bed. It would be safe there until I figured out what to do with it.

Where are you? I sent my question to Zane.

Letting my princess sleep. We're all out in the barn, chatting with our new partners.

Partners? How did that happen?

Go back to sleep. We'll talk tomorrow.

Goodnight, I said, relieved I wouldn't have to face him tonight. Werewolves could stay up for days without sleep, yet another of the many major differences between us.

Flipping onto my side, I realized the window was still open. Not such a good idea. I couldn't handle anymore late night visitors.

Wishing I could flash myself to the window or shut it with my mind wasn't going to get the job done. I'd have to get up and do it with my own two, very human hands.

"If you're going to come in through my window, you could at least be polite and shut it on your way out," I said to no one in particular as I reached up to pull the framed, glass pane down.

A familiar, but unexpected, ghostly face appeared. "I think we need to talk," Alcuin said, looking none too pleased. "By the way, you reek."

"Sorry I'm not up to your smelling standards." I was borderline furious that all the damn supernatural men, who didn't need any sleep, kept interrupting mine.

"Come on in. Everyone else does." I wished right then for a giant eraser that would erase the last hour in one big swipe.

Alcuin slipped into the room's one chair. "Vampires are very aware of each other."

I faced him with my arms crossed, deciding to remain standing in hopes I looked somewhat authoritative. "No. I didn't know. I've been aware of your world for one week now. My entire life has been turned upside down, and I've got werewolf and vampire suitors vying for my attention. I got married when I was drunker than a …"

"Slow down, Doll. I am well aware of your supernatural overload. I've suggested to Zane more than once that he take you to Europe or somewhere far away from here for a month, but he feels too obligated to his pack and their problems."

I was surprised by Alcuin's revelation. I also remembered my earlier desire to talk with him about Valamir. That heart to heart was taking place here and now whether I was ready for it or not.

I decided to spill every detail of my three encounters with Valamir, well, most of the details. I didn't go so far to tell how attracted I was to him or about my erotic experience. From the way Alcuin was watching me, I assumed he already knew. He was, after all, a bloodsucker. Well aware of vampire tactics and tastes, and the potential human responses.

"He brought you the coin?"

Surprised he didn't have more to say, I nodded and retrieved relic from its hiding place. "How do I explain this to Zane?"

Ignoring my question, Alcuin flipped the coin over in his palm, examining it. "I wonder if your vampire admirer could translate these sigils. It's is not my area of expertise."

I had a feeling that Valamir was privy to lots of useful information. Getting him to divulge that information without signing over my soul, and my blood supply, was the problem.

"Sorry to change the subject, but what's all this 'you're

mine' stuff?" I needed to know why my scent was so appealing to Valamir and Zane.

Alcuin stopped rolling the coin and studied my face. "You are quite attractive. And you do smell intoxicating. I detected your unique fragrance that first time we met.

As a rule, vampires can find pleasure feeding from a wide range of donors. On occasion, a specific human catches our fancy. Kind of like a choice dish at your favorite restaurant."

"So I'm a good meal?"

He looked at a loss for words. "It's difficult to explain. We want only to feed from that one special person. I've never experienced it. Not all vampires do. Just like werewolves, and even humans, not everyone finds their own favorite flavor. When we do, we want to hang on, permanently, if possible. I guess the question is: *who* is your favorite flavor, Chloe?"

I found, much to my dismay, I couldn't answer.

Eighteen

I tried to hide my relief when Alcuin presented the fourth, and what we hoped was the final coin, to Zane over breakfast. My vampire confidant didn't stay long, complaining the sun was getting on his nerves and giving him a blistering headache. He promised to return when we were ready for our "ride" to the board meeting.

Zane had readily accepted Alcuin's explanation for obtaining the coin. My late night worry session had been unnecessary. As he'd promised last night, before leaving, Alcuin kept the more sensitive portions of our conversation to himself. Something I knew he disliked in light of his longtime alliance with Zane.

I'd also filled Alcuin in on my parental problems *and* my plans and reasons for traveling to Portland minus Zane. In lieu of time constraints, we determined he'd handle Bob on his own. In truth, I didn't want see my stepdad bedazzled regardless of the reason.

Uneasy, Alcuin swore secrecy on those revelations as well. He had even gone so far to admit that he'd never once chosen a human's wishes over his own, and made it clear he wasn't planning to make it habit.

Whatever his reasons, I was grateful to have him for an ally, even temporarily. He would make sure I arrived at my destination unscathed.

Thank goodness I'd adapted to teleporting since I'd be traveling Air Alcuin twice in one day. Actually, three times — a round trip to and from Seattle, and a one way ride to Portland.

In addition, Luke had remembered his role in my escape-to-Portland scheme. He'd called, as planned, at 7:15 AM to request an evening meeting. I'd explained to Zane that Luke wanted to have a long overdue sit-down with me and Rhonda. Something my werewolf mate was none too keen about. He considered her an arch enemy to be avoided at all costs.

In the end, I'd won the argument by reminding him that Michael or Mack would be close by and that Luke wouldn't let Rhonda harm me.

Overall, he'd been pretty receptive considering he was scheduled to meet with Rita later about the coins, a meeting that promised to be long and arduous, according to Rita's predictions. She'd invited another linguistic scholar to collaborate with them, and believed they might decipher at least a portion of the coins' script this evening.

I promised to let Luke follow me home, and if circumstances warranted, I could even unleash (forgive the pun) Stryder from the barn for additional protection. Zane was planning to release him when he returned home.

Zane and the two M's had determined the mutant should have one final day of captivity to seriously consider the implications of switching sides. I was supposed to read his thoughts later and confirm his decision to leave the mutant cause for good.

Tom, on the other hand, wasn't being quite as receptive. The dreadlocked mutant had so far refused to comply. When I'd taken a peek into his mind, I'd been startled to discover he was crushing big time on the redheaded wolf-woman. He'd seen her from a distance, just once, but it had been enough to ignite his interest. Tom wasn't real intelligent. From what I could tell, he was downright dumb.

Meanwhile, Zane had gone out to feed Tom and Stryder, leaving me to shower and figure out what an administrative assistant should wear to her first ever board meeting.

I'd also asked Zane what would keep the board members from identifying me. After all, they'd sent Zane here to investigate the murders and find the girl who could chit chat with animals. According to him, no one had a clue what I looked like. Logan alone knew my identity, and Zane promised he was to be trusted.

I hoped he was right.

After trying on at least five potential outfits, I decided on a traditional beige suit, ideal for summer weather. I'd purchased it two years ago for my interview at the animal park. Luke had admired its sleekness, but made sure to remind me that wearing it to work would be overstating my position.

"Wow!" Zane said approvingly, causing me to gasp. He'd managed to catch me off guard.

"Don't sneak up on me like that." I pivoted to look over my shoulder in the mirror before facing it again to tuck in my silk blouse.

"No need to check, you look fantastic from every angle. Sorry for the scare." He came closer and looked over my shoulder into the mirror, where our eyes met. I glanced down, my cheeks flushing.

If Zane discovered my indiscretion and lies, I doubted he'd be so appreciative. Pushing the thoughts aside, I focused on my husband. "Are you sure this is appropriate?"

He shook his head, chuckling softly. "Chloe, Chloe. You have no idea just how enticing you are, do you?" He didn't wait for my response. "That suit shows just enough leg to be appealing, but not overly flashy. Ivory is the perfect shade for your skin tone, and by wearing a wine-colored blouse, you've added the perfect touch. Not to mention, I've never seen you with your hair like that."

Taken aback by his detailed appraisal, I eyed my hair. A majority of the time I left my long ringlets to hang loose, or, occasionally, in hot weather, I'd pull my hair up high in what my mom referred to as my "pebbles ponytail," named after little Pebbles from *the Flintstones*.

This morning, I'd used a hair-straightener to force my curls into submission. And, with the miraculous help from some over-priced hair products, I'd managed to manipulate my hair into a smooth twist on top of my head. Zane's continued admiration confirmed I'd made a good choice.

Alcuin's — *who is your favorite flavor question* — continued to harass me.

Who is my favorite flavor? — Vampire or werewolf — bark verses bite.

Standing here in the daylight, without Valamir's vamp magic messing with my mind, I felt certain that the magnificent man behind me was exactly who I needed and wanted in my life. The choice seemed so obvious.

However, I couldn't stop replaying last night's erotic interlude with the vampire warrior. His fangs piercing my neck had caused me to climax — an embarrassing incident I'd take to my grave.

A grave that I just might find myself buried in if I wasn't careful.

Both my so-called *flavors* had vicious sides to their charismatic personas. Should they turn their anger toward me ...

"Are you all right?" Zane leaned down and nipped my neck, sending a jolt of excitement everywhere at once. When had I developed such a sensitive neck?

"I'm just nervous." At least that wasn't a lie.

Nervous. Anxious. Terrified of losing you. The last thought startled me.

After everything we'd experienced together, I couldn't imagine my life without Zane. I didn't want to need anybody, least of all someone whose approval mattered enough for me to fear losing it.

"There's no need to be nervous. You'll do great. Remember, turn on the mini-recorder." He handed me the tiny recording device. "It will pick up everything. That way, you can concentrate on the animals. Make notes about your discoveries and let the recorder handle the meeting. We'll find someone to transcribe later."

"Where do you come up with all this?" I wondered out loud.

Before meeting the werewolves, I'd been pretty much a day-to-day, go-with-the-flow kind of gal. All this planning and plotting was new to me, although I was adapting fast enough to have already devised a plan of my own. I hoped I could find the Smart boy.

I had three plausible locations to check out. The first, not far from my parent's house, was a well-known institution for mentally disturbed boys and girls, ages five to eighteen. It was the largest of the three, and housed the most residents, making it, in my opinion, the least likely. The other two were closer to downtown Portland. One in the West Hill's area served just eight clients at a time. The cost for this program was astronomical. As far as I knew, the Smart's salaries were modest, but what did I know? They could have saved their money wisely, or relied on a rich relative.

Thirdly, and what I considered my best option for finding Joshua Smart, was a newer, state run, research facility that specialized in helping children recover from traumatic experiences. They'd been featured on a special news report awhile back and had a reputation of taking on high profile cases. Joshua fit that category.

One problem with this location was the intense security. Some of their patients had committed pretty heinous crimes. Alcuin had again offered to remedy the situation. I'd make it my first stop, giving him the opportunity to enter and observe.

Worried about the old vampire myths that required blood suckers to obtain permission before entering, I'd made sure to question Alcuin. After all, Valamir had been blocked from entering The Crab Cove without my invitation, but had slipped into my room unhindered.

According to Alcuin, because Valamir had fed on my blood, he'd been granted certain rights when it came to me. In short, wherever I was he could enter — with one exception — a strong ward. The Crab Cove had been magically warded against uninvited, supernatural visitors, making entry for him impossible. Under normal circumstances, vampires could enter public buildings even if people dwelled there. The locations requiring a personal invite were private residences.

I realized then that Zane was staring at me with one eyebrow arched.

"I did that drifting off thing, didn't I?" I shrugged.

"I get it. You're stressed. Did you still want me to answer your question?"

I couldn't even remember what I'd asked him. Not good. If I wasn't careful, he'd figure out that I had more than information overload going on in my head. My husband was no dummy, and he'd gotten to know me faster than anyone else. I'd never felt so many emotions in relation to any one person.

"What are you thinking?" He gave me a longing look. "Tell me it's good."

I was amazed how in an instance we'd gone from a simple conversation to one charged with heated energy. "It's very good."

Watching him watch me in the mirror suddenly seemed very sensuous. I looked so prim and proper in my current attire. He looked all man. No. That wasn't quite true. His eyes were changing to the golden hue I loved so much. The color signaled that his libido had kicked into overdrive.

"How much time do we have?" I asked.

He leaned down and kissed my neck. "Not enough for what I want to do to you."

I shivered at the thought, realizing right then, without doubt, Zane was the flavor I liked best. He didn't need any mind-magic to melt me like butter. He was warm, funny, sumptuous, powerful, and very much alive — nothing undead about Zane.

"That's disappointing," I pouted. "By the way, I was thinking that you are one of a kind, my kind of guy." It wasn't until after I'd spoken that I realized just how corny I sounded.

Much to my relief, Zane seemed to find my comments endearing and rewarded me with a big grin. "I love it when you call me *your* guy."

"Go on. Get ready. I don't want to mess up my hair anyway." I regretfully shooed him away.

"Good point, Mrs. Marshall. Good point."

I was tempted to follow him into the shower, but refrained. We'd have time to enjoy each other later — that is if he still wanted me after uncovering all my secrets.

Nineteen

The one benefit to the packed space was my ultra-close proximity to Zane.

With my back pressed firmly against his front, and his hands deviously teasing my fanny, I was in elevator heaven.

A woman leered at us through wired spectacles. She was focused on where his unseen hands were busily hiding. I decided to ignore her sardonic smile. She was probably just jealous. What woman wouldn't be?

A man like Zane did more than attract attention. He demanded it. His artful caresses were demanding a response that I was unable to give. Had I responded with the level of passion I was forcing myself to ignore, Miss Nosy would have gotten an eyeful.

Not a moment too soon, the doors slid open revealing a long hallway on the tenth floor. The hotel housed its conference rooms on the upper levels. Our meeting was in the *Mystic Mountain Suite*. How appropriate. My life was about as mystical as one could be.

We exited into the hall leaving our snooty spectator behind.

I Kissed a Dog

In less than ten steps, we were facing the only thing between me and a group of potentially adversarial board members. Muffled male voices drifted from behind the closed door, marked with a gold plaque. My stomach clenched, sending a swirl of butterflies through my midsection.

"Use our silent communi …" Zane started.

Well aware of what he was advising, I cut him off. "I know. *And* the recorder." I pushed the elevated button on my new spy device. The minuscule recorder was secure, tucked in my purse's outside pocket. "I need to count and take deep breaths." I prepared to employ my usual calm-down-routine.

Zane instructed with patience, "You need to look at me."

I glanced up. He gave me a look filled with unspoken confidence and admiration. "You'll do great. Once Logan arrives, we'll go in. He'll introduce you. It'll look better if you seem closer to him."

I nodded.

Zane kissed my cheek. "You've got this, Princess."

Hoping his confidence wasn't misplaced; I smoothed my skirt for the hundredth time.

"Looking lovely, Mrs. Marshall," Logan affirmed, as he appeared by my side. I jumped, still not used to people appearing from nowhere, and calling me Mrs. Marshall.

Logan summarized what I already knew too well. "Remember, three of the elders will have their dogs. One German Shepherd, a Lab, and a feisty young Doberman."

Zane had located the canine companions' photos for me to "study." I'd never liked Dobermans. I was almost certain the dog that had sent me flying into the swimming pool, close to a decade ago, had been part dobby. I wasn't ready to forgive the breed for its indiscretion.

"Ready?" Zane asked.

I managed a smile.

Logan entered the room like a Greek god striding into his celestial palace. I envied his distinguished composure.

The men in the room hurried to take their seats. Their reverence for the Pack Leader was evident. One man, his skin tanned and wrinkled like a well-worn hide, seemed unimpressed by Logan Sanders. I made a note to keep an eye on him.

"Here Boss!" the same man commanded while taking his seat at the far table's far end.

I jerked back, when the largest Doberman I'd ever seen, trotted to his master's side. The man flipped his grey-streaked ponytail over his shoulder and turned his piercing gaze on me. I felt like I was standing on a stage under the glare of a spotlight.

The remaining men, and one lone woman, had taken their seats during the few short minutes I'd been occupied by the ancient Indian and his ferocious hound.

Logan had referred to the beast as feisty. Feisty described Terrier pups, not this sleek, black, terror of a dog. I realized then that everyone was watching me expectantly. Talk about making a scene. Wanting to bolt from the room, I did the opposite and stepped toward an open chair next to Logan.

When people talk about things happening in threes, they're right. One: mean man and vicious dog staring me down. Two: table of strangers watching me with eerily chilly expressions. Three: I trip over nothing, and in what feels like slow motion, tumble toward what I somehow notice is plush, mauve carpeting. I hope it's as soft and springy as it looks. I hear several gasps before two super-sized hands drag me to my feet.

"Uh, thank you." I try to smile like nothing happened and find myself looking up at the leathery face from the end of the table. "You …?"

"There now," he soothed like the parent of a frightened toddler. "Are you all right?"

I allowed him to settle me into an expensive, high-backed chair. I was so far from feeling all right responding would have been blasphemous.

He patted my shoulder and returned to his end-of-the-table seat where his dog posed like a regal warrior.

Logan began, his voice firm and steady. "I guess this would be a good time to introduce my newest administrative assistant, Cassandra Carpenter."

Still dazed, it took me another endless minute to realize *I* was Cassandra Carpenter. We'd altered my name just enough to keep anyone from putting together my true identity. "Hi?" I gave an awkward parade wave.

"Welcome," several voices chorused.

"Glad you could join us," the other woman said. Some nodded. A few smirked — so much for instant acceptance.

Unable to leave them with such a horrible first impression, I decided to make my own mini-speech. Something I'd later regret like everything else about the meeting.

"That's me, Cassandra Carpenter. Please forgive my grand entrance."

That earned a few strained chuckles.

"I'll be taking notes and just want to thank you all for welcoming me into your group." I took my seat again in what I hoped was a demure fashion.

Looking to Zane for approval, I noted instead he appeared both puzzled and perplexed. *Chloe, Princess, do you think you could draw any more attention to yourself? Check your recorder and get your notepad.* He quickly looked away, but not before my latest savior noticed our discreet interaction.

What was with this guy? Friend or foe?

I organized myself while the board members took ten minutes to "check in". According to Logan, he was practicing a new ice breaker to loosen things up.

For my benefit, everyone introduced themselves and gave me the opportunity to jot down their names. I drew a makeshift table and put the names in their proper order around the oblong shape, trusting this extra attention to detail would benefit me in the long run.

All dogs were in attendance as expected. The chocolate lab lounged by his owner's feet, head resting on his front paws. The German Shepherd panted, his doggy mouth turned up in a canine grin. Like the Doberman, he sat stiffly next to his owner's chair. The lab and the shepherd were very interested in Logan and Zane's unseen lupine qualities. They stared at the two werewolves, who appeared unaware of their latest admirers. Only the Doberman remained indifferent to Zane and Logan.

The meeting started like any other board meeting. The last meeting's minutes were reviewed. Old business was addressed, and then before I realized it, we were onto new business. I hadn't even bothered to listen in on the pets. *Nice work*, I chastised myself.

Keeping my pen poised over a half-filled notebook page, I searched the lab's mind. I trusted the mini-recorder would take care of anything I missed while nosing around in the canine minds.

The door to the dog's thoughts swung wide open and I slipped in. His owner, Roger Ryker, a Native American male, in his fifties, and sporting cropped, graying hair, materialized in a majority of the dog's visions. It was easy to see this was a good match. As far as I could tell, there was nothing out of the ordinary. Normal dog stuff was all the Labrador had on his mind.

Disappointed, but happy for the two of them, I moved on to the beautifully-marked German shepherd, saving the dreaded dobby for last.

The dog stiffened as I entered his thoughts. I probed as gently as I could, hoping he'd relax and reveal something of interest. I didn't have to wait long.

I was yanked into a recognizable but unexpected landscape. The dog and his owner were walking through the strange medical facility that I'd seen in the cloaked creature's mind. They stopped at the foot of one of many beds, providing a close up view of a male patient. He wasn't resting on his bed.

He was strapped to it.

His body writhed from side to side like an animal caught in a trap, experiencing unspeakable pain. Perspiration glistened on his face, which was turning an odd shade of gray.

The shepherd stared up at his master, who during introductions had identified himself as Martin, one of the Makah Tribe elders. Martin leaned over the thrashing patient along with several men dressed in scrubs, and none other than the infamous redheaded woman.

He met her gaze from across the bed. She gave a slight nod.

"He's not progressing. We all know what that means. But wait; make sure. We've been wrong before," Martin instructed.

"Then?" another man asked, glancing at his clipboard.

"Kill him," Martin said with a shrug. "We don't need any more renegade baldies running around. We've caused enough problems cleaning up our mistakes." He glanced sideways at the woman.

She glared at Martin. "I'm certain you're not blaming me for *your* screw ups." Her eyes flashed crimson. Martin flinched like he'd been stung.

"Of course not, *Mistress*." He inclined his head.

"Blaming me wouldn't be wise." She moved around the table and behind Martin. Leaning over his shoulder, she whispered something that made the corner of his mouth rise.

Without further comment, she strode with hips swaying, down the corridor, making it her own personal runway, high heels clicking on the concrete.

The men gazed after her retreating figure, and then sighed in unanimous relief when she exited through the double doors. Martin was wearing a stupid little grin that gave him a slightly insane appearance. He'd been satiated by her whispered promise.

I started to pull away from the vision, when the dog whimpered, recapturing my attention. Martin and the others stared down at their patient, who was transforming into something not human.

I Kissed a Dog

He shriveled and shrunk, his skin becoming a railroad track of wrinkled lines and creases. His thick, blonde, mane-of-hair was falling out in clumps, making his head look like a shiny orb. I could almost see the veins pulsating beneath the thin cap of skin covering his skull. He looked like an alien featured on the Sci-fi Channel.

What had started out as a normal-looking twenty-something male, had become what I now referred to as one of the ugly creatures, minus its cloak.

Martin pulled a syringe from his pocket.

"Look out!" I warned, realizing my error too late.

Every board member was gaping — their eyes glued on me. So much for my simple administrative duties.

By the strained expression on Zane's face, it was evident I'd blown any opportunity to appear normal. As if I ever pulled off normal.

I hoped the information I'd gleaned from Martin's German Shepherd would redeem me. I dared to take a quick unassuming peek in his direction. He was frowning.

The single person smiling was … I glanced down at my notebook —James McQuillen — the man who'd kept me from the face plant, and who owned Boss the Doberman, the dog I hadn't had time to explore yet.

I know what you are. He sent the message telepathically, lifting his water glass in a mock toast.

◉

The meeting's remaining minutes passed without incident. There were a few heated words in response to Logan's ideas for expansion into more family-friendly markets. The person most opposed to anything he suggested was the murderer,

Martin. He could see no financial benefit to changing their already successful business model.

While they were debating the details of Logan's business plan, I made one unsuccessful attempt to infiltrate the mind of Boss, but the Doberman's thoughts were guarded by a smoky haze. I could make out movements beyond the fog-like barrier, but was unable to latch onto anything of substance. His mysterious owner rested a hand on his pet's head. I couldn't help wondering if his hand somehow shielded the dog's mind from my probing.

The discussion regarding Logan's new ideas had changed the meeting's entire atmosphere. No one seemed the least bit interested in me or my note taking. I sipped coffee and counted the minutes until could tell Zane and Logan about Martin and Mr. McQuillen.

I didn't have to wait long before James McQuillen made the final announcement. "Thank you all for attending. Logan Sanders, our dear friend and business associate, has given us a great deal to consider. I also want to say it's been a pleasure to welcome Cassandra to our group." He nodded my direction. "Everyone is excused except for the elders."

"Back in fifteen," Logan stated.

I practically leapt from my seat, rushing into the hallway. Where was the little girls' room when you needed one?

"Excuse me, Ms. Carpenter?" the other woman, Maureen Harper, tapped my shoulder. "Are you looking for the ladies room?"

Relieved to see her smile, I sighed. "Was it that obvious?"

"Let's just say, I know how it feels to be in a room of chauvinistic men for more than two hours. Follow me."

We exited our stalls in unison and faced the long mirror. I

I Kissed a Dog

scrubbed my hands, wishing I could wipe away the filth of my lies. Keeping secrets from Zane was eating me from the inside out. I'd made a huge scene in Vegas over his supposed secrets, yet here I was carting around several biggies of my own. The biggest being that I'd made out with a very sexy and powerful vampire, not once, but twice. And I'd liked it.

I'd also somehow managed to pull one of his closest friends into my scheming. If I felt this bad, Alcuin had to be feeling worse. Or did he? I wasn't convinced that vampires handled their emotions the same way as humans.

"Are you okay?" Maureen asked, now rubbing her palms together under the dryer.

I was *still* washing.

Realizing how silly I must look, I rinsed and shut off the water. "I'm just nervous. I made an utter fool of myself."

Maureen leaned toward the mirror, and expertly applied a burgundy shade of lipstick. "I've been there. Shake it off. The next meeting is the most important."

"What's different?" I hated to appear so naïve.

"For one, it's just the elders. There will be several additions to the group, and we'll be discussing some pretty serious issues. I'm guessing Logan's at least briefed you on the Plum Beach murders."

Not sure what to say, I nodded, and made a point of finding my own lipstick.

"I'm certain, if you're working in this capacity with him, you know his real identity?" She arched one sculpted brow, anticipating my reply.

Two young women breezed in, interrupting us. I tried not to look too relieved.

Maureen glanced at her Rolex. "We better get going."

Back at the table, I drew another map and scribbled the names of those still in attendance. James McQuillen, Maureen Harper, Logan and Zane, Roger Ryker, and two newcomers — Jonas Kallappa and Theo Secor. The fact that Martin the Murderer was absent renewed my hope that I could end the meeting on a positive note.

"Why'd Martin leave?" Theo Secor asked gruffly.

"Because I asked him to," said McQuillen. "We've all got places to be. Let's get down to our most recent problem. Zane, updates from Plum Beach?" McQuillen crossed his arms over his barreled chest.

"We've had four murders. All young men, none over thirty. It's been a week since the last victim. I've also found the animal reader."

My breath caught. What was he doing? I thought I was a secret. I grabbed my glass, nearly inhaling the water.

Zane wasn't done. "Considering Martin is no longer present, I'd like you to meet Chloe Carpenter." He stood and extended his hand, which I refused.

I was enraged. How dare he do this without warning me? Was he crazy? Now my so-called cover was blown to pieces. Talk about keeping secrets! And to think I'd been ready to reveal mine.

James McQuillen grinned. "I was right."

Good for you! I barked silently for his ears alone.

He had the nerve to throw back his head and laugh, like a maniac as far as I was concerned. Whatever the joke, I missed it, but everyone else chuckled right along with him.

Zane remained stone-faced.

Good for him. Had he laughed, I would have marched out of the room and called for Valamir. Well, maybe not Valamir, but Alciun for sure. I couldn't wait to leave for Portland now.

Bye bye, Zane, and bye bye guilt.

"I'm glad you all find this so amusing; I don't. For all I know, one of *you* is a bad guy." I glared around the table, searching for any reaction to my accusation. No one fidgeted or looked worried.

"Chloe, please, accept my apology. The reason I laugh is because with all your natural curiosity you didn't even wonder *why* or *how* I could communicate with you mentally."

I took a longer look McQuillen and his dog. He couldn't be.

In answer to my silent question, he shimmered and vanished below the table. I heard the unmistakable shifting of bones and stretching of flesh. Then Boss barked and licked the giant wolf that'd appeared in place of McQuillen.

The Doberman looked like a puppy next to the massive silver wolf. He was a majestic creature. Silvery white, McQuillen seemed to shine.

He padded around the table and sat by my chair, placing a massive paw on my lap. I couldn't help myself. My hand was drawn to his lush fur like a magnet to metal.

"You're so handsome," I heard myself coo.

"That's what you said to me," Zane grumbled.

I turned to glare at my mate. "You should probably not talk to me right now."

When I looked back, McQuillen, still in wolf form, was dragging his own clothing into a small kitchenette in the back of the boardroom. Boss followed.

"That's not something you see every day," I muttered. "I

think I'll keep all this out of the official notes." I looked to Logan for approval. His immediate thumbs up signal provided no room for doubt.

A few minutes later, with McQuillen back in his place, I shared what I'd learned from Martin's dog. No one seemed surprised, which surprised me.

"I've found some inconsistencies of my own in relation to Martin," McQuillen offered. "I gave him an assignment to get him out of here. Logan, you know I haven't trusted him for some time."

"Agreed," Logan said.

Maureen grinned at me. "I had a feeling you might be the one. You don't know how much you've already helped. We need to locate this medical facility, pronto. Any ideas?"

No one had a clue.

"I'll have to read the shepherd again." I didn't like the idea, but I couldn't think of a better alternative.

"Don't you worry about that just yet. You've got plenty on your plate staying safe and keeping tabs on the happenings in Plum Beach," McQuillen said.

"Who is this redhead, anyway?" Roger Ryker spoke up.

"Your guess is as good as anyone's. I can't help but think she's somehow tied to Jazmine," Zane said. He shot me a questioning look. *Forgive me? I knew you'd be too edgy. You were ready to hyperventilate.*

What he said made perfect sense, but I ignored him and focused on the brainstorming. No one seemed to know much about the ugly, bald creatures, or anything else of critical importance.

The things everyone could agree on for certain were:

I Kissed a Dog

Martin's status as a traitor; the redheaded woman's involvement; the fact that there were medical procedures going on that created the ugly people; the possibility mutants were rebelling and getting help from inside the purebred or Native American communities; and somehow the Plum Beach murders were connected.

Zane kept several key facts to himself. Facts I wasn't willing to disclose, and as far as I could tell, Logan had no inclination to share either. Neither bothered mentioning the ancient coins, or the new partnership with Stryder, a mutant. Nor did Zane bring up the problems with Agent Green and the mysterious Detective Davis. And they didn't refer to my marriage with Zane.

Zane's next query half answered the reason for my final observation.

"If I may be so bold, Elder McQuillan?" Zane asked sounding more formal than I'd heard him.

"Cut the crap, Marshall. Spit it out," McQuillan commanded. "We've moved past all that haven't we?" He cocked his head and gave Zane an easy smile.

"But this is a matter of major importance."

Around the table, everyone seemed to lean forward.

"My birthday is approaching," he rushed on, "and I'm pledged to Jazmine. I cannot join with a female who is involved in a deadly scandal, maybe even the murder of humans."

The group, minus McQuillan, nodded their agreement. I could see the wisdom in what Zane was requesting. Not to mention, he was already married to me and regardless of my current displeasure over his actions, I loved him.

I'd find a way to kill Jazmine myself if it came to that. I didn't have any idea how I would accomplish such an outlandish feat, but I'd give it my best shot. Maybe I'd take down Rhonda at the same time.

"I will not dissolve this agreement, not yet," McQuillan began. "However, I will extend the deadline another thirty days. In the meantime, should you find your one true mate, a woman who agrees to accept your mark, you will be freed from what I think is a ridiculously old and no longer useful contract."

"Thank you." Zane looked right at me.

It was more than difficult to pull my eyes from his.

How could I be so angry but so in love at the same time?

Twenty

Back in Plumb Beach, I bustled around our tiny apartment, gathering a minimal amount of must-have essentials for my trip to Portland.

Zane and Alcuin were out in the barn with our resident mutants. I was happy for Stryder. As far as I could tell, he'd make a great addition to our growing team.

Tom, I wasn't sure what their plans were for him — probably nothing very pleasant, unless he decided to denounce his mutinous ways. From what I'd seen in his thoughts, he wouldn't be joining our cause anytime soon. A decision he would regret.

With my small travel bag stuffed to capacity, I slipped out front where my car was parked next to Zane's. As quietly as my humanness allowed, I popped the trunk and deposited my bag. The last thing I needed was Zane asking why I needed an overflowing travel case for a sixty minute meeting with Luke and Rhonda.

We hadn't talked much since Seattle. I was still frustrated about his impromptu introduction that had left me at the mercy of strangers. The way I saw it, not warning me about his intentions equaled not trusting me. He thought I was too weak and emotionally unstable to handle the truth. Granted, he had a point. I'd become prone to fainting in his arms since we'd first met.

And, yes, I'd had my encounters with Valamir, but how could he fault me for something I had no real control over. The vampire had vamped my mind with magic mojo. And in the end, I'd rejected Valamir's invitation to become *his* woman. Just because my body was beguiled by the ancient bloodsucker didn't mean I was.

"Hey, Princess." Zane strode from the pole barn looking like the most magnificent specimen of manhood I'd ever seen. All I had to do was confess my eternal love for him and I'd allegedly receive the mating symbol and live happily ever after.

Why did I continue to resist the inevitable?

"What are you doing out here?" He pulled me to his chest where I rested my head.

His heartbeat accelerated as I ran my hand down the length of his muscled arm. I had to tell him about Valamir. He'd have time to process the revelation while I was in Portland.

"I need to tell you something." I tilted my head up, searching his eyes.

"Excuse the interruption," Alcuin said, appearing without warning.

A low growl vibrated in Zane's chest, and he shot an annoyed look at Alcuin. "Why do my partners have such bad timing?"

"Down wolf. No need to howl over it." I could tell Alcuin

was in the mood to bait Zane. I hoped Zane wouldn't bite. We needed to talk before I changed my mind.

Hoping to remind them I needed to be at the park soon, I made a major effort of sighing and lifting my wrist to study my watch.

Zane noticed. "I think Chloe's trying to tell us something."

"I have to meet Luke and Rhonda in thirty minutes. And the wolf here has an appointment with Rita and some ancient coins." I made a point of raising an eyebrow at my vampire transporter.

He refused to meet my questioning gaze. If he abandoned our plan, I'd be stuck traveling the old-fashioned way. Even worse, I'd have to find an unguarded route into a locked down psychiatric facility on my own. Not a feat carried out by any untrained mortal.

Our initial plan had us rendezvousing at the wildlife park, where I'd hide my car on a back road, and teleport, with Alcuin, to our first stop in Portland.

Hopefully, that stop would be our only one. I needed to find out what Joshua Smart had seen. I couldn't understand why he wasn't with his mother. He'd seen something more than his father's brutalized body, as if that wasn't enough. Whatever he'd witnessed that night had scared him into complete silence; landing him, if I was correct, inside a state-funded, psychiatric, research center. Not a place I'd want my kid, regardless of his mental capacity.

"I'll see you at the park, Chloe. Zane would like me to be your escort," Alcuin stated, all business. "I'll keep out of sight; your boss won't know I'm there."

Luke and Alcuin would need to provide the same explanation to my whereabouts, and without Luke knowing about Alcuin, I had yet another thing to worry about.

Alcuin vanished and left me facing Zane, wishing I'd kept my mouth shut. Revealing my most secret sins didn't seem wise under the circumstances.

It was regrettable Zane didn't share my concern. "Babe, you wanted to tell me something?" He leaned back against the Corvette.

"I'm afraid we don't have time. I'll tell you telepathically on my drive to the park." I knew I was taking the — I'm-a-chicken-escape-route — but didn't care. I couldn't bear to see his face when he learned of my indiscretions.

I snuggled against him, inhaling his exclusive wild and musky scent for what might be the last time. He was, after all, an alpha male, not willing to share what he considered his with anyone else, least of all a master vampire.

Even if he forgave my mishaps, there was the chance I could get hurt, or worse, attempting to break into a secured mental facility. Either way, the thought of losing him was almost more than I could handle.

"I love you," he whispered into my mouth before devouring it.

Following an extra long kissing session, I pushed away, blaming the time, and hit the highway. My thoughts remained on Zane, and the way his heated kisses had branded my lips. How I could have thought, even for a moment, that Valamir had anything over Zane. The only explanation was his vamp voodoo. Sure, he was sexy. And indeed he was a force to be reckoned with. But he lacked one very important asset: a pure heart.

I Kissed a Dog

Regardless of Zane's lifestyle as a werewolf, there was something clean, refreshing, even heartwarming about him. He oozed sex appeal, but he didn't use it to control me like Valamir.

I'd be at the park soon. It was now or never.

Are you there? I reached into Zane's mind.

I'm headed to Rita's. Before I forget, Stryder is ready to be released. If you need him, the key is in the kitchen drawer. It's embossed with a number one. What did you want to tell me?

First, I love you. I'm ready to do whatever is required to be your mate.

Are you sure?

I'm very sure. But ...

But what? All you have to do is face a full moon and proclaim your love for me. Claim me as your mate forever, and mean it. A symbol will appear around your ankle, like a tattoo. You've made me the happiest werewolf around.

It sounded easy enough ... if I could just skip the next part. Choosing my words, I shared what happened in Vegas, including my vague memory of Valamir drinking my blood.

Zane remained uncharacteristically silent. I forced myself to continue with the incident at The Crab Cove, and, lastly, I shared last night's bedroom encounter. Ashamed, I told him about my body's betraying reaction to his blood feeding.

He didn't say a word, but growled. The throaty rumbling swelled until it sliced through my mind, shattering my heart.

I slammed on the breaks. A truck I hadn't noticed behind me, swerved, breaks squealing, around my car, avoiding what could have been a fatal crash. Taking a deep breath, I maneuvered the car onto the right shoulder and flipped on the emergency lights.

Zane, are you there? Say something. Please. I'm so sorry. God, I'm so sorry. I would have never done it without the magic. Please, you have to believe me.

I waited, and waited. Realizing I was already late getting to the park, but unable to move.

Oh, I believe you.

Zane! Thank God!

I wouldn't thank me just yet. The kissing part hurts, but not as bad as the lying. You put me through hell over my supposed dishonesty, but have lied to me all week. I thought I'd found a woman I could trust. A woman I could spend my life with. You're not that woman.

Panicked by the coldness in his voice, I did something I'd sworn never to do: I begged a man. *Please, don't say that. It will never happen again. I promise. I need you.*

I realized right then that I was still lying. Alcuin was lying, and Luke too. Going to Portland was yet another secret between us. Somehow I'd put the Valamir situation in a different category, but it was all the same. Lies. Betrayal. He was right.

He couldn't trust me.

Forget what I told you about the mating ceremony. I'll protect you until this is over, but after that you're on your own. So am I.

Zane! Wait! Please!

He reinforced the mental brick wall he'd constructed when we'd first met. I was blocked out — maybe forever.

Alcuin found me slouched over the steering wheel, sobbing. He flashed into the passenger seat and rested a cold hand on my shoulder.

"I was worried. I tried to call Zane, but he didn't answer. What happened?"

I Kissed a Dog

I lifted my head. My eyes felt tight and swollen. I didn't dare look in the rearview mirror for fear of what I'd see in the reflection. "I told him."

"About this?" Alcuin said without emotion.

"About Valamir. I was ready to accept the mating mark and wanted Zane to know everything. Well, almost everything. That's the problem. The lies. We both kept secrets, and rather than protecting each other, we've destroyed everything." The more I talked, the more my grief transformed into anger.

Why was it my burden alone to carry? He'd lied more than once. He'd taken my virginity without my knowledge. In my drunken state, I'd consented, but that didn't count. Not really.

We'd both theoretically had good reasons for our deceit, yet neither of us was able to forgive the other — so much for love.

One thing I remembered from my church-going days was that forgiveness was a huge part of love, the most important part. If we couldn't forgive each other, there was no point in me shouting some ridiculous promise at the moon. Divorce wasn't something I wanted, but considering the situation, no one would blame me.

Zane was right. We needed to finish what we started. Find the killer and get on with our lives. We'd known each other for just one week, for crying out loud. I was being ridiculous.

"Do you want me to talk to him?" Alcuin asked, his face still void of emotion.

Did I? No. As far as I was concerned, we were over. "Don't bother. I'm going to Portland, and then I plan to solve this mystery like Nancy Drew."

Alcuin's blank-faced mask cracked. "Nancy *who*?"

"You don't know who Nancy Drew is?" I guessed vampires didn't read much.

"Should I?"

"She's only the greatest ever girl detective. When there's a mystery to solve, you can count on Nancy Drew."

"Should we contact her?" Alcuin asked, his excitement rising.

That was all it took to send me over the edge. My tears vanished in a wave of uncontrollable laughter. Maybe I'd trade places with the Smart kid and let them experiment on me instead. My mental state was in serious question.

Alcuin had told me to curb my emotions the night we'd first met. That particular memory added fuel to my hysterics. When I caught a glimpse of the baffled expression on his face, it acted like a match thrown on gasoline, sending me even further over the edge.

"Why do you laugh like a maniac?" Alcuin clasped my face between his hands and stared into my eyes.

Dammit! Now *he* was using mind magic on me, trying to calm me down.

It was working.

After a few minutes of strange staring, I'd reestablished a sense of sanity, and was grateful for Alcuin's interference. He'd saved me a ton of time and trouble. If everyone had a mind-melding vampire on hand, no one would need medication.

Alcuin shook his head, still looking somewhat dismayed by what had just transpired. "Chloe, doll, please, I beg you, don't do that again."

I wished I could make the promise he wanted, but considering our current predicament, I didn't dare. "I'll do my best. Though laughter, even somewhat crazy laughter, can be healing. For us humans anyway."

"I'll have to take more time to research human emotions," he said to himself. "When you're seven hundred years old, it's difficult to recall past emotions."

We drove in blessed silence to the park. I'd never enjoyed the quiet so much. Being around a vampire like Alcuin was downright soothing. He didn't require conversation, or music, or anything, as far as I could tell. Unlike Valamir, he didn't seem the least bit interested in my blood. That was a relief. The last thing I needed right now was my vampire friend going berserk for my blood.

Luke was in the gatehouse when we arrived. I'd never seen him so frazzled. He raced to the car.

Alcuin had vanished, keeping Luke unaware of his presence.

I rolled down the window. "I didn't realize how late it was. I'm sorry. Are you okay?" I knew he wasn't.

"I was worried. It's not like you to be late for anything. You've never been impulsive. Now you're married. You're late. I don't know what to think." Luke ran his hand through his hair.

"With the murders and everything, I think I'm kinda losing it."

He relaxed. "Yeah, we all are. It's just if anything happened …"

"Nothing is going to happen to me. I just need some time away. Zane is overprotective. That's why I need you to cover for me. If anyone asks, we had a meeting, and I headed home. No matter what happens, please, stick to that story."

"I'm not sure why I'm agreeing to this. We sure need you here. The animals need you. I can tell they're acting differently. Mack and Michael are great and all, but you, Chloe, are one of a kind." He gave me the warm smile I'd come to love over the past two years. Why couldn't I have fallen for him?

With that question still harassing me, I pulled out of the lot. I hadn't bothered confirming with Alcuin the place where I planned to park my car. I'd have to trust in his vampire honing skills to locate me.

Just to park's south side, there was a little dirt road, hidden behind a wall of brush and connected to the wildlife park's property. No one used it anymore. It led to a tiny cabin that had been boarded up ever since I'd started working for Luke, who'd stayed there when he'd first inherited the land from his grandfather. No one would notice my car tucked conveniently behind the cabin.

I found the entrance without a lot of trouble, because I knew what I was looking for. An old tree trunk, a white cross propped at its base, marked the place I needed to turn.

Glancing in the rearview mirror, I confirmed no one was following me, and made a quick right turn and drove through the undergrowth, trusting I'd find the road on the other side. Sure enough, my tires crunched along as they rolled across the gravel. I slowed to a crawl and flicked on my brights. I saw the old cabin looking as forlorn as I'd ever seen it. It sat off to the left of the road about a hundred feet ahead

A few minutes later, I'd parked behind the now-slanting structure. I was amazed Luke hadn't either remodeled the place, or torn it down. I was partial to the second option. It looked ready to collapse on its own.

Maybe my emotional outburst had made me stupid, but it

hit me like bullet between the eyes just how dumb it was for me to be sitting in a pitch black forest with Jazmine, mutants, and God knows what else seeking my destruction.

I tried again to reach out for Zane. As before, the mental brick wall kept me from entering his thoughts. So much for his promise to protect me despite our breakup, it appeared he was off duty tonight.

Ignoring the insane urge to leave the car like the idiots in every known horror movie, I turned my attention to the landscape. The cabin was boarded up and looked like it hadn't been used in years. I couldn't see beyond the edge of trees and foliage that surrounded the structure. Eerie shadows drifted through the trees — a thick coastal fog was blanketing the area. As much as I hated to admit it, the place looked haunted. I expected an army of ghosts to appear any second.

"Alcuin, please hurry. I need you," I whispered urgently.

From the corner of my eye, I saw one of the shadows separate itself from the trees and dash to the cabins opposite side, then another did the same, and another.

I wanted to believe my eyes were playing a cruel trick on me, but I knew otherwise.

I wasn't alone out here. I was being surrounded.

⁂

Faster than I thought possible, I scanned the area for my supernatural stalkers. Seven showed up on my mental radar. Five were mutants. Two of them, I wasn't certain, which caused my fear to escalate. The mutants made sense. I should have expected an attack. I'd gotten complacent with Zane always around. Tonight, I was on my own. But one thing was certain, I wasn't going to roll over and die without a fight.

I hoped Zane had left behind his pistol.

He had wanted to equip me for the worst during our searches of the murder scenes. It sure wouldn't hurt to have some old-fashioned fire power on hand despite my aversion to guns.

I remembered my stepdad's gun collection with mixed feelings. Bob had made it a priority to show me gun safety basics, too bad he hadn't thought teaching me to shoot was as important.

Frantic with fear, I dug through the glove compartment and was preparing to scramble into the back seat, to access the trunk, when I remembered my very effective, mind-bending barrage in Vegas. I could only hope my abilities had expanded yet again, because I was planning an attack on multiple levels. Reaching more than one mind at time wasn't something I'd ever attempted.

Another shadowy form ducked behind the cabin. They were going to systematically attack me.

I had to act now.

Not sure how to start, I allowed my anger at Zane, Jazmine, and the mutants to soar to the surface like scorching lava rising in an erupting volcano. Until now, I hadn't a clue to the extent of my bitterness.

A rush of crimson and black filled my mind like a whirling tornado. I was somehow controlling the swirling mass. I probed the minds around me.

Picturing a huge weapon, loaded with tormenting pain, I readied myself to fire.

"Three, two, one! Take that you freaks!" I screeched.

Something inside my head burst outward like a series of guided missiles launching from an aircraft carrier. My mental missiles hit their targets at once. I knew they'd made impact by the screams and roars that followed. Opening my eyes that I must have closed during the "launch" provided all the confirmation I needed.

Writhing on the ground, around my car, were the five mutants. They were all gripping their heads. One by one, they stopped moving.

Still wary, I opened my door and leaned out, surveying the scene. The mutant closest to me was staring with blank eyes at the starry night sky. His eyes locked in what I'd come to think of as the death gaze. Feeling bolder, I leapt from the car. The four other mutants were lifeless.

I'd killed them.

A little shiver trailed down my spine. My animal reading capabilities had turned from healing and helping to inflicting pain, even death. I wasn't ready to accept myself as someone who killed. I doubted I'd ever be.

"You had no choice," a familiar voice said from behind.

Not sure who or what I'd find, I forced myself to turn. I was facing two of the cloaked, ugly men. They were very similar in appearance, but I was able to recognize the one speaking as the same creature I'd met before. The other nodded his agreement.

I took a slow step backward — the car's safety beckoning.

"Don't be afraid. We're here to help. We've been keeping an eye on the park's property. The mutants have been congregating at this cabin," the creature explained.

I realized then I was no longer afraid. There was something calming about these misfits. "Who are you? Can you tell me what you know?"

"My name is David," the familiar one answered.

What was it with the ordinary names? I still expected every

supernatural being to have some exotically foreign name. "David? Not what I expected."

He chucked. "It wasn't my first choice either."

"The coins …" I started but was interrupted by a flash of light and the sudden appearance of none other than Alcuin.

It was about time.

My new friends didn't have the same warm fuzzy response to the vampire. I didn't have a clue what they thought, because they'd made a swift exit to nowhere — vanished, without warning, again. I fought the urge to scold my vampire accomplice. He was nowhere in sight when I'd needed him. Now he'd ruined my opportunity to find out more about anything.

Aware of his poor timing, he had the sense to look as disappointed as I was feeling. "I scared off your friends," he said somewhat contrite. "It looks like you were able to handle things on your own." He made a point of kicking one of the fallen mutants in the side.

Realizing I should have shared my parking location to begin with, I decided not to lecture him. "I could've used you sooner, or later," I muttered, unable to resist one final jab.

"What's done is done. Let's get you to Portland, and then I'll return to deal with this … mess." Despite his scolding tone, I could tell he was impressed by my ingenuity.

I should have been the one sprawled on the ground, less an arm or leg or head. At least my mess was bloodless and the bodies were still intact.

"I don't feel good about leaving my car. According to the bald guy, this is a haven for the bad mutants." I hoped he'd have an acceptable solution. I'd already given up my home, at least temporarily, to the two M's, and now that I was on the outs with Zane, I wasn't sure about our living arrangement. The last thing I wanted was to lose my car.

"I will find someone to ward this entire property, and I have a feeling your cloaked crusaders will keep watch until I return."

Reassured, I removed my small travel case from the trunk and made sure the car was locked. I'd have to trust that Alcuin would make good on his promise of protection. There weren't any other options, unless I wanted to postpone my trip.

"I'm ready. Let's go."

I didn't need to say it again. We vanished in a rush of wind, and moments later were standing in field behind one of several, windowless, storage buildings. The research facility loomed ahead of us. Lights around the property brightened up the area.

Alcuin glanced at my bag. "Let's get you checked into a hotel. You can't cart your bag around, and you need a home base. Also, I took the liberty of picking up a rental car."

"Wow. Thanks. I didn't even think about all that." I decided right then that he was forgiven for interrupting my conversation back at the cabin.

Moments later, we teleported into a hotel room. I just had to ask. "You already ..."

"Paid for the room, number 412," He handed me the cardkey. "A black BMW is parked in a space with the corresponding number." He grinned. "I wanted to make sure you had a place to unwind and a car to drive."

I had to give Alcuin credit. For a vampire, he was pretty in tune to a woman's needs.

"We're on Cornell Road. The institution is out by the

Hillsboro Airport. The state purchased a portion of their land to build it. I've also confirmed that the boy you seek is indeed a patient."

I was again amazed by Alcuin's resourcefulness, but now I had bigger things to think about — like how to make contact with a boy who didn't speak. I trusted that Alcuin would get us inside, but facing Joshua Smart, and getting him to open up to a complete stranger didn't seem likely. Why was I attempting the impossible?

Wanting to improve my odds, I reviewed the plan with Alcuin. He would teleport me to the facility. He'd already figured out a way around the guards. I didn't ask how, because part of me was scared to know the answer. All I wanted was Alcuin to get me in and back out uninjured.

There were no hitches getting in. We landed in a long hallway; steel doors with barred windows lined both sides. Alcuin raised a finger to his lips and tilted his head to the left.

A young man in a security uniform sat behind a small desk at the hallway's end. He was hunched over a laptop screen. With his typical boldness, Alcuin stepped into his line of vision. The security guard registered Alcuin's presence and staggered to his feet. "Stop! Don't move."

His eyes darted between Alcuin and a nearby exit. Rather than flee, he scooted around the desk to face Alcuin, pulled out his weapon and raised it, his hand shaking. "What are you doing here?"

"I'd like to visit one of your patients," Alcuin said, as if similar requests happened every night in this fashion.

I almost laughed at the guard's bewildered expression. He glanced at his watch.

In that second Alcuin gripped him around the neck. I

I Kissed a Dog

couldn't hear what he whispered, but it got the guy's attention. He bobbed his head as Alcuin relaxed his hold and moved to face him. They stood eye to eye.

I couldn't help feeling sorry for the kid; after all, that's all he was. I guessed him to be about twenty-one, twenty two. This was probably his first job out of college. I'm sure he never expected to see a fanged-man on the psych ward. Though he'd more than likely met a few patients who believed they could sprout fangs.

Alcuin spoke loud enough for me to hear from my position in the shadows. "What's your name, young man?

"Randy Miller, Sir."

"Mr. Randy Miller, I need you to unlock Joshua Smart's door. I understand he is on this ward. Is that correct?"

"Yes Sir, but he doesn't talk." Randy stared blankly at Alcuin. Vamp mind magic at its best. I decided hiding was no longer necessary and stepped into the corridor.

"Chloe, no!" he ordered, losing control of Randy, who jumped sideways. Alcuin snatched him back by the collar and once again stared into his widened eyes. "Randy, you will not do that again, will you?"

"No, Sir."

"Good boy. You are unable to move or speak without my permission. No matter what happens you will remain at your post. You will do nothing." Randy straightened his shoulders and walked like a robot to his desk.

Alcuin flashed to stand in front of me. "The cameras, I can keep myself from being videotaped, but you don't have that luxury. Everything's being operated by the laptop. I'll need a minute to delete you from the tape and get the room information."

I waited, trying to stay patient under the circumstances. With his vampire speed and abilities, he solved the problems and was rewarded by a door's lock disengaging with a loud clank. "Are you ready?" His eyes met mine.

"How much time do we have?" Not knowing what Alcuin had arranged left me at a disadvantage. This would be my only opportunity to talk with a human eyewitness who'd actually seen the killers. I hoped I had enough time.

I couldn't screw it up.

Twenty-One

I swallowed the urge to cry as my eyes adjusted to the near nonexistent lighting in Joshua Smart's room. The fact that his living space was well-furnished and immaculate couldn't conceal its cell-like atmosphere.

But it wasn't the surroundings that prompted my tears, it was the boy.

Imagining him as a laughing, energetic, baseball player was no longer possible. He resembled a ghost, trapped in a human shell, unable to escape his anguish. His eyes were glazed and unseeing, yet, at the same time, seemed glued to an empty chair below the room's sole window, a window protected by bars.

Uneasy, I found myself staring at the chair wondering if he was envisioning someone or *something* seated there. My fear level amplified, pushing me closer to my own personal fright limit.

Alcuin had advised that I leave the door open. I struggled with his suggestion, but decided to compromise. I pushed the heavy door into the halfway position, allowing us privacy while leaving a quick escape route.

The boy was lost in a trance, or another dimension that I was unlikely to access in the short time we had together. If the last news reports were accurate, not even the best specialists had been able to communicate with the Smart boy.

Maybe I should have stayed in Plum Beach with Zane. At least there I'd felt semi-safe.

No. No. No. I would not allow Zane to invade my thoughts. Just thinking about him made my heart tighten. I never knew a broken heart could hurt so much.

Get a grip, Chloe! Pay attention to that boy. He needs you. Zane can take care of himself. My mental motivation did the trick, and I refocused my attention on the task at hand.

I took a seat in the chair.

During my quick appraisal of Joshua's room, he'd not once looked away from his beloved chair. It was if he'd been waiting centuries for a very specific guest to arrive.

He'd have to settle for me.

"Hi. I'm Chloe." I searched his face for a visual response — a twitch, blink, or movement of any kind — nothing. "I'm sorry about your dad, and I know you saw something that night, something scary. You tried to tell the police about it and they didn't believe you, did they?" I paused, hoping for a miracle and some sign that I was correct about him knowing more than he'd first let on.

He blinked once, twice — the third time his eyes stayed opened.

They locked on me.

All I could do was stare back. I hadn't expected him to respond, yet, here he was, clear-eyed and waiting for me to continue.

"Joshua, can you understand me?" The question slipped

I Kissed a Dog

out before I realized how demeaning it might sound. The kid was traumatized not an idiot. "Sorry. I'm just so glad you're okay."

He scooted to the edge of his bed and grinned, a boy-smile that warmed my heart. I let my mask of concern drop and replaced it with my brightest smile. "It's great to see you smile."

Curious, he looked at me. "Chloe?"

I kept smiling, not sure where to start now that I had his undivided attention.

"You're the first person to talk to me like you believe me. I'm not crazy like my mom thinks I am. She won't even visit." His gaze dropped to his lap where he twisted his hands.

"I'm sorry to hear that, and I'm sorry to rush you, but I don't have much time. Can you tell me what you saw that night?" I doubted he needed me to verify which night I was referring to.

He looked up. "Sure. I'll never forget it. I got home after my game. When I walked in the door, I smelled something awful. Like wet dog, urine, and a pot full of pennies."

Blood and mutant body odor; smells I'd prefer to avoid in the future.

"Did you see a woman?" I pressed, growing more anxious about the time.

"I found my dad …" he gulped. "I guess I was in shock, because after finding him, I started to think I was in a nightmare. I thought I was dreaming.

The sliding door off dad's bedroom was knocked out, into the backyard. When I looked, this is the weird part — I saw what looked like a wolfman from the old horror movies, and the back of a woman disappearing into the trees. She had pretty red hair. I don't know why I noticed that. My dad's all torn up and I'm admiring some lady's hair." He hung his head again.

I wasn't sure what to say, but I couldn't just let him shoulder all that shame. "You know shock does mess with a person's mind. Believe me, I know. The red hair was the one pretty thing in the picture. It's not surprising you noticed it."

His eyes met mine and he gave me the sweetest smile. It was obvious our conversation was doing wonders for his mental health, far more than the psychiatrists and their medications had accomplished. He just needed someone to listen to his story and believe it.

Like Joshua, I understood how hard it was not to blurt out the truth to anyone willing to listen. I was also aware that if I decided to open up about my own supernatural situation, I'd be in a room just like Joshua's in some comparable adult facility.

Society didn't take kindly to people who spouted off about vampires, werewolves, and witches. On the other hand, vampires, werewolves, and witches didn't appreciate blabbering humans spilling their secrets. Talk about feeling nuts with no one to tell.

"Why won't my mom see me? She acted so weird after dad's murder. Not sad, just strange. Like she knew I was telling the truth but didn't want to hear it."

I felt like kicking his mom's ass. I'd already added finding out what her problem was to my list of things to accomplish. This kid didn't belong here, nor did he deserve to be left alone like this.

I Kissed a Dog

Not used to playing the mother role, I forced myself to get up and walk the few short steps to Joshua's bed. I surrounded his small frame with my arms. He stiffened at first, and then collapsed against me. He did what I'd expect any kid in his position to do: he cried.

For one brief moment, I considered taking him with me, but wasn't sure that would be the safest option. If his mom was somehow involved, maybe he was better off here.

"Joshua, I want to bring you with me, but it might be best for you stay here, just for awhile. I promise I'll get you out. Start talking with people; just don't talk about the monster. We know it's real, but they don't. Eventually, they'll see your improvement and release you."

I didn't know how much to say about my other worry, but I had to warn him. "If your mom asks again about what you saw, tell her it must have been a bad dream. I'm not sure you can trust her. I'm so sorry."

I waited for more tears, surprised when he squared his shoulders. His expression turned stern, and his lips tightened into a thin line. "I already wondered about that. I'll be careful. Don't worry." He patted my leg like a parent consoling a child. "Oh! I almost forgot. The night after my dad died, a funny looking guy in a weird cloak-thingy came into my room. He gave me something, a note. I couldn't read it."

I raised my eyebrows. The kid was intelligent, so he not being able to read didn't add up. Then it hit me. *And who's the slow one? It's in a foreign language, like the coins.*

I tried to contain my excitement, afraid to get my hopes up. "Do you have it here?"

He was already facing a dresser in the corner. "They let me

bring a couple of books and my journal. I have all kinds of notes and doodles inside. When they searched my things, they must have thought the paper was just another drawing I'd shoved in my book." He flipped through the worn notebook. "Here!" He handed me the paper. "I hope this helps."

"I'm sure it will. I better go. Remember, be careful. I'll find a way to get you out of here. Now write down these names in your journal: Zane, Logan, A-l-c-u-i-n …" I spelled out. "Misty, Mack, and Michael. Only leave with one of them if I don't come. No. One. Else."

He nodded, his face flushed. I knew right then that he'd be okay.

"Chloe!" Alcuin hissed. "Now!"

I stuffed the paper in my back pocket and gave Joshua a quick hug, at the same time an alarm's siren pierced the calm. A stampede of footsteps pounded in the distance, coming fast.

Without a backward glance, I rushed into the hallway, pulling the door shut. Alcuin flashed to my side and grabbed my wrist. We fazed before I could protest.

"You sure know how to push the limits, Doll."

"Don't call me, doll!" I quipped, relieved to find myself standing in my hotel room.

Alcuin paced to the window, pulling the curtain aside. "That was way too close. You could have been caught, killed even."

"Killed? At a state hospital for children?" For once I thought my vampire protector was overreacting.

Dropping the curtain, he spun to face me. "You may not have noticed, but that was a pretty isolated location, and

I Kissed a Dog

there were men with guns, big guns, not just handguns like Hall Monitor Randy was using. Some of those kids are criminally insane. I got a look inside their minds. I'm a bloodsucking vampire, and even I didn't like what I saw."

For once I was glad I couldn't read human minds.

I didn't want the responsibility of deciding what to do with criminals, children or not. Animals and a few supernatural minds were plenty for me. What bothered me was Alcuin. My never-show-emotion vampire was reaching a breakdown level. He seemed worried about my wellbeing.

"You care about a human," I teased, shocked by this latest development.

He looked appalled. "What human might that be?"

"I think you know."

Rather than bothering to respond, he launched into a detailed explanation of how the additional security force had uncovered the breach he'd managed to create. With no intention of returning in the near future, I wasn't too alarmed. When it came time to free Joshua, I'd worry about the details. Until then, I had way too much on my mind — like the latest message from my new best friend — the ugly man — David.

I pulled the folded paper from my pocket and handed to Alcuin. He spent a good hour examining the letter, with no results and fewer comments. We decided it would be best for him to take it back to Plum Beach and have Rita and the others examine it. From what we could tell, it was the same ancient language engraved on the coins.

It was close to midnight when Alcuin made his usual dramatic exit, leaving me alone in the hotel room. As promised, he again pledged to keep my whereabouts private. For a brief moment, I'd considered returning with him, but was unsure how to handle the situation with Zane.

I felt angry, hurt, confused, and a ton of other unproductive and unpleasant emotions. I'd wanted time to think about accepting the mating mark, and I planned to take that time.

I was no longer sure that Zane would still want me as his mate or wife.

Luke had given me the week's remaining days off. For the first time ever, I had nowhere I needed to be in the morning. The guys could handle things back home without me. My riff with Zane would serve as a distraction for everyone involved. Staying away for another day would give him time to cool off and focus on the latest evidence.

As far as I knew, there were no new animals on my need-to-interview list at the park, and I wanted to see my parents. I hated the way we'd left things. Going home without a personal visit would be just plain rude. The person I wanted to be rude to was Zane, and Jazmine, *and* Rhonda.

So I had a few bones to pick.

What twenty-four year old female didn't have conflicts?

Several hours of fitful sleep were all I could handle.

Disturbing thoughts of Joshua Smart, Zane, and the Plum Beach murder mystery battered my mind like an aerial bombing attack. I'd even had an erotically charged dream about Valamir. Sleeping was out of the question given I couldn't seem to find the off-switch for my mind.

It was 4:02 AM on Tuesday. I wondered if Zane was still

asleep. Ignoring the urge to check his mental status, I made a pot of gourmet hotel coffee, and flipped open my laptop. I'd already mapped out my day. For starters, I'd spend a few early morning hours researching ancient languages to see if I recognized anything, and then, a long hot shower prior to checking out.

Before giving the paper to Alcuin last night, I'd taken a few minutes to appraise the document. I'd even traced some of the symbols. Even a research novice was capable of conducting a simple online search. Maybe I'd get lucky. It was about time one of us did.

Following my shower, I intended to indulge in a hot breakfast before heading to Troutdale and my parents. Mom had used her new texting talents to inform me they'd returned home ahead of schedule, no doubt thanks to Alcuin's assistance. I was torn between calling head of my arrival, and surprising them. For now, I was leaning toward the big surprise.

Bob worked the first shift. He'd always been an early riser and a hardcore workaholic, much to my mother's ongoing consternation. With him gone, I'd have some time alone with her. We needed to talk candidly. Something neither of us excelled at.

I sat on the bed's edge debating whether or not I should prop some pillows against the headboard and get to work, or set up my laptop at the elegant desk in the corner. Unable to motivate myself into action, I rearranged my schedule and moved my shower up to the number one spot.

With the hot water pounding on my aching shoulders, I relaxed. The shampoo's flowery blend provided a soothing aroma therapy session. I ran my hands down my squeaking hair, feeling like the first *Breck Girl* in action. I'd done a research project on her commercial history in my high school drama class, not something I made a regular practice of reminiscing about. I was also contemplating the possibility of switching the water flow and filling the tub. A bath sounded even more tantalizing.

A few minutes later, feeling grateful for the hotel's supersized hot water tank, I sunk into liquid warmth, letting the water envelop every last inch of me; just my face remained exposed.

As a child, my always-anxious mother had made sure to check in on me every five minutes during bath time, afraid I'd fall asleep and drown. Her fear about drowning was valid, but not in the context she'd envisioned. I doubted her paranoia had extended all the way to my fifteenth birthday, and my near-deadly dip in that stranger's freezing pool.

Even in the heat, I shivered at the memory. Pushing the thoughts of that horrible day aside was simple enough, but they were replaced by searing visions of Zane. Why couldn't I stop thinking about him? Sure he was my husband, but ….

The time we'd made love I was in a drunken stupor. Although the few romantic moments we'd since shared were well worth remembering, and repeating.

A loud thump startled me. I pulled myself out of water. What in the world? So far, the hotel had proven to be pretty much soundproof.

Feeling vulnerable, I was anxious to dress.

I rose hastily and stepped from the tub, further chilled by the rivulets of water cascading from my thick curls, leaving icy trails all the way to my feet. Normally, to avoid this unpleasant sensation, I wrapped my hair in a towel right away. But for some reason, all I wanted to do was to cover up. I cocooned myself inside an oversized towel and tiptoed to the bathroom door.

I peered into the suite. *You're being ridiculous! Get a grip!* I scolded myself. Every bump wasn't the boogie man.

This time it was the boogie girl.

The infamous redhead was stretched across on my bed, and two, very large, suit-clad-men, mutants, I suspected, in their human forms, stood impassively by the door.

I hugged my towel tighter and fought the familiar fainting feeling. I refused to tumble over, knowing I'd land in a powerless and naked heap on the floor, without Zane to soften the fall.

Twisting into a sitting position, my tied-for-first-place, worst-enemy-ever, broke the silence. "Well, well, Chloe. We meet at last," she said sounding like a typical movie villain.

Terrified, I took a step back.

A rapidly forming plan featured me hiding in the bathroom. Problem, I had no idea what I'd do next. I considered melting her mind like I'd done to the mutants at the cabin, but without her, I'd lose my greatest link to the Plum Beach murders.

I wasn't even sure my powers would work on a purebred. So far I'd only been able to override mutant minds. What if I tried and failed?

I'd be the one dead on the floor.

Keeping my eyes locked on hers, I took another tentative step.

"Don't bother. We'll just break the door down, and I can't guarantee you won't get," she paused for effect, "hurt."

Her warning worked. I wasn't moving an inch in any direction.

"That's a good girl. And to show you that I'm not a complete bitch, I'm going to have my men face the door so you can get dressed. Just ignore me. Us girls have all the same parts anyway." She raised her brow daring me to refuse.

The men complied without further prompting, giving me a close up view of their football-player-shoulders. Any last minute fantasy of somehow getting past the two of them was doused like a flame underwater. They'd tackle me or toss me aside. Neither option tempted.

The woman scowled. "Any reason you're not moving?"

That was all it took. I sprang into action.

Ignoring her smug expression, I tried to dress as discreetly as my towel allowed; all the while wondering what of use I could rescue from my belongings without her noticing. My purse was on the floor by the bed. There was no way she'd let me bring that a long.

What kidnapper allowed their captive to pack? — Apparently mine.

"Pack up and leave your cardkey on the desk. Everyone will just assume you checked out and took off on your own.

She'd made a good point.

Two people knew my whereabouts — Luke and Alcuin. Only *one* person, if I wanted to get technical. And one vampire. I'd slammed the door on my supernatural support system.

For the first time, I found myself hoping one of my sneaky sidekicks would betray my confidence and tell Zane and the others what I was up to. But I'd have to presume otherwise and act accordingly. I could no longer see myself as a victim of circumstances, especially since I'd insisted to Zane, on more than one occasion, I wasn't some disaster-prone damsel in distress.

If I intended to survive, I needed to get and stay one step ahead of my captors. My powers could provide that extra edge.

One problem: I'd always found it tricky to do multiple activities while listening in on an animal's thoughts. That would have to change. To my benefit, the gift had been expanding every day, and I believed the growth-trend would continue. Believing in me and my capabilities was essential. Without faith in my talents, the woman I despised as much as Jazmine would ensure I died a humiliating and gruesome death.

It was time to push through any self-imposed limits and stay alive. I had to be ready to climb through any window of opportunity, no matter how brief or unexpected.

To my amazement, the first window opened following my personal pep talk.

"I told you! Back to the girl!" the woman barked, whirling to face her two flunkies, giving me a blink of time to shove the traced symbols into the pocket of my jeans.

I made a show of shimmying into the stretchy denim, wiggling my hips like I'd seen Rhonda do more times than I cared to remember. Things had to be bad if I was looking to archenemy number three for survival skills.

The men, being true dogs, sensed my seductive antics, and whipped their heads around. I wouldn't have been surprised to see them panting.

What did surprise me was Ms. Redhead's brutal response.

She vibrated and turned full werewolf with a roar. She'd taken the form I found most repulsive and fearsome, sending me back to the bloody fight in the forest, where I'd seen Zane in the very same shape — on two legs — looking like a half man half beast monstrosity. Eyes crimson with malicious intent.

Her guards dropped to the floor and rolled on their backs, arms and legs up, resigning themselves to her ruling rank.

I swallowed the urge to laugh.

As horrifying as the scene was, the image of two grown, massive men, flat on their backs, submitting to a woman, werewolf or not, would stay with me forever.

Wait! What the …? One orangey pile of something was dangling from the bed.

Her hair! My female captor, in her haste, had changed so fast, she'd torn right out of her clothing like Misty in Vegas. In this case, Ms. Werewolf had also lost her hair.

A wig.

Sensing my appraisal, she swung her massive head around to glare at me. Salvia trickled from the corners of her elongated snout. Although notably smaller than Zane, she was no less imposing.

Her eyes stretched into narrow slits and her horrible lips curled into a feral grin. There was no mistaking that like Jazmine, she detested me.

In some strange way, I could understand Jazmine's feelings, as misplaced as they were. She wanted something I had; at least I'd *had* Zane. I wasn't so sure now. What this beast wanted was yet to be determined.

My stomach constricted, and an unexpected jolt of fear

punched through my midsection. What if I'd lost Zane? *Get a grip! This is no time to ponder bad love gone good ... gone bad.*

I forced myself to stand taller and stared back, not quite sure what I hoped to accomplish by my challenging attitude.

She didn't take well to my unexpected display of bravery.

Asserting her dominance, she growled her threat, running her tongue over the sharpest teeth I'd seen in such proximity.

I closed my eyes, waiting for the canines to shred my throat.

Unlike Valamir's blissful bites, I could expect no pleasure from the rabid she wolf, just excruciating pain. I felt sorry for whoever would get stuck cleaning up my mess, bloody entrails and all.

She still doesn't get it. Stupid stupid human.

Impossible! I was on the verge of a bloody and demoralizing death. It couldn't be another open window this soon. Yet here she was broadcasting her thoughts out in the open for any halfway decent, animal-mind-reader to overhear.

The area around us quivered. I knew then she was shifting back, and allowed myself one huge sigh of relief. Though later, I'd realize I should have waited to rejoice.

With simple curiosity getting the best of me, my eyes opened, seemingly without my permission. I had to know, had to see her face minus the flowing amber wig.

My internal warning bells started tolling the minute I registered her striking and familiar features: The exotic face; the stylish geometrical hairstyle; the commanding presence.

A teeth-chattering chill wound up from the base of my neck down to my finger tips.

I was looking into the icy eyes of one very pissed off purebred she wolf.

Jazmine.

Twenty-Two

"You?" was all I managed, bewildered by the startling turn of events. I wished I could say it all made sense now, but, in truth, I was even more baffled.

The thing I knew for certain: Jazmine and the redheaded-woman were one in the same. Not two separate entities. One. One evil bitch bent on my destruction, and only God knew what else.

Her escorts, now back on their feet, had moved to either side of Jazmine. The two of them, together, could defeat her in combat. So why were they submitting to such castrating treatment? They were at least double her size, but cowered when she blinked. She wielded a powerful hold over them. I needed to find out what fueled her unchallenged authority.

"Finish packing," she ordered, her eyes shooting daggers my direction. "We have someone to meet." She continued to stand — bare ass naked — like it was the most natural thing in the world to carry on a conversation in-the-buff.

The men didn't seem to mind, although they made a point of keeping their eyes diverted, glancing rarely at their mistress. She appeared not to notice, though I expected she enjoyed

I Kissed a Dog

tempting them. Look, but don't let me *catch* you looking. Touch, and I'll kill you — double messages to die for.

I couldn't help thinking that with a body like hers, I just might consider parading around naked too; although chitchatting with an enemy while undressed, not my style, no matter how luscious my curves.

Jazmine snapped her fingers and the tallest guard pulled a bag from under the desk. She snatched up her wig from the floor by the bed where it had fallen. It needed some serious grooming.

The detestable mutant duo must have anticipated her need for new clothing and packed accordingly. From what I'd observed, werewolves had serious anger issues. They were impulsive too. No wonder she had to carry double the outfits wherever she went. Every temper tantrum would require fresh, non-tattered attire.

I couldn't think about Jazmine's anger issues without my thoughts returning to Zane. I hoped again that he wouldn't let his anger shut me out. I needed him now more than ever, especially since I was uncertain that anyone but Zane, or maybe Logan, could deal with Jazmine. She was a real live menace, naked or not.

As she dressed, I finished packing and was able to stuff my cell phone inside my bra without drawing attention, thanks to a little trick I'd used in high school to avoid my stepdad's detection. Bob had been prone to purse checks, for my own good, of course. He didn't think cell phones were appropriate until adulthood. One evening, he'd caught on to my charade when my shirt started rumbling.

This time, if I remembered right, I'd left my current phone

on the silent mode following the jaunt to Joshua Smart's mental hospital. And to my benefit, my captors were not nearly as attentive as I'd anticipated. I'd already confiscated two items of importance. I wasn't sure how or when I'd use them, but if windows kept opening, I'd keep crawling through.

"Give your bag to the guys." Jasmine ordered, again looking her impeccable self.

With the wig in place, she gathered the shredded pieces of her former outfit and stuffed them in her expensive tote. She checked the bathroom, looked under the bed, in the trash baskets, and closets. "Nothing left. Let's go." She dismissed me with rude hand gesture.

The tallest mutant picked up her carrier and collected my bag too, leaving the number two flunky to open the door.

Jazmine stepped through, hesitated, then whirled back to face me. "Here are the rules. You will act like a normal human heading out for some morning sightseeing. Bradley will make sure your car is returned to the appropriate rental retailer and we'll ride in the limo."

"One little warning," she lowered her voice. "Don't try anything out of the ordinary that might draw attention to us. I'd prefer not to kill you, but don't doubt that I will. I want you away from my future mate, understand? But from what I've heard, you might be useful to have around."

I nodded, hoping I looked agreeable.

It was a good thing she couldn't hear *my* thoughts. Because there was no way I'd step aside for her to claim my husband, regardless of our current unspeaking and un-mind-reading status. I loved him. I'd determined that much.

She also knew something about my abilities. I wasn't sure how, or from whom she'd gathered her information, or how she'd even located me. I hoped that her earlier mental blunder was evidence that she still lacked a full understanding of my capabilities. As long as she didn't know I could read *her* thoughts, there remained another possible window for me to escape through. I'd take all the windows of opportunity I could get.

We made it to the limo without incident. Bradley sped away in the car I'd been so eager to drive to my parents. Relaxed against the plush leather seat, Jasmine kicked off her shoes and leaned forward. "I'm sure you understand that Zane is mine regardless of your one-night-stand-wedding. We've been pledged to each other since we were pups. It's critical we're mated. He is the rightful alpha, you know?" She said pausing to peer at her fingernails.

Hoping to hide my surprise, I nodded again. Hadn't I privately questioned Zane's beta position?

I quickly assessed that Jazmine didn't expect me to answer, nor did she give a damn about anything I might say. I was safe for the moment so I allowed myself the luxury of pondering Zane's heritage.

His birthright should have secured him the alpha's lead role in the Pacific Pack. Not that Logan was unqualified. In fact, he was quite the opposite. But there was a certain something about Zane that gave him an edge over the current alpha. Maybe it was his bloodline. Or maybe there was more to the picture than I was letting myself see.

As we sped across the Markham Bridge, following the signs north to Seattle, Jazmine decided, much to my displeasure, to continue our conversation.

"Zane always was concerned about our mutant cousins roaming in human territory without more accountability from the purebreds.

At one point, when his father was preparing to pass him the torch, so to speak, Zane refused to accept. He wanted reconciliation between us and the mutants. The Indians were having no part of it. Most of us were skeptical too. How could we integrate with a subspecies?"

Now I was even more baffled. "I don't understand. You created the mutants, and as you said, they're like relatives. Why all the animosity? Couldn't you have just taught them better table manners?"

She exploded into giggles. So loud, the driver heard through the glass partition and scowled in his rearview mirror. His response led me to believe he was an unsuspecting human, but I couldn't be certain. Jazmine's guard, on the other hand, remained stone-faced by her side.

Staring at the mutant's blank features, I realized that although I'd just discovered the supernatural world, I'd already formed some clear-cut opinions. First of all, after meeting Stryder, I'd accepted that not all mutants were bad. They weren't so different from their purebred counterparts.

The most important discovery: I couldn't tell the good guys from the bad ones based on species alone. Just as humans were prone to prejudice and intolerance, so were the supes.

I wasn't sure why I was so shocked by this latest revelation, but I was. Knowing I could categorize the creatures I met based on their species had made certain groups seem less threatening. Now, all the so-called distinguishing characteristics were blurred. Everything was grey. Bad guys, good guys … it all depended on whose side you were on any given day.

I Kissed a Dog

Making that vital distinction would take far more effort on my part.

As a child, I'd asked my mom why everyone couldn't just get along regardless of any differences. By the time I hit seventh grade, I'd found my answer. People could be mean. They could be downright nasty and cruel.

Religion, race, political views, how much money you had in the bank, where you worked, lived, whatever, all had the potential to serve as dividing lines. Add a whole world of supernatural beings to the mix, and things got even more divisive. Who or what was on my side?

"Deep thoughts, dear," Jazmine crooned. "Care to share? I'm not as bad as you might think. "

I almost laughed. Her attempts at sounding motherly and reassuring fell way short given all I knew. Mothering murderers didn't fit with my idea of a good guy, or girl, period. Nothing Jazmine did or said would convince me otherwise, but I couldn't help my curiosity. Maybe she'd reveal something important if she kept talking.

I smiled and made a beeline into her thoughts, where I expected to find some diabolical plan forming.

What does Zane see in this creature? She's dimwitted. Kind of cute, but too much butt.

Too much butt? I was sitting across from a psychotic werewolf woman and she was thinking about my fanny. As for the dimwitted comment ...

"So you can talk to farm animals?" she asked out of nowhere.

I stayed silent, unsure what I wanted to tell her about my talents.

"Not answering isn't an option. You're my prisoner. Don't let the surroundings fool you."

Noting the flash of scarlet in her eyes, I decided to keep it simple. "I don't talk, not really. I listen or see pictures and sounds." Had she asked the same question a week ago, my answer would have been the truth. Now I could do a whole bunch of other nifty stuff that I would die before revealing.

Unfortunate for me, knowing her violent tendencies, death was a likely reality. But I planned to prolong my survival for as long as possible.

"All animals?"

Taking a more playful tone, I joked, "Farm animals, domestic animals, and wild animals."

"I hate to say it, but I'm impressed."

Following her impromptu compliment, the remaining drive passed in silence. Jazmine spent her time flipping through bridal magazines and daydreaming about her wedding dress and what she mentally referred to as mating with Zane. She seemed to regard my marriage to Zane as an incidental incident, easily rectified.

Sickened by the graphic images of her imagined honeymoon activities, I sent my mental tentacles out, away from Jazmine, seeking *my husband*. I'd never been successful making contact with someone hundreds of miles away, but I had to try.

I was frustrated to find that even with all the recent advances in my abilities, I still couldn't communicate at this distance. We were almost to Seattle. Zane was a good eight hours southwest. I guessed he was out of range. Though I couldn't be certain he'd open his mind to me even if I could reach him.

I Kissed a Dog

After attempting to reach Michael, Mack, and then Stryder, I gave up on my search and gave in to the fear nipping at my thoughts, tormenting me with the endless possibilities of brutality that might lie ahead. My exhaustion finally overrode my fear, and I dozed off, just to be awakened a short time later when the limo skidded to a stop, jolting me sideways.

With my eyes still closed, I determined that I'd been blindfolded during my nap. Automatically, I reached for the offensive fabric blocking my vision.

"No. No. Hands off. Just be thankful you were sleeping. We waited until the last possible moment before putting it on," Jazmine said.

With my head still fuzzy from sleep, I snipped before thinking about the potential consequences. "Aren't you the nice and polite kidnapper? I'll make sure to keep notes on how to treat my future enemies." I didn't need my eyes open to sneer.

Unable to see her reaction, I pushed into her mind.

What an ungrateful bitch. She should be thankful. Maybe I'll torture her later, but I've got to lure Zane here. We'll watch her die together, as mates.

Tempted to respond to her thoughts, I bit my tongue.

"Get her into the dorm and put her in the lower hall. Maybe then she'll understand the importance of pleasing me."

Once again, my mouth had earned me the wrath of another person … a werewolf. Why couldn't I swallow my sarcasm? Now I was headed to some horrible place created for the worst of their prisoners. I didn't do well camping, and I was doubtful I'd survive in some dirty, dank hole.

Deciding it was best not to stir up any additional trouble, I allowed myself to be steered from the limo. I launched more mental probes and discovered I was surrounded by were creatures, primarily mutants from what I could tell.

Without the use of my eyes, I confirmed what I'd noticed before, werewolves and mutants smelled different. Over all, the mutants didn't smell badly, just odd. I still couldn't understand why Jazmine, a purebred werewolf, was hanging out with the mutants she hated.

The more I found out the less I knew. Not a great formula for solving a mystery or saving my life. At least if her last thoughts were accurate, I had some time before she reduced me to a bloody pulp.

She intended to use me as bait — for Zane.

The problem with her plan was the simple fact that Zane was furious with me. Furious enough to leave me to Jazmine's whims?

I'd know soon enough.

I detected the minute we entered a building. The lingering scent of flowers was replaced by the stale, sweat-tinged odor of too many people crowded together.

My blindfold was yanked off, getting caught for one agonizing moment in my tangled curls. "Ouch!" I yelped. "You don't have to be so rough."

Jazmine trilled. A sound that sent shivers down my spine.

Her laughter was minus even a hint of happiness. Rather it rang with perverse pleasure over my discomfort. I figured her attempts at niceties were long over. Part of me was glad. I was tired of playing games with a serial killer who was lusting after my husband.

She grasped my chin in her hand, forcing my face within an inch of hers. "Rhonda mentioned you had a sarcastic streak. She also said you were used to getting what you wanted. I can relate to that. I always get what I want. Which means, you won't." She flicked my chin, hard, before tugging me into a headlock.

Opposed to violence, I was shocked to find my mind reeling with ways to snap the offending finger right off her hand. Revenge, one thing I'd always avoided and discouraged others from enacting, had never looked sweeter.

A crowd had formed, distracting me from my vengeful thoughts. They were watching us, some licking their lips, anticipating more violence.

With my head secured in Jasmine's grip, I could see those standing behind her. They were all women. Attractive women dressed in tan uniforms. There were girls as young as twelve or thirteen and women in their fifties, maybe older.

Their commonality was their beauty.

I remembered my vow at the hotel — stop being a victim.

I'd conveniently forgotten somewhere along the way that dumping the victim role didn't equal being reckless. I was just too tired of Jazmine's abuse to refrain from spouting off more careless words. "You won't get Zane. He loves me. You can't force him to love you, can you, Jazmine? Can you?"

The change came without warning. I barely sensed the vibration before her clothing blasted in every direction.

A black bra strap snapped against my cheek as it sailed by. Jazmine landed on all fours in full wolf form. She circled, snarling and snapping, her gums trembled, drawing my gaze to her razor-sharp canines. I recalled in that instant that wolves had forty-two teeth, and I was pretty damn sure I was getting a good view of most of them.

The ring of surrounding women stepped back. Some had their backs pressed against the concrete walls. They looked as terrified as I felt.

"No!" A male voice shouted. "Honey, please, settle down."

She swung her head in the direction of his voice. Martin, the least-trusted elder, from yesterday's board meeting, pushed through the growing crowd of females. His faithful German Shepherd on his heels.

Although somewhat startled by his appearance, I wasn't that surprised. His dog had already revealed Martin's connection to the redheaded woman — Jazmine. I was still having a hard time accepting they were the same heartless woman.

The regal charcoal wolf she'd become whined, her attention now on the man.

"Remember our goals. You wanted her alive. We have too much at stake," Martin soothed. "Let's get you a hot bath."

She nodded her massive head and turned one last time to glare at me before trotting away at his side. The minute she was out of sight, several women hurried to collect what was left of her clothing. They understood what was expected of them.

I realized then that another window-of-opportunity had opened wide. No one seemed interested in me, and the red wig was splayed across my feet.

Taking advantage of my latest window, I reached down and made a show of massaging my calves while stuffing the tangled mess up the pant leg of my jeans, thankful I wasn't wearing one of my skinny-legged pairs.

I Kissed a Dog

Curious, several women continued to stare at me. I rubbed my legs and rotated my hips from side to side before returning to an upright position. I kneaded my lower back and grimaced.

"Are you okay?" A blonde asked, her striking blue eyes mirroring concern.

"Stiff. Too much tension I guess." I rotated my shoulders.

Her eyes moved from my face and darted around the lobby. She started to speak, but grimaced instead when Jazmine's two musclemen rounded the corner, flanking me. Each grasped an elbow, squeezing harder than the situation warranted.

The blonde woman dropped her head to stare at the floor, avoiding any further eye contact.

I was more than irritated by the men's' intimidating attitudes. "Stop it! You're hurting me!" I snapped. Not only was I annoyed, but I was also getting sick and tired of being manhandled and bossed around. I wanted my old life back. And if that wasn't possible, I wanted to at least hear what the blonde had to say and adjust my plans if necessary.

"You're lucky The Mistress didn't ..." the tallest drew his fingernail across his jugular, adding semi-realistic gurgling effects.

"Wow. So mature," I muttered. Despite their physical prowess, these guys were lacking in the intelligence department.

Several women smiled, encouraging me. One slapped a hand over her mouth, forcing what might have been laughter into submission. The majority still looked shaken, and a few appeared alarmed by the situation. I couldn't wait to find out why they were being held.

Ignoring my last remarks, my terrifying tour guides steered me down a long corridor. The tall rude mutant, on my left, was without doubt leaving imprints where his fingers pressed mercilessly into my upper arm.

I tried once to pull free, but he tightened his grip in retaliation. Between the throbbing in my arm and the wig tickling my leg, walking wasn't easy. Trying my best to ignore these inconveniences, I surveyed my surroundings, searching for any possible escape route.

What I saw did little to increase my confidence.

We were trapped in what appeared to be an abandoned school.

Each passing door had a window, and I could see more women. Some were resting inside what looked like classrooms turned dormitories. Others were seated at sewing machines. Several classrooms were filled with supplies, weapons, and canned food. The place reminded me of a women's minimum security prison combined with a survival training camp of some sort. Cameras were mounted above us, red lights blinking as they monitored our movements. Throughout the hallways, men patrolled with assault rifles resting on their shoulders.

This building was not escape friendly. I'd have my work cut out for me. I needed some major help — supernatural help.

From my brief observations, I'd determined that most of the women were scared, and they also appeared unhappy with their circumstances. If I could gather enough support for my cause, we could overthrow Jazmine and her crew. There were more than enough weapons to go around.

At the passages end, a staircase wound downward.

I Kissed a Dog

Fantastic. This had to be the way to my new home in the lower hallway

Forcing my feet together, I refused to take another step without first testing the loyalty of Jazmine's closest sidekicks. "Why do you listen to Jazmine? She's just using you. You could fight back like real men, you know."

"And why would we want to do that?" Mr. Tight Grip said, digging his fingers deeper into my flesh. I winced, and a little whimper escaped my mouth.

"Because she's a lying bitch," I managed to hiss through gritted teeth.

"Man, let up on her arm," my right-sided captor commanded. He released my arm, taking a long step back. I knew what was going to happen next.

Since mutants no longer required a full moon to shift, I'd guessed right.

In what seemed like slow motion, his snout elongated and his body expanded, sprouting patches of fur in the process. Fingers became razor sharp claws, and his mouth filled with jagged fangs. I wasn't sure how, but unlike the purebreds, his clothing stayed on, sort of. They were ripped and tattered like the Incredible Hulk's after his transmutation.

Instead of shifting, his taller counterpart, whipped out his sidearm and a crackle of gunfire followed, pulverizing my defender's chest. He stumbled and tottered before plummeting backward, furry arms flailing but failing to stop his fall.

What felt like a small earthquake rocked the concrete floor, causing me to topple forward. I landed with a thud next to the bloodied mutant. The holes in his chest were more than bleeding; they were smoking. Silver — of course — the one thing that could kill both werewolves and mutants.

"Listen," with a gurgling, wet sound the fallen creature managed to whisper.

I leaned forward, pressing my ear to his snout. Afraid he might not finish, I plunged, without permission, into what were surely his last thoughts. *I'm in your mind. Think, don't talk.*

I'm Dante. I'm so sorry. I was trying to help. They're creating an army.

I didn't like the sound of that. *For what?*

To destroy the purebreds and take over their holdings, then the humans. His chest rattled as death crept closer.

A hand grabbed my shoulder, ripping me from Dante's shuddering form.

The bald men can help. The old barge …

What barge? I asked hoping to latch onto his final thought.

It was too late. He was already shrinking, his human body replacing the mutant one.

I'd never been inside an animal's mind at the moment of death. What I felt was empty darkness, like the universe without stars. The shell remained, but the soul had departed. Dante, I hoped, was in a better place.

For the first time since my capture, I allowed a tsunami of hopelessness to wash over me. Wave after wave, bowed my body until I was grasping my thighs. A torrent of hot tears followed.

Without comment, my remaining guard yanked me upright. This time, I marched obediently beside him down the staircase. I could hear doors above opening and women screaming. I knew the other guards were already descending on Dante's motionless form.

They'd seen the whole thing. One or two of them had even laughed. Their laughter was what pushed me over the edge. What little faith I'd clung to was washed away with my tears.

It was hard to hang onto hope when your tormentors found death something to laugh about.

Twenty-Three

I entered the lower hall defeated and resigned to experiencing a painful and dehumanizing death at the hands of Jazmine and her followers.

Maybe I'd been wrong to believe a werewolf could love a human.

After seeing how the *other* side lived, I was beginning to doubt Zane's intentions. He'd admitted to deceiving me, and then he'd initiated our Vegas wedding night fiasco, yet another example of his poor judgment and lack of compassion. Jazmine was better suited for him. She'd have no problem standing up to his chauvinistic ways.

I shoved all thoughts of Zane aside. In all likelihood, I'd never see him again, and dwelling on our short-lived relationship did nothing but depress me more. I had one thing to be grateful for. Since my tearful meltdown, Mr. Tall and Rude had loosened his death grip on my arm and was whistling an old Beatles' tune. I made every effort to stay steady as I struggled to keep up with his longer gait.

I Kissed a Dog

Instead of the classroom windows I'd seen on the upper floor, this hall featured doors devoid of any windows.

We reached the corridor's midway point, and much to my relief, Mr. Tall and Rude ceased both his off-tune whistling and brisk stride to scrutinize a door that looked as battered and beaten as I felt.

Deep gouges twisted down its full length, giving the appearance that something with knife-wielding claws had sought entrance. I swallowed hard, a new storm of fear brewing in my stomach.

To make matters worse, the basement corridor didn't have that busy school feeling I'd noticed above. It was sinister, and eerily quiet.

The scratched door loomed in the background. My eyes were drawn back to it like a magnet to metal. I could survive with mold, mildew, and gloom, but living in dread, while I waited for some mystery monster to tear through the door, sent my faith spiraling downward.

A lone guard manning his post at the hallway's end was the single breathing thing in my line of vision. Seeing the casual way he lounged behind his computer monitor drew my attention from the door.

In this hauntingly similar place, I was reminded of Joshua's cell-like room in the mental institution. I was also reminded of my pledge to get him out.

I didn't break promises.

In what seemed like slow motion, Mr. Tall and Rude fished out a key ring. "Home sweet home," he said, sounding cheerful.

I decided to ignore him and keep my mouth clamped shut. I prayed that my current good behavior would earn me a meal.

The gnawing in my stomach was prompting grumbles loud enough to slice through the stillness. If I didn't eat and sleep soon, I'd really be grumbling. Once my basic needs were satisfied, I'd get back to finding some way to keep my promise of freedom for Joshua Smart.

"You're quarters," my escort announced snide as ever. The door swung open revealing a barren and dreary room.

Four army cots with a blanket and pillow lined the far back wall. A sink and toilet were hidden behind a filth-singed room divider. With no windows, I was painfully aware that I would be lucky to have shadows as my constant companions.

One undersized bulb flickered from the ceiling. Day and night would blur.

"Who've we got now?" I recognized the hall monitor as he swaggered past and left a stack of towels and my travel bag on the end cot. "You hungry?" he added, looking my way and ignoring the sudden scowl on Mr. Tall and Rude's face.

Before I could get my mouth open, my original escort answered, adding one more rude reason to detest him. "She's hungry, probably thirsty too. Her name's Chloe Carpenter, and she's a high priority prisoner. The Mistress is unhappy with this one. She's a sneaky one." He shot me a look that dared me to respond. "She'll have fun bunking with Connie and Deb." He paused as if recalling something important. "Deb should be transferring back upstairs by Friday."

The new guard nodded with a look that said Deb's imminent move was old news.

I Kissed a Dog

Whoever Deb was, I intended to discover what she'd done to earn relocation rights to the upper level.

The hall monitor turned his attention back to me. "I got P and J or ham and cheese. What'll it be?"

Certain I was pressing my luck, I forced what I hoped was a semi-sexy smile. "Both?"

Hall Monitor tossed his head back and roared, "A girl after my own heart!"

"Don't get too cozy with her, Dillon, she's trouble."

I plopped on my cot and leaned against the concrete wall, ignoring the chill, and the warning, too tired to protest. After some food and a few hours of sleep, I'd make a point of earning my nickname.

Dillon would have an opportunity to meet Trouble face to face.

I was just swallowing my last bite of P and J when my roommates entered. Dillon patted the blonde on her rear. She giggled, her cheeks flushing. I noted this with an annoying touch from the green-eyed monster. Jealous that she'd somehow managed to find her very own masculine light source in our dreary dungeon. Dillon was cute enough, especially when he smiled. Dimples always helped. Their happiness only made my separation from Zane that much harder to endure.

"This is Connie." He nodded at the object of his interest.

"I'm Deb," said the taller brunette.

I was still gaping at Connie. "You!" I recognized the woman as the blue-eyed blonde from upstairs.

She stopped her flirting. "Isn't this convenient?" She sounded less than pleased.

Not sure what else to do, I extended my hand. "I'm Chloe. You were getting ready to tell me something …"

"I'm not sure what you're talking about. You must have confused me with someone else." She shot me a warning look.

Not wanting to alienate her before I had a chance to pick her brain, I just nodded. "You're probably right. I'm not sure who I saw. I was pretty out of it."

Dillon turned to study me. "You're awful tiny to be so much trouble, but I'll tell you what I told these two …"

"Be nice to me and I'll be nice to you," the women chorused.

"Great. Make me look like a big softy. I'm going to grab Ms. Chloe her surprise desert. You want anything?" He looked pointedly at Connie. Her cheeks glowed. I'd stumbled onto a serious prisoner captor love connection. If my intuition was right, this was no casual flirtation. These two were smitten.

My roommates listed their requests, and I took the opportunity to disappear behind the privacy screen with a partial change of clothing. With great care, I pulled Jazmine's wig from my pant leg and wrapped it in my dirty t-shirt. I tugged on my favorite oversized sweatshirt, and hurried back to my bunk just as the deadbolt slid into place with loud clunk.

I stuffed the wig-wadded-shirt into my bag and collapsed on the bunk. Deb and Connie followed my example, both resting their backs against the concrete wall.

"So?" I glanced at Connie on the bunk to my left. Deb, on her far side, had pulled a paperback from under her pillow.

Connie shook her head just enough for me to notice and

glanced sideways at Deb. Our conversation wouldn't be happening while Deb was awake.

Frustrated that I'd have to wait for answers, I took another look around the room. I hadn't noticed four, three-drawer dressers on the wall opposite the make-shift bathroom. No wonder their bunks were so bare.

Under the circumstances, I wasn't sure I wanted my possessions out of reach, tucked away in a dresser. I still had the symbol tracings to review, and my cell phone was resting secure below my breasts. As much as I hated a too-snug bra, this one was successfully supporting and camouflaging the added weight. I doubted I'd get a signal down here, but I'd damn sure try at the first opportunity.

A second later, I heard thunderous footsteps approaching. They stopped right outside our door.

I held my breath, too scared to breathe, panicking as I envisioned the vicious claw marks. But instead of a mutant monster, the friendly hall monitor entered, laden with more food. At least starvation wouldn't be an issue.

"Your sweets have arrived," Dillon announced. This time he delivered our food but didn't linger, to Connie's obvious disappointment. He seemed preoccupied.

Relieved to exhale, I examined my desert, which consisted of an ice cream sandwich and a little tub of yogurt. The three of us ate in silence.

I still couldn't figure out how Jazmine had found me. Alcuin had rented my room at the hotel. Just he and Luke were aware that I was headed to Portland, and the only one who knew my exact plans and whereabouts was Alcuin. The idea that he'd betrayed me, Zane, and our close-knit group, seemed unfeasible. What could he hope to gain? He was a vampire, not a mutant or werewolf. It just didn't add up.

Considering Alcuin as an enemy wasn't what I wanted. Nothing in my life was making sense anyway.

I stuffed my travel bag under my ultra-thin pillow and turned on my side, making sure to face my two roommates. My stepdad had taught me the importance of that timeless trick. Having my back to them wasn't an option, not if I wanted to ensure I was alive tomorrow.

Deb was buried in her book, and Connie was stretched out on her back, eyes closed. I had no clue what time it was. All I cared about was getting some much-overdue sleep, before I made more mistakes to regret later.

I trudged behind the repugnant, cloaked, bald man, David. We stopped at a square opening in the floor. Stairs, steep as a ladder, started at the opening's top, and disappeared into darkness below.

Somehow, I knew I was dreaming, but this was much more than any ordinary dream. It was a vision. Understanding how or why it was happening wasn't important; I was along for the journey.

"Follow me," David said, before descending with an uncanny ease not customary for a human being.

Clinging to a lone handrail, I followed him down the narrow steps carefully. Every few seconds the building would shift, just enough to mess with my equilibrium. As clumsy as I am, any rocking motion has a potentially negative side effect. Staying upright was my current priority.

I Kissed a Dog

"Not a building, friend, this is a boat. A barge to be exact," my companion explained using his telepathic ability to communicate. He'd read my mind. In his case, I didn't mind the intrusion.

I reached the stair's final level. It was then I realized where we were. A barge. David had just stated we were in a barge.

Yes! That had to be it. I had a vague memory about a barge. I'd heard something before this. At last I'd uncovered a major-connect-the-dots moment.

The mutant guard, Dante, had mentioned a barge right before he died.

Shivering, I pushed the image of his smoking chest from my mind, and turned my attention solely to my guide, who was traveling down a corridor lined with medical equipment and supplies.

We reached a double door with two glass windows. David floated up until he was level with the windows.

"How did you ... never mind." What was a little levitating in my already crazy vision?

I peered through the opposite window into the medical facility beyond. I recognized the location. I'd seen it before, in the mind of Martin's dog.

Without a sound, David entered the room, his cloak ruffling as he brushed by. Not sure what else to do, I followed him through the rows of beds. A number were empty, but at least ten or more had patients strapped to them.

"Just watch, listen," David instructed.

No one seemed the least bit aware of our presence. We were invisible; I hoped invincible too. Without superpowers, I didn't want to face the mutant sentries posted through the room.

Inspecting a patient, Jasmine leaned closer. He was twisting and pulling at his restraints, frantic to escape.

"He's turning! After the last few, I was getting worried." She applauded, her excitement palpable.

"Didn't I tell you not to worry?" Martin rested a tentative hand on her elbow.

Keeping her eyes on the bed, she sidestepped his touch and leaned closer to their writhing patient.

Martin appeared hurt, humiliated even, like she'd slapped him in front of their closest associates. It was far more obvious here, in the vision, just how consumed Martin was with the more dominant Jazmine. It was pathetic watching him grovel for her affection.

Someone nearby called for water. Unlike the thrashing man who'd won Jazmine's approval, this patient was calm and composed despite his precarious position.

Martin's German Shepherd, who I'd failed to notice at first glance, growled a warning deep in his chest, reminding me of Zane.

Even in my dream state, Zane still intruded. He'd beguiled and branded me forever with his kisses and sensuous caresses. As hard as I tried to fight the pull, the truth was in front of me like a larger than life 3D movie.

I belonged with him. I wanted to be his mate; his wife; his companion.

An infuriated command from Jazmine pierced through my passion-filled ponderings. "Kill him! He's going to become one of them. There's too many! We ... "

A guard charged forward, pistol pointed at the bunk.

It was empty.

I Kissed a Dog

The thirsty patient had vanished. The restraints remained intact. He'd disappeared from the room.

"Find him!" Jazmine bellowed, shoving Martin aside when he tried once again to comfort her. "I want David dead! Now!"

I spun to face my cloaked guide. David?

Of course, he was showing me his personal history with Jazmine. He'd been a regular guy, or so it seemed. But some unholy experiment, courtesy of Jazmine and her supporters, changed David from a normal looking man into the hideously-hooded, bald creature still hovering a few feet away.

"They killed those of us who didn't shift into mutant form. They are creating a mutant army, changing humans. Jazmine and Martin are using the earliest recorded fae magic to change the mutants. They can now shift at will, without the full moon. If they recover the coins, they will hold a key to immortality. Those of us with fae blood, turn into this." David dropped his head. "You must stop them, Chloe. Join with your mate. United, you will unveil a powerful magic."

"Fae blood? Magic?" Great, more mythical mysteries, but that still didn't answer the one burning question I needed answered. "David, how did Jazmine find me ...?"

◉

"Wake up! Chloe!" a shrill whisper whistled through my mind, knocking me from my sleep-induced vision and almost off my bunk.

Grabbing the thin blanket, I pushed up into a sitting position and found myself facing a wide-eyed Connie. Deb was snoring obscenely, her book flopped open over her face, several pages fluttering as she exhaled.

I was annoyed by Connie's interruption. I needed to learn more from David but had no idea when he'd reappear. "So, *now* you'll talk to me?" I whispered, sounding harsher than intended.

"Sorry about earlier, but I couldn't risk it. Jazmine and her flunkies are psychotic at best."

I couldn't agree more with her judgment, and I was relieved she hadn't taken my negative reaction to heart. I could use an ally in this Godforsaken place.

"So you know her real name too? Everyone else calls her *The Mistress*," I hissed Jazmine's pathetic, pornographic title, hating the way the words polluted my mouth.

Mistress of Misery and Mayhem fit our captor like a well-tailored suit. I envisioned greeting her with the title next time she materialized.

Connie inched closer, prompting me to do the same, until we were both teetering perilously close to the edges of our cots. Deb chose that moment to groan and then take a haphazard swipe at her blanket before returning to her snoring session.

Right now, it was crucial that we avoid waking our roommate. Connie seemed to agree as she maneuvered off her bed with great skill, pillow and blanked tucked under her arm.

Adjusting my weight, I followed her example and joined her on the floor by the dressers. I attempted to cocoon myself in my lone blanket, making sure I had a clear view of the sleeping, snoring beauty.

"Don't worry; you'll know if she wakes up. The engine will stop roaring." Connie smirked.

I was beginning to like the fresh-faced blonde. She seemed to have the sarcastic routine down.

I Kissed a Dog

Not sure how much time we had before Deb emerged from dreamland, I fired off several questions I'd been dying to ask anyone with answers. "What is this place and why are you here? I think I know why they want me, but what about the rest of the women? And, Jazmine, how do you know her name?"

"This is an old, abandoned high school. All I know is it's on an Indian reservation somewhere in Northern Washington."

The school's location made sense in light of what I'd learned at yesterday's board meeting. Picturing Zane sent a fresh stab of longing through my core.

"As for our mysterious mistress ..." Connie, unaware of my inner torment, glanced at Deb before continuing. "She showed up at the specialty bridal store where I work, about three weeks ago; said she was planning the wedding of the century. That's what they all say.

Anyway, I smelled what she was right away. I was surprised she'd chosen to frequent a mutant-owned shop, being a purebred and all. We helped her pick out a gown, and then she returned a week later to check on its progress even though we'd given her a pickup date."

I seethed at the thought of Jazmine planning a wedding to *my* husband. My. Husband. Thoughts of Zane threatened to generate a river of tears, something I didn't have time to indulge. Swallowing hard, I met Connie's eyes.

"You okay?" she asked.

"Nothing that I can't deal with. Please ... go on."

"Well, like I said, she came back unannounced with two of her boy toys. Sensing danger, but not sure what to do, I did my best to please her. She still needed her bridesmaid dresses. When I bent over to grab our latest sample book, one of her men knocked me out cold. I woke up in a van full of other mutant women. I happened to be seated closest to the front divider. I overheard the driver call her Jazmine. That was the first time that I heard anyone use her given name. She'd listed the name, Zane Marshall, on all her wedding documentation at the shop."

I felt the usual wave of jealousy spiral through me

None of this made any sense. The one thing I was sure about: how much I hated Jazmine.

Maybe she was insane with no hidden motives. She'd certainly made her craving for Zane known to me. Maybe her sole purpose was to marry him and produce a litter of pups.

No. She was doing something far more devious than planning a wedding to an already married man. Her clandestine medical activities proved that. Killing off the men in Plum Beach, and searching for ancient coins weren't part of her marriage preparations either.

Connie glanced again at Deb and lowered her voice. "I know this sounds stupid, but one of the others, a woman who has been here a long time, said *The Mistress* was rounding up all the most attractive mutant females to keep us under control, so she could use us as servants for her new army."

I'd heard all about the whole army thing in my dream with David. "Great. Another take over the world scheme. A modern day Hitler who sprouts fur and …"

The snoring came to a sudden halt. Like an operating switch had been flicked into the off position. I stiffened and felt Connie tense beside me.

A few grumbles and pillow punches later and Deb settled back down.

Giving Connie a warning look, I nodded for her to continue.

By the time she finished, I'd pieced together a theory. One with a number of gaping holes, but it was better than nothing.

Jazmine, her sidekick, Martin, from Logan's Board of Directors, along with a bunch of mutant-wannabe-warriors, were attempting to collapse the current purebred hierarchy and take control of their business interests, and God knew what else.

This wasn't a fight for equal rights, more like a hostile takeover.

And as Connie had explained, it appeared as if Jazmine was trapping mutant women to do her bidding, ensuring she kept the upper hand with her male followers.

Unluckily for Jazmine, more of the female mutants were going to form bonds with their alleged, Loyal-to-The Mistress' captors, following in the footsteps of Connie and Dillon's blissful example.

In addition, according to Connie, Deb had started out as a serious ringleader, stirring up unrest and causing Jazmine more than a few headaches. Rather than killing her, Jazmine now used our still-snoring roommate's popularity with the other women to her advantage.

Deb had been converted to the "lower level" spy; rooming with the women deemed rebellious, thus unworthy to serve their Mistress. In order to keep her circulating amongst the others, the time to reinsert her back into the general population had arrived. The cycle would continue. Deb would seek out any dissenters and report them while pretending to be their accomplice

Dillon had trusted Connie with the secret, warning her to keep any anti-Mistress views to herself. He was determined to protect Connie, even going as far as to start planning an escape.

If I had anything to say about it, me and any other desiring woman would be joining the lovebirds when they decided to leave the nest.

After two hours of hushed conversation, I determined Connie was worthy of my trust. I had to believe in someone. There was no way I'd get out of here alive on my own. Having a guard on our side would be yet another bonus.

Once we'd decided to trust each other, I launched into my own story, skipping the parts about Valamir, the coins, and my own advanced mindreading talents.

As I'd done so many times before, I shared an abridged version of my special skills, sticking to how the animal communication process had worked in the beginning. I didn't want Connie or Dillon aware of my ability to delve into their minds' darkest corners.

Under the circumstances, I could trust just enough to take the next step.

Anymore might prove deadly.

Twenty-Four

By Friday I was going stir-crazy.

Connie wanted to wait until Deb was upstairs before making any specific escape plans. I understood her reasoning, but I was hungry for action.

My thoughts were consumed with Zane. Did he miss me? Would he forgive me? Was he even still alive? The not-knowing kept my stomach in knots. I was more worried about my friends back home than myself.

I'd spent countless hours trying to determine who'd betrayed my whereabouts to Jazmine. Alcuin was the only one who'd been aware of my exact location. He'd arranged everything from the hotel room to my car rental. Luke had known my general travel plans. Unless Alcuin had revealed my detailed plans to an unknown person, it had to be my vampire friend. No matter what, he was somehow responsible.

To make matters worse, he possessed the sketches from Joshua Smart's journal.

What if he failed to pass them onto Zane and the others, and instead turned them over to our enemies?

I hoped David and his ilk would find a way to intercept the

drawings. The cloaked crusaders had proven to be resourceful and discreet, impressing me at every turn. I had to believe they were out there somewhere working on my behalf. I wished that David would take me on another guided dream quest. I'd drifted to sleep each night with the expectation of such an encounter, only to awaken disappointed.

Promising Connie I wouldn't try anything drastic, I'd been the picture of an obedient captive for the past three days. She, on the other hand, had been free from the room on a number of occasions, with her beastly beau, Dillon, whom I liked as much as I could under the circumstances.

At the moment, the two were off wherever it was they went for their rendezvous. I didn't understand why Deb didn't report their dalliances. Maybe she'd use their relationship for blackmail at a later date. Connie wasn't worried, though. If Dillon thought something was safe so did she.

I disagreed, but kept my opinions to myself.

Any comment she perceived as negative about *her man* was defended with great vigor. Creating tension between us wasn't worth my efforts. The last thing I needed was my ally seeing me as a threat to her happiness.

Deb, my closest real threat, was sorting her meager belongings. She hadn't said much to me since my arrival, and I didn't expect it to change now. I'd listened in on her thoughts a number of times.

She spent a majority of time reading or reminiscing about her childhood, which had been ideal until she was bitten at fourteen by an uncle. Jazmine controlled Deb with the promise of revenge. She wanted her uncle to suffer for ruining her life.

When she spoke to me, I was shocked. "Would you like any

of my books?" She motioned to the tower of paperbacks on her dresser.

Not wanting to appear ungrateful before she reunited upstairs with Jazmine, I nodded and wandered over, making a show of examining the covers. "Spicy stuff." That was an understatement.

"Wouldn't have it any other way." She continued folding.

Not sure what to say, I grabbed the pile and plopped back on my bunk.

The book covers featured gorgeous women embraced in passion by muscle-bound men. A number of the titles included the word *desire*. My breath caught in my throat at the sight of a male cover model who reminded me of Zane.

"See something you like?" Deb was by my side before I'd processed her moving. It was the first time either of my cellmates had displayed their mutant powers. I'd almost forgotten they weren't human.

Embarrassed, I hugged the book to my chest.

"Don't think you'll win this battle," she growled, changing the subject. Her eyes flashed crimson. "Jazmine *always* gets what she wants."

She snatched the book away, scanning the cover. "Ah, isn't he adorable? He looks an awful lot like a photo my Mistress keeps. Is *he* worth your life?"

I paused. Was he?

I'd better know what exactly I was fighting for, because it was time to make a stand. Ignoring Connie's warnings, I rose to my feet; certain Deb could smell my fear.

"Is Jazmine worth yours?" I grabbed the book back. "You think she'll keep her promise, help you destroy your uncle, think again. She's using you like she uses everyone else. You're nothing special to her, just another means to an end. She'd use your uncle against you if it served her purpose." The venom in my words surprised both of us. She took a step back, eyes wide.

"How … how did you know that?" Confusion was painted across her face.

"You can't trust her. She keeps putting you off, doesn't she?" I'd latched onto her first thought following my verbal assault, learning that Jazmine had promised Deb, multiple times, that they'd start pursuing her uncle any day. That day had yet to come.

Deb staggered to her cot and collapsed, her eyes glued to the floor. "She keeps making excuses for why we can't go after him."

Knowing this window wouldn't stay open long, I moved to sit beside her. "You don't have to put up with this, you know. You're in the perfect position to do something.

"At first she planned to kill you. It was after she discovered your secret and how she could use the information to control you that she enlisted your help, wasn't it?" I hoped I was right. "From the beginning, you knew how wrong this all was."

"Are you a witch?" Deb looked up, but kept her gaze diverted from mine.

"Sort of, but mostly just another women being held against her will. A woman in love with the wrong man, at the wrong time." *Yes. I'd die for Zane,* I thought, but not if we could find a way to live.

I dove into her mind again and found a wounded, war-scarred woman ready for change, now resolved to helping me, but uncertain how.

Now was my chance.

I Kissed a Dog

"If you want out of this hellhole, here's what we need to do…"

An hour later, we had our plan in order. I'd also learned some valuable information about the mating mark.

I needed to be outside, tonight, during the full moon.

It was then the mating magic would work. Proclaiming my love for Zane would seal our union. He had no choice in the matter, he was already marked. If he couldn't forgive me later for my dishonesty, that was fine, we'd deal with it. Right now, we needed the added abilities that authentic, love-bonded mates received, like unlimited telepathy.

Granted, I already had the skill, but the distance between us was just too far to allow for any communication. I'd been trying with no success since my capture. Deb was worried that my human condition might keep me from gaining full powers. I felt certain it would work. I might be human, but I was also something more.

Besides, we had to try. I was running out of options.

It was my chance to connect with Zane and my team back home. Worst case scenario, I still had my cell phone.

When Deb entered her debriefing upstairs, she would convince Jazmine to let me out with the others. She'd tell Jazmine how terrified I was and that seeing the mutant masses howling together during a full moon would send me over the edge.

A full moon was the one time the compound was open for all the women at once. The special event meant a bonfire outside and a chance to run the grounds. Pent up mutants were difficult to keep under control. Jazmine was no fool. She knew she had to give a little to get a lot.

After the mating ritual, which could be completed quickly

and quietly, I would reach telepathically for Zane, and then call out to Valamir, in hopes he still had me on his vampire radar, however that worked.

After all, if Alcuin was right, my blood was his obsession, and I needed someone to get Jazmine's wig to Plum Beach and into the hands of Detective Davis or Officer Tate, fast, while keeping it far from Agent Green's twisted agenda. I still didn't know the agent's role in all this, but it wasn't to help our cause. It was obvious that he was in Plum Beach to thwart the murder investigations.

A few minutes later, the door clanked open, revealing a smiling Connie and Dillon. Turning to face Deb, he put on a more formal face. "You ready?"

Ignoring me as we'd discussed, Deb grabbed her belongings and bid Connie a brief farewell.

"Good riddance!" Connie barked at the closed door. "Now we can breathe."

"At last," I agreed, pacing the room as I prepared to share the plan.

Before I could say anything, Connie hurried to the third dresser and pushed it aside — the scraping sound, like fingernails on a chalk board, was forgotten at the sight of an oversized ventilation shaft.

"Told you we could count on Dillon." She grinned, her eyes twinkling with mischief. "Hope you're not claustrophobic."

Stunned to find a possible escape route so near, I rushed to crouch in front of the grated metal plate. "I don't want to end up in some creepy boiler room." I shivered, overcome with the heebie-jeebies.

"Where does it go?" I asked, peering inside.

I Kissed a Dog

Imagining myself belly down, army crawling through the shaft, wasn't something I was eager to attempt, regardless of my mom's embarrassing stories about me wearing out the left knee in my pajamas due to my speedy, army crawling technique.

"Where do you think it goes? Out of here," she answered. Before I could respond, she was squatting next to me.

Putting her mutant strength to use, she gave the cover a tug, separating it from the rectangular space.

"But ..." I stammered, hating the way my nerves had surfaced. I just wasn't ready to abandon my plan with Deb.

"But what? Let's take a look. We need to do a test run; see where it ends up."

"Are you saying you don't even know where it goes? I thought Dillon would have at least told you that much." I didn't want to go into the shaft if I could help it. The opening was starting to look like a dark maw eager to devour us whole, and my doubts were increasing the longer I stared into the gaping shadows. "I have a better idea."

"What could be better than a hole in the wall?" Connie grinned, breaking the tension..

"Would you believe that Deb is on our side?"

Connie's rolled her eyes. "This better be good."

Twenty-Five

After an arduous debate with my current roommate, it was decided that we would stick to the course of action Deb and I had concocted, with the secret shaft serving as an alternative plan or emergency exit should we need it.

I somehow doubted we'd make it back to our quarters alive, if Plan A failed.

More likely, we'd be burned alive in the great bonfire Deb had boasted about. A spectacle blatant enough to strike fear in the hearts of every creature present, and one that would squelch any rebellion forming in Jazmine's ranks.

After returning the grate to the duct's entrance, Connie repositioned the dresser to its original place. If something went wrong later, we'd make every effort to meet here and exit together.

After hours of anxious waiting, Dillon entered with two bowls of pasta and two tan uniforms like I'd seen the women upstairs wearing. It seemed Deb had completed the first part of our scheme — getting Jazmine to approve an invite to the bonfire. Being trapped all this time had increased my desire for freedom. I couldn't wait to breathe in the night air.

What I wanted, far more than fresh air, was to wrap my arms around Zane and forget everything but the warmth of his lips on mine.

Noticing my faraway gaze, Connie snapped her fingers. "Hey, daydream later. We've got a prison riot to instigate." She replaced her jogging suit with the perfectly creased uniform.

"That's one sexy ensemble," I joked, attempting to silence the fear gnawing in my gut, making eating impossible.

"*The Mistress* wouldn't want her harem looking hotter than she does." Connie smirked. She looked thoughtful before unbuttoning her shirt enough to reveal an ample eyeful of cleavage.

She'd managed to make herself look sexy in a basic uniform. Dillon would appreciate her efforts even if Jazmine didn't.

Rather than worrying about my appearance, I took special care to gather the items necessary for cracking the case and proving my innocence. Wrapping Jazmine's wig snuggly around my right calf, I stretched the sock up to my knee, securing the hairpiece.

The kakis pants were wide-legged, providing enough space for me to move with ease. I adjusted the cell phone in my bra and slid Joshua's sketches into my back pocket, eager to get on with the big event.

In a few short hours I'd be one of two things: Dead or Alive.

At least we didn't have to wait long before Dillon reappeared with my least-favorite escort, Mr. Tall and Rude. I trooped after my captors, Connie at my side, providing a hint of security.

The air of anticipation in the compound was palpable.

Women dashed from their classrooms intent on reaching the great outdoors. I couldn't blame them. I felt like running too.

I scanned the hallways. The number of mutant guards had increased. I decided it was time to let Connie in on the full extent of my silent communication capabilities.

Hey, don't panic and don't look at me. I'm speaking to you telepathically.

Chloe? Despite my warning she glanced my direction. Thankfully, in the bustle no one seemed to notice.

None other. I don't have time to explain how I do this.

O-k-a-y, she agreed sounding somewhat reluctant.

Where did all these extra guards come from? This is going to make it difficult for me to do my mating magic.

Can you talk like this to anyone? She asked.

Anyone who is of the animal persuasion.

Does Deb know? Connie sounded wary.

We'd reached what had to have been the school's cafeteria/gym. Neat piles of clothing were stacked throughout the room. *Changing room?* I asked Connie silently.

Yes. And you didn't answer my question.

She knew about some of my abilities, enough to know I could reach out to Zane following the mating ceremony and with any luck contact a vampire friend.

We were guided though doors that opened to reveal what could have been a picture book scene under different circumstances.

Dillon steered Connie into the night, leaving me to admire my surroundings with my favorite sidekick, who for the moment was intent on standing at my side.

An expansive, grassy field, freshly mowed, stretched past an

I Kissed a Dog

old playground. The forest beckoned in the distance. The summer sky was clear, and the stars spread seductively overhead, the moon their master. A bonfire popped and crackled, shooting sparks upward, surrounded by women in uniforms.

As evidenced by the discarded clothing, others, already in mutant form, romped through the field, remaining inside the ring of armed guards. Their ranks expanded to cover at least half a mile in all four directions. Anyone attempting a mad dash to freedom would be executed.

The gun-totting watchmen were a serious reminder that this was no high school, homecoming bonfire. This was a way, granted, a pretty cool one, to further manipulate those in servitude to *The Mistress*.

So absorbed by my surroundings, I jumped when a heated hand clamped around my arm. "Enjoying your little recess," Jazmine purred. "Try not to be too frightened when everyone takes off their clothes and shows their inner beauty."

Struggling to control any sarcastic rebuttal, I nodded, remembering Deb's extensive efforts to convince Jazmine of my mutant phobia. It was show time, and I had a starring role to play. I wasn't hoping for an Oscar, merely survival.

"They're all going to turn into mutants?" I asked.

Jazmine tossed her head back and roared with what I considered unladylike laughter. "Why, of course they are. Don't worry, though, I'll protect you from the wolf monsters." Her grip tightened on my arm. "Won't you join me at my table?"

She didn't wait for my answer, instead prodding me to an elevated platform that featured a table set up for six, and a good-sized podium.

What I hadn't counted on was her wanting to hold my

hand all night. How the hell was I going to do my moon mating ritual with her stuck to my side?

Deb, Connie, can you both hear me? I'd blasted more than one enemy at a time with my mind powers, but had never mentally spoken with more than one animal at time.

My head tingled, energy thrumming through my body. Again, something unpredictable was happening. I suspected my powers extended beyond anything I'd ever imagined. Talking to two or two hundred wouldn't be an issue.

I can hear you. Loud and clear, Deb answered.

Me too! Connie confirmed. *Dear God, she's got you cornered.*

I saw Connie watching from about twenty feet away.

It appears I'm her hot date for the evening. I need you to create a distraction. It has to last long enough for me to seal the mating.

You'll know when, Deb assured.

I hoped they could pull it off, because right now the air duct was looking like the better option.

"Entertainment! Start the entertainment!" Jazmine barked through a handheld microphone. "You'll love this," she whispered to me.

Awkward didn't begin to cover how I felt seated like a pagan god atop a created dais. Jazmine, dressed like a queen, was presiding over her loyal subjects. I wanted to vomit. How had Zane ever found anything appealing about her?

A low growl rumbled at the bottom of our platform. Martin's German Shepherd glared up.

The despicable dog that'd caused my coma-catastrophe reminded me of Martin's dog; I mentally screamed into the shepherd's head, *I hate you!* Then to make sure the beast knew I meant business, I slammed a vision of me shaving off all his

I Kissed a Dog

luscious fur into his doggy mind. The growl turned into a yelp, and he fled into the crowd.

"Dog? Jazmine ..." Martin whined from below.

I swallowed a snort when I realized the dog's name was Dog.

"I don't care about your damn dog, Martin. Get the entertainment started," Jazmine ordered.

I stifled my laughter. Martin was an idiot. He was the one man on Logan's board stupid enough to fall into the clutches of someone like Jazmine. How together they managed this growing empire was beyond my comprehension. I was still missing something, or more accurately, someone.

Alcuin. He was the traitor. He had to be.

Before I could contemplate further a woman screamed, "Oh no, you don't! I like him! He's mine!"

The other voices subsided as the altercation accelerated. With grace, Jazmine dropped to the ground, slinking toward the distraction. *My* distraction!

I crept down the stairs, hoping the commotion would serve its purpose.

Dillon roared, "I don't know what you're talking about. I don't belong to *anyone*, and not either of you." Ouch! I knew Connie wouldn't like that shocking proclamation regardless of the reason. Dillon sounded like he meant every word.

The yelling escalated as I headed the opposite direction. As planned, everyone was drawn to the potential dogfight, the animal part of them unable to resist the impending bloodshed.

I found a dark corner by the school, blocked from view by a shield of overgrown Emerald Green Arborvitaes, or as some referred to them, "Instant Privacy" trees. I slipped between them and ducked, praying their promise of privacy would apply to me. There wasn't much time remaining. The girls could only argue so long before a full-fledged fight was expected.

"Tonight, as I look upon this amazing moon ..." I stalled. This was ridiculous. I was talking to the moon. How would proclaiming my love for Zane under a full moon bind us together? The whole idea was absurd. *Why am I thinking about this now? These don't feel like my thoughts. This isn't me.*

"Mating with a werewolf is not in your best interest, my beauty."

Turning, I faced the voice's soothing source. I knew right then who'd been planting the confusing thoughts. Damn it! I'd wanted to talk with Valamir, but not until *after* I'd completed the mating ceremony, and not now when I was on a life or death time schedule.

"You!" I snapped. "I've been held hostage for days and you choose now to ride in on your white stallion. And who are you to tell me who or what I can mate with?" I was beyond tired of being bossed around. I didn't care if the delectable man towering over me had two very pointy teeth. I was saying my bit before he or someone else tore me to pieces.

"You should watch your tone, my dear. I may lust for you and your blood, but I do not take kindly to disrespect." He glowered, arms crossed.

"Go ahead! Do me a favor. At least I'll have a moment of ecstasy while you're sucking me dry. Go on! Bite me!" I took a very dangerous step forward and tilted my neck in submission.

He shrugged, fangs extended. "I think I will have a bite, since you're offering."

I Kissed a Dog

Warmth pooled in my belly and spread down my thighs as his teeth sank in. This wasn't what I wanted, was it? Death by vampire? No. I'd simply challenged the wrong foe — one older, stronger, and ultimately sexier.

My eyelids fluttered shut and I allowed myself to drift away, floating on waves of pleasure and pain.

Dying in his arms made death seem delightful.

Dying without telling the world how much I loved Zane was unacceptable.

Through the fog-like-dizziness of severe blood loss, the words I'd longed to speak floated from my mouth, barely audible: "Zane, I love you ... *you*. I want to be your mate, your wife, your everything. It's too ..." My next word, late, was drowned by Valamir's snarl.

He released me and leapt back.

I straightened up, an unfamiliar power coursing through my limbs. A ripple of heat ringed my ankle, forming what felt like an anklet of fiery metal.

Ignoring the vampire's snarls turned hisses; I bent to examine my leg. I yanked the red wig from my stocking and tossed it at Valamir, who despite his discomfort caught it with ease.

A circle of sigils bordered my ankle. They seemed to writhe on my skin like miniature snakes. Unable to restrain my curiosity, I touched the foreign markings and was sucked into a portal of black nothingness. Not the response I'd expected.

Valamir, the bonfire, Jazmine, *everything* had vanished.

I stood somewhere, but nowhere.

For the first time, I noticed a metallic taste in my mouth. Searching my recent memories, I recoiled. At some point during Valamir's little blood bath, I'd consumed his tainted blood, and then I'd activated the mating mark. The repercussions of these two interrelated actions would without question cause some future abnormality — yet another group of bizarre gifts or talents to unwrap.

Approaching footsteps drew my attention. Despite the gloom, I was able to make out a familiar figure. My worries were swallowed by the joy exploding like fireworks in my heart.

Zane.

No longer held hostage by fear, I raced toward him.

Flinging my arms around his neck and wrapping my legs around his waist I clung to him, tears streaming down my cheeks. Our lips met and he kissed me with such ferocity I thought he might devour me whole. I felt his presence everywhere. My tongue strokes matched his, and I wondered how I'd ever thought Valamir had anything over my werewolf.

"Princess," he murmured stroking my hair. "We don't have long …"

Ignoring his warning, I pulled his head down and kissed him with zeal. Forget the mutant war; I wanted my man.

His hands roamed, leaving trails of sizzling pleasure in their wake. I arched, pressing my pelvis against his hardness, embracing a refreshing, new brazenness. "I'm so sorry," I whispered between kisses. "Can you forgive me? I love you."

Gentle but firm, he held my shoulders, untangling himself from the web of my arms and legs. "I forgave you the minute I thought I'd lost you. Alcuin broke his code of silence." Zane gazed down at me, his eyes glowing amber.

At the mention of Alcuin, panic returned, overriding my passion. "Don't trust him! He may have sold us out."

"He'd never ..." Zane paused, looking thoughtful. "He said he'd explain everything this evening. Logan wanted to speak with him first about the spell he suspected we'd translated from the coins."

"Just Alcuin knew my whereabouts."

"Speaking of, where are *you*, right now? This place ..." he glanced around, "is a temporary dimension where mates are united if they're not together when the final markings appear. I always thought it was just a legend. It seems the legends are real."

I noticed then that the darkness was receding, and Zane was fading with it. "I don't know where I am. Some abandoned school on an Indian reservation in Washington. Jazmine's the redhead." I blurted.

He nodded. "I know. Chloe ..."

"Zane! No!" A rush of anger tore through me as I was swept away, back to the school.

I felt cheated. Would we ever have time together, alone, without some supernatural tsunami looming over us? Would we even survive? Now that we were mated, the idea of living without him was intolerable.

To make matters worse, Valamir was waiting where I'd left him, looking smug, surrounded by the overgrown shrubbery. I could hear shouts in the distance.

"Your fighting friends have lost the spotlight and your captors have noticed your absence," he announced, as if I wasn't well aware of the mess I was in.

Under the horrendous circumstances, and not sure what else to do, I begged. "I know you hate me. I'm sorry, but I love Zane. You're gorgeous, sexy, and all that, but you keep biting me." I shook my head, hoping to clear it enough to make sense. It was obvious by Valamir's twitching mouth that he was fighting to keep from smiling.

"Will you help me, please?"

"Chloe, I have never refused the passionate plea of a lady. True, you are, for the moment, not mine. But I have an eternity to win your favor. So, I'll start now. What do you want of me?"

"That wig! Will you take it to Plum Beach and give it to Detective Davis or Officer Tate? No one else. Especially not Agent Green," I warned. Loud voices and stampeding feet were drawing closer.

"It would be my pleasure. Anything else?" He let his gaze linger on my breasts a moment too long, despite my rejection.

I was frantic, there had to be something more I could request, a way to take advantage of his attraction. "Will you return and help us get out of here?"

"And what will I get for my efforts?" His lip curled. "You've asked me to complete not one, but two tasks, Chloe Carpenter. And Vampires, although chivalrous, at times, do not offer their services for free."

Panicked by the chaos closing in, I sealed our deal with something far more dangerous than a kiss. "I'll owe you a favor when you need it." I realized too late that I'd pretty much left the door wide open. A favor for a vampire could mean any number of things.. How could I be so stupid?

"It is as you wish."

The glittery trail that was Valamir vanished into the night sky, leaving me to face a furious Jazmine and her army of traitorous mutants.

Twenty-Six

Surrounded by Jazmine, her private guards, a perspiring Martin, and an assortment of mutant women wasn't reassuring. I didn't see Connie or Deb anywhere. I hoped their attention-diverting-scam hadn't been uncovered. Dillon was suspiciously missing as well. I was, however, more than a little happy to see Martin's dog cowering off to the side, too afraid to approach any closer. My fur-shaving vision had castrated the now pathetic pooch.

"What are you doing *back here*?" Jazmine demanded. "Escaping isn't possible, or practical in your case." She appeared uncertain how to handle my strange behavior. What was I guilty of? Playing Hide and Seek.

Ignoring her question, I pierced her mind's barrier, and rather than scanning her current thoughts, I reached for her memories. Seeking the actual school's location, I flipped through thoughts like a file clerk scanning files in a filing cabinet.

For some reason, I now understood my multiple, mind-manipulating capabilities, and they were beyond anything I could have dreamed up. Evidently, the official mating ceremony and blood sharing with an ancient bloodsucker had enhanced my supernatural skills.

Supernatural — I'd never dared attach that particular word to what I did.

Confident in my abilities, for the first time, I blasted my exact location to Zane, Logan, Misty, the two M's, and even Stryder, who should now be working with the others. This was instant messaging at its best. I could have avoided all the discomfort my cell phone was causing inside my too-snug bra had I known the extent of my own preternatural messaging system.

The confirmations poured into my mind, affirming they'd received my mental memo loud and clear. They were coming. All of them. Except Logan. His RSVP wasn't amongst the others. Then I remembered; Alcuin was meeting with him about the coins. What if Logan had been injured, or worse, by the vampire?

"Is there some reason you aren't answering me?" Jazmine grabbed my wrist, twisting.

"Ouch!" I yelped, hesitating for a moment, before firing a mental-missile into her mind. No one was going to grab or grope me again without my permission. I'd had enough to last a lifetime.

She dropped to her knees, clutching her head. Her pain-fueled shrieks slicing through the night.

Bull's-eye! At last Jazmine was where she belonged, bowing to me.

Martin, to my amazement, took charge. "Somebody, do something! Call our onsite medic! Now! Jazmine, honey, talk to me. What's happening?"

I Kissed a Dog

She continued to writhe; her screams turning to whimpers as her eyes rolled back, revealing the whites.

I could sense she was struggling to shift into her werewolf form, but whatever I'd conjured kept her trapped.

The mutants, somehow realizing that I was the cause of the assault on their mistress, were howling with a singular, mournful purpose. Answering calls echoed from every direction. Whatever army existed was being deployed to deal with me.

Yes, I had plenty of cool and painful weapons in my mental cache, but I didn't think I could overcome several hundred creatures at once. I needed my back up.

"Whatever you're doing to her, make it stop!" Martin commanded. "She could have killed you and she didn't."

"And that's supposed to make me feel what … sympathetic?" The nerve of some people was mind boggling. "First, she threatens me; then almost runs me down: kidnaps me; and holds me captive …"

"That sounds about right," a male voice affirmed.

A wave of awareness crashed through me. I'd heard that voice before in Vegas, and again at the board meeting.

Closing my eyes, I took a deep breath and released Jazmine. She remained panting on the ground. One of my liberators had arrived ahead of schedule.

"My, my, did we underestimate you," Logan drawled. Even in human form, he was beyond intimidating. "You're everything I'd hoped for, and so much more."

"What?" I stuttered, still trying to process his presence and strange behavior.

"Before I explain, I need to warn you. Alcuin!"

In a flash of shimmering light, Alcuin appeared, gripping

Misty's arm. Her face was etched with anger and fright. Her eyes met mine, pleading.

"Misty!" I cried, and started toward my friend.

Logan blocked me. "I don't think so. My little sis, here, has become far too independent for her own good. And I know just how much you two bonded. Very sweet. So, if you want to continue your friendship, you'd both do well to remember two things: I'm in charge. You're not."

A few mutants chuckled in agreement. I was utterly dumbfounded. Logan? The bad guy? He was the pack's alpha, well, not by blood, but nevertheless, the current leader. What the hell?

I chanced a glance at Alcuin. By his dejected state, I could only presume he was feeling self-conscious, even defeated. He wasn't displaying even a portion of his normal confidence. It appeared things were happening outside his control. He looked almost as lost as I felt. His eyes, for just a moment, met mine. He inclined his head, just enough for me to notice.

Alcuin would come through for us before this was all over. I wasn't sure how he'd ended up with Logan, but it wasn't where he wanted to be. I'd bet my life on it. Logan was the true, tyrannical traitor.

The Alpha paced through the crowd, turning every few seconds to look my way. "I can see you're trying to make sense of what's happening. Let me help you. But keep this in mind, Ms. Carpenter, if you attempt to use any of your mind magic on me or anyone here, your friend, my dear sister, will be destroyed."

I swallowed my frustration, hoping I appeared unruffled by his threats. I couldn't, however, help rolling my eyes.

Misty, on the other hand, wasn't so composed. She lunged at her brother, growling. Alcuin held tight, keeping her from breaking loose.

"Oh, come on, Misty. Give it up. You're such a pacifist. War is part of life," Logan chastised, choosing that moment to launch into an extended discourse on the many benefits and necessity of war.

Jazmine, Martin, and the others, turned their attention to the werewolf, hanging on his words like a life preserver. More than a few of the women blushed when his eyes rested on them for longer than a second. I felt certain if he offered poisoned Kool Aide, they'd drink it. That was a scary thought.

Disregarding his warning, I sent out another communication to Zane and the others, explaining the most recent developments. I figured as long as The Alpha didn't notice any visible or harmful reactions to my mental activities, I'd be safe enough.

In addition, I'd created an effective mental barrier that would keep any unwanted intruders from entering my mind. Logan, I assumed, was worried about my more destructive talents anyway, like turning Jazmine into a moaning mess of meekness.

Remembering how she looked writhing on the ground gave me a sick sense of satisfaction. In the future, she'd know better than to provoke me ... if there was a future for me — for any of us.

I sensed Zane attempting to push into my thoughts and allowed him entrance.

We'll be there, Princess. I promise. Keep Logan talking. One thing he has always loved is attention. That's why I let him take the Alpha position without a fight. I didn't want to be in charge. I'll explain later. Without Alcuin's teleporting talents, we're stuck traveling the old fashioned way. Hang on, baby. Hang on.

I will. You can count on it. Hurry. Please.

Knowing we'd need all the help we could gather, I sent a beacon out to David and the cloaked creatures. With David's advanced telepathic abilities, I was certain he'd hear me. I was uncertain, however, if he'd respond. I hadn't heard from him since the guided dream encounter.

If everyone showed, we'd have a chance to defeat Logan's clan.

Given the opportunity, Misty and Alcuin would join us, I was sure of it. Valamir had promised his services, and I felt certain he'd return. He wanted to collect a favor from me and would do whatever it took to gain that favor.

Zane, Stryder, the two M's; they were a sure thing. With any luck, Connie, Deb, and Dillon were lurking close by. They'd come to our aid if they could. And we had one weapon no one else did: Me. When the time came, I'd use my powers like a nuclear weapon, melting the minds of our enemies like butter in a microwave.

I hoped there'd be some other way, though. I wasn't real keen on becoming the cause of ultimate annihilation, and not all the women here wanted to follow Jazmine or Logan. They were trapped in forced training to serve as slaves.

How did all this fit together? What did the medical facility on some old barge have to do with Vegas hotels, random murders, and mutants? With me? How did Logan keep his evil agenda from his board members and Zane? I had too many questions and no logical answers.

I Kissed a Dog

Any logic I'd known before had pretty much vanished with Zane's grand entrance into my life.

"Ms. Carpenter," Logan snapped. "Were you listening?"

Feeling like I was back in a high school social studies class, I half stuttered, "Uh, well, I was kind of trying to figure all this out. Like ... what are you hoping to accomplish? And what *are* you doing?" I hoped I'd earn points for honesty. I had not a clue what he'd been rambling about for the past ten minutes.

"If you'd listened, you might have learned something." He shook his head. "No problem, we'll chat over dinner. Won't you join me at the table? I'm sure you'll see the reasoning behind what might look otherwise ..."

Jazmine blurted, her eyes on fire, "Why explain anything to her? As soon as Zane comes for her, she's dead. And I'm doing the killing." She was vibrating, ready to shift.

"Think again, bitch!" Misty snarled, infuriated. "This vampire isn't going to be able to hold me much longer."

"Enough!" Logan roared. "Jazmine, I am in charge here, just in case you've forgotten. I will handle all matters related to this lovely lady." His eyes made a quick, but deliberate sweep of my most female assets. "And, Misty ... my little sister, I regret to say this, but I fear I must. Another outburst from you and your blood will be nourishing the ground we stand on."

A sudden, heartbreaking shadow darkened Misty's face, one of making her appear like a baby sister whose big brother had just abandoned her to a pack of rabid mutants. I yearned to comfort her.

As we made our way back to the platform, I sent a message.

Misty, I am so sorry. We'll make it out of here. I promise. Be ready for anything, and remember, you've got a family with me and Zane. I had no way to measure the impact of my words. I prayed that they provided some sort of assurance.

From atop the dais, Logan extended his hand. I grudgingly allowed him to pull me to the table and seated myself amongst what amounted to werewolf royalty. I was far from impressed.

I was worried and afraid, afraid I couldn't keep the two promises I'd made: one to Joshua Smart, and one to Misty.

A vision of the mutant at Luke's abandoned cabin, eyes glazed in death, flared to life in my mind like a movie screen in a dark theatre. I was a killer. The truth no longer repelled me. It gave me a sense of power. I could and would protect those dear to me.

I'd kill again, without hesitation, to ensure my promises were fulfilled.

Twenty-Seven

I couldn't help wondering if the renewed determination I felt was reflected on my face.

Jazmine continued to glare, while Logan and Martin made a show of enjoying the feast (blood saturated meat) that was delivered to our table courtesy of several attractive mutant women still remaining in their human forms.

A majority of the captives had shifted and were frolicking in the moonlight, unaware of the inevitable conflict.

Refusing Logan's halfhearted solicitations to tempt me with food, I allowed my powers to roll over the area, seeking any new or concealed supernatural elements.

With no new blips on my mental radar, I turned my attention to Logan, who made Zane's table manners seem impeccable. "I'm ready to hear about your unholy alliance." I glared with venom at Jazmine, who slurped blood off her fingers.

"You are disgusting. What a pity that this is the last meal you'll enjoy," I said through clenched teeth. I was banking on Logon's promise to protect me from her sure to be violent response.

As expected, she lunged across the table, and was subdued by her own two guards, who now appeared to defer to Logon.

"Undoubtedly, our guest needs some attention." Logan suggested with a smile.

Jazmine sulked, and Alcuin and Misty appeared baffled by Logan's sudden surge of friendliness. Martin remained indifferent, still ripping his blood-soaked dinner from a bone.

I wasn't fooled. The Alpha was hoping to sweeten whatever deal he planned to offer in hopes of gaining access to my powers. I'd play along to gather my own intelligence.

Scanning the faces, I noted the one empty place setting. We were minus our sixth dinner companion. "Are you expecting someone else?"

Logan, cheery grin still intact, nodded. "A person I'm confident you will remember, but I'll start without him.

A purebred, loyal to our pack, was visiting your wildlife park and overheard a conversation that piqued his interest. In response, I sent Zane to search for you and investigate your town's *unfortunate* increase in murders." He gave Jazmine a meaningful look. "Regrettably, for Jazmine, Zane fell for you in the process, adding additional complications to our already complicated situation."

"He'll return to me," Jazmine said sounding unconvinced.

Logan sneered, "You keep believing that, Jaz. *Anyway*, one of our Native American brothers discovered an ancient document, referring to a set of coins …"

"What kind of coins?" I said hoping I sounded casual.

"Stop playing coy. You know Alcuin has kept me apprised of your house-to-house searches. Zane, as my second in command, was also giving me detailed accounts of your activities. Why wouldn't he?"

"He wouldn't if he'd known what a ..."

"Now, now, let's forget the name calling and move on." Logan's smile remained, but his eyes blazed crimson. I'd hit a nerve.

"Would you like to see the coins, Ms. Carpenter?"

I turned to glare at Alcuin, the one person who could have delivered them personally to Logan. Again I sensed his shame and doubted that he'd willingly wanted to partner with the alpha wolf, but he had. Why?

I didn't have time to ponder further before Logan nodded at one of the guards, who pulled a briefcase from the podium's inside shelf.

Eager to see all the coins together, I leaned forward.

I wasn't disappointed. They'd been polished with professional care and glowed in the moonlight. The magical sigils writhed across their surfaces, reminding me of the markings on my ankle. Alone they'd seemed special, but as a set, spectacular. An almost tangible force radiated from the case. I couldn't help but reach out a hand.

Just missing my fingers, Logan closed it with a click; extinguishing the preternatural flame I'd felt so powerfully only seconds before.

"What are they for?" I wanted to caress the coins. The need to have them in my possession was almost overwhelming. I knew they were somehow central to everything I'd endured.

Logan, as Zane had implied, loved to listen to himself talk. He launched into the details I'd been waiting to hear.

I listened with a mixture of awe and increasing terror as

Logan, with a few insertions from Martin, explained his intricate plot to rule as the unquestioned leader of all werewolves and mutants. Something his father had aspired to, but failed to embrace following a death match with Zane's father.

Pretending to be appalled by his father's devious plan, but in reality devastated about his death, Logan had used Zane's guilt, and his lack of desire to lead, as a means to take over the Pacific Pack. Zane, the true heir, became second in command, where he was content to wander for weeks, returning when he was needed.

Logan had also formed a secret alliance with a power hungry Jazmine, knowing very well that few men, purebreds, or mutants, could resist her sexual allure. He'd hoped she would keep Zane in line while manipulating any male they needed.

Just over a year ago, one of Logan's Native American partners, working for Martin, had after years of looking, located the fae document Logan's father had been seeking. It had been buried in an ancient Indian burial ground. The fear of angry spirits, had kept treasure hunters away until the US government proclaimed the sites historical, religious landmarks, off limits to outsiders.

The legendary text described a medical procedure capable of altering mutants, giving them the ability to sun walk in their changed forms like their purebred counterparts.

In addition, a process for creating mutants out of men, without being bitten by a purebred was revealed. The men, changed in this manner, were less likely to die from infection or other complications. In the past, a high percentage of those who were bitten didn't survive the change, and it was also against the treaty to create more bitten mutants.

I Kissed a Dog

The fae, or fairies, as humans called them, were the most powerful supernatural beings, second only to God's holiest angels. Divided into the Seelie and Unseelie courts, they spent more time battling each other than worrying about the other supernatural creatures, which they deemed inferior to their own ancient race.

Overwhelmed by information, I would have considered fantasy fiction two weeks ago, I cleared my throat. "So, you were performing medical experiments on unwilling men?" I'd seen their so-called medical procedures in the visions from David and Martin's dog.

Logan shrugged. "Chloe, my dear, there's always been a price for knowledge. I need to build an army fast. To exert my authority, and garner the respect and support needed to rule, I had to cut corners. Besides, I'm doing them a favor. They end up with super strength and abilities they'd never acquire in their weak human bodies."

A jolt of anger kicked my adrenaline into high gear. I trembled with energy. "How dare you decide for someone else who or what they should be? And you're still lying. Not all your *patients* are surviving, are they?"

"She's right. Remember, Logan, she scanned Martin's dog at the board meeting. She's seen the unwanted results," another familiar voice agreed.

"You've got to be kidding?" I spat as James McQuillen, the man who'd saved me from my untimely face plant at the board meeting, slid into the sixth chair, his ever present dobby, Boss, at his side.

I almost expected Zane to join us and admit his involvement, but I knew better. He was one of the good ones. "Who else should I expect?" Maybe the two M's would now appear, making the father and son duo the best actors of all.

James McQuillen grinned. "We're all here now. I promise. No more surprises."

"And I should believe you, because?"

"Good point," the big Indian agreed. "I think Logan was just finishing up his story when I so rudely interrupted."

Still trembling, I looked around the table. It was starting to make sense. Like I'd predicted, this was a hostile takeover. Certain purebreds, humans, and mutants had joined forces to seize power. I doubted they'd be content with ruling over the werewolves and mutants. Who would be next? Other supernaturals? Humans ...

"The coins. I was almost to the wonderful, incredible, life saving coins," said Logan.

"Please do continue. I'm not sure it can get any worse," I said the words knowing it was about to get much, much worse.

To confirm my belief, James McQuillen took over. "The coins, once translated, reveal the formula for eternal life. Your friend here," he nodded toward Alcuin, "was unable to accomplish the task as promised."

I glanced back at Alcuin. Wait a minute. Yes, they did accomplish the task, or were close to it. Rita and the others had been working nonstop on the translation. I was sure they'd made significant strides.

This was information I'd be keeping to myself. After all, Logan was the one who'd implied that knowledge was worth a price, maybe, in this case, a small fortune.

"You still haven't explained why some of your patients aren't surviving. Why you're killing them when they don't turn," I questioned, remembering the gruesome murder of one such man in his hospital bed on the barge.

"Some humans aren't exactly human. At least not all the way human. Many have fae blood. Their polluted bloodline causes them to mutate. They become hideous beasts with untamable supernatural abilities. We can't have them running around interrupting our mission, Ms. Carpenter. That would be bad press," explained McQuillen.

I thought of David. He was "bad press" waiting to happen. Just the press I needed about now to wipe the snide expressions off a few unfriendly faces.

Shoving thoughts of revenge aside, for the moment, I determined to learn all I could while my hosts were in the talking mood; I asked the one question that hadn't been answered. "Why kill the men in Plum Beach then? They didn't turn into the bald guys."

"That was my work," Jazmine said with unmistakable pride. "We'd been testing the process for months before it actually produced the desired results.

In the beginning, no one was changing into anything. We used a vampire associate's powers, and erased the memories of our patients' time spent on the barge.

Unluckily, for a few of them, it came to our attention they were regaining their memories. We couldn't risk having news of our operation spreading. So, I eliminated the problem and obtained an added benefit. Law enforcement was focused on solving the murders, keeping their attention off the other unusual happenings in their town.

They kept Zane busy too, so busy he didn't see what was right in front of him."

"How convenient," I muttered, sickened by her compassionless explanation. She was beaming.

I took a quick peek in her head and was appalled to find her reliving the murder of Josh, including the violence-laced sex beforehand. I pulled out, revolted.

A subject change was in order. "How did you learn where the coins were hidden?" I directed my question to James McQuillen. "We weren't the only ones searching for them."

"We applied certain physical pressures on one of the bald abominations."

"You mean you tortured him."

"To death," Logan answered.

I looked away from his gloating face.

I didn't want to hear anything else about death and dying. What I wanted was to get those coins away from Logan's henchman. The possibility of Logan and Jazmine gaining immortality was downright horrifying. They'd murder, without any qualms, anyone or anything that got in their way.

That would include me and everyone I cared about.

I couldn't let that happen. I wouldn't let it happen.

If my supporting forces didn't show soon, I'd see exactly how and to what extent my powers had expanded.

⟲

Martin clapped his hands, "We're way overdue for our evening entertainment."

Logan moved to the podium and adjusted a handheld microphone. "I can see you are all enjoying your night of freedom to its fullest."

His comment was met with a strange combination of howls, yips, and human cheers. It seemed that everyone had forgotten their captive status and the fact at they normally spent their days on a rigorous and tightly supervised schedule inside the old school.

The unrelenting brainwashing was working.

As was the case with any minority, equal rights were deserved and desired, but Logan had failed to explain the price they'd pay for what they thought would be equality with the purebreds.

These mutant women would become even more enslaved. Freedom for them was a beautifully crafted illusion that would crumble under the weight of truth. And there was a strong possibility that I'd be the one telepathically delivering that very truth in a few short hours. I hoped I could wait for my backup, but I'd do whatever was necessary to stop this madness.

With any luck, the entertainment segment would end with my comrades bursting into the mix and giving the masses a true taste of freedom. Although, I wasn't real comfortable counting on luck; mine had taken an unexpected turn for the worse when James McQuillen had joined Logan's already powerful posse.

I remembered his extensive mental capabilities; they'd rivaled my own in many ways. I'd prefer him as an advocate not an adversary, but it was clear that the choice wasn't mine to make. He'd chosen his side. We were now chasms apart.

Stealing a glance his direction, I was startled to see him watching me.

Things are not what they seem, Ms. Carpenter.

Before I could answer, a group of Native American drummers and dancers entered the clearing. When I looked back at James McQuillen, his attention rested on the dancers, leaving me to wonder if I'd imagined the mental message.

I was sure I hadn't.

What did he mean? Like I didn't already know that things were not what they seemed. That statement could be the opening line in a book about my life. What if …?

The musicians pounded their drums to life, drawing the crowd closer, stopping Logon from any further grandstanding and interrupting my silent debate.

Dressed in traditional ceremonial attire, the group swirled into action, their musical whoops and hollers sending chills down my spine. In the distance, a chorus of howls complimented the performance far more than any traditional backup singers.

I'd attended a Pow Wow many years ago with my parents and had loved the theatrical dancers and musicians. But tonight's performance had the opposite effect. It felt eerie, wrong somehow.

Everything was wrong tonight. Even the moon had morphed into a sphere of seducing shadows, casting a suspicious, crimson-hued glow for as far as I could see.

Chloe, I'm here, Zane announced into my mind, making everything, for one brief moment, right again.

Just knowing he was near, sent my libido into overdrive. I'd never believed the scientific studies on pheromones acting as aphrodisiacs, but I was willing, when this was all over, to reexamine the data. Maybe it was the whole mating thing, but I could swear I smelled Zane's distinctively masculine scent over every other fragrance, and there were scents abounding in the night air, not all of them pleasant.

I Kissed a Dog

Forget the moon; I was heady with visions of my mate. Never mind the possibility of death; I wanted my man, my werewolf. I wanted him at my side.

Together we'd defeat our enemies.

Chloe, your fanged admirer showed up and offered to transport us here vampire style. I decided I'd kill him later. I had to get to you first.

Who's here with you? I couldn't help wondering just how extensive Valamir's teleporting abilities were. Envisioning the vampire bringing Zane to me was difficult considering his self-proclaimed obsession with my blood. My promise of a future favor must have provided the precise amount of motivation.

"*Mack, Michael, Valamir, of course, since he* drove, *Rita, Stryder, and several friends of Stryder. I think some of your cloaked crusaders are here as well. I'm not sure how many. They're harder to pick out.*"

I was again aware of McQuillen's gaze on me. He nodded just enough for me to notice. For certain I wasn't imagining things. Maybe he'd fight for us after all. Having him, Alcuin, and Misty would increase our odds significantly. Factoring Connie, Deb, and Dillon into the equation would be even better.

I sent out a mental probe, hoping to locate my newest allies, informing them the time was now to do what we'd planned all along. There was no response. I hoped they'd found a way to escape. If not, we'd have to attack without them.

Be ready, Chloe. Valamir's circling around to teleport you away from the frontline. I can't fight and worry about you.

What? I screamed into his mind. They needed me. My mind magic was vital to our winning. What was he thinking? He clearly wasn't.

It's temporary. Just until we remove some of the danger. Don't worry, Princess, you'll get your chance to blast their brains.

So not funny.

We're already taking out mutants around the perimeter.

Zane, some of these women want out of this crazy cult. Please don't tell me you're killing at random.

I already thought of that. We're asking if they want to join us. They have ten seconds to decide. That's the best we can do.

I froze. Valamir was behind the platform, preparing to grab me. When that happened, all hell would break loose.

Right now, my team was functioning under the radar. They had the advantage. In a few seconds that would all change. And I'd be forced to hitch a ride behind someone's eyes to see the fight firsthand. That wasn't good enough.

Before I could gather my thoughts enough to think of an argument that would persuade Zane to change his mind, icy arms pulled me close and I was spinning out of control,. If I had to choose, I'd pick Alcuin as my transportation source. I preferred his less dramatic technique.

"I think I'm going to barf." Bending over, I clutched my stomach.

Valamir looked at me with a strange intensity. "Please forgive me. I just teleported your entire entourage in one trip. I am a bit unsettled. I promise a better experience in the future."

I didn't tell him what I was thinking. Teleporting again, ever, with him, wasn't on my top ten list of things to do. I

I Kissed a Dog

hoped Alcuin would prove to be a good guy so I could ride home with him.

Straightening to my full height, I cautiously took in my surroundings, almost afraid to see where he'd delivered me.

"No way, uh uh. I am not staying down here. Whose idea was this?" I demanded at the sight of my familiar basement room/cell.

"I was instructed to place you somewhere no one would expect to find you. I didn't realize you had an intimate relationship with this room. Again, I apologize."

"Don't apologize. Move me! Anywhere but here. Please!" I'd begged Valamir earlier to return and help me. Had I known this would be his ultimate act of kindness, I'd have kept my mouth shut.

"I must go. They are in danger. I will return for you as your mate permits."

As always, he disappeared in a cloud of pretty particles, leaving me in my dreaded dorm room alone.

I knew something he didn't.

I was no longer that timid and terrified girl Zane had dragged to Vegas.

I was a confident and cunning woman with skills. Supernatural skills that just might be what saved all the tough guys' supernatural asses.

Oh no, I wouldn't be here waiting like a good little girl for Zane's approval and Valamir's arrival.

I'd be on the bloodstained battlefield with the rest of my *entourage* well before my motherly mate deemed it safe enough for me to return.

Carol Van Atta

No way was I missing the final showdown. I had a serious score to settle.

Not even Jazmine's surrender would suffice.

I was seeking absolute silence.

With her mouth shut permanently, I'd be satisfied.

Twenty-Eight

"Chloe, is that you?" a muffled voice put a rapid halt to my vengeful thinking.

I turned expecting to see one of my former roommates behind me. "Deb? Connie?" I questioned the silent room, listening intently. It was impossible to gauge where the voice had originated.

Besides my ragged breathing, the other perceptible sound came from just outside the door.

I remembered with horror the first time I'd seen the entrance to my room. The deep gouges had supplied the visual evidence of some sadistic monster's attempts to tear through the door.

What I heard right now sounded like something making forceful strokes — like razor-sharp claws scraping the door's full length.

The image sent a spike of terror through my chest. Being mauled to death when freedom had been so close was unacceptable.

Using my mind magic, I thrust my mental feelers out and

into the formidable enemy's thoughts now ripping at the door, like a dog digging for its long lost bone.

Kill. Kill. Kill. Kill Ki ...

Halfway through the fifth *kill* I pulled out. Whatever was pawing so maniacally had a mental makeup unlike any I'd ever explored.

Its psyche was blacker than black, obsidian — a pool of swirling darkness with the audible word — kill — rising from its murky depths with increasing volume and intensity.

The clawing creature's sole purpose was to cause my death.

Zane had supposedly delivered me to safety. Wouldn't he be surprised?

I took advantage of an unexpected stretch of silence. Was it gone? Maybe it had given up after breaking a claw.

Cautious, with all my senses screaming for me to stop, I crept toward the door, I could picture The warning sign, "Abandon all hope, ye who enter here" from Dante's *Inferno*. A well-crafted description of hell's portico and possibly my door.

What waited on the other side was as inhuman as they came.

The devil himself? — I doubted it, but whatever it was could inflict diabolical damage that I wouldn't survive despite my increasing arsenal of supernatural weapons. I wasn't sure how I knew this. But I did.

I was aware that I'd met my match. I had to escape. Beyond that I didn't have a clue what my next steps would be. Before I could change my mind, I spun to face the four familiar dressers.

My claustrophobic fears paled in comparison to whatever

waited in the hallway. I'd navigate the hidden air shaft rather than risking a faceoff with the beast.

Maybe there was another way. I had allies, and one committed purebred-protector. For an instant, I'd forgotten the war just beyond my little prison. It had to be raging out of control.

Sending out a mental probe, I located and latched onto Stryder. I needed to see Zane. I didn't know what I'd do if he was injured.

To my relief, he was very much alive and fighting viciously in his more mutant-like form, his teeth shredding through the thick neck of a male mutant.

Tracking the movements of my group was nearly impossible. Everything was happening faster than my human eyes could process. Fur, blood, and body parts were blasting from the moving mass, and I had no clue who was slaughtering who.

Stryder was shielding a small group of mutant women, who'd switched to our side. Others were attempting to join their cluster. I wondered why they weren't advancing against Jazmine's hordes. It appeared they were cowering instead.

With every breath I drew, I wanted to contact Zane for help, but resisted the urge.

Popping into his, or one of my other friends' heads, in the midst of this merciless carnage, was bound have unpleasant consequences. Ones I wasn't willing to risk in order to save myself. They needed to keep their thoughts undivided. A blink at the wrong moment could equal a gruesome death.

Instead, I continued my surveillance, hoping to catch sight of James McQuillen. After a few minutes, I gave up. Getting back to the battle and away from whatever was lurking beyond my door was my present priority.

Slipping from Styder's mind, I hurried to the dresser. I was able to pull it away from the wall, revealing the shaft's murky maw. I wouldn't be surprised if it spouted teeth and chewed me to pieces.

Hesitating, I glanced one final time around the room. Part of me wanted to curl up on my cot and bury my head under the flimsy pillow until danger passed.

Renewed clawing jolted me into action.

I entered the duct head first and made every attempt to distribute my body mass evenly, making sure to keep some weight on my legs. I forced myself to slide along rather than crawling.

Deb had mentioned that this method of travel would prevent the joints in the sheet metal from breaking. I hoped she was right. I'd heard that crawling through an air duct was a myth, but I was doing it. Granted, I was pretty small and this was a large vent. I hoped it would support me the entire journey.

Wishing I had a flashlight, I inched forward. The shaft slopped downward, leading, I guessed, to the basement.

The darkness felt alive, chilling me all over, and to make matters worse, a foul odor grew stronger the further down I progressed. I pictured dead rats just ahead, and waited with dread for one of my hands to come in contact with an animal's decomposing corpse.

After what felt like forever, I came to a drop. A light was more than necessary at this juncture.

Remaining statue still, I attempted to shut off the rising

panic constricting my throat. I sucked hard, gasping for breath. Then I remembered my cell phone.

Slowing my breathing, I retrieved it from my bra, and powered it up. It provided just enough illumination for me to identify an eight foot drop down a narrower shaft.

Taking several more deep breaths, I considered my limited options. One, slide down the shaft and hope I didn't crash through; two, scale down with my back on one side and my feet across from me.

"Chloe, is that you?" A female voice filtered up the duct, sending my adrenaline soaring.

"Deb?" I asked my voice shaky. "Where are you?"

"In a shaft above the basement. Don't jump!"

"Wouldn't think of it," I confirmed, striking off option one as an alternative for my descent.

Confirming my chosen travel mode, she instructed, "Put your back against one side and your feet on the other; keep pressure on your feet and lower one leg, followed by your back, and then another leg. You can do it," she encouraged.

Terrified, but without another choice, I followed her directions.

Eight feet felt like twenty as I inched my way down. At the halfway point, something gouged my lower back. Pain seared through my right side.

"I think I'm bleeding. Oh, God, it hurts," I whimpered.

"Chloe, don't stop. You've got to keep moving."

She was right, but I knew if I didn't alter my course, the sharp protrusion would damage more of my back.

With great care, and extra encouragement from Deb, I slid

sideways, away from the source of what had become an agonizing intrusion to my escape.

Descending with greater caution than before, I managed to reach Deb, who was stretched out on her belly. Our faces almost touched.

"Thank God you're all right." She reached around and managed a half hug with us lying down.

She pulled her arm away and grabbed my cell phone, shining the light on her hand. I saw the blood the same time she did.

"Let's get out of here."

"How —?" It was her voice I'd heard from the room, and I was desperate to know what'd happened to her and Connie.

"I'll explain when we're out of here, for now, keep your eyes on the prize," she encouraged.

With her mutant agility, she was able to maneuver into a new position with ease, her feet now in my face. But before I could complain about her shoes so close to my nose, she began her advance, using a strange army crawl to slither through the duct like a snake with appendages.

I followed her example to the best of my human ability and tried to keep up.

She could sense when I'd fallen behind, and slowed her pace to accommodate my lack of dexterity.

Sooner than I'd expected, we reached a grate. "This is it," she said, sounding excited.

All I felt was relieved.

I heard the grate rattle before she tugged it off. She shimmied through the small opening and dropped to the floor.

I Kissed a Dog

"You made it!" Connie said from below.

Another flood of relief rushed through me at the sound of her voice. They were okay. But where was Dillon?

"Come on, Chloe. Stay on your stomach and lean through the opening. We'll do the rest," assured Deb.

Once my feet were on solid ground, I turned to embrace Deb, then Connie. "Thank you."

"Here, sit down." Connie led me to a card table with folding chairs around it. Several decks of cards were stacked on the table's otherwise clean surface.

"What is this, the custodian's lair?" I asked, surveying the room full of cleaning apparatus and supplies.

"None other." Deb gave me a lopsided grin that belied the tension barely contained beneath her cool exterior. "Connie, grab the first aid kit. It's on the shelf over there."

While they cleaned my wound, which thankfully, wasn't too deep, I learned where my friends had disappeared to. Although *they* were safe, Dillon hadn't fared as well.

He was dead.

Dillon's killer was none other than the monster attempting to make mince meat of my door.

Connie, once she was assured of our current safety, reverted to silence, allowing Deb to share the details of Dillon's death and their escape. Connie's grief was palpable. There was nothing either of us could say to comfort her.

According to Deb, once they realized Dillon wouldn't fit through the shaft, she and Connie had decided, with his insistence, to go on without him, but he'd wanted to try one final alternative before they separated.

Jazmine's guards had locked them in the lower level room

following their deliberate distraction. She'd been suspicious of their squabble and wanted all three locked away until later when she could interrogate them. Their escorts, eager to return to the bonfire, had failed to search Dillon for his keys, and he was able to leave the room.

He'd warned the women about the feral creature that was kept isolated in a secured room turned holding cell. Dillon wanted to ensure it remained in lockdown before leading Connie and Deb out through the back entrance.

The last they'd seen of Dillon was him sprinting around the corner with a hideously mutated creature pursuing him. Almost to the door, Dillon had slipped. The beast, seizing the opportunity, had grabbed Dillon by the neck and dragged him away.

At this point, Connie erupted into tears. "He yelled for us to go back inside and lock the door. There was nothing we could do. That thing was like a mutant that had survived a nuclear holocaust. Oh, God, I don't know what I'll do without him."

I moved to put an arm around her shoulders; she continued to cry, shuddering every few seconds.

"We were in shock," Deb continued. "Connie was beyond consoling. I didn't know what to do. But I knew Dillon would have wanted her to get out. About the same time, *that thing* returned and started slicing at the door.

I'm not sure how, but I convinced her we couldn't allow Dillon's death to be for nothing, and we made it to the basement. On our way down, I heard something. It was you talking to someone. I called out, but you didn't answer."

"But I did!"

I Kissed a Dog

"Who knows what happened." Deb shrugged. "The acoustics are off in the shaft. I wanted to get Connie as far away as possible. Then I returned to look for you."

I wasn't sure I could express my gratitude to them, but I tried. "Thank you so much for coming back for me. The dresser was in place, though. That confused me. I thought maybe I was hearing things."

Despite Connie's still flowing tears, Deb chuckled. "Oh, that. I kind of punched a hole in the dresser so I could pull it back into position. I didn't want to roll out a welcome mat to our getaway route."

I nodded, my thoughts already flipping to the next phase of our escape. "We have to leave and join the others. They need us." I couldn't stand the thought of remaining down here with Zane and my other friends fighting for *our* lives.

"No! We can't! What if Dillon is still alive?" Connie blurted, surprising us both with her outburst.

I glanced at Deb, uncertain how to handle Connie's resistance.

Understanding my dilemma, Deb responded. "Babe, we need to get out of here. There is no way Dillon could have taken that thing down. I have no clue where it came from or why Jazmine kept it imprisoned here, but we don't want to end up anywhere near it. Dillon would never have wanted you to involve yourself. He wanted you free."

Connie stared up at the ceiling. "No, I can't just leave him. The beast came back to the door when Chloe was inside. That was right after we entered the shaft. Maybe it put Dillon aside for dinner later on." She swallowed hard. "Maybe it wanted to capture us all before mealtime."

I hated to admit it, but she had a point. If it was Zane, wouldn't I want to be sure?

"I'll compromise," Deb stated. "We go and get help from one of Chloe's friends, and then we look for Dillon."

"What if we're too late?" Connie pleaded.

Deb countered, "We can't beat that thing alone. We need help. We're wasting time arguing."

"Let's go already!" Connie half-shrieked. She leapt to her feet, tossed my arm aside, and glanced around the room a final time. Then, without warning, she charged to the far corner, and loped with inhuman grace up the stairs with Deb on her heels.

I caught up with them as they opened the door at the top. We all stood, just listening. It was obvious the battle was still underway by the woeful wails of the dying, and the vicious victory roars.

"We need a plan," I whispered, afraid they'd shift into their mutant forms before we decided our best course of action. I was just in time.

Connie whipped her head around, her eyes glowed red. "Kill Jazmine and everyone fighting on her side. That's *my* plan," she snarled.

Almost afraid to answer, I offered a compromise. "Sounds like a good plan, but we can't just dash out there like madmen, women," I amended. "There are two purebreds besides Jazmine that are not on our side. Logan and James McQuillen are with her now. I'll identify them as soon as I can. Try to gather any …"

Midsentence, my friends, thrilled by the extensive violence, and no longer able to contain their bloodlust, morphed into the mutants I so feared. Without a glance my direction, they bolted toward the raging bonfire, leaving me in the shadows alone.

Cautious, I picked my way through the grass, staying close to the school's wall. No one would expect to find me out here. That was something in my favor.

With my back pressed against the cool concrete, I slowed my breathing for what felt like the millionth time, counted to ten, and I launched myself into Stryder's mind. I located the ideal vantage point behind his eyes, and made sure to block my presence, making certain not to disrupt his efforts, which had paid off noticeably during the time I'd been absent.

He'd organized the defectors and they were advancing stealthily against their former companions.

Bodies and bloody entrails were strewn across the field. I retched, unable to handle the choking stench of blood and smoldering flesh. It seemed the welcoming flames had served as a wicked and effective weapon of deathly destruction.

I tore my attention away from the surrounding horrors, and using Stryder's keen eyesight and heightened senses, intently sought a glimpse of my mate. It was plain, despite the carnage, our side was winning. A hint of relief heightened my emotions, providing my first twinge of optimism in a long while.

David and his bald men stood steadfast, arms crossed, along the sidelines. Every few seconds, for no observable reason, a mutant would crumple to the ground. I suspected David and his kin were using mental powers similar to my own.

Misty was standing, shoulders thrown back, in scary-wolf

monster form on a small mountain of bodies, her howls declaring victory.

Alcuin and Valamir, the two lone vampires, were fighting back to back, brandishing gore-stained blades, and slicing through any rival that dared approach.

Where was Zane?

I counted Mack, Michael, and a purebred I assumed was Rita. They were bloodied, but still fighting impressively. Connie and Deb had joined Styder's group and were making serious headway.

Still no Zane; it was as if he'd vanished from the scene, but I knew he wouldn't leave me or his pack mates behind.

An unexpected feeling of despair intruded, demolishing my confidence and drowning the pleasure I'd felt watching my entourage as Valamir referred to them, kick some serious mutant ass.

Chloe … a choked voice whispered into my mind. *Is that you?* So faint were the words, they barely registered.

Uncertain, I swung to the left and spotted a solitary figure I'd missed at first glance. The person was sprawled on the ground near a tree. Tentacles of incoming fog hovered over the area where he lay, making it difficult to see.

I looked closer.

Zane? No! It couldn't be.

He was twisted in an unnatural position but had managed to shift back into a human.

Without thought for my own safety, I half ran half stumbled to his fallen form, collapsing on my knees beside him. I slapped a hand over my mouth to stifle the cries of anguish fighting to explode. My mate had taught me well. Even as I stared at his broken and brutalized body, I had enough sense to avoid attracting any unwanted attention.

Understanding that talking would be impossible in his condition, I entered his thoughts. *Zane. Oh. My. God. What can I do? You can't die. I won't let you. I love you. I need you.*

Press your mating mark against mine. Legend says this will heal ...

Unable to finish his instructions, a rasping spasm tore through his chest. Blood spewed from his mouth and nose.

"You will not die! I forbid it!" I heard myself shout as panic threatened to override my senses. I refused to succumb to the old Chloe's fainting-in-a-time-crisis routine.

I needed to think, to focus. Becoming hysterical was not an option.

Zane wanted me to do something simple. I struggled to organize my jumbled thoughts.

Our marks. He wanted me to join our mating marks.

Spurred to action, I yanked off my shoe and sock and was pushing up my pant leg when Jazmine, in her wolf form, skidded to a stop behind Zane. She changed shapes and faced me as a flawless naked woman, hands on her narrow hips.

"Isn't that sweet. You were going to activate the healing process," she paused for effect. "Well, I don't think so! If I can't have him; you won't!"

"Just take me," I pleaded. "Isn't that what you wanted all along? Me out of the picture? Then you can have Zane as a mate; you can use the coins to give him eternal life. You love him, remember?"

No! I will never touch her. Don't do this! I. Forbid. It.

Ignoring Zane, I made myself look up and meet Jazmine's crimson eyes.

The smug look of defiance pasted across her face flipped a switch inside me. Inhuman fury boiled to the surface and overflowed, giving me the burst of inner strength I needed to resist.

Without effort, I fired a mental missile into her scheming brain with such efficiency and force it blasted her onto her ass; her feet flew from beneath her. She collided with a breath-sucking thump against a trio of boulders. What sounded like bones cracking followed.

Scooting myself next to Zane, I prepared to press my marks, now glowing amber, against his.

Out of the mist came Logan Sanders.

Snarls and guttural growls preceded The Alpha leaping at me as if he'd sprouted wings; his claws extended, and lips curled back, with unrestrained hostility. His fangs appeared more lethal than a saber-toothed tiger's.

Terrorized, I lost my mental grip on Jazmine, who though unsteady, grappled to her feet as another massive wolf plummeted into Logan, forcing him onto his back.

Logan responded fiercely, knocking his attacker off. The two rolled, each one struggling for purchase. Jazmine, to my amazement, backed away and fled.

Now! Zane's pain-laced roar spurred me into action.

With speed I didn't know I was capable of, I wrested my pant leg up and pushed Zane's over his knee. His sigils were writhing, welcoming mine. Instead of amber, they shone black.

I pressed my calf against his and watched in amazement as our marks intertwined, tattooing an extra, matching ring of sigils around our ankles. His turned the same vibrant color as mine.

I Kissed a Dog

"You did it, Princess," he said, his voice steady and strong, and his eyes glowing with pride.

"I did, didn't I?"

Healed by deep magic I couldn't begin to comprehend, he pulled me into a long-awaited embrace, and kissed me. First tenderly, and then more insistent, his mouth ravaging mine. Running my fingers through his hair, I heard myself whimper his name.

Momentarily sated and with a look filled with promised pleasures, he lifted me to my feet, where I clung to him, unwilling to let go. Losing him wasn't an option.

"Well, Zane, are you prepared to be our Alpha?" asked a masculine voice.

Staring up at the moon, Zane looked thoughtful. "I can't ignore that destiny has made my purpose so obvious, old friend," he said, serious.

Seeing it was James McQuillen who'd spoken so casually to Zane, sent a jolt of electricity down my spine; I readied my torpedoes. Target, the betraying bastard's manipulating mind. This Judas wouldn't have a chance to hang himself. I'd beat him to it.

Zane, sensing my intention, pressed his lips to my hair. "He's one of the good guys."

Staggered by this latest revelation, I intruded into McQuillen's thoughts.

He didn't erect any barriers, allowing me to snoop through his mental file cabinet. My findings confirmed Zane's statement. He *was* one of the good guys.

"Logan's dead," McQuillen stated what I was already well aware of. The Indian had defeated Logan, returning Zane to his rightful position as Pacific Pack's Alpha.

Naked and torn apart, Logan's blood soaked the ground around him.

I couldn't help replaying what he'd so cruelly said to his sister. Something about her blood nourishing the soil. He'd picked the wrong Sanders sibling. Misty Sanders was just fine, alive and breathing. Her big brother, not so much.

Coincidently, at the moment, Misty, along with our core group, was trudging across the schoolyard; a sizeable crowd of women and a few men who had surrendered in tow. I'd examine their motives later to ensure their future loyalty to our pack.

Our pack, I thought, inwardly cheering. I was married/mated to a pack leader. Who would have visualized predictable me as part of a werewolf pack?

On a somewhat less pleasant note, I still had some in-depth questions for Alcuin about his loyalty, or lack thereof, but they could wait. He'd come through for us in the end. That's what mattered.

"Where's Jazmine?" someone asked.

It was then I remembered she'd disappeared during Logan and James McQuillen's fatal clash. "Oh, no! I think she got away."

"She couldn't have gone far!" Stryder barked. "Let's spread out. Find her! If our new alpha agrees, of course." He inclined his head in honor of Zane's position.

"To our new alpha!" Misty shouted. She dropped to her knee in reverence.

I watched in amazement as both werewolves and the remaining mutants bowed in submission, accepting and acknowledging Zane as the uncontested leader of a new, more diverse pack, a pack where purebreds and mutants would work and live together as one family.

I Kissed a Dog

Being a bi-racial woman with supernatural powers, I was for the all-new, all-inclusive Pacific Pack.

Our victory celebration was cut short, not by a search for Jazmine, but a thundering roar that raged louder than any lion, tiger, bear, mutant, *or* werewolf.

Working at an animal park, I knew that a male lion's roar could be heard up to five miles away, the loudest of any big cat. What I was hearing far surpassed anything I'd ever heard, including the King of the Jungle.

I realized right then we wouldn't have to hunt Dillon's killer.

It was hunting us.

Twenty-Nine

Misty responded first. Blasting into the air, she shifted into a wolf before her front paws hit the ground.

The nearby air swelled and rippled as the others followed her example, morphing into their fighting forms and circling their prey, a predator unlike any they'd faced before.

The newly formed pack radiated a sense of confidence that came from having the numbers advantage.

Our increased numbers offered me little assurance.

I'd been inside the creature's mind. Its sole purpose was to kill. There would be no reasoning. No surrender. Its death alone would stop its murderous cycle. God only knew why Jazmine had kept the monster in her possession.

I needed to find the answer, and with it, the means to crush her rabid *pet*.

Zane glanced from the menacing demon back to me. I didn't need any mindreading skills to decipher his thoughts: Stay here. Stay back. We'll handle it.

I nodded, well aware I would be disappointing my mate for what I hoped would be the final time.

The pack bordered the demon. There were no other words

but hell-spawned demon — to describe what we faced. Demonic might prove too kind a description by the night's end.

A thunderous bellow erupted from the fiend's mouth.

Even from my position I could see its lethal fangs. Several rows of what resembled ice picks lined its cavernous maw. A thick tongue-like appendage rolled from its mouth, reminding me of a humungous frog seeking to capture an unsuspecting insect.

If I had any control over the outcome, no one I knew would end up in its protruding and malformed midsection.

To make matters worse, my thoughts flashed to Dillon. The idea that Dillon, or a part of him, was being digested inside the beast revolted me. I swallowed the bile rising in my throat. I would not allow myself to think about the slain guard. Any mourning would have to wait. Connie was doing enough of that already. I needed to think about locating Jazmine and bringing a rapid conclusion to this monster-sized problem.

Closer inspection revealed three sets of arms protruding from either side, all ending with scissor-sharp claws. I had no doubt the extent of damage those claws could render. I didn't have to wait long to see the results.

One of the new mutant converts lunged, reaching for the beast's throat. For the briefest moment I was fooled into thinking the creature was embracing its attacker. An instant later, all six arms sliced across the mutant's back, gouging so deep, her spine was severed.

Gagging, I turned away and caught a glimpse of what might be our last hope.

From the tree line, David and his mutated brethren floated forward, forming a perimeter around the conflict.

In the interim, more mutants rushed the beast, and were gruesomely dispatched before they could deal out any damage of their own.

David, what is this? I was almost afraid to ask. *Can you stop it?*

What you see is a loathsome mistake created on the barge. Jazmine is able to control it, to a degree, with a mechanism she alone possesses. She's eluded us all night.

We can restrain the beast not defeat it. It too is filled with fae, unseelie to be exact, magic. Yet to our benefit, it is of very low intelligence, operating by brute force and the instinct to kill.

An unstoppable idiot for a monster, we were facing the worst kind of enemy — dumb *and* deadly.

I had to find Jazmine. We needed the device she used to command it.

Contain it! I'm going for Jazmine. I had to act fast.

Zane and James McQuillen signaled for the pack to cease their frontal attacks as David's cluster approached cloaked in silent secrecy. Without Zane's command, the pack would have turned their aggressions on the fae-blooded oddities. Jazmine had warned them repeatedly about the dangers presented by the so-called abominations. The true abomination was shrieking and grasping for anything breathing.

In unison, cloaked arms raised igniting an unprecedented pressure that whipped through the field like a sudden storm. Low growls and snarls rumbled through the pack.

I could understand their uneasiness. Despite my trust and faith in David and his followers, I, too, was fighting the urge

I Kissed a Dog

to come unhinged, unglued, or more simply stated: go stark raving mad.

Miraculously, whatever numinous spell they were weaving had the desired effect on the demon.

It skirted backward, arms waving, terrified by the newest intruders. Its black, pupil less eyes darted sideways, searching for the source of its distress. Spears of light arced over it, forming a cage of energy the demon was powerless to escape from.

Its temporary capture was my prompt.

Closing my eyes I extended my mind, allowing it to expand.

Jazmine, with Martin, appeared on my mental radar, shoving boxes into the trunk of an old car. Slipping into Jazmine's mind as easily as Cinderella's foot into the glass slipper, I surveyed the scene. Seeing Martin still alive baffled me. How could such a big coward have survived?

I noted with some satisfaction his prized Doberman was no longer by his side. It appeared my mental barrage had reaped permanent havoc on the dog's mind.

Realizing time was too scarce to spend gloating; with speed that surprised me, I perused Jazmine's mental agenda, flipping through her mind's file folders. The device she used to control the demon wasn't hard to locate.

A necklace! She wore a chain around her neck. A silver whistle, resembling what an owner might use to train a dog, hung from the end of her chain, along with several keys and a heart locket.

I searched deeper and was rewarded with the sequence needed to complete the process. The commands were simple.

Two short whistles: kill everyone but those I've branded. One long whistle: Kill anyone you see. Another directed it to return to its cell, a different one for remaining silent, and, finally, I located the cease all activity signal. Three long bursts of piercing sound. That's the one I stashed in my own memory files.

Now I just had to retrieve one tiny, seemingly insignificant instrument that could alter the course of our lives by shutting down the greatest threat I'd ever seen.

No big deal, I thought sarcastically hoping to inspire my courage. But considering Jazmine loading a car on the property's far side wouldn't make my task any easier. Glancing at David's men, I ensured their magic-powered cage was still standing strong, its captive secured inside.

Zane and his inner circle, including the two vampires, were gesturing wildly as they attempted to strategize their next move. He'd for a moment forgotten me, so it seemed.

Testing this theory, I dashed into the ever-thickening fog. When I was sure no one was following, I slowed my pace, directing my full attention on Martin.

Using my powers I infiltrated Martin's mind and flipped the off switch.

He slumped to the ground, dropping the box he'd been lifting. The picture of a puppeteer snipping the puppet's strings came to mind. Martin was my very own pliable puppet.

Since accepting the mating mark, I had experienced yet another expansion of my gifts. It was if a sealed book, overflowing with instructions, had been unlocked, revealing the mysteries and methods for managing my powers.

All I had to do was wish for a desired outcome and the solution materialized. Persuading someone to act in a specific manner was, after years of trying and failing, at last an option. I'd developed a form of mind control. Instead of causing debilitating mental anguish, painful and potent enough to kill, I could also now command my target to behave precisely as I wished. How convenient! And terrifying.

Such power could prove corrupting if I didn't keep a firm reign on it. I'd worry about putting safeguards in place later, after our current mess was cleaned up.

Speaking of messes, I'd reached the school's back parking lot. I peered around the wall. Martin lay on the pavement with items from his box strewn around him. I couldn't make out what had spilled.

The limo we'd arrived in was nowhere in sight. Just the rundown car and two other vehicles were visible under the dazzling moonlight. Jazmine was stooped over Martin.

I wasn't sure what to do. I wanted her necklace, but for some insane reason, I felt the overwhelming urge to confront her first.

There were plenty of reasons to do just that. She'd nearly allowed Zane to die. She'd victimized Plum Beach by gruesomely killing its inhabitants; she'd experimented on unsuspecting men, turning them into inhuman creatures; captured and tormented countless mutant women; *and* she'd ensured that a little boy spent a portion of his life in a secured mental hospital.

If those weren't reasons enough, the fact remained I despised her.

Looking into her eyes before I destroyed her seemed appropriate. On some level I understood that I should perform another mental trick like I had on Martin and be done with it, but an unfamiliar burning sensation swept through me, igniting a blaze of rage I wasn't certain I could douse, nor was I sure I wanted to.

Ignoring the sensible voice telling me to grab the whistle and return to the others, I took a tentative step away from the school. But before I could advance further, a chilling wind gust swept through the tree branches, whipping through my hair. As I inhaled the resulting crisp fragrance, Jazmine did the same. She kept her face lifted, sniffing.

I knew before she spun to face me she'd smelled me.

Convinced of my ability to overpower her with my mental magic, I strode forward, feeling for the first time in my life, invincible.

She shifted with such speed, I failed to see the usual vibration preceding the change.

A biblical warning my stepdad often quoted flashed through my mind in the moment before she sprang.

Pride cometh before a fall.

My pride was about to get me killed.

Thirty

Several unforeseen events happened at once.

All surrounding movement shifted seamlessly into slow motion. Including Jazmine arcing through the air, making me think of Logan before James McQuillen cut his life short; saving mine in the process.

This time no one was waiting in the wings to rescue me.

I was alone, and to make things worse, I felt something altering inside me.

My mating marks were alive, animated. A fiery ring of heat swirled insistently around my ankle igniting something unfamiliar yet exhilarating. I acknowledged the warm sensations spreading up my legs and expanding through my torso.

My head tingled like a million tiny pins were pricking my scalp in a perfect chorus. An image of my hair separating from my head threatened to send me into hysterics despite my looming death.

Even more bizarre, what looked like ripples of water floated past me in a fuzzy haze, reminding me of the strange vibrations that occurred before the werewolves shifted forms.

No. It wasn't possible. How?

In answer, my body bowed forward, knocking me to my hands and knees. The warmth flooding through me was no longer pleasant, and was scorching me from within.

If blood could boil, mine was.

Throbbing pain racked every nerve, muscle, and bone in my body as I felt myself split apart, reshaping and reforming into something not me, something not human.

I lifted my head and howled just in time to see Jazmine plow into my crouching form, sending me flying.

The next seconds were a blur of fur and teeth.

Animal instinct took over as we rolled across the grassy field fighting for dominance. Frantic, I sought my mental powers, praying they were still accessible.

They were.

Using them, I slammed into Jazmine's mind paralyzing her like a fly trapped in a spider's web. My teeth sank into flesh and her blood flooded my mouth, increasing my lust for vengeance.

She shuddered then stilled. The faintest heartbeat remained.

The human part of me hesitated, feeling like I'd cheated and fought dirty, but I quickly focused on the evil she'd birthed and the lives she'd destroyed. She'd never agree to surrender, nor would she cease her villainous agenda.

There was no choice. Not anymore.

Picturing her brutalized victims, I clamped down, pressing my fangs deeper into her neck and shaking my muzzle. I could feel the now sporadic beat of her heart as it slowed, and then stopped altogether, her life force at last extinguished.

Afraid she might somehow rejuvenate herself I refused to relax my hold.

"Jazmine, oh God, no!"

Martin's sharp cry served as the signal for me to stop. Releasing my grip, I swung my head around meeting Martin's eyes with my own.

He took a step back, another, and looked at the pavement near the car. Keeping his eyes trained on me, he crouched, and using both hands, began sweeping the fallen items into a heap.

With my improved werewolf vision, or whatever it was I'd become, a glint of something shiny caught my attention.

The coins! Of course! They were trying to escape with the coins. That's why Jazmine had fled in the midst of a battle. She had wanted the formula for eternal life more than victory tonight. Rebuilding her army would come later as long as she possessed the coins. Her cause had now been inherited by Martin, who was scrambling to locate the prize.

With some relief, I realized Martin didn't have the translation. As far as I knew, unless Rita and the others had deciphered it, which was indeed a possibility, no one had it.

Regardless, I couldn't allow something so important that had destroyed so many lives remain in the hands of a madman. Martin, with his misguided loyalty to Jazmine, certainly qualified as mad.

Wanting my human hands back so I could gather coins, I pictured myself as Chloe Carpenter, human female, and following renewed bodily rearrangements, I was rewarded with my original, God-given shape. Naked shape, but who was complaining at this stage of the game?

Once more taking advantage of my mind magic, I froze Martin in place and dashed to the car. I found two of the coins, and was just starting to sift through the spilled contents of his suitcase, when an earth-shattering roar shattered any semblance of momentary sanity I was feeling.

I'd forgotten the demonic beast and the whistle I was supposed to be retrieving.

So caught up in my hatred of Jazmine and our subsequent fight, I'd failed my friends again.

Gripping the two coins, I scurried back to where I'd overpowered Jazmine.

It wasn't a pretty sight.

The grass was trampled and torn. Splatters of blood dotted the landscape. Jazmine's throat yawned open like a gory mouth. Her eyes, no longer filled with anger and loathing, were void of anything. They were empty. Lifeless.

I'd killed her.

And in the process I'd emerged somehow victorious, and also unscathed.

Trying to ignore the unfamiliar feelings that resulted from taking a life, I continued my frantic search for the one thing that could control the rampaging monster.

Without any concrete way to determine how long I'd been away from the others, I had to consider that the demon might have freed itself from David's magic-made prison.

With that horrible thought urging me on, I dropped to my knees, running my fingers through the grass. At this rate, it would be dawn before I found anything.

Sensing a nearby presence, a chill swept across my exposed back.

I rocked back to sit on my heels, more mortified by my bare ass on display than who my stalker might be.

"Chloe, are you hurt? What happened?" Zane rushed to

help me while pulling off his tattered and blood drenched T-shirt. He knelt and lifted my chin, his eyes searching mine.

Unable to meet his gaze, I dropped my head. "We have to find the whistle," I whispered. Afraid if I said more, or acknowledged his gentle touch, I might break. A breakdown would have to wait. We had a demon to exercise.

Pulling away, I yanked on his filthy shirt and stood, relieved to see it reached mid thigh. "The whistle's silver," I added, before sending Zane a mental summary of my fight with Jazmine and subsequent search for the coins.

"Here. Put them somewhere safe." I pressed the coins into his hand. He shoved them deep into the front pocket of his jeans. To my relief, he didn't press for more details.

Turning his attention to the ground, his eyes rested on Jazmine, but again he didn't comment. "We have to hurry. That *thing* is testing the barrier. They can't keep it up much longer. They've expended too much magic."

We had to help David and his fae-blooded friends; they'd done so much for us. Without them, we'd all be dead.

With that in mind, we explored what felt like every blade of grass. My frustration increased the longer we looked. The beast was barking excitedly, a sure sign it was closer to freedom.

"Dammit," I groaned. "Oh no!"

"What?" Zane looked up, puzzled.

"I figured it flew off Jazmine during our … anyway, maybe she's still wearing it."

Zane stalked over to gaze down at his former fiancé. I hurried to join him.

"There, in her hair." I pointed; shocked to see the chain

tangled in her blood-matted bob, the whistle still intact. I couldn't help remembering her sleek coiffed hair the first time I'd seen her. She'd seemed indestructible.

I knew better now. No one was indestructible.

Without a hint of compassion, Zane ripped the chain from her bloodied throat and grasped the one thing that could silence the beast.

"Let's move!" He grabbed my hand.

Relieved he didn't expect me to stay behind, I matched him stride for stride as we raced around the building, another benefit of my mating marks and the magic they'd unleashed. I now had supernatural speed, and it felt incredible.

"I know the whistle sequences," I yelled. We were close enough for me to see the demon flailing at the cage's dimming lights, the enchanted energy failing.

Zane halted, handing me our last hope. "No closer. Try it from here."

Three long blasts through a little silver cylinder and it would be over.

Finally, something simple.

※

The metal felt cool, even comforting, secured in the ring of my lips.

I breathed in and readied myself to blow.

That's when the mystically-warded enclosure collapsed, right along with David and his men, their magic spent.

Hell on earth had been merely a terrifying theory until the demon erupted from its cell with such force the ground trembled.

I Kissed a Dog

The first line of defense went down in its initial rampage; a significant number of our mutant comrades were crushed underneath its massive weight.

The slow motion phenomenon was happening again.

And I was shifting — all over again — without *my* permission. Zane, seeing my dilemma, grabbed the whistle midair as it flew from my grasp.

Three long blows! I mind-shrieked. My front paws hit the grass with a thud.

I'd had enough of this madness. A feral fury, birthed from every bad and rotten thing that had happened in my life, roared to the surface, providing a dazzling shot of determination and strength.

Instead of fighting it, I surrendered control of my human nature and let the beast in me reign.

I charged through the mass of what remained of my future pack, and plowed into the six-armed ogre.

From faraway, I heard Zane shouting my name, calling for Valamir to transport me out. I wondered why he was wasting his breath when he should have been blowing the damn whistle, but I didn't bother stopping to find out.

I had a mission to complete.

In a burst of fur and muscle, Zane appeared by my side. He'd shifted into his monstrous seven-foot form, the one I'd despised in the past. Now all I recognized was much-needed power and skill.

Next to him, Valamir materialized, along with Alcuin, Misty, and the two M's. Connie and Deb, along with Stryder and Rita, joined what would be our final stand.

Using my mental advantage, I sent instructions to everyone

at once; and in perfect unison we attacked from every angle, using our personal areas of expertise to our greatest benefit.

Surprised by our onslaught, the beast stumbled, and then rapidly righted itself, only to be knocked back again by Zane and Alcuin. I torpedoed its mind, hoping to hit the off switch like I had with Jazmine and Martin.

Infuriatingly, its mind didn't respond to my masterful manipulation.

In the midst of my efforts, I diverted my attention, for an instant, and our adversary, aware on some level of my unique capabilities, directed his rage at me.

Without warning, I found myself caught up in tangle of claws, propelled skyward, high over its head. Then I was dropping into its gore-drenched mouth.

Searing pain speared through my neck, and I felt myself drowning in a sea of agony, no longer able to stay afloat or maintain my link to the others. I was back in that suburban swimming pool all over again. Drowning. Dying.

Everything flashed to black, swallowing Zane's face as I slipped into oblivion.

The first thing I noticed when my eyes popped open was my mate.

He clutched me to his chest, releasing a sigh of relief. I was nestled between his legs, and we were seated on the ground with a small assembly of familiar faces standing around us.

"Hey, Doll, you did real good." Alcuin grinned down at me.

"More like superb, possibly exceptional," Misty added sounding almost cheerful.

I Kissed a Dog

More remarkable than Misty's good cheer was the fact that Zane didn't bother correcting Alcuin's doll reference.

Feeling kind of woozy, I clung tighter to Zane, his skin feverish under my hands. His dark hair, a tangled, but still sexy mess, draped over me like a protective curtain that I had to peek through to see the others.

Everything felt right, although I guessed there were still a ton of things still very wrong.

For one, my throat had been ripped open. "My neck," I moaned, recalling my last moments in the Jaws of Satan. If that wasn't the devil, what was?

Zane, stroking my hair, murmured, "I had a chance to return your healing favor. You're quite the trooper."

"Definitely a trooper," Mack agreed.

"Okay guys, enough already. I'm feeling like Dorothy in the *Wizard of Oz*. The part when her family surrounds her bed at the movie's end. And what aren't you telling me?"

"It can wait. Let's burn this place to the ground and get out of here," said Zane with a note of finality.

It was then I realized we were missing part of our pack. "Where's Stryder?" I glanced around. "James McQuillen, Rita …"

Zane interrupted. "We lost Stryder. He fought valiantly. Rita was badly injured, beyond her werewolf regenerating abilities. McQuillen is with David and his clan. They'll take care of Rita, don't worry. After that they'll head to the barge and clean up there and free any remaining prisoners. Valamir is pursuing Martin."

It hit me like an arrow in the chest.

We'd forgotten Martin, and had left him back in the parking lot. I'd obviously lost my grip on his mind. He'd surely found the other coins, escaping with them to another secret stronghold.

There was still one question that hadn't been sufficiently answered. "Who killed the monster?" Someone had saved my life. I wanted to thank that person.

For the first time, everyone smiled. "Who?" I asked again with more force.

The ring around me opened and a powerful looking male strode through, the rising sun shadowing his face.

My rescuer stepped closer. "I'd had just about enough of that bastard." Dillon grinned.

Thirty-One

Seeing Connie secure and smiling serenely, snug in Dillon's arms, was the perfect ending to a very brutal and very long night of death and destruction. Two words that followed me like a kid with a bad crush, a crush turned dangerous obsession.

It was as if death and destruction had been compulsively and exclusively stalking me. Maybe now they'd turn their malevolent attention elsewhere.

A girl could hope.

Hope was one trait I refused to relinquish despite my recent history. As rocky as my life had become, I'd never felt so right. I belonged in this world with the man seated beside me lost in his own thoughts. And now, with everyone off on separate missions, I had my long-awaited time alone with him.

I stifled a mischievous giggle, convinced Zane falsely believed I was dozing as we cruised down I-5 hovering to the posted speed limit. He might be obeying the speed limit, but my mind was speeding in every direction.

He'd arranged for a car so we'd have time away from everything but each other. Teleporting back to Plum Beach would have put us right back in the mix without a moments rest, and I needed some serious R and R.

Stealing a glance to my left, I studied Zane from beneath my lashes. I needed *him* far more than any rest and relaxation.

Squelching those tempting thoughts for now, I considered our plan to meet up with the rest of our group at his property tomorrow. We had some major ground to cover. Everyone who had survived the altercation with Jazmine and Logan, and who'd pledged themselves to the Pacific Pack, would be making their way to Zane's.

He'd decided to purchase the property and build a ranch of sorts to house the misplaced mutants who were now part of our growing supernatural family. I was curious how we'd deal with appearances; scrutiny about our living arrangements was bound to be an issue, but we needed a central location to operate from. Zane had a lot of reorganizing and rebuilding ahead of him. I was looking forward to meeting the challenges and helping him.

I hadn't forgotten my promise to Joshua Smart either. When we returned, I planned to speak candidly with his mom and see if we could gain her approval. Maybe she'd been threatened into giving up Josh. Whatever the reason she'd allowed her son to be institutionalized, she was still his mother. Removing him without her permission would lead to all kinds of legal troubles that our pack couldn't afford.

At least we had today and all night alone before switching back into full problem solving mode.

"I know you're awake," Zane teased. "Your breathing changed about five miles back."

I Kissed a Dog

I had to laugh. "You are most observant, Dr. Marshall." I rarely referred to his veterinarian status, which I'd discovered was legitimate, not just another ruse.

"When it comes to you, Chloe, I am very, *very* observant."

Clenching my thighs together, I attempted to turn off the fiery heat his words ignited. How could one man's voice send waves of sensual pleasure crashing through my core?

I was aware that our connection had deepened since the mating ceremony.

Valamir's mind-magic, at one point, had sent me over the edge, but now his erotic powers paled in comparison to my mate's. I was thankful for that. It made life so much simpler and my marriage that much stronger without the lure of an ancient vampire repeatedly distracting me.

"Okay, I'll play nice, for the time being," he chuckled, aware of my arousal. "Later, you can forget it. Playtime won't just be nice, it will be unforgettable," he assured, promise of untold pleasures evident.

Energy hummed through me as I imagined his tongue trailing down my neck, over my breasts. Everything about Zane was overwhelming me, drawing me to him. My pheromones were wreaking havoc with his heightened senses. His presence was doing a number on mine, especially in the car's enclosed space.

Eager to arrive at our destination, I prodded him, sounding like an impatient kid on a road trip: "How long till we get there?"

"Soon."

So far he'd remained secretive about where we'd be spending the next twenty-four hours, stating that it would be worth the travel time. I wasn't so sure of that.

Ripping off his clothes in the backseat would be pretty thrilling, and there'd be no waiting involved. But I knew better; considering our initial, ill-timed encounter in Vegas, he was going to do everything in his power to ensure I remembered every single caress and kiss.

I had no doubt he would accomplish his goal.

"Chloe, open your eyes."

I did.

And found myself looking out the car's front window, facing the bluest water of any lake I'd ever seen. Even Crater Lake, a place I loved to visit as a kid, couldn't quite compare.

I was reminded of my computer's screensaver; the one displaying an ocean inlet with water so tempting it made a person want to dive into the monitor. This body of water was real. All I had to do was get out of the car and walk to the sandy shoreline where the tiniest of waves crested.

"You like?" Zane's voice was filled with pleasure.

"I love it!" I unbuckled my seatbelt and leaned against his broad shoulder. "You were right, this was worth the wait. How long did I sleep anyway?"

He clicked a button releasing the doors' locks and opened his. "About an hour. We're not far from Klamath. This property belongs to one of our board members."

Seeing my expression, he added, "A trusted and loyal board member. Remember the woman …"

"It's okay." I stopped him mid-sentence. "I'm sorry. I know you wouldn't take me someplace unsafe."

He exited the car with the masculine grace I loved.

It never ceased to amaze me how a man with such a muscular frame could move the way he moved. I doubted I'd ever get over the shock, or pleasure, of watching him.

I joined him beside a professionally-maintained, A-framed structure that overlooked our own private lake. It was just the right temperature outside, and the trees kept the afternoon heat to a minimum. A colorful hammock swung in the breeze between two trees, beckoning me.

Excited to explore further, I hurried to help Zane unload the trunk, before realizing I had nothing *to* unload.

I was wearing a pair of worn jeans and t-shirt that Deb had scrounged from her own belongings before the school went up in flames, destroying all otherworldly evidence.

Seeing my dilemma, Zane smiled. "Don't worry. I had Alcuin make a quick stop when he brought the car." He grabbed a Nordstrom's shopping bag, stuffed to the brim.

Gleefully, I snatched it away and dashed up the steps. I spun to catch the keys, in one hand, again surprised by my newfound agility, and ability to actually hear Zane toss the keys in the first place. Maybe my coma-induced clumsiness had been vanquished for good.

Once inside, I raced through the rooms like a child seeing her new home for the first time.

I wasn't disappointed.

I felt like I was standing inside a giant, cozy, furnished triangle.

There was a quant kitchen, dining area, and large living space with a well-used fireplace. A short hallway, just off the main room, had two doors; one I hoped was a bathroom with a full shower and tub.

What captured a majority of my attention were the steps

leading up to a loft that was home to the biggest bed I'd ever seen. California King? No way. This thing had at least an additional two feet added to both its width and length. Someone had designed this bed with room for …

"I see you've found the bed to your liking?" Zane had managed to slip up behind me and wound his arms around my waist, drawing me back against his chest.

I tilted my head back to further scrutinize the loft, more specifically the gigantic bed. "I think I know why it's so big."

"You do, do you?" Zane teased.

"Werewolves have more than one form they can take, not to mention, they're pretty wild. Maybe more room is needed …" I stopped, embarrassed.

Zane nuzzled my ear. "No need to be shy, Mrs. Marshall. Nothing you say, or do, will shock me. Although you always do seem to find ways to surprise me," he chuckled; his breath tickling and teasing my neck.

Leaving me marveling over *the bed*, he carried an armload of groceries into the kitchen.

Seeing the heaping grocery bags, I remembered my own bag of goodies.

I couldn't wait to examine its contents, and I was more than a little curious to see just how effectively a vampire shopped. I couldn't picture Alcuin at the mall interacting with an eager salesclerk. But by the look of my bounty, he'd made the right selections.

It was possible he'd sent a very realistic impression of my measurements right into the salesperson's mind, helping her, who'd in turn located all the right sizes, colors, and styles.

Alcuin had thought of everything, including a saucy, black

bikini shimmering with glittery stars. Zane would find great satisfaction seeing me flaunt my figure in the miniscule material. My stepdad, on the other hand, would have a stroke at the sight of me wearing so little in front of a man, even if that man was my husband.

With all the chaos from the past twenty-four hours, I'd forgotten my parents. Meeting with them was yet another activity to add to my growing to-do list. I hated the idea of them hating Zane and worrying about me.

Sooner or later, probably sooner, Bob would use his associates in law enforcement to investigate Zane. I was reasonably certain Zane had cloaked his past enough to hold up under scrutiny, but I also knew that my stepdad could be relentless if he felt it necessary.

If he somehow found the connections between Zane and Plum Beach murders, all hell would break loose. We needed a reprieve without my parents going berserk.

Interrupting my worries, Zane called from the kitchen, "Why don't you take advantage of the sunshine and soak in some of those rays you love so much. I'm sure if you dig far enough, you'll find that Alcuin purchased swimwear for you."

I had to laugh. Of course, he'd instructed his vampire friend to buy an itsy bitsy bikini. The one I was already slipping on, keeping an eye on the kitchen should Zane decide to come out before I was ready.

"You'll join me, right?" I was anticipating his massive hands smoothing tanning lotion over my back. I made sure the send him the mental image.

"Wouldn't miss it, Princess," he replied, his voice laced with anticipation.

Tingling with the promise of Zane's expert touch, I finished digging through the bag. I wasn't surprised to find a zebra print beach towel at the bottom. Wrapping it around me, I headed for the sunshine. "Don't be long!" I commanded, trying to sound sultry.

The truth was I did feel sultry, sexy, in fact, pretty damn alluring in my swimsuit. And as I let the cool lake water envelope my feet, I tossed the towel, realizing how glad I was for the one thing I'd almost hated Zane for — the loss of my virginity.

Because of our earlier wedding night encounter, today there would be no pain, just passion. No fear, only the fulfillment of our fantasies. No worry, just wonder.

Where was my mate? What was taking him so long?

Realizing he might take awhile to arrange the house, making it perfect in his mind, I treaded further into the lake, allowing the water to cool my heat, but not extinguish it. Bringing it down a notch, allowed me a moment to mull over my recent experience as a werewolf.

Zane didn't know how or why I'd shifted into what resembled a purebred. He'd never heard of it happening before. Once again I was an anomaly.

On our drive here, we'd stopped at a rest area and taken a stroll along one of several hiking trails. Away from prying eyes, I'd tried to shift and failed. I'd retained the other benefits, like super speed, agility, heightened senses, and an unbreakable confidence in my mental powers; however, I couldn't switch forms no matter how hard I tried.

Zane had promised we'd find someone who could explain what was happening to me. But despite his noble intentions, I doubted it would be easy.

I Kissed a Dog

Two red-tailed hawks, flying overhead, drew my attention, their magnificent wings lifting them higher as they rode the air currents, giving me a personal show in the sky.

Tilting my head, I watched their airborne acrobatics and found myself drifting deeper into the water. "Beautiful," I murmured, soaking in the ambience of my surroundings and wishing I could somehow fly.

"Indeed, you are beautiful." The sound of Zane's voice sent my heart soaring, giving new meaning to the concept of flight.

I turned. He was already reaching for me.

Oh, yes. With Zane I could find a way to fly, without ever leaving the ground.

Thirty-Two

Several long kisses later, we found our way out of the water to a blanket Zane had spread by my towel. We dropped in unison, landing on its sun-saturated softness.

He pulled me close.

Resting my head on his chest, the late afternoon warmth erased the remaining moisture from my skin, adding to the fire already kindling inside me.

I trailed my fingers over his mouthwatering six-pack, afraid I might drool as I anticipated my mouth exploring those perfect ripples. His skin, so smooth, felt like silk under my hand. He groaned and twisted a strand of my damp hair around his finger, tugging gently.

Despite our rising intimacy, I sensed him holding back. Something was bothering him, even now, with our bodies pressed together. Whatever it was would continue to haunt and harass until we exorcised it from his mind.

Respecting his privacy, I made no attempt to infiltrate his thoughts, waiting instead for him to take the lead and open up.

His jaw clenched and his muscles tightened. He pulled

I Kissed a Dog

away, and propped his head on his hand, allowing him to gaze down at me.

The golden flecks, expanding through his irises, were confirmation of his increasing hunger. Yet his tension was plain, evidenced by the hand resting on my bare hip, trembling just enough for me to notice.

My mate was beyond self-assured, especially in the art of seduction. The strain he was exhibiting had nothing to do with any shortfall in that area.

With this realization, a knot of fear tightened in my stomach, squelching my desire, and freeing a barrage of menacing uncertainties.

Another secret, something left to reveal; that had to be it. But what?

We'd bared our souls during the first hour of our drive, committing to keeping nothing hidden from the other, no matter how uncomfortable confessing might be.

I guessed if I wanted to share one final revelation, I could mention my ill-fated vow to Valamir. But I'd come to the conclusion that that particularly annoying promise was mine to deal with alone.

The Master Vampire had helped us overcome our enemies. And he continued to prove himself useful by tracking Martin and the missing coins.

If I told Zane now, he'd spend all his time worrying about me and would end up confronting Valamir. It seemed unfair to burden him with something that could happen years down the road.

I'd tell him when the time came to fulfill my vow. Until then, it seemed irrelevant in light of everything else. I didn't want to think about it either. The implications were too terrifying. Valamir could request anything of me, and I'd be forced to oblige. Considering how bad he wanted my blood …

"I need to tell you something," Zane started, sending another jolt of fear down my spine. I hadn't realized how wound up I'd become thinking about my own predicament.

Rolling onto my side, I faced my mate. "I knew you were upset. You know you can tell me anything. I mean it."

"My Princess, always perceptive *and* gracious. Thanks for staying out of my head. I just needed a second to piece together the puzzle floating around in there." He tapped the side of his head, smiling, but the attempt to lighten the moment didn't quite reach his eyes.

I ran my hand over his shoulder and down his arm, distracted, as always, by his sculpted muscles. "I'm no mind reading bully," I teased, holding his gaze, and hoping to inspire confidence.

Taking a deep breath, he exhaled. "Okay, here I go. First, you know I love you, right?"

"Ye-s-s-s …" I narrowed my eyes, suspicion overriding my fear. This wasn't good. We were dealing with a major revelation here. I wasn't sure I wanted to know. My mom always believed denial was bliss. Maybe she was right.

"I have one last confession to make. On our wedding night, when you were so intoxicated …"

"Oh, no! What else did I do?" His problem was with something *I'd* done. A secret he'd kept about me for me. "Can't we just forget it?" I pleaded, before realizing the irony of my request. I had no recollection of anything following our blurry wedding ceremony. He was the one who remembered the details.

"Babe, you didn't do anything. That's the point. I lied.

I Kissed a Dog

When you threatened an annulment, I panicked. The mating marks had already ..."

Struggling to comprehend, I sat up. "What exactly are you saying? What didn't I do?"

"You, *we*, did not make love that night. You're still a virgin. Please forgive me. I couldn't lose you. There was too much danger, too much at stake. We needed each other. I couldn't risk you leaving."

In one smooth movement, I leapt to my feet, unsure what to do next. This wasn't some simple white lie. This was a life-altering admission with the potential to disrupt everything I'd grown to accept and love about my life, about Zane.

Still a virgin? No wonder I hadn't felt anything different that morning. And Zane had sent the sheets to be laundered before I'd had a chance to spot any traditional, telltale signs of our supposed night of passion. There'd been nothing to see, nothing but clean, unblemished sheets.

His words, *"I couldn't risk you leaving"* suddenly made sense. He'd needed me for the board meeting and to help investigate the murders. What if he'd been using me all along?

"Chloe, please, you know what we have is real. The marks, your new powers, none of it would have happened if we weren't fated to be together. You are my mate; my chosen one." He paused for a moment, gathering his thoughts. Shockingly, he offered, "Explore my memories. Maybe that will set your mind at ease. You'll see I had the best intentions."

Facing the lake, I shivered, no longer feeling sexy, but vulnerable in my skimpy bikini. Not able to face him, and uncertain how to respond to his mind-reading suggestion, I hurried to the cabin, keeping my eyes on the ground.

Once inside, I grabbed my pile of new belongings and darted into the second bedroom. The one I'd discovered across the hall from the bathroom. Dumping everything on the bed, I quickly located a pair of underwear, bra, and jogging suit.

Clothes in hand, I crossed the hall and locked the bathroom door. Leaning against the wall, I allowed the tears to fall.

I'd half expected Zane to follow, but he'd stayed behind. Part of me was relieved, but a bigger part was disappointed. He should have pursued me. He should be begging my forgiveness. Not that I'd accept his apology. How could I?

A few minutes later, the shower was massaging the kinks out of my neck with strong streams of near-boiling water. My skin was developing a pinkish hue from the blissfully brutal heat. I wanted the temperature hot enough to burn away the pain in my heart. If only it was that easy.

The fact remained: I loved my brutish, bossy, lying, but deliciously desirable werewolf. He'd been willing to open his mind to my probing, giving me access to all his darkest secrets. Would I be willing to do the same?

I didn't like my answer.

Gazing down at my mating sigils, I watched the soapy water slide over them, pooling at my ankles, all the while wishing they'd offer some cosmic cure for my latest impasse.

But I knew better. The one with the cure was me.

Thirty-Three

Dressed in the designer jogging suit, with my curls cascading like an untamed mane around my face and down my back, I looked like what Melanie had always referred to as Lady Diva All-natural. All through high school, she'd been jealous of my ability to appear exotic without any help from the cosmetic counter, where she'd spent countless hours trying on every shade known to woman to highlight her plainer features.

I missed my friend.

I could use a female's listening ear right now. Positive girl time was way overdue. One of my top priorities after returning home and calling my parents would be to contact Melanie. Hopefully, she wasn't off on some extended promotional tour for her latest book.

Putting thoughts of Melanie on hold, I intended to make peace with my husband. There was a slight problem: He was nowhere to be found.

He'd left a bottle of expensive wine on the counter, and soft music playing in the background. The one ingredient missing was him.

After wandering the house, and then patrolling the grounds,

which were, thankfully, well-lighted, I'd given up my search and was brushing my teeth and wishing Alcuin had known what hair products to purchase. When it came to my copper-streaked tresses, I was picky. Without a hair band, I was stuck with what my mom had referred to as my ultra-big hair.

After several more attempts to smooth the raging ringlets, I gave up. Who cared if my hair was rebelling? I had more concerning things to worry about.

Like Zane.

I trusted that he was somewhere close by, keeping vigil over the house. Despite our current relationship crisis, he was far too protective to leave me unattended.

Despite the precarious circumstances, I felt an unexpected wave of heaviness as exhaustion invaded my limbs. I'd been through so much; now I had an opportunity to rest my weary body on a massive bed fit for royalty.

With one final look in the kitchen, I trudged up the stairs connecting to the loft, eager to stretch out on a balanced mattress, firm yet yielding.

I didn't get the chance.

Reaching the landing, I froze.

The bed looked as inviting as I remembered, but more tempting was Zane, who blended into the shadows like a predator waiting for its quarry. His eyes glowed amber, flecked with hints of red, focused and alert, and trained on me with a look of desire and restrained anger.

He was lounging languidly against the bed's backboard, pillows propped behind him, his hair flowing around his face like waves of black satin.

"Took you long enough," he growled, his voice both raspy and sultry.

I Kissed a Dog

It appeared that Zane had been concealing a great deal of his commanding, Alpha presence, drastically toning down his feral nature since we'd first met. Tonight it was on full display, sending ripples of fear and tingles of excitement rushing through my entire body.

I took a step back, reaching for the railing, unsure how to handle this new, darker Zane.

He seemed to relish my increasing heart rate, evidenced by his narrowing eyes and mischievous grin. "You're not scared of me, Princess; are you?" his voice positively purred.

"How did you get here?" I asked dumbly, knowing he had the supernatural capabilities to avoid detection.

"The better question might be, how did *you* miss me?" He held my gaze, remaining inhumanly still.

Before I could answer, he was in front of me, cupping my face. "You are mine, Chloe. I am The Alpha, and you are my marked mate. You chose me and will learn to abide by my decisions. I am fair and just, and have, since the moment I met you, thought only of your best interests.

Had you walked away in Vegas, you would have broken my heart, and many of the people you now call friends would have died. And, ultimately, so would've you."

I started to respond, but he placed his index finger over my lips.

"And, if you remember, you feared, at one point, that I was a vicious brute, capable of raping a helpless female, one too drunk to remember. You better believe, had we made love, drunk or not, you would remember, *and* you would have been willing. I would never have taken you without your consent, ever."

Gasping, suddenly fearful, I attempted to flee, but instead his hands grasped my shoulders, keeping me facing and focused on him. As if I could look anywhere else in light of his powerful presence.

Somewhere in my mind, it occurred to me that I should be flaming mad. The only problem was the harsh truth he'd so clearly articulated, and the way his aggressive wildness was igniting my own animalistic passions.

Dipping his head, he brushed his lips against mine. "Wolf got your tongue, Chloe?" he chuckled deep in his chest, and proceeded to slide both hands around my neck, seizing a mess of my curls in each fist.

I heard myself groan, all anger forgotten, released for good, as he stared into my eyes, his own saying everything I needed to forgive.

Hungrily, his mouth covered mine. I relaxed; my tongue danced in perfect rhythm with his. "By the way, I'm willing," I whispered huskily into his mouth, my voice filled with expectancy.

In answer, he tightened his grip on my hair and kissed me harder, his tongue swirling.

Without removing his mouth from mine, he lifted me into his arms and carried me to the bed, tenderly placing me in the center, and then stood again to look down at me, his expression sinfully heated as he pulled his t-shirt over his head, revealing the glorious pectoral muscles and flat board abs I appreciated so much.

Those Calvin Klein underwear models, splashed across the billboards, had nothing on my mate.

By the gleam in his eyes, I had the feeling he wanted to love me hard and fast, but I knew he'd honor my virgin status. In spite of his animal nature, he'd proven to be a gentleman in every way. I could anticipate having all my needs met.

The seething passion that seemed to hang like a haze between us, made it impossible for me to halt my own hands as they worked overtime to remove my jacket and tank. I wiggled out of my pants at the same time Zane dropped his on the floor.

Rushes of burning heat flooded my face and pooled between my legs when I caught the first glimpse of his very impressive manhood, thick and heavy with need. My legs parted automatically.

A throaty moan rushed from his lungs, as his eyes lasered in on my black-laced panties, soaked by my arousal, the only item remaining between his erection and my flesh.

He moved over me like a silent predator, crouching above his captured prey.

There was no doubt; I was certifiably Zane-captured.

I quivered wildly when his mouth found the soft mound of my breast, his hand possessing the other. He tasted and tugged, devouring me

Rising up, his knees on either side of me, he looked ferociously at my splayed legs, his gaze once again resting on the triangle between them. "I hope you're not too attached to those panties." The sensuality in his voice created a raging inferno between my legs that I knew he alone could extinguish.

I whimpered, "Take them off, now." I arched my pelvis to meet his hand.

With one swift motion the lacy material was tossed to the floor with the rest of our discarded clothing.

I lay bare; my legs open in invitation for this god of men,

my very own werewolf, who I realized, without any lingering reservations, I couldn't live without.

Instead of thrusting in as I expected and half-hoped for, he repositioned himself and began leisurely tormenting my body, bringing it into complete and utter submission.

Squirming beneath his touch, I gave myself over to his skilled hands.

His tongue taunted and teased my nipples, while his hand circled my stomach, creating a trail of fire as it made its way lower.

A moment of insecurity invaded when his hand caressed my mound for the first time. Being a sun lover and avid bikini wearer, I shaved a majority of my hair off.

My worries were squelched, at the sound of his appreciative groan.

"Oh, baby, you are so smooth, so sexy," he crooned, parting my folds and exploring my wetness.

A primal moan escaped as I rocked in perfect rhythm to his expert touch, begging with my body for more. Sensing my urgency, he slipped one finger inside, fueling my passion. One finger was joined by another, than a third, stretching me impossibly wide. The thrill of such excruciating pleasure, overpowered the sting his fingers triggered. I grew slicker and hotter as he increased the speed and growled wildly.

"I can't take this. I ..."

In a blur of motion, Zane was poised over me, his manhood nudging, pressing against me, seeking entrance.

"Yes," I pleaded, grinding my hips and pushing myself eagerly against his shaft, opening my legs even wider. The idea of a gentlemanly love making session no longer appealed. I wanted it to be fierce. "Don't hold back, please."

I Kissed a Dog

"I love you, need you," he groaned, meeting my eyes.

With a conquering roar, he plunged inside my folds. A searing pain and tearing sensation sliced through me, to be almost instantly replaced by penetrating pleasure. I rose to meet his deepening thrusts, wrapping my legs around his back, and gripping his shoulders to gain purchase.

Something was building inside me, a hot throbbing response to his smooth stabs. I felt myself stretching wider to accommodate his increasing size.

"Oh, Zane ..." I cried, bucking beneath him.

Feel everything, my Princess, Zane spoke into my mind. *Experience what I'm feeling.*

I was totally unprepared for what followed.

My core shattered into a million tiny pieces of unparalleled pleasure as everything that Zane was experiencing exploded into my mind, intensifying every kiss, touch, and thrust.

Wanting him to have the same experience, I flooded his thoughts with my own overwhelming ecstasy.

Hearing myself scream, I reached a place of fiery release so intense I sobbed as the aching swirls of pleasure mounted and erupted, sending stars shooting behind my eyelids.

In that same moment, Zane cried out, a roar feral and inhuman, overflowing with gratification. I dug my nails down his back, whimpering his name over and over. He flung his head back, pounding into me harder, and then he shouted my name, sending me further over the edge as his release poured into me.

A few minutes later, I rested securely against his chest.

He stroked my hair. "I hope I didn't hurt you. I was having difficulty controlling my wolf. I think you put a spell on me."

"Hey, no pain no gain, right? I've never hurt so good," I giggled softly.

"That's my girl, singing the lyrics to some old song to soothe her savage beast."

"When it comes to you, Zane Marshal, savage is damn seductive." Wasn't that the truth? I couldn't wait for round two and three.

I glanced at the glowing clock on the bedside table. We had plenty of time before dawn to explore his softer side and take another walk on the wild one.

I think I'd like some more ravaging savagery, I encouraged, flipping over to straddle him.

Already ready, Princess. Prepare to be appropriately savaged.

I was dazed and perfectly dazzled to discover just how ready. It was going to be a long night.

Thirty-Four

We were nearing the outskirts of Plum Beach. I rested a hand on Zane's thigh. My thoughts continued to drift to last night. I'd never felt so cherished, so loved. So sore.

We'd spent the remaining hours until dawn exploring every inch of each other. I hadn't realized my body could twist and turn into so many positions. I felt like a very happy human pretzel. And I couldn't wait to do it all over again, sore or not.

Zane was right. Had we made love in Vegas, I would have remembered. He was unforgettable, and I knew without a doubt that he felt the same about me.

"Five more miles," he stated, breaking the companionable silence.

Grumpily, I groaned, "Five miles too soon." I wanted to grab the steering wheel and insist that we reverse course, heading back to our lakeside hideaway.

Reading my thoughts, he laughed, "Princess, we have a bed, counter, floor, and any number of potential places at home for me to ravage you. I'm flexible."

"That you are," I agreed, squeezing his leg and picturing the tree house on the property. Hum … interesting location.

"What now," he muttered, his attention diverted to something in the rearview mirror.

Curious to view the object of frustration, I twisted around to see what was behind us.

A charge of adrenaline fired a fresh dose of unwanted anxiety when I spotted the police car. I'd gone from calm to climbing the walls in two seconds flat. Probably because our last interaction with law enforcement, more specifically, Agent Green, hadn't gone so well. His unveiled threats were resurrected as the flashing lights indicated the necessity of pulling over.

I was relieved to see Officer Tate approach the car. Agent Green was nowhere in sight.

Zane already had the window down and was reaching for his license.

"I'd like both of you to exit vehicle," he said all business.

"Officer Tate," I greeted him with a little wave. "Please tell me he wasn't speeding again."

"Ms. Carpenter … pardon me, Mrs. Marshall, could you please exit the car with your hands up?"

Zane was standing beside the overweight officer before I could get my door open.

"What's this about?" Zane squared his shoulders, sending a don't mess with me or mine message loud and clear.

Officer Tate scanned the area. "I'm sorry, you two, but I don't have any choice."

I made my way around the car and stopped next to Zane,

I Kissed a Dog

puzzled by the normally friendly police officer's strange requests. "Is every okay? How's Barney?" I asked, hoping to diffuse the situation before it got out of hand.

"I'm sorry, Chloe, but I have to bring you in for questioning. In fact, you're under arrest for the murders of …"

I didn't hear a word he said after "under arrest." He clamped the handcuffs around my wrists, apologizing in the process. He recited my rights and escorted me to his cruiser.

Zane, who remained at my side, had grown quiet. *This is all wrong, Chloe. I can smell his fear and uncertainty. I'll contact the pack's lawyers and will bail you out as soon as they process you, okay? Be strong, baby. We'll be back together by bedtime.*

Wishing I could believe it would be that simple, I allowed Officer Tate to guide me into the back, where I was left to stare at the divider that kept me separated from any front seat passengers.

I pressed my face against the side window, my nose touching the glass. Zane followed my example, imploring me with his eyes to stay strong and trust him. I nodded, hoping to reassure him.

Zane, I love you. Please, get me out of here, after you meet with the others. We have to secure the coins and stop Martin.

Stop worrying about everyone else. I'm the pack leader now. I have more resources than you can imagine. My first priority is you. Make sure to send me updates once you arrive. At least we can communicate this way. He pointed at his head.

Knowing I could stay in touch with Zane and the others via mind messages was the one thing keeping me from succumbing to hysterics.

I heard Officer Tate apologize again to Zane, assuring him

he'd do his very best to take care of me, and not to worry because the Plum Beach City Jail was small and safe, *and* clean in comparison to other locations.

I guessed I should be glad. A clean jail was better than the alternative.

Officer Tate slid into the driver's seat and adjusted his rearview mirror in order to observe me better. "Chloe, I'm out of line saying this, and I'll deny it if asked, but I know you didn't do this. But that bastard, Agent Green, has managed to collect some pretty compelling evidence implicating you as a key participant in the murders."

I gasped. What could Agent Green possibly have to use against me? I'd sent the one piece of evidence that would lead to Jazmine.

Leaning forward, I prayed Officer Tate would remember how I saved his dog and answer one question for me. "Can you tell me, please, what in the world does he have on me? I promise I won't say anything. I just don't want to be blindsided."

He nodded and gave me an answer I wasn't prepared to hear, "He found a wig. A woman's red wig with your prints all over it. He remembered your comments at Will's house about seeing a woman with red hair. You're the one who mentioned the redheaded female. He doesn't believe you have any ability to communicate with animals."

"How …?" I shook my head, overwhelmed by the implications. "*I* sent that wig. It was supposed to be delivered to you or Detective Davis."

Valamir — of course — he must be working with Agent Green, who was indebted to Jazmine and her crew in some

I Kissed a Dog

screwed up way. Like everyone else, the twisted agent wanted me out of the picture so he could focus on finding the coins and discrediting everyone I knew. That way he wouldn't have to worry about us spoiling his plans.

I needed to inform Zane of my vow to Valamir. I'd have to wait, though; we were pulling into the station, where an onslaught of news reporters hovered like they were waiting for some Hollywood celebrity.

Cameras spun toward the police car; hands with microphones extended my direction.

Dear God, they were waiting for me.

So was a leering Agent Green, along with my parents, Melanie and Luke.

My best night had just turned into my worst day ever.

"Did you kill your coworkers? We heard you hated Rhonda, is that true?" one reporter shouted over the other clamoring voices.

Coworkers, as in more than Will? Rhonda? What was he saying? Was Rhonda dead too? This was way too much information for me to process.

Lowering my head, and refusing to make eye contact with anyone, friend or foe, I allowed myself to be hustled into the station. When my cell door slammed behind me, I called for Zane, hurling a mental fastball his way.

A vicious pain knifed through my forehead, piercing my mind. It was if my message had bounced back, refusing to transmit.

It was then realized my worst fear had come to pass.

Agent Green had somehow erected a magic-borne barrier,

efficient enough to keep me from communicating with anyone.

He'd skewered my lifeline.

The shrewd agent believed my powers were real. He'd known all along and had made arrangements to ensure I couldn't rely on them.

Unsure what else to do, I wept.

Once I released all my tears, I would do what any other innocent person held unjustly by a psychotic, unidentified, supernatural creature would do.

Break out and prove my innocence.

Epilogue

Valamir paced his small quarters. He'd already located Martin and the small band of warriors assigned to guard him. There was ample time to apprehend the pathetic human and procure the ancient coins.

At present, he had more vital issues harassing his mind — a woman. One he couldn't have, at least at the moment.

The human female, Chloe, was keeping him from important business, disturbing his life like none before had dared. Even from behind bars, her unique scent tempted him. Her tangy sweet blood sang to him like a seducing siren, drawing him to her.

If only Chloe desired him with the same intensity he coveted her.

Although he'd assisted her revolting werewolf mate take down a mutual enemy, he was now plotting that same werewolf's demise. It wouldn't be easy. The purebred was a formable foe, skilled in martial arts and weaponry, and full of magic he wasn't yet aware.

In addition, the new Alpha had a loyal and increasingly adept pack at his disposal, making his destruction a challenge.

Feeling his fangs extend, Valamir chuckled. He'd never been one to turn away from a challenge. In fact, he relished the idea of a worthy opponent. He hadn't found one in centuries, other than that deplorable demon they'd conquered together. That creature didn't count, though; it was spawned unnaturally, obeying its obsession to kill, more like a machine than flesh and blood.

Unable to ignore his overwhelming need to see the woman

that would one day be his, he dematerialized, teleporting to the jail in Plum Beach.

He'd given the wig to the greedy FBI agent, making sure it would implicate Chloe, keeping her confined, safe behind bars, while he completed the task of dismantling Zane's precious pack.

Then he would return for her, coins in hand, becoming her hero and comforter following the untimely death of her mate, which of course would be blamed on another.

With silent precision, he landed outside her cell and glided to the window.

Her heartbeat beckoned him, the blood flowing through her veins igniting his bloodlust.

She owed him a favor. Anything he wanted, and she'd have to comply.

As much as he wanted to collect what she owed tonight, he restrained. It might come in handy later.

An unfamiliar presence approached, staying just outside his line of vision, cloaked in the woods behind the jail.

Valamir was unafraid, just curious. After all, he was the fiercest of predators.

He said a silent goodbye to his soon-to-be woman, and prepared to stalk whatever or whoever was brave or stupid enough to taunt him.

TO BE CONTINUED ...

Watch for the next installment in the **Werewolves of the West Series:** *She Kissed a Vampire*, featuring Chloe's best friend, Melanie Larson, and the continuing adventures of Zane, Chloe, and the Pacific Pack.

About the Author

Like most authors, Carol Van Atta is no stranger to the written word. She penned a short novel at age 12 (somewhat frightening illustrations included) and had a creative writing piece published in her high school newspaper. Devouring books from numerous genres, she developed a deep thirst for more reading materials, and could almost always be found with her nose in a book.

She has contributed to several, popular inspirational anthologies and devotional books, and lives in the rainy wetlands of Oregon with her terrifying teens and a small zoo of animals. She is taking an undetermined hiatus away from inspirational writing to delve into her darker side. It's been rumored this genre-jumping occurred after Carol discovered two suspicious red marks on her neck, and experienced an unquenchable urge to howl at the moon.

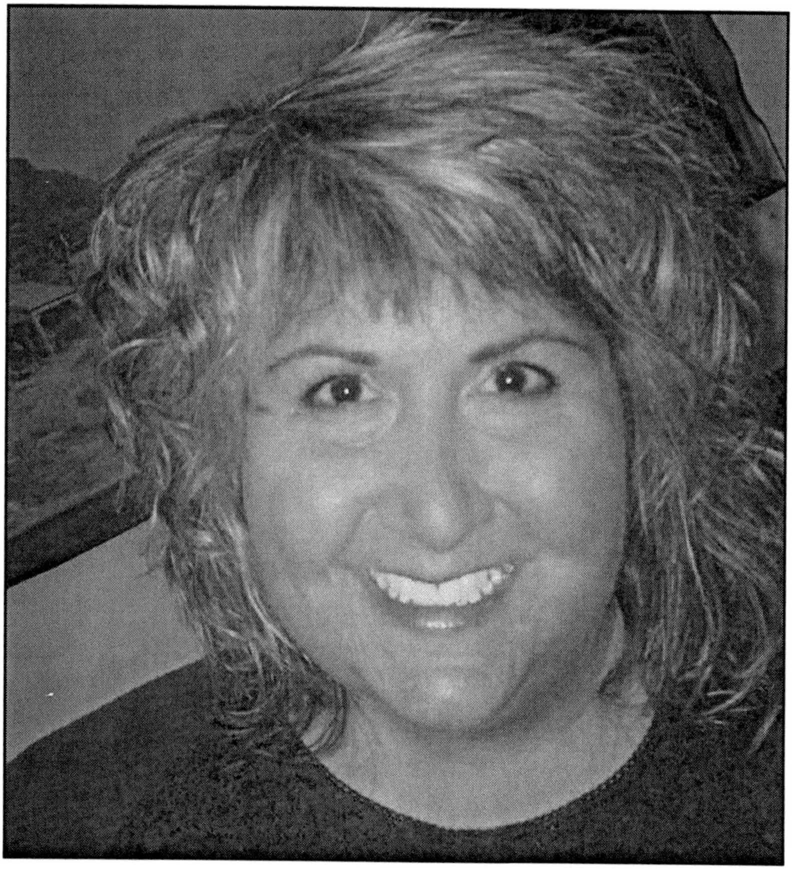